DATE DUE		
NOV 19 Ret		
JUL 1 Ret		
SEP 5 Ret		
FEB 25 Ret		

HONEYMOON, BITTERMOON

Honeymoon, Bittermoon

Ramón Pérez de Ayala

Translated from the Spanish by
Barry Eisenberg

University of California Press
Berkeley   Los Angeles   London   1972

University of California Press
Berkeley and Los Angeles, California
University of California Press, Ltd.
London, England

LUNA DE MIEL, LUNA DE HIEL and
LOS TRABAJOS DE URBANO Y SIMONA copyright © 1923, by
Ramón Pérez de Ayala

Editorial Mundo Latino
Imprenta Helénica
Madrid, Spain

Editorial Losada, S.A.
Buenos Aires, Argentina, 1941

First English translation copyright © 1972, by
The Regents of the University of California
with permission of the heirs of Ramón Pérez de Ayala

Library of Congress Catalog Card Number: 79-116667
ISBN: 0-520-01727-7
Printed in the United States of America

Contents

Translator's Preface

It is fifty years since the writing of this novel and nine since I undertook its translation. I would like to thank the following for their help: the National Translation Center, for a grant of financial aid; Mr. Lysander Kemp of Austin, Texas, and Mr. Grant Barnes and Mrs. Diane Beck of the University of California Press, for editorial assistance, and the Zen Center of San Francisco, for moral and spiritual support.

Introduction: Ramón Pérez de Ayala

Ramón Pérez de Ayala is one of the most important figures of that authentic intellectual and literary renaissance that took place in Spain in the first half of the twentieth century. With its triumphs and misfortunes, his life reflects some of the basic problems that the contemporary Spanish intellectual has had to confront.

A convincing biography of this writer still does not exist. We know very little of his literary beginnings and not too much of his latter period, after he was appointed Spanish ambassador to London, through his life in exile in Latin America and his return to Spain. I will not record here the facts we do possess (which I have already done in the introduction to my critical edition of *Tinieblas en las cumbres,* published in Madrid by Editorial Castalia). Here I wish simply to mention some fundamental biographical details, and comment on the possible meanings they may have and on their influence on the formation of his thought and creation of his work.

Ramón Pérez de Ayala was born in Oviedo in 1880. His first important works were produced around 1910. Thus, he is somewhat after the generation of 1898, which inaugurates contemporary Spanish literature. Notwithstanding, some of the men of '98, such as Azorín and Valle-Inclán, were his best friends. He inherited from the spirit of '98 that critical preoccupation with the problems of the Spanish people which has since the end of the sixteenth century followed a path of progressive decadence. Nevertheless, Pérez de Ayala's attitude coincides more with that of those who made up the so-called *novecentista* group; Ortega y Gasset and Doctor Marañón, for example, were his two colleagues in political activity. This *novecentista* group is characterized by a serious intellectual background, a decided attitude of openness to Europe, and a progressive social and political consciousness, starting from the end of the First World War (whereby Gonzalo Sobejano proposes speaking of a generation of 1914), which culminated in public action in behalf of the Second Spanish Republic, proclaimed in 1931.

Pérez de Ayala was the son of a Castilian businessman established in Asturias. He belonged, thus, like so many Spanish intellectuals, to the relatively well-off middle class. At the age of eight, his parents sent him to the Jesuit Academy of San Zoilo, in Carrión de los Condes, Palencia Province. In this period and almost up to the present day, the religious orders dominated the education of Spanish youngsters coming from the middle and upper classes; the social influence of the orders was enormous, whether the educational system was agreeable to the youngsters or whether—as happened, for example, in the cases of Ortega y Gasset and Ramón Pérez de Ayala—it aroused reaction. In education, the Jesuits have predominated for years by virtue of the selective, almost aristocratic character of their education and the sentimental sweetness of their religiosity.

The child Ramón Pérez de Ayala had a very bad time of it in the Jesuit boarding school. Years later he was to write an autobiographical novel, *A.M.D.G.*,[1] relating his experience, which he also commented on in various articles. We may call to mind only some few sentences in which he paints with very vivid colors this youthful experience: "The most anguished dejection overcame me when at the close of the day, ever-uniform, like stretches across a cold open plain, they shut each one of us up in his small room, little sepulchers, all white with whitewash and linen. It was the moment of the void of night, and the night was the void of the world." (From a piece included in the book *Amistades y recuerdos*.)

It is not necessary to be much of a psychologist to understand the imprint that these youthful sufferings left on the soul of the future writer. Jesuitical education truly marked his spirit forever, for good and for bad. On the one hand, the Jesuits provided him

1. *Ad Majorem Dei Gloria,* the Jesuit motto.—Tr.

with a solid humanistic foundation, which distinguishes him from the usual in Spanish novelists of all periods. Pérez de Ayala had a serious classical background; the reading of Greek and Latin classics, in the original, constituted one of his greatest pleasures to the end of his days. It goes without saying that this classical background reverberated through all his writings and, specifically, gave to his novels an intellectual complexity that makes them not especially suited to enjoyment by the masses.

On the other hand, the Jesuitical education coincided with (or provoked) a serious religious crisis. To a journalist who asked him if he had faith, the writer replied with implacable laconicism: "No. I've studied with the Jesuits."

This brings us to try to specify somewhat the religious attitude of Pérez de Ayala. Like many other Spanish intellectuals (Galdós, Clarín, Ortega, et cetera), he is anticlerical but not antireligious. The distinction is very clear and is worth underlining sharply so as not to falsify the terms of the problem. The anticlericalism of these intellectuals is no more than the logical reply to the great influence (excessive for them) of the clergy on Spanish society and the traditionalism and lack of culture of many ecclesiastics. In his youth, Pérez de Ayala adopted a position of polemical anticlericalism; this is, perhaps, one of the reasons for his popular fame. His attitude toward the Catholic religion was always strongly critical and could be compared somewhat with the Erasmist movement in the sixteenth century: criticism of external ceremonies and defense of an "interior Christianism" joined to the practice of the essential virtues. With time, Pérez de Ayala's attitude toward religion softened a great deal.

Here it may be interesting to record an anecdote. During the years of the Republic a dramatic adaptation of his anticlerical novel *A.M.D.G.* was put on in Madrid. One of the performances was attended by the government with its president, the leftist intellectual Azaña. The work caused a scandal and occasioned mob scenes: at one of them a priest and José Antonio Primo de Rivera, the future founder of the Falange, were arrested for noisily opposing the work.

Pérez de Ayala undertook law studies in Oviedo. At the time this university had a roster of professors of high quality and liberal bent, influenced by the current of Krausism that so powerfully entered Spanish intellectual life from the second half of the nineteenth century on: Altamira, Alvarez Buylla, Sela, Arambaru, Adolfo Posada—and, above all, Leopoldo Alas, "Clarín," the great novelist.

Pérez de Ayala felt authentic adoration (that is the word he used in one of his youthful articles) for Clarín, who was to be his true spiritual master. Pérez de Ayala's novels were not to follow the realistic line of Galdós, whom he likewise admired so greatly, but in actuality that of Clarín: the intellectual novel, rich in ideas and concerns, centered in the very critical vision—bitter, ironic—of the social reality in a Spanish provincial capital. Oviedo was to be portrayed implacably as well by Pérez de Ayala (as Pilares) as by Clarín (under the name of Vetusta).

Clarín and Pérez de Ayala are at one and the same time novelists, thinkers, and critical spirits of great intelligence—also, great pessimists. But their pessimism is softened by the presence of two elements typical, so it seems, of the Asturian spirit: lyricism before nature and a very mellow sense of humor, alien from the Castilian crudity of a Quevedo, for example.

Young Pérez de Ayala then went to England. We possess scarcely any concrete facts about his stay (the first of several that were to take place throughout his life), but we do know that it must have been a formative trip, in a broad and diffuse way: English language, literature, art, philosophy. Pérez de Ayala was, throughout his life, a great lover of England. In this too he differs from the usual Spanish writer of the period, who was wont to receive literary news from France and to revere German culture mythically. Pérez de Ayala coincides with the English spirit in his sense of humor and in his profound liberalism, which in the case of the Spanish writer is not solely political opinion but basic belief, general attitude toward life, almost a religion which has very deep roots in his personality and finds expression in the most varied sectors of the human spirit. For Pérez de Ayala, in short, the fundamental virtue was tolerance, respect for the ways and thoughts of others.

The placid life of the son of a well-off family was shattered by a brusque tragedy. Upon the bankruptcy of the bank where he kept his money, his father committed suicide. It is not necessary to emphasize the burden of pessimism that this event must have provoked in the young mind of Pérez de Ayala who, besides, now saw himself obliged to consider literature as a way of making a living and not as a mere amateur's distraction.

When Pérez de Ayala appeared on the Madrid literary scene, he did so with a slightly disdainful aristocratic attitude tinged with snobbery. Antonio Machado said of him at that time that he had "the petulant appearance of an Oxford undergraduate or a student in Salamanca."

He began a very intense literary life: books of poetry, novels, and essays. He achieved popular fame above all as a result of the scandal of *A.M.D.G.*

Upon the outbreak of the First World War, Pérez de Ayala stood firmly on the side of the allies, like the majority of Spanish liberal intellectuals. He visited the front and wrote a book *(Hermann encadenado)* both against the Germans and as a biting criticism of the Kaiser's speeches. At the same time, a change of orientation took place in his career as novelist. The first cycle of his novels, of strong autobiographical basis, ended, and he wrote three short novels in which the perfection of style is joined to strong criticism of Spanish social realities to give rise to some authentic masterworks. These are the *Tres novelas poemáticas de la vida española: Prometeo, Luz de domingo, y La caída de los limones.* The second, *Luz de domingo,* perhaps his most successful work, is dedicated to

Araquistáin, well-known writer and leftist politician, and supposes a fierce criticism of the system of *caciquismo* [2] that ruled in many Spanish towns.

Pérez de Ayala, now a devoted writer, continued writing novels from time to time and many articles. He adopted a firm attitude against the dictatorship of General Primo de Rivera. His articles of this period, which demonstrate once more his great critical capacity and his sharp analysis of Spanish realities, were collected in the volume *Las máscaras.* (The latest edition, in pocket book, carries the title *Escritos políticos.*)

Pérez de Ayala took part in various political enterprises of intellectual cast. All of them had liberal, Republican, and lay tendencies. The most important was the Association in Service of the Republic, which he founded together with the philosopher Ortega y Gasset and the doctor and essayist Marañón. The advent of the Republic (April 14, 1931) supposed the triumph of this association and these intellectuals. The Republic came into being with a very marked intellectual character; the proof of it is that it sent out as ambassadors figures of recognized prestige—among others, Pérez de Ayala, who was named ambassador to his beloved England.

The story of the writer in his embassy is still to be written; but from what is known, we can affirm that he found himself very much at ease in the country and among the citizens, whom he knew well and esteemed, so that he was able to carry out his task effectively. Nevertheless, his position as a moderate liberal (like that of his friends Ortega y Gasset and Marañón) was being undermined by the most extreme elements of the Spanish Republic, to the point where he ceased to be ambassador after the triumph of the Popular Front in 1936.

His dedication to politics, furthermore, was fatal to his work as a novelist. His last novel carries the date 1926. At that time he was forty-six and was fully recognized by the most exacting inter-

2. Bossism.

national criticism. (He had won the National Literary Prize and was spoken of now and again as a possible Nobel Prize candidate.) He was still to live for thirty-six years. In this long period he wrote many newspaper articles, later collected into books, but not one novel. The matter is rendered especially striking if we recall that Pérez de Ayala insisted several times on his theory that the novel is the proper vehicle of maturity, the fruit of a life experience accumulated over the years—a theory, as it were, belied by his own example. To what is this narrative silence, so difficult to explain, due? Nobody knows for certain. I myself, in my book *La novela intelectual de Ramón Pérez de Ayala,* have treated at some length the possible causes. Here I will summarize the principal ones: (1) the laziness and apathy of the writer; (2) his need of earning a living by means of frequent journalistic contributions; (3) his growing pessimism, increased by the Spanish Civil War and by the death of his son; and (4) the exhaustion of a certain novelistic line.

For the intellectuals who collaborated on the coming into being of the Republic, the Spanish Civil War must have come as a very strong psychological shock. To comprehend it, in the case of Pérez de Ayala, I set down some words that are part of a speech he delivered in London as ambassador in May 1934. Commemorating the third anniversary of the Republic, he is pleased that those three years have demonstrated that "there can be a perfect union of Spaniards, irreproachably united and in concord, whatever might be their inevitable and even useful discrepancies . . . ; that Spaniards are as fit for fruitful social solidarity as anyone else; that it is not true that the Spaniard, by a kind of constitutional fatalism, carries within himself the inevitable tendency toward contradiction, toward injunction, toward lack of discipline, toward separation; in short, that he find himself impelled, despite himself, as the unique manifestation of his personality, to adopt extreme positions of civil war, actual or potential, as if all Spaniards, by a kind of Biblical curse, could be nought but Cains or Abels, hangmen and victims of ourselves. Here is proof to the contrary: the Spanish colony in

London. . . . If on the contrary, we were to fail (I speak not of Republicans but of Spaniards) it will be necessary that with Boabdil's[3] tears in our eyes we prepare to abandon the world stage for the background and cry like women over what we did not know how to preserve as men." Thus it was, unfortunately; the beautiful intellectual idea of peaceful national coexistence was shattered and Spaniards found themselves once more launched (as in so many instances throughout modern history) into fratricidal battle. It is not necessary to underline what such a failure of his civic ideas must have meant to a man of Pérez de Ayala's sensitivity. In these words I believe I see the germ and the explanation of the writer's future attitude, of much of his pessimism and radical skepticism.

With the Civil War of 1936-39 there began for Ayala, as for many other Spaniards, intellectuals or not, bitter years of exile— preoccupation for the fortunes of his country, separation from loved ones (his sons, above all), economic difficulties, uncertainty about the future, and growing nostalgia. After a stay in France, he went to Latin America, visited various countries, and settled in Argentina around 1943. He worried over his family's future. He earned a living any way he could, giving lectures or writing articles on the most diverse topics. His situation was relieved somewhat by the Argentinian re-edition of his principal novels and his appointment to the Spanish embassy.

Little by little, the ties with his homeland were renewed. In June 1948 he published once again in the Madrid newspaper *ABC*, which he had attacked as a youngster. He undertook a short trip to Spain in 1949; and as the experience was a happy one, he returned definitively to his homeland and was reunited with his family and friends on December 20, 1954. To Spanish public opinion. Pérez de Ayala was one of the "wicked" writers who contributed to bringing the Republic to Spain; but there also existed a very generalized desire to let bygones be bygones and to reincorporate into national

3. The last Moorish king of Granada.—Tr.

xvi

life figures of such undisputed intellectual quality. The same was
to occur with Ortega y Gasset and Doctor Marañón.

Pérez de Ayala's return to Spain was purely private and did not
signify any public stand on the problems of his country. He contributed regularly to the newspaper *ABC,* for the most part in articles that repeated or extended essays already published years before.
He received the prestigious March Prize. He left his house infrequently; he limited himself to family life and to friends. All signs
point to a serene pessimism and skepticism, now after so many
things had passed. He died in Madrid August 5, 1962, at the age
of eighty-two. For youth, he was now a figure of unknown signi-
ficance; it knew only his academic commentaries on the fabulists or
Greek and Latin lyric poets and knew nothing of the very polemic
articles or novels of his youth. Because of censorship, *A.M.D.G.*
has not been included in the Spanish edition of his *Obras Com-
pletas.* His first novel, *Tinieblas en las cumbres,* was reissued in
1971, for the first time since the war.

As we have noted previously, the Pérez de Ayala novel belongs
to the type usually known as "intellectual novel" and inclusive
"essay novel"—somewhat similar to what has been done, in our
century, by the Englishman Aldous Huxley, the German Thomas
Mann, and the Argentinians Ernesto Sábato and Julio Cortazar.
In Spain a distant antecedent is Valera; the immediate master,
Clarín; it coincides in part with Unamuno's *nivola* concept and is
prolonged, after the war, in the works of Francisco Ayala and Luis
Martín Santos. Pérez de Ayala inserts in his novels digressions on
very varied themes. His characters, besides, embody or state permanent problems of man, in all epochs and all countries; but that does
not mean that he disregarded the here and now, the concrete Spanish reality of his time.

The danger that threatens this type of novel is coldness and
dehumanization. We do not believe that that occurred, in general,
in the narrative works of Pérez de Ayala. His profound vitalism
(parallel to that of Unamuno and Ortega y Gasset), his sense of

humor (at times close to the grotesquerie of Valle-Inclán), and his great critical capacity (undoubted inheritance from Clarín) give his works an undeniable human and vital importance.

The novel we treat here belongs to Ramón Pérez de Ayala's second period, in which the accent now fell not on personal autobiography but on human problems of universal, almost philosophical validity: love, sexual education, human language and communication, matrimonial honor, Don Juanism. They are problems —I repeat—that interest men of all times and countries, but Ayala focuses on them from his Spanish and particularly Asturian perspective.

In the year 1923 Ramón Pérez de Ayala published two narrative volumes, under the titles *Luna de miel, luna de hiel* and *Los trabajos de Urbano y Simona*. Actually, only purely editorial reasons (the excessive length of the original, in comparison with what was then customary) determined this publication in two separate volumes with separate titles, since it is a matter of a single novel and, what is more, of a perfectly unified work. Therefore, the only sensible solution is that of publishing these two volumes as one, as the recent Spanish re-edition in pocket book has done (under the title *Las novelas de Urbano y Simona*) and as does this translation into English.

In this novel Ramón Pérez de Ayala presents us with a limited situation, that of two youngsters who arrive at matrimony in the most absolute sexual ignorance, as a result of the education that has been given them. The consequences, naturally, are catastrophic.

The novelist fixes on a problem of undoubted magnitude in the Spain of his day and which extends as well, in modified form, to our own: insufficient, inadequate sexual education, based on silence and ignorance. Taking off from there, with implacable logic, Pérez de Ayala derives the ultimate and tragicomic consequences.

The theme of Spanish eroticism, of the mental attitude and

social context of love, has preoccupied Ramón Pérez de Ayala at length and is the theme of many of his writings. In this case, the problem is not only of his protagonists but also of the parents of Urbano; it is that of Paolo, the old bachelor devoured by maternal domination; it is that of Cástulo; and that of the old maid sisters. The novel has offered us a very intelligent and critical sampling of the erroneous attiudes toward love that are typical of Spanish social reality. His book is a plea for a very open and reasonable sexual education (somewhat similar, relatively, to what D. H. Lawrence proposes in his novels), made from a vitalistic point of view, of respect for nature. We have, in sum, a kind of modern *Libro de buen amor,* a "Book of Good Love."

Sexual education, in short, is no more than a section of a broader problem, that of education in general, a theme that obsessed Pérez de Ayala, as it did all the men of the Free Institute of Instruction. The posture of our novelist is clearly liberal: defense of an education based on liberty and not authoritarianism, which seeks harmony with (and not negation of) natural impulses.

In Urbano and Simona the classical figures of Daphnis and Chloe are revived. But, at the same time, they set forth a burning problem for Spanish youth of the present time.

Pérez de Ayala bases himself, thus, on reality; but the literary technique he employs here is not realistic but follows the method of exaggeration, of caricature (so that the evil he wishes to censure may stand out more prominently), of expressionism or of grotesquerie.

The name of the protagonist is significative: "Urbano" means man of the city, educated, civilized. In short, it is a question of making us see how society, by means of an absurd education, can make us unhappy; how the individual, once social obstacles are painfully and laboriously overcome, achieves human and vital fulfillment in love, of body and soul.

In this novel the habitual qualities in Ramón Pérez de Ayala shine forth: very classical style, intelligence, irony, vision of life as tragicomedy, lyricism, very calculated structure. But, at the same time, there comes across in the novel a rootedness in Spanish reality and a critical capacity that make it especially attractive. For Pérez de Ayala, as for the intellectuals of his line, the change that Spain needed was not only in politics but above all in ways of thinking, of mentality, of customs, of attitude, in order to face up to the permanent and daily problems that confront men—in this case, specifically, sexual education, eroticism, and love.

ANDRES AMOROS
Madrid, Spain,
Spring 1971

(Trans. by B. E.)

HONEYMOON, BITTERMOON

[Luna de miel, luna de hiel]

WANING MOON

That after-dinner discussion on the eighth of June was, like all great historic turning points, a seemingly commonplace occasion, except that Destiny, who was present and invisible, tossed his dice of fate, and the participants—whose fortune was decided right there, though they could not contemplate or even guess at the enigma of the future—felt a sort of insidious shudder in the marrow of their bones.

"All of us, *némine discrepante*—isn't that the way you say it, Cástulo?—are anxious for the wedding to take place as soon as possible. We've already petitioned Simona's hand. The children can't live without one another any longer. They're two purest angels. Neither one of them has ever been grazed by the wing of an evil thought. It will be an ideal marriage, something like Adam and Eve in Paradise; except that, of course . . . Urbano, leave the room. Go to the parlor and don't come back until I call you."

The afternoon meal was over, and four people were seated around the table.

First and foremost was Doña Micaela Cano de Fano, who was, as usual, dominating the conversation. Around forty-five, more or less; dressed in a white dressing gown, rather low cut in front and back for coolness, because the heat oppressed her and she suffered from dizzy spells; her hair loose down her back, since she was prone to migraine headaches; an aquiline and lean profile—very similar to that of Dante—with the skin, as if cured and cordovan colored, taut against the bone; the eyes deep set, hard, and alert. She had turned her chair around and rested her arm on the back, her man-

3

ner a composite, between overbearing and romantic. She occupied, imposingly, one head of the rectangular table. There was no one at the other end.

To her right, the husband, Don Leoncio—lined forehead, olive complexion and steely beard: the head of a crushed Huguenot—sat with an air of resignation, stirring his coffee.

At the señora's left was the tutor of the only child, Don Cástulo Colera, a gallant conspicuous alike for his extraordinary meekness and his myopia; gold-rimmed spectacles, with a fine little chain that ended in a hook fastened to his earlobe; little blue and squinty eyes; thinning hair, once upon a time golden, nowadays a little— just a bit—whitish, divided between head and chin. His face, altogether, gave the impression of an October morning, one of those honey-colored ones.

Finally, sitting close on his father's left side was the only child, Urbano, urbane by nature and so baptized; a lad of twenty, large headed, his body underdeveloped for his age, the beginnings of a mustache, a milky complexion, like that of fruit ripened in the shade; very timid, exceedingly susceptible to blushing and even to tears, and by way of contrast, a broad jaw, which denoted a strong will, perhaps beneath the surface and still in germination.

Urbano, obedient and very intimidated, left the dining room, stumblingly. When his footsteps had died away, Doña Micaela continued, "They'll be like Adam and Eve, before the fall, except that now, in these corrupt times, a house and clothing are necessary."

"Which cost an arm and a leg," added Don Leoncio.

"There goes the big skinflint, at it again," said Doña Micaela. "Money, money. You don't talk about anything else."

"Because we don't have as much as you insist on believing."

"A pack of lies, because you don't want to spend what the occasion calls for. And, above all, please be so kind as to not interrupt me, because, among other things, I consider it very rude of you. Now then, as I was saying, the children are like newborn babes. Greater innocence doesn't exist. They're just like Adam and Eve.

I'm quite sure that should we leave them in a garden on their own, like our first parents, nothing bad would take place at all."

"There's not the slightest doubt of it," corroborated the meek and mild Don Cástulo.

"No doubt," the husband dared to say.

"Well, *rara avis*—isn't that the way you say it, Cástulo?—by some miracle you are in agreement with me," Doña Micaela exclaimed, with sarcastic relish.

"I'm happy to hear you say that, my dear, since it means you must be in agreement with me too. Since what you suppose about the children is true, what's your hurry in their getting married? How are they ever going to live as man and wife?"

Doña Micaela fixed her eyes severely on Don Leoncio, who, even without looking, felt the crushing weight of the conjugal stare and sought to explain: "I didn't make myself clear. I was trying to have it understood that the marriage is premature. What do you think, Cástulo?"

Before the tutor might reply, the señora broke in, "Premature! How ridiculous! Listen carefully, for it's just because Urbanito is in a state of absolute innocence that he must get married, so that he can never lose it, since love sanctioned by God is as innocent and pure as chastity itself."

The quiet Don Cástulo squirmed furtively in his chair.

"Why are you fidgeting there? You've got something on your mind," the señora pried.

"Nothing, nothing, oh heavens!" Don Cástulo exclaimed.

"You said 'oh, heavens.' That's a sure sign you're keeping something back."

"Dear, don't force him to be a hypocrite," said Leoncio.

Don Cástulo kept making mute protestations, raising and shaking his hands and opening wide his gentle eyes, two oxidized turquoise spheres.

"I'll answer for him," said Don Leoncio. "Don Cástulo thinks such a marriage would be premature and therefore risky."

"Say whatever's on your mind, Cástulo, I won't take offense," the señora directed peevishly, drawing back her head.

"On thinking it over," said Don Cástulo, uneasily and unconvincingly, "I'm of the same opinion as Micaela."

"What were you fidgeting for, then?" asked Doña Micaela.

"Oh, just idle thoughts that pop into one's head," replied Don Cástulo evasively.

"Out with them, out with them; give out with those idle thoughts."

"Without intending," Don Cástulo said, compunctious, "I recalled Daphnis and Chloe."

"*Da finis sicloen?*" the señora inquired, smiling. "Look, Cástulo, spare us the Latinisms now."

"It's not a Latinism. They're the names of two Hellenic lovers."

"Anything that sounds funny to me I call a Latinism. This is my house and what I say goes. But tell us, what happened to those Edenic lovers?"

"Hellenic," Don Cástulo corrected. "But also Edenic. You've hit the nail on the head, Micaela. You see they were a little shepherd and shepherdess, stricken by mutual and burning love, who lived off by themselves, babbling and frolicking all day long through woods and meadows; but even though Nature, no farther away than the flocks that they themselves were tending, offered doctrine and example, their innocence and ignorance of amorous practices were such that they didn't know how to gratify the passion. A delightful eclogue, just precious."

And Don Cástulo in ecstasy opened wide his blue eyes, wherein trembled a faint glimmer of the skies of ancient Mytilene.

"All such indecencies," declared Micaela, "which, sugarcoated in sweet talk, you've made us swallow, would go on in pagan or Moorish times. Our own case is quite different. It's a matter of a Christian marriage, between two innocent youngsters, as God commands. And the Guardian Angel will inspire them with what they have to do."

6

"No more, no less. Just what I meant to say," Don Cástulo added. "Marriage, according to the disposition of God and of Nature as well, which is God's creation, must begin in idyll, or in honeymoon, as it's commonly called. For which the newlyweds have only to be innocent as newborn babes. Since, were it otherwise, how will someone find honey sweet to taste who is glutted on it?"

And on speaking of honey, even though he might never have tasted it, Don Cástulo assumed an air of sweet authority, as though his head were anointed and coated with honey.

"You come around like a philosopher, Cástulo; for that I respect and trust you. How wisely you perceive my deepest feelings. You, who are no relation to me, understand me. On the other hand, God has given me a heavy cross to bear: to be tied down to a man who differs from me in everything," Doña Micaela expostulated with a martyred expression.

Then she directed her gaze, contemptuous and askance, at Don Leoncio, who from olive green turned ashen green, and who furtively tossed a look over at Don Cástulo, in which he sought to relieve some of the suffering of his spirit.

Don Leoncio meant the glance to say, "My wife is domineering and foolish. You, Cástulo, sympathize with me, much to your credit. Well, I sympathize more with you, for disdain is preferable to the favor of this viper."

On his part, Don Cástulo returned to the patient husband another cautious and enigmatic look, which said, "You're having a bad time of it, Leoncio. Forgive me; I've been the occasion, unwillingly. I too am having a terrible time of it; I'm going to get an upset stomach from the tuna fish. Reflect, to make yourself feel better, that your wife is an irresistible force, a cosmic energy. They're all like that, the quiet ones and the loud ones. One must accept them as manifestations of the malignant and rancorous will of the hostile deities, like sickness, old age, and death. But, ay! we need them for a transcendental end: the perpetuation of the species. Lucky you, who have had a son. Me, poor me, I've had no access to them except in conversation and books. They've not cared for me, they've not paid me any attention, unless to be using me as a term of comparison to encourage or annoy a lover or a husband. A sad role."

After the inaudible dialogue, in which the two interlocutors guessed one another's thoughts intuitively, Doña Micaela resumed her harangue: "I would have that sentence engraved in marble. How can the glutton enjoy honey? How disgusting, dear Lord, to hear what some people say! The decent woman must arrive at the altar immaculate, a lily. That's all. The man marries reeking of vice, contaminated with filth—and is considered an upright citizen. Isn't this your standard, Leoncio?"

"Dear, you've never heard any such ridiculous thing from me."

"There's something worse than saying certain things: doing them."

"My dear, before and after marriage, my whole life long, I've been nothing but a beast of burden."

"You'd do better to own up to it. Confession perhaps brings reform along with it. Beast of burden . . . and you've heard of the saying: honey wasn't made, let alone the honeymoon, for the ass's mouth."

There was a pause. Doña Micaela shouted, "Urbano, come back in."

The only child appeared, skittish as a mule. Looking him in the eye, the mother said, "You are already formally engaged. Your fiancée's mother and grandmother are impatient. My impatience is no less. That Simona and you are eager is self-evident. Who, then, is standing in the way of the union desired by everyone? Are you standing in the way of it, Leoncio? Obstacles?"

"They're much too young. It's a premature marriage."

Don Leoncio had taken a fancy to the word *premature,* even though he might not quite appreciate its full import; but it felt to him that it contained incontrovertible suasive power and carried a vague catastrophic threat.

"Your eternal mulish stubbornness," Doña Micaela asserted.

8

Don Leoncio was deeply hurt by this insult in the presence of his son. He kept the pain to himself, rather than reply in anger and scorn of his wife. "My son," he thought, "is so used to the vilifications and taunts his mother makes at me, that how can he respect me even on the face of it, let alone deep in his heart?" But he realized that if he were to return his wife's affronts, it would only worsen matters; the boy would end up not respecting his mother either. The main thing was that Urbano respect his mother. A goodhearted and untutored man, Don Leoncio shored up his unassuming and modest spiritual life with various props or noble myths: one of them was the cult of idolatry toward The Mother, in the abstract, and for all mothers. His own, in fact, had been a saint. From an illustrious but bankrupt family, from Burgos, the wife of a small-time lawyer, she was left widowed with four sons, the oldest being Leoncio, who was ten. By means of heroic endeavors and without conceding a shred of her dignity, she had proceeded to bring up her orphaned offspring. At fourteen, Leoncio left home, came to Pilares, and went to work as an apprentice in a hardware store. He worked with entire unselfishness to send money home. He was able to find jobs for his younger brothers in different places and businesses. He provided, from afar, comfort and rest for his mother in her old age. Even though he was a partner in the store and was very much in love with Micaela, he didn't want to marry until he had lost his mother; for only at that time did he feel free to act on his own. Thus he thought, "Let Urbano love and respect his mother. Never mind about me. Life would be unbearable without the holy memory of one's mother." What he didn't suspect—the poor fellow!—was that Urbano, by virtue of the rather clandestine suggestion or delicately subtle insinuations of Don Cástulo, respected and loved him more than Doña Micaela. Because he was too afraid of her, Urbano hated his mother a little, unconsciously, with a kind of deeply repressed discomfort and tension. With Don Leoncio, Urbano permitted himself little outbursts of energy and petulance, partly following his mother's lead and infected by the household routine, wherein Don Leoncio

9

was something like low man on the totem pole; partly, because feeling himself so weak and belittled under his mother's authoritarianism, he gave in at times to the adolescent impulse of imposing his will, in revenge, on someone even weaker and more submissive, and for that his father was just the person; but, above all, because Don Leoncio attracted Urbano with a kind of friendly and loving trust. Urbano had but a single friend, split into two halves. One of the halves, which corresponded to daily usage, the passive half of the friendship, was his tutor, Don Cástulo. The other half, dark and silent, where true love reposes, was Don Leoncio, his own father.

"I want to get married, I want to get married, I want to get married," Urbano burst out, looking at his father and in a voice he tried to make sound firm. His jutting jaw trembled, as if his volition, latent and still untried, were trying out its first baby steps.

The father gazed for some time at the son; and seeing him at once so childish and so serious, a feeling of great tenderness and pride came over him. With a benevolent smile, he replied, "Grow up first. Your mother claims you're like a newborn baby."

"I'm twenty years old. I've graduated in law. It's time for me to stop being a newborn baby," argued Urbano, locking his eyes onto his father's face, since whenever his gaze wandered to his mother his voice was paralyzed and the blood rushed to his cheeks.

"Enough of this," said Doña Micaela. "Today is June 8; the wedding will take place on July 8. All opposition is futile, unless it be from the Papal Nuncio."

The human psyche is made up of opposites in unstable equilibrium. Obeying a law of psychological dynamics, Urbano, eager to get married and the sooner the better, upon hearing his mother set the date felt terrified. Goose bumps rose all over his body. With anguished eyes he looked at his father, pleading, in a comical manner, that the wedding date be postponed.

"Doesn't your heart of stone melt before that angel's prayerful face?" murmured Doña Micaela with emphatic phony tenderness.

Don Leoncio, with true tenderness, reserved, deep, and tragic,

10

replied, "Because I am soft hearted; because I want my son's happiness; it's because of that that I'm against the wedding—which is premature."

Don Leoncio, in a sudden broad picture, caught sight of all his personal history, in relation to love matters. Before marriage, Leoncio had made scarcely any attempt at the sowing of wild oats. He was preoccupied only with work. He had married at around the age of thirty (Micaela was three years younger), after an engagement of ten years, with interruptions arising from the coolness and lassitude of the fiancée. After the first birth, Micaela rejected a second maternity and from that time on, fanatically, in accordance with her strange ideas and extremely austere methods, lived solely for the care and education of the only child. Her husband ceased to exist for her. Over the course of time, Don Leoncio had become involved with a harlot, with whom he spent both his passion and his income. Doña Micaela suspected nothing of these affairs. Don Leoncio summed up his amatory and conjugal experience in a couple of axioms: "He who does not kick up his heels as a bachelor will do so as a married man, which is worse. If I, before getting married, had only had some practical experience with women, I would have known how to treat my own in such a way that she might love and respect me, instead of having gotten bored with me right away. Let my failure be a lesson to me to avoid the same misfortune for my son." Besides, Don Leoncio had other overriding reasons, of a monetary nature, against the "premature" marriage of Urbano.

"Urbano is a minor and cannot marry without my consent," Don Leoncio said.

"The wedding will take place on July 8. That's final," declared Doña Micaela, stiffening.

This was the very moment when Destiny, present and invisible, tossed his dice of fate. *Alea jacta fuit.* The die was cast.

"Micaela, without my consent, there is no marriage legally." Drops of sweat rolled down Don Leoncio's wrinkled brow, lined by years of toil, almost bovine toil.

11

"Don't be stupid, Leoncio. Urbano must be married right away. Think of the Parras boy. Do you want a scandal?"

(Urbano, whom his mother kept jealously isolated from all dealings with and news of the world, wondered to himself, "What can scandal of the Parras boy be?")

"What happened to the Parras boy backs me up. The Parras woman was just like you. Here you are. Keep the son locked up in a lighthouse and suddenly, wham! the abduction. The little angel runs away from them with an old and one-eyed maidservant. By luck, they've caught them."

"Shut your mouth, libertine," bellowed Doña Micaela. "I won't have you besmirching your son's purity with abominations. And you, Urbano, forget what you've just heard from your father, who doesn't know what he's saying; he's raving."

But Urbano, inside himself, was musing, "An abduction? What is an abduction? To run off with a one-eyed maidservant? What for?" And he felt weak and pale.

Don Leoncio's head hung down on his chest, his eyes starting and cloudy, like a hanged man's.

Don Cástulo, like the simple-hearted theater goer who watches a tragedy from the first row of seats, with eyes half closed and heart thumping, caviled, "Now the knot is drawn tight. Dreadful auguries pierce the air. What is going to happen here?"

Doña Micaela's mainspring was ambition—not fuzzy, romantic desire, for self-improvement and showing off, but a clear-cut, persistent ambition toward some few practical, well-defined and concrete, though certainly difficult, goals. These objectives, time tested and constant, Doña Micaela, in her inner soliloquies, had never called ideals, but *ideas*; for, closing her eyes, she saw them stand out with marvelous clarity and precision against the obscure background of her consciousness. Since early childhood, she had down there, beneath her serious brow, her *ideas*. There are people endowed with a sense of topographic direction, who through unfamil-

12

iar territory, in the woods or among crags, never lose the way. Doña Micaela had an even rarer gift: the sense of direction in life. She had gotten oriented, barely come of age, to never more deviate from the route; for, besides the idea that guided her and the anxiety which drove her, she was aided by qualities well subservient to ambition—suspicious temperament, cold bloodedness, and stubborn will. The greater part of humankind never cease to be, as long as they draw breath, little children, passive beings; at the moment of birth, children of the past; and in every one of the moments of their existence, children of circumstance. Doña Micaela, on the contrary, did not accept the reality that so spontaneously offered itself, but, instead of accepting it, sought to convert it into what she, Doña Micaela, wanted it to be and believed it should be. Instead of submitting to reality, she made it submit. Dante defined nature as a craftsman with a shaky hand. Though ignorant of this judgment, Doña Micaela was of the same opinion as the Florentine. Of course, she didn't use the same intellectual expressions; reality, nature. Everything exterior to and beyond her skin and senses she referred to as "life" and "things in life." For her, "life" was an occult power, which created and changed the world ceaselessly. All the rest— people, animals, events, and material objects—were "things in life." She was certain of life's omnipotence, and equally certain of its blindness and stupidity. Life was capable of everything, but, as it groped in the dark and without intelligence or design, it created nothing but blunders; ugly objects, ugly animals, and ugly brutes, ugly, brutal, and bad people. Life needed someone to take it by the hand with a knack for taking advantage of its mysterious all-powerful energy, in accordance with a clear idea and an elevated purpose. Doña Micaela did not wish to be dragged along or pushed by life; she was determined to lead it by the hand.

The first of Doña Micaela's ideas was social position; it was the first in time and the deepest in the geology of her heart, something like the ancient, crystalline substratum of her spirit. At around the age of eight, she had already made up her mind to be a señora and

to rub elbows with important and prominent people, a hard undertaking.

Her mother was a shopkeeper who had an open-air stall selling
Catalan notions and textiles in the market plaza. The market plaza:
a great quadrangular space, bounded by decrepit and tumbledown
old houses with porticoes, which in the morning hours filled with
the village throngs in a vast bubbling of colors, smells, and noises of
the most violent and blatant kinds; all manner of carmines, vermil-
ions, veronese greens, and yellows of the fruits and vegetables; scar-
lets, cadmiums, indigos, and purples of the peasant skirts, capes, and
parasols; the balsamic aroma of the mountain grasses, the cloying
odor of the pimento, *afuegaelpito* and *pata de mulo* cheeses, scent
of damp earth, stink of corral and stable; cock crows, duck quacks,
lamb bleats, mongrel barks; sounds of hurdy-gurdy and of bagpipes,
laughs, agreements and curses, the barber's oratory, and psalmody
of the little storyteller, the grumbling of the blind man, reciter of
tales of crimes and shipwrecks. In the early afternoon, the plaza
faded out and fell into a pallid and deep quietude, without any sign
of life. In the still air there wafted the bells of the neighboring
church of San Isidoro, pealing *Ánimas*.

There Micaela spent the years of her infancy, adolescence, and
youth. Her education might have been even worse than that of the
streets, as is the education of the market, were it not that Micaela
had not been born to allow herself to be shaped by the surrounding
reality or to be carried along by the flux of life, but rather to correct
and channel the reality at hand and the flow of life that had fallen
to her lot, within herself and about herself. Primordial character
trait: the absence of sensuality. Her senses did not dominate her.
She almost, almost, did not have senses, since she did not use them
to surrender herself to the world or to delight in its beautiful spectacle, but as spies and witnesses for the prosecution, which brought
news and information from outside to the internal tribunal of her
intelligence, which almost always handed down condemnatory judgments. In the center of the market, submerged in that flood tide of

raw, dense, motley, and tumultuous life, Micaela sat abstracted from
the sensations at hand; the colors did not dazzle her, nor the movement excite her, nor the smells stimulate her, nor the music soften
her. Her skin was lemon colored and as if cured, nerveless—an insu-
lator—skin, on the other hand, matte, firm, knitted, and very beautiful. And, not judging with her senses but with her mind, the market, which was the sunlit sky of her world, seemed to her like a
shapeless and repugnant jumble of greed, lust, ignorance, deceit,
hatred, and misery. And the nighttime sky, the evening and empty
plaza, like an unending tedium, a premonition of death.

Now at the age of eight, Micaela asked her mother (a large,
ruddy, tanned woman, all heart and instinct), "That man who lives
with us isn't my father, right?"

The mother became even ruddier; she tried to explain and did
not know how. She wanted to scold the child and couldn't.

Micaela, looking at her mother haughtily, with her pertina-
cious black eyes, added, "That's bad."

The mother was going to get angry; but she burst out crying
without knowing why. It was not out of shame nor repentance, since
she was satisfied with and proud of her man, who was just a poor
fellow, docile and hard working. He was doing quite a lot by sup-
porting a child who was not his own only because she was her daughter. The mother thought of herself and of her man as decent and
very respectable people, who did not quibble or quarrel or owe a
penny to anybody. And, nevertheless, she burst out crying upon
hearing her daughter. She embraced her and kissed her repeatedly,
stammering, "What do you know about it, little one?"

And Micaela, impassive, repeated, "That's not right."

The mother's man was afraid of Micaela. He used to say to his
mate, "When the child looks at me, something comes over me, I
don't know what. She stares at you in a way that's sharp and cold,
like an owl, an owl that might have the devil inside. That she doesn't
love me, that goes without saying. She doesn't love you either. She
doesn't love anyone. Mind what I'm telling you."

But the mother pretended to reject these apprehensions and warnings, saying, "You're an old worrywart. Let me be."

It is too much to demand love or, still less, affection from infancy. Love is the egoism of youth, whereas affection—that habit formed over many years—is the egoism of maturity. The young fellow loves the person whom his passion needs at a given instant, for it is the essence of love to flourish instantaneously. The older man becomes fonder little by little of the person his passion needs over a period of time. These superior and generous forms of egoism have no place in the incipient humanity of the child, which, closer to pure animal life, does not express its egoism through love or through affection, but by clinging attachment to the people who regulate, sustain, and caress it, without whose support and protection it would see itself lost.

Micaela, being ambitious—radically ambitious—was not at all egoistic. The farthest thing from ambition is egoism. And not being an egoist, she felt no attachment toward anyone. There was only one human being who might merit not quite her attachment, but her sympathy or, better still, her assent and approval; and he was a little boy, some three years her junior, named Cástulo. Reddish hair, big light blue eyes, prominent cheekbones and a slender little nose, a startled expression, Cástulo's was the tiny face of a fox cub. His spirit, a butterfly's, with much golden powder on the wings. Micaela overawed him and he adored her; he followed her everywhere, dying to make himself agreeable and hardly daring to raise his glance toward her.

Cástulo was the legitimate son of another stallkeeper in the market, a serving maid previously in the house of some devout señores, who sent the little boy, at the age of eight, to a Dominican monastery as a serving boy and in his spare time to study for his high school diploma and later a liberal arts certificate.

Micaela remained alone and taciturn, for short spells in the midst of the crowd and tumult of the market; most of the time—in the afternoon and evening—in the darkness of that lethargic plaza.

16

She kept stubbornly to herself, with her nascent intelligence, like a buoy with a little light on top, floating now on the primeval, confused, and turbulent powers of life, now enclosed by silence and solitude as absolute as death.

Micaela, in her ambitions, quested for arrival at a sweet land of dreams, terra firma with an unchanging climate, which was not life at its thick roots, matted still with lumps of earthen clods, symbolized in the market, nor a cemetery-like extinction, as the bloodless and empty plaza appeared to her.

But a little while after Cástulo's leaving, there dropped into that tiny universe of sharp contrasts two lady catechism teachers. They recruited Micaela and took her every morning to the sacristy of San Isidoro, where they instructed her for her first communion. Those ladies came to Micaela as emissaries from the sweet land she had dreamed of, which was neither the unnecessary, painful extreme of the market nor the tedious and unnecessary extreme of the empty plaza; neither primitive and low life nor the absence of life; it was well-employed leisure, the manumission of vile necessities; it was Aristocracy. And Micaela swore to herself, "I'm going to be a señora, come what may and whatever the cost."

After the first communion, she continued frequenting the church. It was not the sensuality of the liturgy that captivated her: precious ornaments, incense lamps, organ music, all that seduction and magic. On the contrary, it annoyed her to see the main Churrigeresque altar, twisting in contortions by the trembling glow of the candles, because it brought to mind the image of Pacholo, a market beggar, who suffered from Saint Vitus dance.

What impressed and pleased her in the church was the darkness and the impression of coldness. She became very religious—a kind of cold and puritanical religiosity; consciousness of duty more than of feeling. Religion demanded of her exactly that vigilant and disciplined conduct to which she aspired; not to let herself be carried along by life, but to rule life. Therefore, religion and aristocracy she fancied as inseparable.

17

She entered puberty without emotion or discomposure, she lengthened her skirt a palm's width, and felt her will more toughened. One day she said to her mother, "You must marry that man who lives with us."

Her mother did not reply. Micaela reiterated the command. The mother spoke, at last: "It cannot be. We're happy the way we are; we're not under any obligation to anyone. If I made him marry me, he'd be miserable, and I'd be unhappy. Besides, what am I going to say to make him marry me?" She spoke from kindness and instinct.

Micaela, unmoved, insisted, "Take your choice: you get married or I'm leaving home."

And as the mother might be disconcerted, Micaela added, "I want to have two last names. To give me only your last name is as if you were to hang a sign around my neck: 'Daughter of sin.'"

That argument convinced her mother. Instinct at times is more amenable than reason. Though with the couple's reluctance, what Micaela ordered was done.

Man, the more enslaved and uneducated he is, the more jealous he is of his freedom; of the immeasurable and illusory freedom which he imagines himself enjoying and which to his thinking consists in the disregarding of some civil law.

This poor illusory freedom does not consist actually in being exempt from the law, living contrary to it, but in ignoring it, even though living in conformity with its dictates—omission of legalization, rather than exemption from the law, which is as if a tuberculosis patient were to believe himself free of that illness simply by not allowing the doctor to diagnose it.

That individual who cohabited with Micaela's mother was a slave to poverty and its ferocious henchmen, routine, ignorance, and toil; in servitude as well to his mate and tied to her by a bond no less formidable than marriage. But he felt himself free because he was not formally married. He gave up his freedom out of fear of Micaela. And, in fact, no sooner was the situation legalized than he began to turn moody and vexatious, as his wife feared. However, the old servitudes—ignorance, routine, and toil—proved stronger, and in the space of a year he forgot about having been married officially.

Micaela used to go with her mother to make purchases in The Nineteenth Century, a notions and hardware store. There she met Leoncio, from Burgos, who was a clerk. All the other clerks flirted with Micaela and told her off-color jokes. Leoncio, short on words, waited on her solicitously and gazed at her with amorous and pure eyes. Leoncio's was one of those Castilian heads, virile and stoical, pinched by the physical effort of not revealing agitations of the spirit; faces which, after so much striving to achieve the serenity of a block, end up by being like sculptures in wood. Micaela, ever alert to scrutinize and size up reality, discovered at once Leoncio's concealed passion.

Several lads had sought Micaela's favors already. Love in all of them betrayed itself as disorder and appetite, undissimulated, but instead cynical and boastful, of the senses. Micaela was, above all else, rationality; and since rationality, the reverse of feeling and imagination, is a simplifier, Micaela had formulated a theorem: "All men are disgusting creatures."

After her resolution had matured, Micaela asked Leoncio, "Are you thinking of marrying me?"

"If you accept me . . ."

"When?"

"When I am able to."

"When will you be able to?"

"When I am free."

"You're not free?"

"My mother is living. I'm not earning enough yet to support her and you," becoming ardent and tender, "and what may come."

"Aha! So, if you love me, you must wish for your mother to die; and if you don't wish for your mother to die, you can't love me. I feel sorry for you."

19

Despite its wooden impassivity, Leoncio's face twisted in a doleful grimace. He replied abjectly, "It depends on what I earn. The chief has already given me a commission on sales."

Absolute ideas do not admit exceptions. Micaela thought, "Just as I guessed. This fellow, maybe not so much, nevertheless is a disgusting creature like other men." Still and all, in expectation and for what might come of it, she consented in Leoncio's considering himself her fiancé.

Micaela was twenty-two when Cástulo reappeared in the market. First of all he went to greet his childhood friend. Cástulo now had his doctorate. He was wearing whiskers, golden as corn, and spectacles. He looked more than thirty years old, and he remained as timid as in childhood. On his arrival, Micaela, busied in housework, had a watermelon red Vergara kerchief tied on her head down to her chin, covering her hair and falling to a point at the nape of her neck, like a cowl. Cástulo stared and stared at Micaela, open mouthed.

After warm greetings, Micaela asked, "Why are you looking at me so funny?"

"My friend, you seemed to me exactly like Dante, as painted by Giotto."

Micaela wanted to know more about it. Cástulo explained to her whom Dante had been and something of *The Divine Comedy*. He also related that Dante, in exile in Verona, met a rather simple old woman, who believed literally in the poet's trip to the Inferno; on seeing him go by, she said, "Your skin got burnt down there," for he was dark complexioned. Cástulo concluded, "And your skin is very sunburnt, Micaela."

Micaela, pensive and furrow browed, thinking of the clamorous market and the deserted plaza, replied, "I've seen the Inferno, and Purgatory; and I have a vision of Paradise. The similarity you find in me to that ancient gentleman is very true. I have traced out my circles in thought." She closed her eyes. "And I see them, I see them clearly: smoke, fire, light, crystal."

"I always said you would become an extraordinary woman."

For Micaela, the only man in the world who was not a disgusting creature was Cástulo; true, she couldn't accustom herself to seeing him as a man, but as a being of some other genus. Micaela wondered whether he was an angel or a simpleton, with all his learning and erudition.

Two years slipped by. Leoncio was earning more all the time, but not enough to get married. Micaela wondered whether the engagement with Leoncio would not be a false trail in her ambitions.

Around then a young dandy began to court her; he was not shy in confessing that he didn't intend her for a wife but rather for a mistress, and he proposed to deposit in the bank, in her name, a regular amount. Micaela, convinced that "all men are disgusting creatures," heard the proposition without surprise or anger. She replied that she would think it over. Her cold body and austere spirit recoiled at the deal, but the easy and secure wealth was an enticement to her ambition. In her cogitations and uncertainties, she happened to recall a certain María Egipciaca Barranco, daughter of a president of the Town Hall, who, tearing herself away from home, had embarked on a life of easy virtue and now, a target for scandal, strutted through the town all dressed up and provocative, without anyone deigning to speak to her in public, not even the very lovers who paid for her finery. "No," Micaela told herself, "money without dignity is not aristocracy." Keen-eyed ambition struck down the false image of ambition.

From where did she get this idea of aristocracy, core of her spirit, which she carried inside her head since time immemorial, since, one might even say, before being born? She had a revelation. Catching her mother off guard, she suddenly asked her, "Whose daughter am I?"

The mother instantly lost her indelible red coloration. She stammered . . .

"What I mean is, what was my father?"

The mother pulled herself together instinctively to prepare the narrative and melodramatic scene which might move Micaela's clemency and bring forth her forgiveness, since the most sincere and simplest beings are the most impoverished in expression and do not know how to project what is in their hearts except with exaggerated theatrical gestures. Only the hard nosed are devoid of histrionics. Micaela's mother began the tale: "A señor . . ."

And before she might pronounce the third word, Micaela interrupted, "Enough!"

"For God's sake, let me explain to you! You'll understand and forgive me."

"I have nothing to forgive you for. I know what I needed to know."

Leoncio, now a partner in The Nineteenth Century and orphaned, married Micaela. The couple settled down in a middle class neighborhood. Her ascetic type of religiosity, frigid puritanical fervor, infused Micaela with fortitude to undergo the conjugal initiations without repulsion, with resigned passivity.

Urbano was born, and after a while the second of the fundamental ideas in Doña Micaela's mind took shape. At times she had been overwhelmed by a longing: "Why can't I be a man?"

Now a mother, one day while holding in her hands the little creature—soft, pliable, and unaware, like clay that awaits the shape the potter may wish to give it—she thought, "Now I am a man; my son is I myself; I will make of him whatever I like. Here I have life, blind life, which can be evil and sorrow or goodness and happiness, subject to my decision." She suddenly glimpsed twenty years' future compressed into the present moment. Her skin grew cold, and she nearly fainted. She would make of her son the exact opposite of what she had been. She knew everything repugnant in life at the age of eight. Her son would come to marriage without having suspected let alone known anything. He would be the first example of a perfect man. Like an apprehension or a buzzing, she thought she heard inside her head: "What a foolish dream!" Rigid, Micaela replied aloud, "It will be! It will be! It will be, just as I make it!" with such desperate energy that she drove her fingers into the baby's flesh and made him cry.

For four years she kept the child close to her breast without anyone else's touching him. This was the time when she brought him as companion and tutor Don Cástulo.

Don Cástulo was so addlepated that he had failed in everything. He had tried for several professorships, but on taking the orals he panicked and was overcome by dizziness. He was living then as a private tutor with a meager income.

Doña Micaela placed complete confidence in Don Cástulo's honesty and learning. He was the mentor destined by the Almighty for Urbano.

"Listen to me carefully," Doña Micaela told him. "My son will be a man and he must get married pure as the snow."

Then she gave him precise orders and outlined for him the blueprint of the future, with the aplomb of an architect who has checked all the calculations and tolerances. Her severe face was not set vaingloriously, but with firmness and confidence.

Don Cástulo exclaimed, "I always proclaimed you an extraordinary woman. That plan, without your knowing it, had already occurred to none less than Plato and to Calderón de la Barca."

"Who are those gentlemen? People of old lineages?"

"Very old indeed; the one goes back more than two centuries and the other more than twenty-four. So then. And not only to those two gentlemen did your plan occur, but also to a king. May I read you a short paragraph from one of my books?"

Don Cástulo returned with a slender volume.

"This book is called *Novellino*; it's in Italian and was written in the fourteenth century." He searched for the passage and read: *"Of how a king brought up a son of his in a cave, and afterward, showing him all things, what pleased him most were women.* To a king was born a son. The wise astrologers forewarned that he must remain twenty years without seeing the light of day. Then they kept watch over him and kept him in a dark cave. After the stated time they took him out and set before him many precious things and beautiful maidens, calling each thing by its name, and of the maidens they told him they were demons. They asked him then what was the thing that he liked most. He replied, 'the demons.' Then the king marveled exceedingly, exclaiming: 'How much tyranny and beauty there is in woman!' "

"It's not that my son," replied Doña Micaela, "must not see women. For now he won't be leaving my side. Neither will it be possible to avoid his seeing women in the street or in church. The point is that my son not see the woman in women. I've already told you; Urbano must arrive at marriage pure as the snow, with his mind as clean and unsullied as a newborn babe's."

"But, carried to that extreme, won't that be impossible?"

"I only condemn as impossible what should not be, even though it be and right before the eyes. If tomorrow you were to relate to me something obscene my son had done, I would reply to you: impossible. And I will not mean that it might not be true, but that it cannot continue being true. But everything, all that should be, can be and must be; it's a question of deciding it. Are you in doubt? Remember, I'm the woman who has seen the inferno."

"You're an extraordinary woman. Whatever you want, you'll achieve."

And with what assiduity and sharpsightedness did Doña Micaela, assisted by Don Cástulo, go about imposing arbitrary form on the helpless clay of Urbano! Over the course of many years, Don Cástulo characterized Urbano's education as a sublime work of energy, ingenuity, and art. Don Cástulo was proud of his collaboration as a journeyman; the master artist was Doña Micaela.

Doña Micaela expurgated the books her son studied, beginning with the Catechism, in which she found coarse and overly explicit references. She likewise censored in the Devotionary certain expressions about divine love conceived in terms of erotic love. She instructed Urbano's confessor so that he might not ask him indiscreet questions, which most of the time, instead of serving as relief and outlet for troubled consciences, are disquieting and suggestive of sin for virginal consciences.

In the household there was no other woman servant than the cook, a recluse who stuck close by her stove. Doña Micaela cleaned the house and a young peasant boy, changed periodically, waited on the table with white cotton gloves.

Don Cástulo did not part from Urbano's side. They slept in the same bedroom. The child did not leave the house, except for mass very early on Sundays with his mother and for a walk to the village, on occasional afternoons, with Don Cástulo. On the country walks Don Cástulo sometimes used to tell Urbano fairy tales and stories of enchantments, those most infantile ones which were approved by Doña Micaela, for example, "Open Sesame"; but most of the time they enjoyed themselves in puerile games, for the tutor was as ingenuous as the pupil.

Don Cástulo was, yes, superlatively ingenuous in his heart and conduct; not so in his imagination. Don Cástulo lived two parallel lives, autonomous and without mutual contact; a real life and a fantasy life. His spare and leisure time was spent in reading erotic authors, Greek and Latin. His imagination was crammed full of literary and vaporous eroticism, which was never inserted in real life, for want of empirical data and experiential points of reference. In his head, he was always going about lamenting, with epigrammatic atticism, the indifference of some Ionic, Corinthian, or perhaps Boetian courtesan: Erisila, Prodicea, Melissa, Heliodora, Berenice. Some nights, Urbano in bed, Don Cástulo said that he was going out for a breath of air. It was the conjuncture at which his imaginary ramblings assumed form and action. He lost himself in the back alleys, and sitting down on the threshold of some unknown mansion, supposed residence of the disdainful courtesan of the moment, would sigh, with the words of Callimachus, "Sleep without care, while I am lain on your porch, beneath the frost. May you some day come to find yourself in a bed like this in which you leave, cruel one! your lover. And you are merciless. The neighbors pity me; but you, not even in dreams. Soon enough white hairs will remind you of these wintry rigors and will avenge me." Afterward he returned home, quite refreshed. These erotic escapades belonged only to his fantasy life, and they were like an esoteric exercise that Don Cástulo permitted himself. He would rather have bitten off his own tongue than mention love in Urbano's presence: *maxima debetur pueris reverentia.*

On Urbano's reaching the age of eight, they enrolled him as a nonresident in the institute. Doña Micaela reviewed the textbooks beforehand and tore out the pages she considered suggestive or dangerous. In the history books she blotted out any reference to bastards, court favorites, and the tribute of the hundred maidens. On discovering in the physiology and organography text a chapter with plates on sex and its functions, Doña Micaela went white with rage.

"This," she declared, "is a plot of Jews and Freemasons to pervert Spanish youth."

Don Cástulo accompanied Urbano even to the point of going into the room where they gave him his final examination and waited for him to leave, so that he might not speak with and be contaminated by any other student. Thus he concluded his secondary education.

For the law course, Don Cástulo abridged the lessons of each subject into respective synopses, which then, after being well scrutinized by Doña Micaela, were given to Urbano to study, until he repeated them by heart, without giving them nor seeking in them the least meaning. Moreover, Doña Micaela snipped out chapters and even entire sections from the texts, without fear of penalty in the examination, since shortly before the end of the course Don Leoncio, on his wife's orders, bribed the professors by sending them objects from the store as gifts—plaster of paris figurines, lamps, and razor cases.

Don Leoncio disapproved of Micaela's system of education; but, stymied by his wife's despotism, he did not dare to grumble. On one occasion, he asked Don Cástulo secretly, "Don't you think that the education being given to Urbano is absurd?"

26

"Psss. In this manner royal princes are educated."

Nevertheless, as the years went by, Don Cástulo was assailed by serious doubts whether Micaela would not be making—with unheard of thoroughness and talent, true enough, and even as it were with genius—an enormous and horrible mistake, because the fact is that Micaela achieved the full measure of her idea. At the age of twenty, in love and set to marry, Urbano was as innocent of the mysteries of physical love as at the moment of coming into the world. Or, in the words of Don Cástulo, "*Tanquam tabula rasa,* strange as it might seem."

Doña Micaela's other idea, social ambition, had been realized in part and was on the eve of being realized to her heart's content. People of rank and quality, like the Boscosos, mother and son, frequented her company, and she was about to be related through marriage with the Cerdeños, old bluebloods of the province.

For the past twelve years at the beginning of summertime, Don Leoncio, with his wife, his son, and Don Cástulo, spent a fortnight at the sulfur spa of Fuenfermosa, for the good gentleman suffered from shingles. This matter of shingles confirmed in Doña Micaela's mind that her husband, as a bachelor, had carried on a wild and despicable life.

On one of the first of these stays, Doña Micaela struck up a casual acquaintanceship with the widow of a certain Cea, an army officer. She was a childish woman, her hair cut in bangs, saffron colored, and curly as parsley; nervous and possessed by a swarm of facial tics. She was accompanied by her mother, a respectable señora of the old school—shawl and bonnet—a handsome young priest, and her only daughter, six years old, Simona.

Doña Micaela felt from the first a kind of awe and ineffable devotion for that so strange and out of the ordinary little woman. She treated her always with great respect.

One afternoon, going for the daily dose of stinking water, the widow Cea, Victoria by name, who was strolling between the priest and Doña Micaela, said out of the blue to her new friend, "Urbano

27

and Simona are almost the same age. If right now, between ourselves, we were to decide to marry them some day . . ."

Doña Micaela, dissolving in curtsies, almost breathlessly, replied, "Oh! Mercy me, Doña Victoria!—You're aristocrats; we're
shopkeepers."

With an automatic twitch, the young widow replied, "Pshaw!
But you're rich."

Doña Micaela said, "You're richer."

And the widow, "Well so much the better."

In the weakest voice, Doña Micaela dared to ask, "Are you
serious about it?"

The widow extended her hand: "Shake on it."

They sealed the bargain.

On returning from the walk, Doña Micaela said to Don Cástulo, "The rule that Urbano not play with any other child has one
exception. He must play every day with Simona Cea."

And, at the age of nine, Urbano fell in love, after his fashion,
with Simona, the only little girl he had ever encountered; and Simona, who customarily lived on without leaving a large country
estate, fell in love with Urbano.

The late Captain Cea, a frenetic gambler, had left pressing
debts. For her part, his wife threw money around freely. As a widow
she had gotten a yen for traveling. She took the young priest along
with her, as her chaperon. By the time of her widowhood, the combined Cea and Cerdeño fortune was already no little bit depleted.
The widow had recourse to loans and mortgages, concealing this
from her mother, Doña Rosita. After the pact with Doña Micaela,
the widow began to borrow money from Don Leoncio, who gave it
to her on nominal interest with only her word as collateral. Of these
unprofitable transactions, Leoncio said nothing to Doña Micaela.
The Fano family and the Cea family lived in separate towns, several
hours apart by stagecoach. They met infrequently. The two señoras
kept in touch. They never neglected to reconfirm the pact relating
to the future marriage.

"Twenty," said the widow Cea, "is the perfect age. Simona is going to school in the Salesas convent. She will stay there until she's nineteen. Until then it's not prudent that he or she find out that they are destined to be husband and wife. Then, a few months of engagement and marriage."

Doña Micaela adjudged the plan admirable.

No sooner had Simona left the Salesas convent than Doña Micaela took Don Leoncio one Sunday morning, led him to the coach line, and on the road, in the berlin of the stagecoach, explained to him that they were going to ask Simona's hand.

The provident mother opened a small traveling bag and displayed a jeweled bracelet: "The engagement bracelet. It cost only fifteen hundred *pesetas*. Menéndez, the jeweler, will send you the bill at the store."

Don Leoncio's eyes and his brain suddenly fogged. The horse-bells of the team echoed inside his hollow skull. In a fleeting transition, his head turned into a resonant horsebell, inside of which tinkled a phrase, beating against the interior walls: "Oh-my-God! Oh-my-God! Oh-my-God!"

Doña Micaela added, "I see you're delighted, as I am. It was my life's dream."

Don Leoncio pulled himself together and asked for some history of the unexpected news. Doña Micaela replied triumphantly, "What will a mother not do for the good of a son? Victoria and I arranged this together years ago. Recently, we've worked it out down to the smallest details. The children will go to live in a flat in one of the houses on Calvario Street which are owned by Victoria, who, in addition will send them a thousand *reales* a month. We will send them two thousand *reales* more. Victoria pledged to pay for the furniture and wardrobe. I've arranged to have those expenses billed to us. The little couple will have around two thousand *duros* a year and free lodgings. They can have a carriage. I even think we'll be able to have them granted a title. Simona has a right to it on both sides of her family."

Aided by the jolting of the carriage, Don Leoncio replied with quavers of seeming violence, "In the first place, Victoria is riddled with mortgages and at the mercy of moneylenders. It will be public knowledge soon enough. From me, she has gotten at various times, over the last eleven years, more than fifteen thousand *duros,* which I consider down the drain."

"Are you sure?" asked Doña Micaela, with a horrified grimace.

"If only it weren't so," sighed Don Leoncio.

The woman was not long in recovering from the bitter surprise: "It doesn't matter," she said, "if Victoria is ruined. We have more than enough money."

"That's where you're wrong,' Don Leoncio confessed, crestfallen. "My business is going badly. We can't permit ourselves the least luxury. I hadn't wanted to tell you anything to spare you worries and because the situation is still not irremediable."

"Bah, bah, bah!" replied Doña Micaela, laughing. "I see what you're up to. Your stinginess; you've always been a skinflint. Tomorrow I myself am going to the store and I'm looking over the books."

In the books there were juicy entries, for love offerings, which Don Leoncio could not possibly explain to his wife. (The one who, over the years, had captivated Don Leoncio's fancy and his income was María Egipciaca Barranco, that highborn prodigal, target for scandal in the town, who had served as an example for Micaela as a young girl in deciding to reject a seductor, the strongest temptation of her life. Now, Doña Micaela, wrinkled, her bosom flattened by a denim corset cover, dressed in black, looked like a scrawny Lenten image; María Egipciaca, plump and sleek, a pre-Lenten feast puppet.) He felt faint. He whispered, "You don't have to go to that extreme. I've told you that the situation isn't irremediable."

"I had a feeling it wouldn't be so bad. Today, we are asking for Simona's hand. Tomorrow, it will be another day," Doña Micaela said.

And Don Leoncio, cowed, let it pass, trusting in the near Future to fatally thwart the wedding.

The confession of his shaky financial affairs Don Leoncio had made was certain; highly certain that of the bankruptcy, snarled accounts, and bad debts of the widow Cea. But beyond the monetary question, which was no little matter, what sorely troubled Don Leoncio's heart was a prescient revelation of how very unhappy his son was going to be marrying under such circumstances, so young and, above all, so without any experience even of the simplest facts and fancies of love, which not even children in knee pants are wont to be totally ignorant of.

Husband and wife arrived at the town of Regium and from there, in a hired cab, headed for Collado, the estate where the two widows lived, not far from town but already the country.

It was in the beginnings of summer.

The estate, which was very extensive, was enclosed by a battlemented wall, a walk atop. Within the precinct, in addition to a park and gardens, there were large vegetable plots with borders of several kinds of fruit orchards, pastures where a large herd of spotted cows grazed, hen coops, rabbit warrens, and beehives.

From the entrance gate—a Roman arch between two emblazoned guardhouses—there rose in a smooth, ascending slope an avenue, festooned with rose bushes, hydrangeas and geraniums, which, like an ivory knife split in half a green hill on whose height there sprang skyward a small forest or tuft of deep green cedars, laurels, and elms, almost black against the sun. Within the grove, cloistered in thick and caressing shade, the mansion lay hidden, showing just scant dark fragments of its granite walls or fleeting bluish glints from its slate roof, through the close arboreal jalousie.

At the foot of and beyond the crowned and stately hill, against the background of the sweeping and craggy terrain, there rose with even and gentle modulations a panorama of pastures and cultivated fields, framed and protected within the battlemented wall; an ex-

31

quisite bucolic poem, come alive, on the rustic sleepiness of the country, of eternal hours and blurred horizons. The sun chanced to strike against the copper of a cowbell dangling beneath the chin-fold of a matronly cow, and one did not know whether the clear and long and oscillating tinkling was a reflection of the sound or an echo of the light. The golden voice of a shepherd spread abroad in vibrant waves, one with the day's splendor.

The carriage was crossing the threshhold of the property, when Doña Micaela, from the coach, took in at a glance the idyllic surroundings, from which emanated a smooth and fragrant feeling; she saw, ahead, the florid hill from whose wooded height the cream-colored avenue descended, which seemed to her a torrent of the sweetest milk which overflowed in her heart and drowned her in unknown pleasures. She murmured, as if in a trance, lightly resting a hand on the thigh of her intimidated and dispirited husband, "Have you seen the escutcheons at the entrance? What an estate! This is the happiest day of my life. The next, happier still, will be before the year is out, when they get married; the next, even happier, in around two years, when God presents me with the first grandchild."

Don Leoncio, unable to contain himself, exclaimed, "A son of our son? Good grief! Really, that's going too far."

Doña Micaela did not hear. She went on, "This princely home will be Urbano's."

Don Leoncio raised his voice, "Wake up, Micaela, wake up. This home will not be Urbano's. Even now it almost doesn't belong to the widow, who has it mortgaged to the swine Forjador for eighty thousand *duros*. And, where is she going to raise that?"

Doña Micaela spun around, furious: "You've always got to mix aloes in the bread of good fortune, you wretch. If the estate is mortgaged, we'll raise the mortgage."

Don Leoncio mumbled, "You're out of your mind."

The carriage stopped at the entrance to the mansion.

The widow Cea came out to receive the couple, with her short and curly forelock of saffron and parsley, her amber complexion dappled with freckles, vitreous and greenish eyes, diminutive figure, and the convulsive movements of a mechanical doll.

They went into the drawing room.

There the old Doña Rosita, widow of Cerdeño, was waiting, garbed in the air of upstanding and ceremonious excellence that fine old silks possess; silken ivory complexion, silken white hair, coif and gloves of black silk cord, black brocade dress, purple silk mantle, black silk stockings and shoes. She did not seem like a creature of flesh and bone, but a precious idol, adorned with silken materials, so weightless that, taking her up in arms, she would crumple. The only thing about her that gravitated downward was a huge medallion hanging from her neck, half a palm in size; inside it was a miniature which portrayed, from the knees up, a young girl dressed in the style of the First Empire.

Doña Rosita inspired Don Leoncio right off with a desire to kneel down. Doña Rosita presented herself in his fancy as a church image; the Mother of God, but even more deserving of respect and adoration, since—Don Leoncio felt, intuitively—they depict the Mother of God as young and beautiful; now then, inasmuch as the mother is young, neither a son nor anyone else can see in her the mother, but the woman. The symbol of maternity, as Don Leoncio understood it, not as the act of procreation but rather from the point of view of filial homage, had to be embodied in an image of an old woman, beautiful and without material humanity; and thus was Doña Rosita. Don Leoncio, transfixed by an almost religious ecstasy, stood trembling, contemplating in detail the miniature that hung on the bosom of the old woman. In fact, Don Leoncio, keyed up and feverish, took the miniature for a reliquary of the kind that he so often had seen in altars; open niches in the torso of statues, where bones or relics of ancient saints' lives are contained. Behind the glass of the miniature there extended a brilliant and diurnal hollow, which was the secret boundary of Doña Rosita's soul; and like a crypt one looked into it from without to see the past from afar, and at the same time the present, of her youth, incarnate with miraculous virtue of perpetuity in the just-pubescent and fresh lass of the Napoleonic era. As Don Leoncio was not versed in history, he took it for granted that that girl was Doña Rosita as a youngster.

"Are you looking at the miniature?" asked the old woman.

Don Leoncio assented tacitly, nodding

"Whom do you think it is?" she asked once more.

"It's you," Don Leoncio replied, unhesitatingly.

"Come closer, examine it well," Doña Rosita invited, extending the miniature with her hand.

Don Leoncio, respectful and deferential, approached. From the old woman there emanated a penetrating perfume of bergamot. Don Leoncio scrutinized the miniature. It bore a perfect resemblance to Simona.

"It's your granddaughter," Don Leoncio said without hesitation.

Doña Rosita laughed, with a young but hollow laugh, which came swirling up from the depths of long ago, and finally she commented, "Well, it's my grandmother. Life's strange tricks."

And she placed the enameled child's face side by side with her own, of faded ivory silk.

Meanwhile, Doña Micaela, as she chatted with the widow Cea, was glancing sideways at the family portraits around the room. Two details vexed her, thinking of her son, and she hoped to God that the innocent might not enter that room until after his marriage: one, the shockingly low necklines of the ladies; the other, in the likenesses of the gentlemen in jousting garb, the excessive prominence and ostentation of that piece of armor which was denominated "codpiece."

The engagement petition was verified. The reading fell to Doña Micaela. The widow Cea, twisting around toward Doña Rosita, as if controlled by a spring, said, "Mama, it's for you to reply first."

The old woman spoke: "In my time, this marriage might not

have been accepted, because the groom is not of our rank and blood. Today it is different. Wealth, honestly earned, is the same as high rank. I accede and I am honored. I remark only that the wedding is somewhat tardy. My grandmother married at fourteen. I married you off at fifteen. It's all right all the same, because my granddaughter is like a little girl of six, and I know for a fact that her fiancé is just the same as she."

The chaplain of the household was present, Don Eleuterio Muñiz, the one who escorted and chaperoned the young widow on her travels, a man slightly under forty, of reserved and yellowish countenance.

"And you, what do you say, Don Eleuterio?" asked the widow Cea.

"*Placet*," answered the cleric, tracing a sign in the air, which as well could have been a benediction as a gesture that disembarrassed the mother from the care of the daughter, tossing her to one side.

The two widows, Doña Micaela, and the priest were for an immediate wedding, in two or three months. It was clearly apparent that the young widow, Simona's mother, was in a great hurry.

Don Leoncio thought, "Poor woman; you hope that with my money you'll get out of trouble—I, who am up to my own neck in hot water."

Doña Rosita desired a quick wedding for other reasons, especially for the sake of tradition. She was totally unaware in any event that her daughter and her son-in-law might have squandered the family fortune.

Don Leoncio, allying himself as a last resort with the most powerful arbiter of conflicts, time, insisted on an engagement period of at least one year before the wedding.

They called Simona. Doña Micaela placed the engagement bracelet upon her and kissed her on the cheeks.

Don Leoncio kissed the young girl on the forehead. Simona's face was aglow. On kissing her, Don Leoncio, softened instantly into tenderness, said to himself, "How strange things are! Why do I not want Simona as a daughter? How well suited to be the child's wife. Ay! If in this next year I might make a man out of Urbano . . . then, let them marry, even without a *cuarto*. He would earn it later, and they would be lucky. Lord, who is it Simona reminds me of? That coppery, shiny hair; that white, creamy skin; those eyes so round and so black; that mouth so red and tempting; that splash of charming freckles. How luscious this little girl is! Like a sweet dessert, rice pudding with little spots of cinammon, the freckles; a little fiery red cherry and two sweet black berries on top, which are the mouth and eyes; and the whole, served in a dish of reddish beaten gold, which is her hair. But, besides, she reminds me of someone else. Who?"

Almost the whole year went by, and Don Leoncio had not been able to intervene to make a man out of his son. Urbano remained under his mother's dictatorial thumb, as much a child, simple and helpless in the face of the world as on the day he was born.

During the courtship, Doña Micaela directed and coached her son, sometimes directly, with maternal solicitude, in the most frequent and clearest cases; sometimes indirectly, through the passive and thoroughly instructed Don Cástulo, in the more delicate and embarrassing exigencies—for example, epistolary correspondence.

Firstling lovers, even the most discreet, feel the necessity of communicating with and unburdening themselves to someone. This insuperable desire is like a physical necessity, by which is exhaled the anxiety and aspiration which the soul is continually generating and inhaling; a kind of sigh, but far more profound than the pneumatic sigh of the lungs. In order for the lover to venture to relieve himself of these oppressions, with superabundant expirations, it is necessary that there assist him one of two unique propitious conditions: solitude, in which case he talks to himself, or perhaps carries on with trees, rocks, and stars, which is the poetic manner; or the confidence of a bosom friend, which is the more satisfactory and relief giving. Urbano had a half friend: Don Cástulo. To him he revealed himself, and with him he consulted over the rudiments of epistolary romance. He would write daily and throughout most of the day. The letters were minute annotations of all his acts: "I awoke at seven-thirty. I washed up. I got dressed in my everyday clothes. I put on the violet-colored tie, which you told me last Sunday you liked so much. I breakfasted on hot chocolate, because I'm tired of coffee with milk now. I went to mass, with Mama. I prayed for you. It's raining and this makes me sad. I've been indoors in my room all morning, studying forensic practice and international law with Don Cástulo. What a bore! I don't know what such gibberish is good for. At noontime we ate greens soup, stew, and croquettes to start out with," etc., etc.

"What do you think of it?" Urbano asked the preceptor. "Simona will be happy. I tell her everything."

Don Cástulo, obeying orders from Doña Micaela, who secretly read Urbano's letters and those of Simona, replied, "The letter is to the purpose; but it ought to be livened up a bit with little sweet and affectionate touches. Such as: my dearest, my treasure, queen, I dream of you, I cannot live without you, I adore you."

Urbano, with moist eyes, exclaimed: "What beautiful words! I feel all this and much more. My heart is as if bursting and I don't know how to express myself. My dearest, my treasure, I dream of you . . . . It's true, it's true. I cannot live without you. True, true, true. Sometimes I think I'll die. I adore you. It's also true; but, won't it be a sin?"

Don Cástulo was touched and smiled.

"Hush, foolish boy. That's just a manner of speaking."

"No; it's the truth, it's the truth."

"It is the truth, yes," assented Don Cástulo, who was passing through a new imaginary existence, having come to believe he himself to be the protagonist in the love affair and author of the love letters, though he imagined them as directed to an ideal woman, his feminine archetype. As his ingenuousness and inexperience of the world in any event rivaled Urbano's—leaving aside his chimerical, disdainful courtesans—he came to fantasize by imperceptible pleasant stages the arbitrary fantasy that he, and not Urbano, was a young lad, brought up on the orders of his father, the king, inside a cave, avoiding all human contact in order that one day he might know a single woman, the Woman *par excellence*, and that he might enjoy love, One And Only Love, as no one had enjoyed it since Adam. And imagining these pipedreams, he thought of Segismundo of *Life Is a Dream*, from whence he came back to advise Urbano to incrust, like a gem, in one of his letters the verses that Segismundo breathes from the depths of his heart on first meeting Rosaura:

> Each time I see you
> you fill me with admiring,
> and when I look more
> still more to look desiring . . .

Going on in his fantasies, almost as real as reality itself, Don Cástulo saw himself now as married to the Archetypal Woman, all alone, in the chamber of Hymen. And at this critical moment, his heart failed him, his limbs turned to jelly, he swooned with mortification, and in the end he saw himself running away madly, like an ox stung by a horsefly. And transferring this situation, exceedingly critical and tragicomic, to the imminent future in the life of his pupil Urbano, he inferred that that ideal marriage, incubated and hatched in accord with a scrupulous moral standard, could no less bring in its wake ridiculous and unhappy consequences.

Doña Micaela was not of the opinion that the couple should come together often before the wedding. During the year of engagement, Urbano went but five times to visit Simona. Don Cástulo accompanied him, not only on the stagecoach journey but afterward, on Doña Micaela's orders, all the time the youngsters were with one another. Old Doña Rosita was also present at the amorous colloquies, which were not colloquies as such, since they neither spoke to nor looked at one another, except with reservedness and alternately, not being able, because of confusion, to sustain a shared look. There weighed upon them the preoccupation that the affection of man for woman, and its corollary, matrimony, were serious and bitter dangers from which they could not be saved without the guidance of the grownups. Previously, when they were children, there in the Fuenfermosa spa, they were allowed to meet freely. They sometimes held hands and were happy. Now they felt doubly unhappy, because a greater appetite for happiness fired them, which was suppressed and annulled by a type of unyielding and unclear obstacle: social conventions and misguided education. The desire for happiness in them was something like the seed of a little flower that by chance germinates in the subsoil of a street and, on trying to break forth to the light, happens to run into the bottomside of the urban pavement.

The business affairs of Señor Fano went from bad to worse. Those of the widow Cea from worse to dreadful. But Don Leoncio kept afloat, the widow did not declare bankruptcy and time, Don Leoncio's ally, in spite of a campaign of nearly a year, had not defeated the wedding.

Every day, after dinner, a familiar polemic scene was played out over whether the marriage was or was not premature. On rare occasions, the performance was canceled when there came to visit and have coffee Doña Encomienda, the widow Boscoso, and her son Paolo.

Although Paolo was past fifty, his mother always called him "little one" and treated him like a child. Little one had had a fiancée since his adolescence, that is for a period of thirty-five years; but his mother did not consent to his marrying yet, because, she explained, "Paolo is too young. At his age, one should enjoy oneself. Obligations and worries will come in due time, and perhaps all too soon. Meanwhile, let him amuse himself with his collections of antique harnesses and treatises on bridlery and horsemanship, and with breaking colts; for you must know that Paolo is the best horseman in Spain and the most learned in equitation."

He was seen continually parading through the streets, now one, now another, creaky old nags of all sorts, saddled with historical brocaded trappings; six meters to his rear, a footman, on another nag, sorrier still than that of the master. Don Cástulo, the Hellenist, used to say, "There's nothing so beautiful as a hexameter followed by a pentameter; it's like a gentleman escorted by his servant, likewise a gentleman. And a gentleman, with his escort, is like a hexameter followed by a pentameter, the happiest and most majestic metrical combination."

Upon the mother and son's going away, Don Leoncio advised Doña Micaela: "Take a look at that case. Paolo is older than I and, nevertheless, to his mother it seems that it's too early for him to marry."

And Doña Micaela replied disdainfully, "You never get the point. It's not that he's young, but that the fiancée comes from a lower class family. Doña Encomienda is in her place. On the other hand Urbano is marrying a girl who is a blueblood from head to toe: the daughter of General Cea."

"My dear," objected Don Leoncio, "Simona's father was a captain."

"And since he died sixteen years ago, now he would be a general. That's plain as pudding," concluded Doña Micaela.

And so it went, up until that after-dinner discussion of the eighth of June, when invisible Destiny tossed his dice, and Doña Micaela, whose will was also crass, supine, and affected, like that of Destiny, decreed the same date of the following month for the wedding.

The wedding was celebrated in the Collado chapel. Among the guests were found Doña Encomienda and her son, Paolo, the Centaur, in riding boots, which he never took off. His mother said to the other guests, "All of you are invited to the forthcoming wedding of my little one, some time in the space of the next five years. There's no hurry until he reaches sixty, a man's age of maturity."

Don Eleuterio Muñiz, the widow Cea's chaplain, officiated.

Doña Micaela wore some large black feathers on her head,

which she shook from time to time with pomp like a horse in a funeral cortège.

The widow Cea fluttered about, pompous, tiny, and wound up, like a music box doll.

Doña Rosita was like an image with processional trappings; she had put on, beneath her black toque, a ruffle of white and very fine thread, and trailed a train of otherworldly silkiness.

Don Leoncio wore his new cutaway jacket, which pinched him in the armpits—and also in his conscience, for he feared not being able to pay the tailor for it. In order to hide the dejection and sadness in his heart, concentrating all his energies on his expression, he compressed his brow and lips and held erect his head, grayed and yellowed, in a pose as severe and hard—on the outside—as that of a Huguenot.

Don Cástulo, in the tribunal of his conscience, found himself as shaky as Don Leoncio. He recalled certain times, as a spectator in the theater when, if firearms were brandished in a scene, he would cover his ears for fear of the explosion. There, a front row spectator at the wedding—it was decreed that he be the eternal spectator—he might have liked to stop up the ears and eyes of his soul, so he would not have to witness the cataclysm that of necessity had to supervene.

After the nuptial banquet, the newlyweds were to go in a landau alone as far as Regium and take the stagecoach to Penedo, where they would spend their honeymoon at the seaside. It was Doña Micaela's firm conviction that, now married and by mere virtue of the sacrament, the newlyweds were converted all at once into grownups and were able to get along by themselves without outside assistance.

At the moment of the farewell, Doña Rosita, who prided herself on having a safe, sound, and almost pessimistic philosophy of life, in the old manner, said sententiously, "You are now, my children, on your full honeymoon. From here on begins the waning moon."

Urbano clung tenaciously to his father's neck, crying and blubbering into his ear: "For God's sake, don't let me go. I'm scared."

Doña Micaela came up to her husband, furious and fierce, and in a hoarse whisper so that the others might not hear muttered, "What dirty thing have you said to him, you devil? Don't pay him any mind, Son, even if he is your father."

Don Leoncio did not reply for he too was crying.

Doña Micaela added, directing herself to her son, with imperious eyes, beneath her austere brow, "The Guardian Angel will go along with you."

Paolo said, "I'll go with them on horseback as far as the stage-coach, as a mounted escort."

And he retired to summon his steed.

At last the couple left, in the landau. From Collado to the stagecoach office took a little over half an hour. Urbano and Simona rode along with their heads down, not looking at one another; she awaiting she knew not what and he fearing he knew not what. Twenty minutes out along the road, within Urbano's foggy brain some ideas began to form and take shape. He thought, "Why am I frightened? I felt, and Mama confirmed it for me, that I would be happy getting married. Then I should be happy now that I am married." He sighed aloud, "How happy I am!"

Simona, without raising head nor eyes, returned, in a hollow echo, the exclamation, "How happy I am!"

And in the ten minutes remaining that they took in reaching the stagecoach office they considered themselves exquisitely happy.

On boarding the stagecoach, they behaved with so much uneasiness and nervousness that the passengers looked at them with irony and suspicion. Though very confused, Urbano chanced to overhear a bad-smelling fellow, probably a fish seller, say, among other unintelligible things, these two words, "Abduction. Parras."

The newlyweds had seats in the front of the coach. Also traveling in the berlin were two French nuns.

Since the nag Paolo was riding was worn out and dilatory, despite much spurring the landau had gotten far ahead of him, and the

42

newlyweds were already departing in the noisy stagecoach, swept up in a whirlwind of sparks, dust, horsebells, and whipcracks, when the horseman appeared at the end of the street.

Paolo, standing up in the stirrups, flung his arms about in wildly enthusiastic good-bye waves, whereby the passengers in the stagecoach were convinced that Simona was being abducted and that that aged rider, perhaps the offended father, had come, a moment too late, in pursuit of the fugitives.

Urbano rode along hunched up, next to a little window. The noisy and strong swaying of the vehicle made him close his eyes, as if he were falling precipitously through an abyss. From the bottom of his heart a desperate prayer rose to his consciousness: "If only it were true that we were falling over a precipice! I would seize Simona and die with her in my arms!" But as the fall went on and on, without reaching bottom, Urbano at last had to open his eyes. The stagecoach was going along a shabby street on the way out of town. The townsfolk, barely clothed in filthy rags, were seated on low stools outside their hovels. One girl, in a corset, bust and arms exposed, was combing herself right in the street, looking in a piece of mirror that she had in her lap and moistening the comb in a cracked china bowl that lay on the ground. The girl did not even turn her gaze on the stagecoach's passing. A mother was washing a baby, naked from the waist down, which she lifted up by the armpits and showed to the travelers by the back, as if by chance, for she as well as several neighbors burst into peals of laughter. Some incredibly feeble old men were sunning themselves, mummified and impassible, their hands resting on the crooks of canes. The local dogs ran on one side and the other of the carriage, so scrawny that, for lack of breath, their barking sounded like groaning; a flock of ragged urchins begged for a *cuartín* or an *ochavín,* stretching their bare and skeletal arms toward the carriage door. Diverted by these novelties, Urbano forgot Simona and himself. The stagecoach went out into the open country. The light—white, thick, and palpable light, mixed with the dust—entered in torrents through the berlin's little windows. But to Urbano it seemed then that he was short of light, along with breath. He pressed further into his corner, so as not to make contact with Simona. If with a lurch of the coach he came perhaps to touch her, there spread throughout his body a sickening faint. He closed his eyelids once more. The two words that he had heard from the sardine-smelling man came back to mind. "It's the second time," he thought, "that I hear that word: abduction. The other time I heard it from Papa, a month ago. Juanito Parras, it seems, went off on a trip with a one-eyed maidservant; alone, like me now with Simona. They call Juanito Parras' trip an abduction, and add that it was a scandal and that they were stopped. Why was Juanito Parras traveling with the one-eyed maidservant? Why am I traveling with Simona? Our parents call this a wedding and honeymoon trip. What will strangers call it, those who don't know us? They call it abduction, I've clearly heard. Then I've no doubt that we're occasioning a great scandal. Really, this is very confusing, very distressing. I could cry. How I'd like to go home. Guardian Angel, help me." As a long time passed without the summoned angel deigning to take note of him, Urbano went on thinking: "I'm very sorry not to be in agreement with Mama, but I think that it would have been much better if instead of the Guardian Angel Don Cástulo might have come along with us." Suddenly his heart began to jump for joy; a solution had occurred to him: "If they were to stop us, like Juanito Parras and the one-eyed maid . . . For that it will be necessary that I commit some outrage." He began to consider outrages. "They arrest thieves. If I were to steal something from one of these little nuns . . . My God, what a dreadful thing! That wouldn't be merely an outrage, but a sacrilege." And he looked once more at the nuns, with contrite eyes, as if he were begging their pardon. As his mind was drifting and unfocussed, his attention now remained fixed on the nuns. Something strange was happening to them. From time to time, the two, simultaneously, gave a little jump on the seat, something like a twitch; then they muttered some words in French and crossed themselves with rapidity. At first Urbano attributed it to a

44

violent hiccupping. He discarded this explanation, it being impossible that two people might hiccup so in unison, not even under the same monastic rule.

Then he observed that the twitches and subsequent crossings took place when the driver ejaculated certain round expressions that Urbano had never heard previously. "It must be," he thought, "that they're nervous and that brutal coachman startles them with his shouts." But neither did this explain the periodic and fleeting tribulation of the nuns, since after some of the fierce coachman shouts they remained quite calm while on the other hand they went through the whole routine at times when the driver did not raise his voice. "Now I understand," Urbano said to himself. "It's not a question of the tone, but of the word itself." He applied himself to studying the words that were alarming the nuns and found that they were three. "It means there are words that have the virtue of producing magic effects, like in the fairy tales Don Cástulo used to tell me. I'm going to try repeating one of them aloud." No sooner said than done. The nuns jumped, crossed themselves, and muttered. Simona turned her sweet face toward Urbano: "Did you say something, Urbano?"

Until that moment he had forgotten that he had Simona by his side, that she was his wife, and that they were traveling as newlyweds. An uneasiness crept over his breast, a shadow of irritation with Simona for having recalled him unexpectedly to real life, problematical and painful.

At this, the stagecoach stopped. A horse had fallen. The coachman rained furious blows on it in the kidneys, clutching the reversed whip by the lash end, and repeated curses and blasphemies in number equal to the blows. The nuns crossed themselves and crossed themselves, dizzily. They ended up covering their ears, for which they had to slip their fingers inside their fastened hoods. Simona hid her head in the bosom of the nun at her side. Urbano, trembling in all his members and more in his heart, thought, "Oh, God! Oh, God! This I understand. And what I said before would be the same, an indecent swear word, only I didn't understand it. Heaven forgive me! I didn't know. I know nothing. They haven't taught me anything. Lord knows. Those nuns are Frenchies and they know more Spanish than I, for they understood but not I. It's not my fault. Did Simona understand what I've said? Certainly not. All you had to do was look at her face."

And as soon as the stagecoach continued along the road, Urbano did not come out of himself for a long time, until they stopped in front of an inn.

Urbano saw that several of the passengers got down and entered the inn, and he got down and entered too. The others ordered white wine, and he ordered white wine. With the wine, there spread through his body an anxiousness to run and jump. He felt his cheeks inflamed, and his throat dry, as if in reality he had run and shouted a lot; but now he seemed to be master of himself, as never before. With glass in hand, he approached a circle of conversation and stood listening, like one of the boys. An astonishingly simple idea took hold of his mind: "If I were to make as if I were distracted and let the coach go off, and then . . . There's the way out."

There was a disturbance, because the coachman cracked his whip outside. The passengers pressed hurriedly out to the coach, and Urbano, swept up, saw himself spurred along with equal haste. On getting into his seat he was in very high spirits and was laughing. The stagecoach resumed the journey. Simona asked her husband, "What are you laughing at?"

"Well, you'll see, for a moment, I had an idea, but it's gone now, completely gone. It occurred to me when they were talking down there, in the inn. It was a marvelous idea. Never mind, it's gone now. Those people were saying . . . , wait. It's very funny. They say that our seven horses are blind and all are more than twenty years old. Since they've made the same trip thousands of times they know the road by heart, make the turns without being guided and stop where they're supposed to stop. Isn't that funny?"

"It's very funny," repeated Simona, and taking advantage of

the fact that Urbano was looking at her for an instant, she submerged herself, literally submerged herself, in his eyes and then let herself sink down, down, little by little into Urbano's soul as if into a bottomless sea.

She caused some sensation in Urbano. He left off looking at her, frightened; he closed his eyes, but now he carried Simona within himself and he saw her falling, falling upon his heart, crushing it, so that it was paralyzed and not allowed to breathe. "Why have I gotten married?" Urbano groaned to himself. "To be with Simona my whole life and to be happy, as Mother said I would be. This then is the happiness—and yet, I feel like breaking down and dissolving in tears. I'm choking. If only this trip were over. And what am I going to do with Simona?" The coach was descending a steep grade. The driver applied the axle brake, whose large plate screeched. The stridency infected Urbano, setting his teeth sharply on edge, and he was so far abstracted now from the outside world that to all his sensations he attributed spiritual origins, though at this moment it was nothing but a matter of a scratchy discordance on his overtaut nerves. "My teeth are gnashing; I could sink them into my own flesh," he said to himself. "My fingers are itching, with an urge to destroy and tear something to bits. My arms are tingling, with an urge to squeeze and squeeze something between them. Why can't one hug and kiss one's wife, like one's father and mother? Oh, no, no! It would be delightful, but terrifying. Simona would repulse me, if I were to try it. Only . . . if we were to make as if we were playing mother and son, she my mother . . . then . . . Oh, I feel sick. This must be what they call drunkenness. But how can I dare to suggest it to her? I'll die of shame first." Another idea occurred to him; in the inn, they had spoken of bandits, the Squinteye of Laredo and his gang, who a few days before had held up and robbed the stagecoach from Santander. "If bandits were to hold us up, and take me off with them—that would be a way out."

Simona, for her part, in her irreproachable simplicity, found everything natural. She supposed that thus it had happened and had

47

to happen in all the marriages there ever were, are, and will be. Being married now to Urbano she ought to be happy. And she was. With her faculties in delightful suspense, almost anguished, yet unhurried, but reveling in that delicate expectation of the body and the spirit, she awaited something marvelous—a shower of gold, a blinding splendor. The tinkling of the horsebells sounded to her like faraway and crystalline music, as in the ether of a swoon. A chance contact with Urbano flooded her soul with a loving, caressing, balsamic fluid, which was transmitted to her from her husband, in a mysterious and exquisite way, and which was flooding and swelling her heart, like a saturated sponge. Her longing was at once so heavenly and painful that she felt a need to direct her eyes toward the infinite, and she cast her glance out to the horizon. Behind some purple clouds, a nacreous mist was rising, incandescent, as though of otherworldly light. A formless little cloud floated in the light, of a supernatural rose color; a color that emanated from within and was not reflected from the surface, like the colors and hues of the world. The little cloud assumed the figure of an archangel, with silvery wings outstretched. Simona was hit by a sparkling dart in the breast, which passed straight through her; and without even thinking, she interpreted that divine vision by identifying it with the miracle of the Annunciation to the Virgin. Her insides crawled and a voice of seraphic timbre said within her, "You are going to be a mother." Her head slumped, completely pallid.

"Have you gotten sick?" asked Urbano, solicitous.

"It's nothing, it's nothing. I'm all right now," and she looked at her husband, blissfully, dissolving herself in the look.

And this look was the one that finished off frightening and dismaying Urbano, who shifted his terrified eyes, curling his lips and brows, to contain the exacerbated pain that was impelling him to break into a mad shriek.

The coach came to the end of the line in Penedo, at the door of the Don Bermudo Inn. This Don Bermudo was not an allusion to

48

the owner of the inn, but to a king of long ago who founded the town.

At the journey's end, Urbano was about out of his wits. He moved with great difficulty and without knowing what he was doing, following, instinctively like a herd animal, the group formed by the other people. And thus, he found himself in front of a counter which was the inn's office. Simona followed at his heels.

"One or two rooms? Are you a married couple, sweethearts, or brother and sister?" the manager asked indifferently.

One of the travelers, who had a mean look and a comic face, pushed forward to reply, waggishly, "They're a little brother and sister, can't you tell?"

Urbano's jutting jaw tightened. He marshaled his energies to resist the furious desire to escape running, running, running, until falling down somewhere bursting.

That they might be taken for brother and sister gave him some hope, and he judged it a singular divine favor.

"Yes, we're brother and sister. Two rooms."

A short while later, after changing, with a tongue dry, stiff, and light, like a cork, which hardly allowed him to speak, he explained, haltingly, to Simona, "I'm not having supper. I'm going to bed. I have a headache that's torturing me."

Simona, fervently, offered to take care of and sit up with him. He refused, choleric. Simona, meekly, said that she was not having supper either and that she was going to bed too. Simona slept the whole night through. In her dreams, she saw herself as the happiest of women; she was floating in a lake of aromatic oil, a transparent amber color, and over it the moon sprinkled its white and sweet glitter, like powdered sugar.

Urbano did not sleep a single instant. With his teeth he tore the pillow, beat his face with his hands, and did not cry only because his eyes were arid, parched by the fire of sterile love. After a long struggle, he lit the candle and paced about the room. The inn was built by the seaside. The surf resounded, vibrating against the walls with coarse and persistent rhythm, as if a saw were gnawing at the foundations of the house.

In the room was a dressing mirror. On passing by, Urbano saw himself reflected. He saw a phantasm, which was him and was not him. It was the Urbano of the moment, so different from the Urbano of the same day in the morning, the last time he had looked at himself in the mirror. Owing to the duplicity of images (that of he himself, in the flesh, which he touched, in order to be sure of its reality; and the other flat and phantasmagoric figure, under the moon of the mirror, like a glass image case), Urbano, insensibly, split and divided into two persons—the Urbano of always, and the Urbano of the moment, wretched and most unhappy. The Urbano of always finally had been disembodied and reduced to the Urbano of the moment, who was there, looking with a washed out and supplicating expression, like a soul in torment, at the Urbano of old. And the Urbano of old, he murmured in a broken and hateful voice to the Urbano of the moment, "You're an idiot."

But instantly he corrected himself: "No, no, poor fellow. The idiot is your mother."

And the Urbano of old felt so much tenderness and pity for the Urbano of the present moment that he got dizzy and wanted to kiss him on the forehead. He approached the image and on tilting his head to reach his forehead, the other, likewise, leaned his head back; and they kissed on the mouth. They had their lips glued.

He stretched out again on the bed, wishing it were a tomb. At this point he reasoned with some clarity: "I'm in a ridiculous position," he thought. "Why? What have I done to deserve it? I don't know anything. Well, that's why. I'm in a ridiculous position." As his mother's son, the feeling of being ridiculous exasperated him. He suspected that there must be some secret conjugal obligations, and the ignorance of them brought upon him the feeling of ridiculousness and stifled rage. "But," he went on, "what if there were no such obligations? Mightn't I be foolishly confused? Since Don Eleuterio has married us, isn't that all there is to it? What more is there to do?" He considered his situation one of absolute desperation: "Because," he went on, "desperation doesn't come from what's beyond repair. In what's beyond repair, since it is certain, one sits back. The cause of desperation is the uncertain. It's better to die once and for all than to be condemned to death, which is to die sixty times a minute. The cause of desperation is darkness, when we know that in its fearful hiding place our treasure is calling out to us, but we have no torch at hand. Cursed be the one who denied me light for the torch. I'm a man and I'm like a child lost between the forest and the night. Let this uncertainty end or I'll have to kill myself."

His will, beneath the surface and still not exercised, became taut.

For lack of other terms of choice, he preferred absurdity to indecision. He got up early and wrote to Simona: "I'm going to my home. You go to yours, in the first coach. We'll see each other soon, when the time comes.—*Urbano*"

And he took the wagon to Pilares, where his parents lived.

On Simona's waking, the first thing she did was to read Urbano's note. She stood confused for some moments, distracted. She thought it over for a while. She considered that decision of Urbano's also natural and in line with the usual practices in marriages.

Simona had received her very few notions about matrimony from her grandmother. She remembered then having heard the old woman say one time, "All men, one as another, fall short for us; and this is better than their being too much for us. In our family there is a sign that the newly married women lose their husbands. My own was very good, but he was always rambling far and wide. He was a frigate captain. I couldn't complain about him; but I was very unhappy; I cried a lot." Recalling these words, Simona felt under the obligation of being very unhappy and crying a lot.

When the maid came in with breakfast and asked the reason for the crying, Simona responded, without conviction, trying hard to cry with great dignity, "I'm very unhappy!"

The maid, believing her seduced and abandoned, lavished kind words on her, embellished with crude amatory examples, which Simona could not make hide nor hair of.

On her return to Collado, Simona found her grandmother alone. Her mama, the widow Cea, had gone off on a trip, chaperoned by the clergyman, the afternoon before, a little after the newlyweds.

Simona came in crying and saying, "I'm so unhappy," in childish and stilted tones.

Doña Rosita crossed herself: "And your husband?"

"I don't know."

"But, what's happened?"

"What always happens in marriages in our family; it's the sign. What happened to you," replied Simona, quite certain, leaving off crying. "I've lost Urbano."

"You've lost him? Where?"

"I don't know."

"Is it that you've quarreled? A tiff?"

"Quarreled? A tiff?" echoed Simona, openmouthed. Those were two words and concepts which didn't exist in Simona's vocabulary or understanding.

"Then," insisted Doña Rosita, "tell me, tell me."

Simona told in detail of her honeymoon trip. She concluded, "It's our family's sign. I've lost Urbano. Until he comes back, and he will come back (he's written it to me), I'll dedicate myself with my heart and soul to the child in my womb. Anyway, I'm very unhappy." And from repeating it so much, she began to feel unhappy for real.

Doña Rosita, avid, leaned forward to take her granddaughter by the hands.

"The child? What child? You're going to have a child? How can that be, from what you've told me?"

"I'm going to have a child. I didn't tell you everything just now.

You should have guessed it. On getting married one has children. It was on the trip, when we were going along in the stagecoach."

"In the stagecoach? God have mercy! Weren't there also two nuns with you?"

"Yes. And I believe it is partly due to the influence of the two holy women."

"Hail Mary, Mother of Jesus!"

Simona, then, narrated the apparition of the Angel of the Annunciation on the horizon. Doña Rosita had to struggle hard to hold the laughter back: "Good, my little one. First of all, let's hope that the father of that child that you must have returns. And now I'm going to tell you something, in your ear. Come close. Since the world began, there hasn't been a honeymoon more beautiful than yours."

But Simona insisted that she was very unhappy. Above all, for not being able to cry as profusely as she would have liked.

For his part, Urbano dropped into the paternal household as his procreators and tutor were finishing the midday meal. On seeing him appear, with a cadaverous face, eyes as though frozen in a vision of eternal terror, his strong jaw awry, Doña Micaela lowered her head for the first time in her house.

"Papa was right. I've learned from experience. I don't want to get married."

Don Leoncio was the one who recovered his voice first.

"Son, you're already married."

"It doesn't matter. I don't want to be with Simona."

"Whatever you wish, Son," replied Don Leoncio.

Confronted by Don Leoncio, Doña Micaela's just abated ferocity reared up with looming brusqueness.

"What are you saying there, you fool? He'll return, he'll return this very day, come what may and whatever may have happened. Who's in charge here? Would it be my husband, who only by the grace of God and the resignation of a martyr I put up with? Would it be my son, whom I have brought up for perfection on earth and blessed happiness in heaven?" Doña Micaela was speaking excessively, for abandoning herself to loquacity she gave herself the illusion of going about recouping energy and intimidating the others.

Urbano smiled with bitterness: "I won't go back!"

"Yes, you will go back, Son. Your mother says so," advised Don Leoncio softly. "Mothers are always right."

"I'll go back, Father, because you say so, and because . . . I love Simona." And he broke out crying. "But I won't go back without first having a talk with you. And I won't go back alone nor with just the Guardian Angel for company."

"You'll go back with Don Cástulo," said Doña Micaela, regaining her dictatorial mien now that the rebel was bawling.

"A pretty role! The one that's always fallen to my lot," exclaimed Don Cástulo. He was pensive a short while and added, "I accept it. I have an idea, provided Doña Rosita is willing to collaborate with me. The youngsters will stay a short while at Collado."

And, finally, as if he were speaking to himself, he murmured, "Daphnis and Chloe, reborn. *Nihil novum sub sole.*"

CRESCENT MOON

"*There's no time to lose,* Cástulo; off to get your things ready. Move. The second stagecoach for Regium leaves at midafternoon," urged Doña Micaela.

Don Cástulo went out, with rhythmic, somewhat effeminate movements, which were habitual for him and which, on occasions of perturbation or of hurry, would become even more exaggerated.

The family remained alone and in a strained silence—Don Leoncio, Doña Micaela, and Urbano. After some moments, the first to speak was Urbano, despite himself, like a glass vase that, from a sudden change in temperature, breaks and emits a *crack*, which in its turn breaks, along an imperceptible line, the transparent and hard, crystalline silence.

"How weighed down my body feels! How weighed down my spirits are! I could sleep for hours and hours, and days and years. I've been without sleep two nights, the last night and the first night," alluding, of course, to his last night as a bachelor, in which, as the saying has it, one cannot sleep, and his first night as a married man, which had been the saddest of his life.

His father came to his support, with tenderness and pity: "The child's right. Let him rest up today as much as he likes. There's no reason not to put off the trip for tomorrow."

"You speak, as usual, like a fool," Doña Micaela said severely. A married couple who don't sleep a night under the same roof is a broken marriage. Urbano will go today to rejoin Simona. If he doesn't make the stagecoach, he'll go in a cart; if there's no cart he'll go on foot; if he gets worn out, you'll carry him piggyback."

"Yes, yes, whatever you say, Mama," replied Urbano, with a gesture of absolute resignation and passivity. "Send me off on a trip to wherever you like. I'm not responsible for myself. I'm a thing. I'll go, just like a piece of baggage. It's all the same to me going in the berlin as going in the baggage compartment."

It was an act of submission by Urbano, but of insolent, critical submission, which by its novelty left Doña Micaela perplexed.

Don Leoncio, directing himself mentally to his wife, thought, "There, harsh and cold woman, the fruits of your despotism. You haven't wanted to bend to anybody else's feelings or ideas. You know it all, better than anyone. You've attempted to change the world and improve on what Don Cástulo calls infallible Nature. You haven't consented in life's sweeping you along, floating like an object without a will; I've heard it from you millions of times. Listen now to your son. You've gotten what you wanted. But what have you made of him? Just what you didn't want for yourself: a thing. You've heard his terrible expression: he'll go just like a piece of baggage." To Don Leoncio, this about the piece of baggage seemed a well-turned phrase, a locution exceptionally suggestive. He imagined an enormous and symbolic suitcase, containing the person and destiny of Urbano, ticketed already for the land of no return. Luckily, from these anguished and poetic imaginings, he was brought back to reality by the sight of a real suitcase, one of those whose bottom half is a leather case and the upper part of corduroy carpet, in the shape of a bag. It was Don Cástulo's suitcase, which the owner himself was toting in his right hand.

"I'm ready. No delay for me," said the tutor with an ambiguous look, which denoted awe, pride, and consciousness of responsibility, faced with the extraordinary, rugged mission with which they had entrusted him.

Doña Micaela, looking daggers at her husband, said, "Emotional scenes are forbidden by royal decree."

And then, kissing her son on the forehead, "Go with God. Enough childishness now."

Don Leoncio had an inspiration and, instead of kissing Urbano, shook his hand, like a comrade, saying to him with a counterfeit smile, "You're leaving us now, you rascal you. And you'll find yourself so happy in your new life you won't even remember us. I have a strong feeling that those extreme measures of which your mother was just speaking to get you off today will be what we would have to use within a few days to bring you back."

Urbano's heart swelled with sudden and baseless joy. He replied, cracking an unusual smile, "What do you mean, to bring me back? You mean us, Simona and me?"

"Naturally, naturally," replied the father. "It wasn't necessary to state it. It's well known that the bucket follows the rope and the calf goes with the halter."

Hardly had Don Cástulo and Urbano gone off, than pessimism regained its sway over Don Leoncio's spirit.

Down the street they went, a man and an adolescent, master and disciple, tutor and pupil, the oddest pair ever seen. Man, master and tutor, had now to exercise the office of catechism teacher and initiate the boy, disciple, pupil, and catchumen in the rugged duties of connubial love making. And it so happened that the catechism teacher was as ignorant and naïve as the catechumen, if not more so. Had only the venerable Plato run into them, what a delicious occasion to display his eloquent and divine irony!

Master and disciple arrived at the stagecoach terminal at the very last moment. There were no more seats in the berlin, so they had to go in second class, squashed among the other travelers, which Don Cástulo was glad of, because he feared the interrogations, sure to be disconcerting, which were they alone Urbano might put to him.

During the journey, Don Cástulo pretended to be reading a Greek book. It was a pretext behind which to think things over and meditate on them. His reflections did not bring him any peace of mind. All he could think was, "What a hideous mess I've got myself into." He was angry with and cursed himself for having offered himself stupidly to mediate in such a hazardous crisis.

Urbano rode along, he had forseen it, like a suitcase, vacantly, loaded down perhaps by thoughts and emotions, but dark, hermetic ones. This state of heaviness and swollenness gave him a sense of physical well-being. He felt as if he were of greater size than before and as it the stuff of his body were stronger and weightier. He sensed within himself a gathering of forces which, for the present, demanded quietude and later had to be released in diverse and fiery activities.

They arrived in Regium at nightfall.

"Well, little fellow," Don Cástulo said, "now to take a little hired gig and straightaway to Collado, as your good and wise little mother has decreed."

Pusillanimity and trepidation induced him to overuse the diminutive. Man in great conflicts instinctively makes himself smaller; he becomes a child again and tends toward using puerile expressions. Don Cástulo was even more frightened now than when he sat for his professorship examinations.

"What's the hurry?" Urbano said. "We can have supper here, since at Simona's they aren't expecting us and won't have a meal ready. We'll go there after supper."

"That's an idea, except that I don't have any appetite and couldn't eat a bite."

"Me either."

"Then . . . Look, Urbanito, take it from me; don't put off till tomorrow what you can do today. Your mother, who's an extraordinary woman, has said: no more childishness. I'm not a little child any more. So then, upsy daisy to take the little hired gig."

And so it was. En route for Collado, Urbano, though fortified by the presence of his teacher and friend, worrying that the vague anxieties of the previous day might return to gnaw at him, asked in a loud voice, "Well, then; and me, what do I do with Simona?"

Don Cástulo felt a lump in his throat. Unspoken words rushed through his head with torrential rapidity: "This child is a silly goose. Micaela is an evil witch. Where else was a nonsensical, illogical education, against all the principles of classical pedagogy and the dictates of common sense going to lead but to this stage in which the comic is mixed up with the pathetic, as in the romantic dramas? But I have no dealings with romanticism and its hybrid ways. I'm not a romanticist. I'm a classicist. I like things clear, well defined, and situations intelligible. Although . . . are you sure, poor Cástulo, of not being a romanticist?"

"What do I do with Simona?" Urbano repeated. Don Cástulo replied in a brusque tone of ill temper, which lent him, unexpectedly, a kind of authority: "What have you got to do, my boy? Why nothing. You've married Simona, and all you have to do is to keep on being married to her. To the devil with the enigma! Someone would think they had obliged you to undertake one of the labors of Hercules."

"What a load you take off of me! I don't have to do anything but keep on being married to Simona. That's the natural thing; it's what all married couples do. The natural thing is always the easiest."

And Don Cástulo thought, "Poor child! What will he know of what the natural thing is when he dares to say that the natural thing is the easiest?"

"For the foolish and silly things I did last night," Urbano continued, "I'm not wholly to blame. They surround the wedding with so much solemnity, the grownups get so serious, everyone cries and gives such somber and frightening words of advice that I felt overwhelmed and believed they had imposed the gravest of obligations on me. As I couldn't even suspect what my duty was, I thought I'd go out of my mind. You will admit that the wedding ceremony is enough to throw fear into the heart of the calmest."

"The grownups' little jokes and tomfoolery."

"I'm happy to hear you say it. When we get to Collado, Simona will already be in bed. I'll go straight to bed in my room, I certainly need the sleep; and tomorrow what a surprise she'll have on learning I'm back! We'll go out together to the garden and the orchard. We'll hunt butterflies . . . and like that forever."

"Exactly like that, little one. Always hunting butterflies. What joy!"

Simona had spent the entire afternoon in the belvedere of the large tower staring, like sister Anna in the story of Bluebeard, at the dust of the roads toward the horizon. One minute she shouted, "Here he comes!" and the next she sighed, "He's not coming, nor is he anywhere in sight." Until night fell and Simona got into bed. She lay drowsing and dreaming in the twilight between sleeping and waking, when her heart seemed to her to become a fiery coal which flew from her breast and plunged into the sea, making a long and sorrowful hiss. She awoke with a start and discovered that that noise, half dreamt, came not only from her heart but from a carriage that was arriving, making the gravel crackle on the avenue through the grounds. Simona leaped out of bed and leaned out the window.

"Urbano!"

Urbano had just stepped down from the carriage. He raised his eyes and soul toward the magnetic voice, which attracted and held him like a lodestone. It was a moonless night. Sheltered in the shadow of the old woods, darker than the night, the house was darker than the woods. Urbano was only able to make out, up above someplace, in the frame of a window—blacker still than the house—a thin whitish vapor, a kind of glow, swallowed in the darkness. It was Simona, made quite ghostlike by the darkness.

"Simona!"

"Are you there?"

"Here I am."

"I'd come down to greet you; but I'm alone and in a night-shirt."

Don Cástulo, who for once was in a bad humor, could not help mumbling a sarcastic witticism: "Damn the obstacles."

"It doesn't matter," Urbano said. "Go to bed. We'll see each other tomorrow, bright and early. Good night, my sweet."

"Good night, Urbanín."

Urbano, in a transport of enthusiasm, hugged and kissed Don Cástulo, who had a passing notion of saying to his pupil, "You clown; that's what you should have done with her"; but he restrained himself, considering that, in his own case, he mightn't have dared either.

Urbano, after greeting and kissing the hand of Doña Rosita, went off to bed and hardly stretched out fell into a leaden sleep, as if they had trickled in his ear some drops of henbane.

Doña Rosita and Don Cástulo remained in the dining room to talk the matter over. The old woman insisted, firmly, on the tutor's having some supper. The table was set by Conchona, a country girl, stockily, massively built; her head the color and dimensions of a regular pumpkin, as there was no difference between the color of her skin and the shade of her hair, one and the other between bay and crocus color.

"This maid is just like one of the family," said Doña Rosita, who was as always doing needlework, "but she's still somewhat crude. She's meddlesome and forward and has to stick her nose into the conversation. I put you on notice. Don't pay her any mind; don't place any trust in her, worse. Don't say anything private in her presence. Let's talk, in between her comings and goings. I find you dispirited, worried. What's the matter?"

"If you think it's a small thing . . ."

"I don't know the first thing about it."

"Well that's what's so serious, that not one of the four of us know the first thing about it."

"Which four of us?"

"Which four could we be? You and I, Simona and Urbano."

Doña Rosita broke out laughing: "I don't follow you, but it's tickled me to see myself hitched up with you and making a team with some newlyweds. We make a lovely couple. I must be at the very, very least twenty years older than you."

"I'm under forty-five and over forty. I'm in the prime and sweet October of my feelings."

"Good age for a man to get married."

"I'm of your opinion. But back at fifteen, I thought I was at a

61

good age to get married, and so on since then, year after year. And you, how old are you?"

"Speaking of years, a mule drivers' conversation. Explain what you were trying to tell me before."

"I thought you were taking it all in."

"As all you say . . ."

"My dear Doña Rosita; Urbano is so innocent, ignorant, and bumbling that if someone doesn't instruct and push him, with gentle artifice and craft, toward the completion of the marriage, he will be *per secula seculorum* by his wife's side without daring even to kiss the tip of her little finger."

"And what harm would come of that?"

"Tragedy, Señora, but a comic tragedy, which is a despicable type, hybrid, in short, romantic. I'm no romantic."

"Tragedy?"

"Yes, Señora. Yesterday it was on the point of coming to a climax but it was smoothed out, thank God. It's a true miracle that Urbano didn't kill himself last night."

"Good gracious, good gracious! Either I'm simple or what you're telling me doesn't make sense. Kill himself? Why?" dropping her knitting.

"For love, for blind love, for unsatisfied and never satisfiable love, since it is blind. Allow me to read you a paragraph from this book, one of my favorites. Just today, on the trip here, I was reading it. Its author was a Greek of ancient times who was called Achilles Tacius. He says, 'Woman is a bittersweet. Her nature is like that of the sirens, who attract in order to kill; the very pomp and ritual of the betrothal affirm the magnitude of the injury: a flute lament, closing and opening of doors, the going and coming of torches. Before so much mystery and tumult, who will not cease to exclaim: Woe betide the poor man they are betrothing? For my part, it looks as if against his will they are recruiting him for war.' Very learned words, indicative of the slight or nonexistent change in men and customs in many centuries. Is there anything unusual in Urbano, frightened, having right off lost his head like a raw recruit, and his perhaps seeing Simona as his most cruel as well as his sweetest enemy?"

Doña Rosita interrupted: "Bless me if I understand you one bit, absorbed as I am in hearing how you say it, more than what you say. What language, Jesus and Mary! You should have been a preacher and preached. Or devoted yourself to politics. Why don't you speak in public?"

Doña Rosita's ingenuous flatteries were like a breeze that dissipated the fog of melancholy and ill humor that dampened Don Cástulo's spirit. He continued, "Because I would die of fright. I'm more timid than a country mouse. Besides, you attribute to me a gift of eloquence that I am far from possessing. A thousand thanks, all the same, my dear Doña Rosita. And let's get back to our business. Urbano came home this morning sputtering, on the point of perishing, like a shipwrecked sailor. I, quite charitable and more deluded, thought I could throw him a line with which he might save himself. Here, aloud, is what I then thought: I, I said to myself, with my amorous knowledge acquired from illustrious authors, and Doña Rosita, with her long years of experience, proceeding concertedly and artistically will go about infiltrating into the minds of Simona and Urbano clear notions of complete love, of which they've heard neither hide nor hair as yet. We will submit them to a poetic discipline, so light and gentle, that not even they themselves will take note of our dominance. This I thought, foolishly, at first. Later on, on my way here, the true nature of things made itself clear to me in all its crudeness. What am I going to teach anybody on the subject of love? Or what are you going to teach, my venerated Doña Rosita? That's why I've said to you at the start that not one of the four of us know the first thing about it. Yes, Señora, we're characters in a comic tragedy—a truly romantic situation. But, I repeat that romanticism repels me. Give me clearly defined situations. I don't see any other

63

rational way out than to put Simona and Urbano together, inside a basket, for a whole night, as is done to mate a male and female dove. And then, let nature take its course."

At this point, Conchona came in with a basket of vegetables, which she placed in front of Don Cástulo. Then she planted herself with her arms akimbo to dumbly scrutinize the guest: "Are you a colonist, lordyship?"

"No, I'm not a colonist," replied Don Cástulo, disquieted under the maid's intense, unblushing stare.

"Well, you look just like a colonist—so dandy, so fine with those eyeglasses. Are they gold?"

"Yessss, . . . Ssseñora," said Don Cástulo, his voice weak and shaking, as if he were before a board of examiners.

"You are a colonist, and you don't want to tell me so. I never saw such a beautiful colonist." And she contemplated Don Cástulo, with languorous and maternal eyes, like a cow with her calf.

"Hey, Conchona," Doña Rosita intervened, extending a hand gloved in black silk, "off to the kitchen and don't be rude."

"It's so hard for me to stop looking at this lordyship! Ay!" and she went out, between heavy sighs.

"You were talking before," said Doña Rosita, "about nature. Since I was a little girl, I've been taught that education consists precisely in resisting and, often as not, in overcoming nature. Nature is lightning in the sky, gales on the sea, earthquakes, torrential rains, cold that bites, and heat that suffocates. We'd be in a pretty fix if in all these cases we were to let nature operate, without combatting her or at least defending ourselves from her. The animals are beasts of nature; cows and bulls, mares and stallions, sheep and rams, hens and roosters—all of which are in abundance on this estate. What do you propose, my friend; that Simona and Urbano instruct themselves in the ways of love by means of the examples which, without passing beyond even the walls of our property, the animals provide them?"

"Just so."

"No, for not even with that will they be instructed, because they are innocents, and only unchaste eyes know how to see unchaste things. I'm approaching sixty; hardly have I ever left this house and its surroundings; it's probable I may have seen innumerable times nature take its course, as you say. But no, Señor, I've not seen that; or if I've seen it, I haven't taken notice."

"Me either, which doesn't mean anything in particular, since I've moldered in the city and between four walls." There's no spur for the timorous like flattery. Flattered by Doña Rosita, Don Cástulo now felt anxious to put on parade the arsenal of his erudition and of his rhetoric. "The Holy Spirit has just spoken through your lips, Señora. *Omnia munda mundis,* Saint Paul's words, in his Epistle to Titus, Vulgate edition, and it means: for pure persons all things are pure. I also know how to say it in Greek, if you like, but let's not get away from the main point. You maintain that education opposes or overcomes nature. In some circumstances, yes. But education must also adjust itself, that is, be in accord with that same nature. Though we are rational, we are animals. It would be absurd to oppose or overcome good digestion or to undertake to digest in some manner other than as the animals. On the contrary, good education should teach how to digest well, starting by teaching how to chew well, which the animals know to a *T,* without need of education. Well, with love, three-quarters the same. There is in human love an element of nature, common to men and beasts, which the beast knows without your educating it, but the man is ignorant of if it's not taught to him."

"I, frankly, in my simplicity believed that men were all born to this knowledge and that the only ones who had to learn were we women."

"How silly! *Homo sum,* and I only know that I don't know anything!"

Doña Rosita gave herself up to laughter and let her needlework fall on the table.

"That makes two of us."

"You're a widow . . ."

"Ay! That was a thousand years ago. My memory grows dim. I don't remember except in dreams—and then like a nightmare."

"My dear Señora Doña Rosita," continued Don Cástulo, infected by the old woman's laughter; but his laugh was disconsolate, "I'm coming to recognize that love is an enigmatic and painful thing, as those fools the romantics maintain. Or else this society in which we live is the enigmatic and painful thing."

"There you go with your cavilings, which to me seem woven of cobwebs," said Doña Rosita, gathering up her knitting and starting in on it again with rekindled vigor. "Since I was a child I remember having been busied ceaselessly with needles and crotchets. My mother, may she rest in peace, instilled in me this saying: The woman rightly will have her hands occupied so her head may be unpreoccupied; for when the hand is idle, the brain works and consumes itself. Let me be with cogitations and hairsplittings. No one has ever pressed me to discussion, like you now. Knitting is my forte; don't bollox me up with theologies."

"An ancient maxim of Publilius Sirius: *mulier, cum sola cogitat, male cogitat*—the woman who sits thinking by herself is cooking up something evil."

"Well, it's the gospel truth."

Conchona came in, with a veal stew, and went through the same fetishistic rites as before in front of Don Cástulo, ever more nervous and harried with the novelty of feeling himself the object of feminine admiration.

On Conchona's going out, very reluctantly, Doña Rosita said, "Why are we straining ourselves and wracking our brains figuring out what love is. The girls around these parts, what madness, aspire as their supreme desire to marry a colonist, that is, one of those immigrants coming back from the isle of Cuba. And not for money's sake, oh no! They marry them, even though they be *in albis* and flat broke, because for these half-civilized creatures the colonist is the ideal of beauty and manly elegance. All of them are a sickly yellow color because of I don't know what ravages of the insides, the liver or the spleen. A lot of them carry filthy diseases, as Don Arcadio, the doctor has confided to me. Then, they dress up in *flounces*, which is what they call their outfits, bright as strawberry and cream sherberts. Well, the more outlandish they are, the more the local girls like them. Why is it so? I'll tell you in a wink. Because the village girls, and they know it, are half animals, savages practically, and the colonists seem to them like fine and cultured people, which is what they wish to be. You may say that education consists in accommodating oneself to nature, which is the same as getting down to its terms. No, my good man, education will always be to rise above or to wish to rise. Around these parts each of the local lads is as handsome as a statue; I say it without offense to modesty, because I'm an old woman. And all the same, these country lasses look down on these handsome lads, as clumsy, ugly, and common, while they fall for any old beaten up and stringy colonist. Of course," added Doña Rosita laughing and peering roguishly at Don Cástulo over her spectacles, "some of those big tropical birds are something to look at. But, flattery aside, you put them all to shame."

"Ssseñora," stuttered Don Cástulo, in the height of his disquietude lifting his fork, with a piece of oily meat impaled on the prongs, to his nose.

"Easy, gentle knight, I'm not wooing or courting you. The one who's doing that, plainly enough, is Conchona. Why, you've made her fall in love with you at first sight, because she's taken it into her head to find some semblance or trace of a colonist in you. And so that you won't take offense at appearances, I've said the aforesaid, which otherwise might be taken as joking or brazen soliciting. Truth is, that brute gives the highest offense, daring to fall in love with you."

"For my part, I wouldn't say brute," Don Cástulo corrected, as if speaking to himself, "but rather primitive, uncomplicated soul."

"Primitive all right; her stink of the stable and the hovel so heavy, it still hasn't worn off; and her big head a pumpkin of the highest order."

"I haven't looked at her closely, but I perceive in her I don't know what of idyllic, wild beauty."

"You're no little joker, a failing common to all very learned men, *vervigracia,* priests."

"Señora Doña Rosita, in failings or virtues, don't compare me with the priests, for God's sake!"

At this point reentered Conchona, who was now Pomona, with two large porcelain fruit baskets, cornucopia shaped, stacked up and overflowing with a plenteous harvest of colored fruits. And among the diversity of smaller fruits, the formidable pumpkin of her face loomed up, with its great rent of a mouth and two large albino eyes, windowless holes as though cut out with a knife. This clownish deity set the fructiferous abundance within reach of the more than disconcerted guest; she joined her forearms in such a way that each hand was couched over the opposite elbow, thereby making the twin gelatinous abundance of her breasts swell out, shaking it practically in the diner's face; and as she now dominated him in an above to below perspective, after a thorough examination, she exclaimed with all her heart, "Holy Saviour of men, look how this poor heart is! Full of dust and filth, like Jesus bound for Calvary. Ay! Veronica I'd like to be and clean him and shake him and leave him like the coral from the seas. And his hair too, this gold and silver hair, all covered with dirt and grime. The dust clouds of the road have left my lordyship like a sack of flour. And nobody dusted us off on arrival. We'll fix that. Kerchoo! Kerchoo!" and she launched into raining blows upon the shoulders of the anguished Don Cástulo, whereby she raised in the air a kind of dusty cloud. And not satisfied with this, she seized him and worked over his head between the fingers of her two hands, like an enthusiastic barber who gives a massage to a high tipping customer.

Doña Rosita, struggling to keep down suppressed laughter, gave a shriek: "Ass! How dare you carry on like that in front of your mistress? Out this instant, or I'll come after you with a whip. And don't set foot in this room again."

Conchona fled, with the sullenness and wariness of a driven animal, but right on the doorstep she stopped, turned her large head, and said, passionately, before rushing out, "He's as pretty and fine as an Antilles parrot."

"Please do me a favor, if you'd be so kind," Doña Rosita said. Get up and lock the door inside, so that that beast won't plague us again."

And when Don Cástulo had complied, Doña Rosita said, choking on great bubbles of laughter, which popped successively, "That, my dear sir, is love, love that lets nature freely take its course. Watch out! Or, don't watch out, since as a tutor of love, you must first of all pass a practical examination. Weren't you saying that you knew nothing? Come now, calm down, and let's come back to our point."

"I should calm down? We should come back to the point? Has there ever been any other point for me? Señora, I'm a frustrated lover," he sighed from the depths, his eyebrows knitted to inverted *V*'s, and raising a hand over his heart.

"Ah, egoist! This has nothing to do with you, but with Urbano and Simona."

"It's true; I had forgotten."

"You were maintaining that the difficult thing was to surrender oneself to love. The case that stands out, and how it stands out, which has presented itself to us with Conchona, perhaps shows you that the difficult thing is for one to resist love. Would you care to change your opinion?"

"No Señora, I rather reaffirm my opinion," becoming uneasy. "I've told you that Urbano, though joined *per secula seculorum* with Simona, will not dare to kiss the tip of her little finger. The tip of her finger? Not even the tip of a glove."

"Impossible and ridiculous."

"Ridiculous, yes. Impossible? If it were impossible then it would no longer be ridiculous. Señora, if you were familiar, as I am, with Urbano's character, with his soul and mind, with the execrable education that was given him—excuse me, that we have given him —you wouldn't judge impossible what unfortunately is irremediable. I've been inseparable from him since he was born, and I swear to you that he continues being a newborn baby. In the face of so much purity and innocence, I, great man of learning, which is as if to say, great fool and blockhead, from that time gave myself the illusion of being like an Olympian god who presided at the reborn eclogue of Daphnis and Chloe, now Urbano and Simona. In this deceitful volume," and he took up with a trembling hand the book that was lying on the table, "along with Achilles Tacius I have bound the pastoral romances of Longus, which I saw as being my manual of erotic pedagogy. Listen to what the author says at the end of the preface: 'May the gods permit me to stir the emotions of others without my own emotions being stirred.' Woe is me! Hardly did the child and I leave the paternal household this morning when I realized that, as more conscious, my feelings had to be stronger than those of Urbano."

"So much the better, my friend. How is one going to teach what he's totally ignorant of? Calm down and pull yourself together. You were proposing, so to speak, to be a teacher in the school of libertinism, to educate in sin these newlywed toddlers and that I help you as assistant professor. I'll help you with advice. Your theory, by what you have told me, includes in the section of good breeding a chapter of instruction in bad breeding and encouragement in evil."

"That's my theory?"

"You've spoken of digestion, that one must be taught to digest; and you've insinuated that making love would have to be taught, making love in the physical sense."

"Yes, Señora, but that wouldn't be bad breeding but good breeding."

"Exactly; I was coming to that. I've been taught, since I was a little girl that anything that can't be done in front of others falls under what commonly is called bad breeding. But you add that these things of the old bad breeding have to be submitted also to good breeding. A happy discovery! Yes, sir; you enlighten me. It had never occurred to me. You're quite right. So that from tomorrow on you've got to get busy in giving Urbano some bad breeding. How funny!"

"Are you serious?"

"Look me in the face."

"Yes, you're serious."

"I don't see how you can give bad breeding but with bad examples, so to speak. Really, do you really think that Urbano even in a century wouldn't kiss Simona *motu propio*?"

"He'd sooner put his hand in the fire."

"Well, you teach him. For you to kiss me in front of them and pretending to believe they didn't see us, I don't think wise. Given the difference between you and me in age they'd consider it a filial kiss. But, there you have Conchona. How would you feel about giving her a kiss on the mouth? Sacrifice yourself. Ah! And watch out, for at the worst these country nymphs defend their honor with slaps and punches."

From Doña Rosita's eyes there peeked out a jovial and malicious demon.

"Oh my dearest Señora!" Don Cástulo exclaimed, abandoning himself to despair. "My case is like that of Urbano, only hardened by years of abstinence and useless cogitations. What have I got to teach Urbano! They could set before me the pink Venus and the white Diana, and all the beautiful courtesans of Corinth, Alexandria, Rome, and Paris, enticing me to love with exciting gestures and supplicating words, and I would die on the spot, before touching their smooth and mortal skin. And let them not venture to touch me, for I would explode like a firecracker."

"Well, this certainly is a case. You leave me dumbstruck. All right; it's getting late. Let's go to sleep. Now then, I hope you will stay here a few days, at least about a week. Today is Friday; until next Thursday I'm not letting you go. You'll see how much good the country life does you. Give me your arm to go up the stairs, my old legs creak."

"Eclogue or tragedy? Well, I give up. I'm a convert to romanticism. Love is a thing tragic and grotesque at the same time. No doubt there are hybrid literary types just as there are hybrid animals and hybrid people. Forgive me, Doña Rosita, if my thoughts slip through the bony wall of my forehead."

"Tomorrow, the early morning air will clear your head."

Saturday morning, the first to arise was Simona. She awoke like a calendar lark; in a nightshirt, she jumped up, mad with indecipherable anxiety, and almost bumped against the roof inside her little cage, which was her virginal bedchamber. She dressed quickly. She went downstairs. Only the servants were up. She went out into the garden. On seeing the lawns pearled with dew, she took off her shoes and walked a good way on the damp grass.

From the line of the horizon to the east, there arched a mound of violet-colored clouds, like a mountain of amethyst rock, on whose flank, toward the midpoint, there gaped a luminous cavern, topaz color, such that there might be being celebrated therein the lingering moments of a great fiesta, nocturnal and secret, of gnomes and fairies; it was the sun, just rising, which, perforating with its rays the mass of clouds, made a funnel or golden windmill. Simona felt enthralled by the sight, drawn toward that windmill. She thought of Urbano, of waking him, so he might come down and the two of them together go flying to be swallowed up in the vortex of the sun. She took some pebbles from the walk to throw against Urbano's window. She desisted, deciding that it was overbold and incorrect, and also from reluctance of awakening him out of sleep. She imagined him in the bed; she imagined him like a baby in the cradle, like the baby that from one moment to the next she was going to have, due to the simple and mysterious fact of being now married to Urbano; for she had always heard it said that baby boys are the spitting image of the father, and therefore, the fathers of the sons. Then she had a disquieting thought: "When I have that child, I'm not going to have clothing to put on him; that of my dolls is of no use to me, since they're clothes for older girls. I can just see my child, dressed up like a doll! I have to hurry up and make him some little things and swaddling clothes." And she determined to apply herself to the task later on that same day.

She put her shoes back on and went off to ramble through the garden. She went, like the Homeric Aurora, waking the flowers with pink fingers, caressing them without damaging them. On returning to the house, her face was as fresh and aromatic as a morning flower. Her grandmother, who of old was an early riser, was in the kitchen giving instructions to several servants. Simona gave the old woman a good morning kiss on the cheek and immediately went off, as if in a hurry. She returned soon, bringing along her largest doll, some scraps of white cloth, and bits of lace. She sat down on a sewing stool and, the doll in her lap, began to take its measurements with the cloth.

"What are you doing there, child?" asked Doña Rosita, half bemused and half serious. "A grown woman playing at dressing dolls?"

"How naïve you are, Grandma! Dressing dolls? How silly! I'm making little clothes for my child. Do you realize that he's coming tomorrow or the next day. The little angel won't have anything to wear."

"Goodness, I hadn't thought of it," replied Doña Rosita, feigning seriousness. "But it's not necessary for you to trouble yourself. You would do it badly for lack of practice. It's best to buy the clothing ready-made."

"And what if the child comes right away?"

"There's always some advance notice, little one."

"What other advance notice than our having married?"

"I'm sure to know more about it than you, Simona. Come now, how do you figure he's going to come to you?"

"In a little box, all packed up," said Simona, very reddened, after a pause.

She said this, because they had taught her that babies come from Paris, packed up. But she had the conviction, a deep, dark, and disturbing conviction, that she was going to have the baby some other way, inside herself; she didn't know how, only sure that it had to be inside herself; she guessed that she would have to expel it through breathing; she felt it move, in the marrow of her very being. She had felt it, almost formed, and it rose to her throat, during the stagecoach trip. But these feelings were so strange and ineffable that she didn't dare to communicate them to the grandmother.

"Quite so, in a little box, all packed up," the grandmother said. "Do you reckon by mail?"

"No, not like that."

"By the stagecoach?"

"Not that way either," replied Simona, more and more reddened.

"Then it will be by special messenger, little one. Or a little bird will send it down the chimney. Be that as it may, there's always some advance notice and ample time to get clothing ready. For now, what I'm most anxious to tell you is, hide the doll and scraps, so that Urbano doesn't see them; and don't think of alluding, let alone speaking openly, to your husband about that nonsense of the expected child." And she added, unthinkingly, "If you infect him with your fantasies, we're really in trouble."

"You call fulfilling a mother's duties fantasies and nonsense, Grandmother? Why, what do we get married for, but to have children as God wills?"

"Yes, God wills it, but good manners also will that the wife not speak of that to her husband. It would be little short of a shamelessness."

"A shamelessness?" Simona stuttered, quite confused.

"Oh dear," thought the grandmother, "I've gone too far. This is going to get into mischief. Well, it had to come about sooner or later. But I'm afraid I've used an inappropriate and clumsy word."

Aloud she amended: "I've expressed myself badly. I meant to

74

say, an indelicacy, something that's not in very good taste. The wife's modesty imposes silence on these things. When the time comes, the woman communicates it to her husband whispering it in his ear, and if it can be in the dark, so much the better."

As she was speaking, Doña Rosita was thinking, "By beating around the bush, circumlocutions and explanations, I'm just making it worse and worse. I don't know what I'm saying."

Simona, as though speaking to herself, murmured with her head lowered and red, "Something in bad taste? A wife's modesty? In his ear and in the dark?"

At this point Don Cástulo came in, pallid and bleary eyed; his shirt without collar and with only the neckband, from which protruded an Adam's apple so robust that it made one see at a glance why Don Cástulo cleared his throat with such frequency; velvet slippers in episcopal purple, bordered in gold thread, a gift of Doña Micaela. Don Cástulo reverently went to kiss Doña Rosita's hand.

"How have you slept, my good friend?" the señora asked.

"Don't ask, excellent and respected friend; horribly."

"Tossing and turning? The strangeness of the bed perhaps?"

"Not tossing and turning; worse. Not the strangeness of the bed but of the dreams—in other words, nightmares. And that when I'm never one to dream, for I go to bed good and tired, from among other things daydreaming. Well, I dreamt that I was being kidnapped. Absurd and romantic? Absurd and romantic, I concede, wise and most discreet friend. A bandit was abducting me, was carrying me off on horseback to a cave, in a dense forest. Then, behold the bandit is female, a woman, in male garb—an Amazon. I will remind you, in parentheses, that the original form of marriage, which we call holy matrimony, and I would almost add, the only rational form, was abduction. Coming back to my fearless Amazon. Do you know that the Amazons of mythology were missing their breasts, for they cut them off in order to shoot the bow better. Well, my Amazon had them, large enough and of wonderful softness."

Doña Rosita winked, signaling that Don Cástulo was overstepping himself, in the presence of Simona. But, Simona was not listening to this last, eager to say something herself, and she said as soon as silence offered, "I too have had a similar dream; a robber who came in through my balcony."

"Nothing more?" inquired the old woman.

"Nothing more, Grandmother."

"Well, I dreamt about my frigate captain," said Doña Rosita, sighing, her eyes misting.

"We've all dreamt, except for that lazybones Urbano, it would seem; for when one dreams a lot, he wakes up early, and he's still like a log," opined Don Cástulo in a tone of mock reprobation.

"What do you mean, lazybones? You mayn't use that word," Simona replied, in the same tutorial tone.

"I say it because by now he should be up and by your side."

"He's got plenty of time to come, to be up, and sitting down, and in all postures, for at some time one and the other will weary of togetherness," commented Doña Rosita.

"Oh no," Simona corrected. "Neither he nor I will weary. The truth is that I can't live without having Urbano by my side."

"So be it," the grandmother concluded. "Before I forget, Don Cástulo; if you want to write letters, the writing table is over there. Around this time a messenger leaves who takes the mail to Regium."

"I did have two missives to write, very short ones."

He wrote them, sealed them, handed them over to a servant, and said to Doña Rosita, "If you, my noble and kind friend, knew the contents of these epistles, you would laugh. You may know that I'm almost a convert to romanticism. I'm writing an acquaintance asking him to send me by return mail some little works by a certain Rousseau, whom until quite recently I've considered the bogeyman and who is, in a manner of speaking, the Mohammed or prophet of the romantic religion."

"Religion no less?" asked Doña Rosita. "And who is the God who inspires that prophet?"

"Whom do you think? The devil."

"Oho, oho!" the old woman exclaimed, making a pair of horns with the index and little fingers of her right hand. "And the other missive, if it's not an indiscretion?"

"I'll tell you later," Don Cástulo replied, laughing.

Breakfast was brought in by a maid whom Don Cástulo had not seen before, which caused him a certain surprise that he didn't know how to conceal.

"I've ordered that Conchona not wait on the table," Doña Rosita said, "because of the great nuisance she was to you last night."

"Oh! Really, I wouldn't call it a nuisance."

Don Cástulo swallowed his breakfast silently, lost in thought. After half an hour of silence, he jumped up with his hands on his head and in great agitation begged: "The messenger, the messenger with the letters. They've got to get the letters back from him. One of them must be torn up. Another must be written."

The messenger had left long ago. It was impossible to reach him now.

"What's the matter? Do you repent of your conversion, I mean diabolical perversion?" asked Doña Rosita sarcastically, who could not take Don Cástulo entirely seriously.

"No, Señora, I persist with growing perverseness in drawing ever closer to that devilish romanticism. It's about the other letter."

"Something serious?"

"I can't confide it to you unless we're alone."

"A confessional secret. So be it. Simona, pretty one, please go out, would you. Now we're alone. I'm all ears."

"The fact is that Micaela, before our departure, asked me to send her daily a brief word of how the amorous relationship between Urbano and Simona was going, until the point when by sufficient indications, I might send her the happy news that the marriage was then consummated, which in legal or canonical terminology is called 'passing the unconsummated time.' One or two words would serve the purpose according to Micaela's dictate; for example, 'still terrified,' 'looking up,' 'commencing caresses,' 'clandestine kisses,' 'imminent solution,' et cetera, et cetera. Now, then, my opinion which I declared to you last night, is that days and days will go by without Urbano coming out of his stupor and passivity. And so I have just written Micaela this sentence, which I now realize is amphibological: 'We have passed the time uneventfully,' as if to say 'Nothing for now, unless it be that time passes peacefully.' "

"Well, that's perfectly so."

"But am I not telling you that the time is the unconsummated time of the marriage. If we've now passed it, Micaela will understand that the marriage has been consummated. She's well acquainted with and very keen on subtle interpretations."

"So what? Sooner or later, we will really pass the time."

"No, Señora, we won't pass it. I know myself—I mean, I know Urbano."

"Well, so what? After all, tomorrow unsay it and write with more clarity."

Urbano came in, with a shiny and alert face, cheerful and radiant eyes. Before saying good morning, he said, forcing the words,

"Is it late? Did I oversleep? What time is it? And Simona? Has Simona gotten up? Where is Simona? How come Simona's not with you? When does Simona come down?"

"Will we or will we not pass the time, Don Cástulo?" Doña Rosita asked, merrily.

Urbano looked like a new man to Don Cástulo. Nevertheless, he replied, "We'll continue passing the time, as up until now, illustrious and ironical friend."

Upon Simona's appearance, much of the steam seemed to go out of Urbano. He gave his hand to his wife, but then, as if on contact he had burned himself, withdrew it rapidly. During breakfast, with Simona by his side, he regained some of his naturalness and wound up being expansive and jovial, a bit to excess under the pressure of nervous tension.

After breakfast, Simona proposed to her natural lord and

master their going out together and taking him to visit the vast estate.

"I'll get my hat," said Urbano.

"Hat, what for, if we're in our home?" said Simona, taking her husband by the hand and leading him to the garden.

And so they went out to take a walk hand in hand and on their own, just as when they were children in the Fuenfermosa spa. Nature presented itself to Urbano in a showy light, somewhat scenic, which reminded him of the one time that his mother had taken him to the theater to see a magic show.

The sun was beginning to scorch the air, but the breeze, festive and aromatic, tempered the solar breath. A gracile and rich mist lay over the countryside, a gauze with spangles of gilded silver. Perching in the tops of the trees, the linnets sprinkled their song, minute and fresh like a pizzicato; hidden in the shadow, the redwings launched a long melodious lament, a plush violin sound. Into the distance extended the pervasive chirping of crickets and cicadas, in slow beats, like waves—now more intense, as if approaching; now more turned down, as if going farther away—a tenuous and alternating pressure.

Urbano and Simona crossed the garden quickly and came into the fruit orchards. Urbano had never seen the country in these morning hours, which are like the infancy of the day. A pleasant feeling of self-forgetfulness deliciously blurred his senses and spirit. He saw it all without looking at anything in particular and heard it all without listening closely to anything. It was as if he were floating over things. In his state of almost absolute passivity, which he perceived, vaguely, as a sensation of almost absolute liberty, he felt himself to be receiving and storing up in his body a copious influx of energy. Never had he felt so happy, and his happiness was like an intuition of growth. He knew that he had Simona with him, because he found the world perfect, Simona being the complement for the perfection of the world; but not because his soul was concretized toward the presence of Simona. Without Simona he might not have felt happy, nor might he have noticed the perfection of that magical world in which he now found himself plunged. With Simona, he enjoyed not so much her nearness and beauty as feeling himself alive, with abandon and fullness, almost feeling himself born to life and to light. Simona was one among many things, the most important, no doubt, but one among many things; she was exactly like the light, hidden in the footlights of the proscenium, whose function consists in making all other things visible, in revealing them, being invisible in itself. On the other hand, for Simona the world and all other things were annulled and negated to the existence of Urbano, who was the one who uniquely and truly existed. Like Jehovah in Eden, who gave names to things for the only man being then on earth, giving him to understand that he had no other end than to solace and serve him, so Simona conducted herself, giving possession of her elders' estate and its contents to the only man on earth for her. And Urbano, allowing himself to be conducted about, amorous and ecstatic, by Simona in those diaphanous moments was not characterized as her husband but as her child. And she contemplated him with heavenly pride and maternal tenderness. Her happiness was nearly complete—nearly complete, for she felt a shade of anxiety.

And thus they spent the morning, in paradisiacal idleness and innocence. When, on returning for lunch, they rested a moment in the shade of the grove around the house, Urbano emptied his overflowing heart all at once in a phrase immemorially banished from human lips: "This is Paradise, Simona."

At lunch, Don Cástulo noted a new change in his pupil; his wan skin, the color of fruit ripened in the shade, had gotten red, and not, as up till then, now and again, in the passing scarlet of boyish blushing, but in the pink of a sunburn.

At the table, Urbano and Simona acted uninhibitedly, but neither were they at all flirtatious. Their glances did not cross except when in the course of the trifling conversation it happened that they spoke at the same time. Doña Rosita and Don Cástulo listened to them, without being able to figure anything out clearly. Rather than two spouses they seemed like brother and sister, in familiar concourse.

The newlyweds' afternoon was a replica of the morning. Simona wound up showing Urbano, point by point, all the lots and appurtenances of the extensive estate. They were followed about by a corpulent mastiff, a friendly animal, Cerezo by name.

At night, after supper, Doña Rosita and Don Cástulo awaited uncertainly what perchance the two youngsters were going to do. After a few yawns, Urbano said "Good-night" and went tranquilly to his room. A short while later Simona followed him, to her room.

"Didn't I tell you so, my venerable and mistaken friend?" said Don Cástulo. "Each one of them has gone to his roost, the same as each owl goes to its olive tree."

Sunday morning, Urbano experienced a new sensation; he heard bells for the first time. And thus it was. The chaplain being absent from Collado, having left on a trip with Simona's mother two days earlier, the señores of the house and the greater part of the servants went in caravan to hear early mass in the church of a nearby hamlet, Pendueles. The day was dawning splendorously. Swallows crossed the heavens with prodigious rapidity, as if the air at that hour were thinner and more navigable.

Don Cástulo, who gave his arm to Doña Rosita, said to Urbano, "Offer your arm to your wife."

"Of course," the boy responded diligently, obeying.

Simona grasped her husband's arm with sweet but undisguised eagerness, as if she were exercising an act of possession. Urbano felt at his side his wife's warm weight; a light and pleasant burden, which on contact transfused currents of energy through him. For a few moments he had a fancy to lift her up and carry her on his shoulders, symbolizing in this way what for him was the essence of matrimony: a kind of gymnastics with which to carry the constant weight of a different person who for a series of reasons—among which, in Urbano's case, perhaps the least determining of which

81

had been the free will of the husband—happens to be one's own wife. Evidently, Simona was a burden in Urbano's life, a burden full of fearful secrets and, notwithstanding, a desirable burden.

At this point, the bells of the church rang out. From the diaphanousness and stillness of the atmosphere, they sounded as though right next to one's ear. The metallic vibration spread through Urbano's flesh, moving him. He said to Simona, "I guess I have heard bells infinite times; but to tell you the truth, I hadn't heard them till now."

"How silly!" Simona commented almost absently, absorbed in the adventure of going arm in arm with her beloved.

For just as for Simona under the influence of Urbano, the outside world was ceasing to exist by moments, for Urbano under the influence of Simona, the reality of things and the reality of his own body and spirit were wakening by moments from the nebulous void which was the previous condition, his own and that of the universe.

His soul set in that stirring and vibrant tonic chord, Urbano entered the village church. The priest was already on his way toward the altar. It smelled of cyprus and rosemary. The walls of the church were white, bare of ornamentation. Only the *Via Crucis* was seen, painted with thin traces of pitch; its coldness, blackness, and starkness made one think of gaunt death. From the cylinder vaulted roof there hung down toward the presbitery two models of brigs and a four-masted corvette, among whose fine rigging the spiders had woven gossamer and rainbow hued webs. Through its porthole skylight, red curtained, entered a puff of air, and the three miniature ships set sail in unison on clouds of incense, while the curtain shook with the flapping of a sea sail. The humble retable was a stranger to the gaudiness of gold leaf; it was painted in dull white, indigo, and red lead; in the niches were lodged a few saints, those of good-natured and bovine expressions in the Byzantine style. Urbano gazed reflectively at everything. He began—other people arrive at the end of their days without having undertaken this operation—to analyze and define on the one hand sensible objects and on the other the intimate impressions by means of which he went about linking himself with them. Since the first days of his childhood, he had heard tell, as a general and day-in-and-day-out fact, of the religious fervor that naturally accompanies devotional practices—saying the rosary, taking communion, hearing mass. But he had never felt that fervor, even though he continually called it up and invoked it, perhaps with anguish. Now—for the first time —an uneasiness crept over him, a kind of itch or prurience of the soul. The black and grim crosses on the cold wall made him afraid. He lifted his eyes from them and directed them toward the ships, which were nodding and swaying gently. The boats hung there like offerings of the shipwrecked. How fragile life is, how at the mercy of storms! He thought again of death, and he averted his glance from the little toy boats. Out of the corner of his eye, but fixedly, he contemplated Simona, all self-absorbed, her fingers interlaced, her eyelids lowered, hidden in the shadow, which veiled her, giving her an extraordinary pallor, and by a chance of the perspective, on one side and the other of her head, two clematis yellow candles. "She looks like a corpse," he thought. "What would I do if Simona were to die?" And Urbano turned his heart to God, like a child toward his father. The hand bell rang. The priest elevated the host. After some moments of self-abnegation, Urbano, little by little, began sinking into a state of serene and wordless meditation. His temperament agitated by the crisis of the last few days, the ratiocinative maternal inheritance, submerged in the deep regions of his spirit, flourished to the surface. He was thinking now of his recent immediate religious experience. For him, the world was beginning to come out of the void; but he understood that it would never come out entirely, that, as far as he might advance, he would always reach a limit beyond which he could not advance; in the shadow of this zone of mystery he would have to raise his heart imploringly toward the Father who is in heaven. He was making himself into a man rapidly; he felt within himself, beyond possible

83

doubt, the development. But all the same, he would not cease to be conjointly a child, like all other men. Was not Don Cástulo a man-boy? And his father. Doña Rosita a woman-girl too. Well every time he might feel childlike, he would feel religious. In the past, he did not feel religious because he did not feel childlike, since he was one; to know what it is to feel oneself childlike, it is necessary, first, to know and feel oneself a man. To becloud this most clear meditation, an exception presented itself: that of his mother. His mother was a thoroughly adult person. In her there were no signs of puerility. And nevertheless she was the most religious person, with an awesome piety. There did not remain in her remnants of childhood; one might say that she had not been a child, but that she had been born a grown woman. If she had not been one, she would have to become one on some future occasion; the contrary would be absurd, monstrous.

The mass concluded; to shake Urbano from his meditation, Don Cástulo had to tug his arm.

Until lunchtime, seated in the park beneath the trees, Doña Rosita, Simona, and Urbano received visits from some rustic señores, local people from the area, who came to congratulate the newlyweds and with gifts in kind: hens, pies, fruits. Don Cástulo went roaming about the estate.

Since it was Sunday, Doña Rosita wanted the family to be together the whole day, and after lunch they returned to sit beneath the trees.

Urbano fidgeted in his wicker chair, impatient and bored, ("yes, bored," he thought), in spite of the nearness of Simona or perhaps because of her nearness, which was beginning to fatigue him. That tumefaction, or enlargement and heaviness of his body, which seemed to him to have been acquired coming in the stagecoach two days earlier, from Pilares to Regium, with Don Cástulo had increased during the short stay in the open air at Collado, as if his organism had been enriched with a multitude of mature cells, which demanded to be released by means of physical exercise. This was what he felt: need for physical exercise, the nature of which he couldn't succeed in imagining. How strange! Until then, he looked forward to the coming Sunday as a day of repose, and on such a day, lazing about deliciously, he figured to rest. Now he sought also to rest, but with a relaxation that could not originate but in some manner far from lassitude.

The sun's heat abated, and Doña Rosita suggested taking a walk to the beach at Boves. It was necessary to go looking for Don Cástulo. They found him absorbed and wandering in a thicket of oaks, his hair awry, declaiming aloud. Blushing, he excused himself: "Scars from my humanistic education. Alone, in the darkness of the forest, I forgot myself and broke into reciting my beloved classics, according to old habit."

"So, then? Do you repent of your conversion to romanticism?" asked Doña Rosita.

"Ah, my charming and perspicacious friend! I vacillate, I vacillate. Or rather, some few of the classics I now note were fiendishly romantic."

"To blazes with devils and fiends; don't talk to me about that romanticism bogeyman any more, which darned if I know what it is, and don't toss in hell to boot. For me, everything that ends in *ism* gives me the shivers; like cataclysm, cubism, gargarism, rheumatism, exorcism, anarchism."

"Me too, but it attracts me like magnetism."

"Another *ism* that frightens me."

"Well, among them there is a parallelism."

And they began to laugh at the comic turn the dialogue had taken.

The beach at Boves was a semicircle, of white shining pebbles. On one side the sea, on the other green meadows; a half moon on a background of blue and of emerald. On one of the tips of the moon sat the huts of a little fishing village. There was no harbor. On landing, the fishermen dragged their boats up on the beach.

At the very moment of the arrival of the family from Collado, the fishing launches were coming in, their triangular sails of white canvas spread, which the afternoon sun enlivened with changing gleams of pink silk. At first glance, they seemed to be sailing helter-skelter, in competition to be the first to arrive at the shore. But this was not the case, for they were arriving in geometric order, quite patterned.

"Notice," said Don Cástulo, "that the boats form an angle or wedge, like cranes in their migratory flight. With a wedge of that sort, Nelson split us up the middle, Spaniards and French who were sailing in a straight line, at the battle of Trafalgar—which goes to show that sharpness always beats rectitude in everything; in letters, in politics, in business, in life, in love."

"They do come in a wedge, and I am aware of the reason," Doña Rosita said. "Look at the boat in the lead."

The boat that was advancing at the vertex of the angle, heading for land, was decked out in streamers and pennants. At the top of the mast waved a strange flag, which was none other than a sash of the kind village girls use at festivities. It was clearly visible, with a yellow background and a border of roses and hibiscus flowers. Perched on the prow, like an old-time figurehead, a young fisherman readied an oar to soften the landing.

"Quick, quick," Doña Rosita ordered, "let's hurry to the meeting with the townspeople."

Women, children, and old folks were running from the huts to receive the boats. Several voices were heard, one after another, as though in practiced chorus:

"They're calling for a wedding in Leonardo's crew."

"Who'll the groom be?"

"Who'll the bride be?"

"Examine the banner."

"The banner never lies."

"It's Silvina's."

"Long live the betrothed!"

"Long live Nolo!"

"Where're the parents?"

"Over there, with the net."

"A net for a big day's catch, judging by the size of it."

Left behind, an elderly man and woman were walking, laboriously carrying a reddish and voluminous net, its cork floats dragging on the sand.

Doña Rosita, who, with her party, maintained a discreet distance, interpreted the events. It was a local tradition. When a sailing boy asked a girl's hand in marriage, it was only in a symbolic and timid manner, hoisting in his boat the sweetheart's sash. The girl's parents presented the suitor with a net. The owner of the boat donated a day's catch with that net toward the wedding expenses.

Urbano, recently initiated in the use of the critical faculty, was enthralled by it. He said, "They're all pretending to be surprised, as if they hadn't a suspicion of anything until having seen the sash hoisted up over the sail. But how were they not going to know, unless they were idiots, that that Nolo and that Silvina were lovers? And the parents, how did they get the net ready if they're only finding out now?"

"My boy," Doña Rosita replied, "there are many things one knows that one pretends not to."

"On the contrary," Urbano answered, "there are many things one doesn't know that one pretends to."

"But don't you think these simple and innocent practices are very beautiful, very poetic?" Doña Rosita inquired, to draw Urbano out and to discover where his thinking led.

"I don't know what innocence is or poetry is."

"You don't know what innocence is?"

"No, Señora."

"I will rescue you from ignorance. In the words of a poet, I tell you: innocence is you."

"Then I loathe innocence, Doña Rosita."

"You loathe yourself?"

"The way I am now, yes."

"Well, how do you want to be?"

"If I knew that, I'd no longer be the way I am."

"It's plain to see who your teacher was, child. You speak the same backward language as your tutor," Doña Rosita said smilingly.

"Oh, cruel and implacable friend!" Don Cástulo intervened. "The boy has spoken with Lacedemonian clarity and conciseness."

"Didn't I tell you?" the old woman commented. "Lacedemonian. To me that sounds like female demons. And back to hell again."

"I don't know if I'm making myself clear," Urbano added, thrusting his jaw forward. "What I do know is that I've never been answered with clarity."

"Did you want to ask me something, if you please?" the grandmother asked, gently.

"Whether or not the surprise of the town and the parents is sincere," Urbano said, "one deduces that Nolo and Silvina were engaged secretly and because they wished it, not because the families arranged it for them. Is this the proper and usual way among simple and innocent people? Is it so also among other people? Do you think that it's good or that it's bad?"

"Is it that on your own and freely you might have chosen someone other than Simona?" inquired Doña Rosita, more and more interested in the conversation.

"On my own and freely, I might have chosen Simona, only Simona, Simona and Simona. But I might have liked to have chosen her myself, without you or anyone else choosing her for me, or even having an inkling about it. I would have liked, how should I put it? I might have liked to abduct her."

A fragile flutter of enthusiasm crossed Simona's face.

"I've answered the question whereby you've avoided answering mine," Urbano continued. "Will you answer now?"

"I don't remember now, child."

Urbano suddenly fell into pallid silence. When he had spoken, the others looked only at him; but he, though involved in the conversation, did not cease to observe what the inhabitants of Boves were doing while awaiting the landing: how the parents approached with the net; how the girls surrounded the bride to be with smiles and bows; how they pushed her alone, toward the shore, to the place where the bannered boat touched land. Then, the fellow who was handling the oar in the prow, jumped onto the beach and kissed his fiancée on the mouth, one, two, three, four times; Urbano, amazed, gave up counting. At this moment was when Urbano fell into a pensive muteness. The other three presumed he was silent in irritation.

Suddenly, the gaiety in which the fishermen, women and children, and old people were caught up was cut off. Doubling the cape opposite the town, there appeared a rowboat that was flying a black cloth from a pole in the stern. It was towing something that barely broke the surface of the sea. Lamentations filled the air, grievously.

"Let's go home, let's go home," murmured Doña Rosita, trembling. "It's a drowning. May God rest his soul."

"I want to see it," said Urbano, "You go, I'll catch up with you."

"What do you want to see, little one? It's horrible. Perhaps he's been eaten by the fish," advised Doña Rosita.

"I want to see it all," Urbano concluded.

"I'm staying with Urbano," said Simona.

"Oh no, that no," the grandmother cut in, taking her by the hand.

The dead body was naked and almost intact, except for the earlobes, and the eyes, now empty. Rigid, reddish and bluish, shiny, as though varnished; it looked like a sculpture in wood. To Urbano it recalled the saints of the church of Pendueles. Urbano contemplated it with passive curiosity, without a feeling of repulsion or of sorrow. He heard from a sailor beside him: "Hands and feet are like a gentleman's, thin and uncalloused. He's killed himself, this one."

"How do you mean, he's killed himself?" asked Urbano.

"That he's killed himself willingly."

"Willingly?"

"Or unwillingly."

Urbano went off, with perturbation in his mind and heart. How clearly he had begun to see it all, a few hours before! How mixed up it all appeared once again! "It doesn't matter," he thought. "Now, I feel myself having a will and faculties, which I never had. I'm becoming stronger, I'm becoming a man. The scales are falling from my eyes." He seized some stones from the ground and hurled them far away, out of an urgent need to expend energy. He caught up with the others. Simona took him by the arm.

"Angry with Grandmother?" asked Simona.

"No."

"You seemed angry."

"With myself, who's the only one I'm ever angry with."

"Why?"

"Because I don't know how to express what I want."

"Well, I understand you well enough. You're right. How happy I was to hear you!" Simona was alluding to the hypothesis of having been abducted by Urbano, though she did not dare to say it directly. Confused, with the desire and the fear that Urbano might guess it, she dropped a glove, which Urbano picked up. Simona said to him, "Keep it for me, so I don't drop it again."

Urbano kept it mechanically. Doña Rosita whispered to Don Cástulo, "What do you think will happen tonight?"

"Where and to whom?"

"To whom else? To the youngsters."

"Ah! Like yesterday, and like tomorrow, and next year, till the end of time. Each owl to his olive tree."

"How can you be so sure?"

"I know myself . . . I mean, I know Urbano."

"What a queer mania of confusing yourself with your pupil!"

"In these matters, my delightful and kind friend, confusion is our style, his and my own."

After supper at the table, an overseer of the estate presented himself, saying that on the following day he had to go to get some stone from a quarry to restore some walls. Urbano decided to go too. They couldn't dissuade him. He had a kind of hunger for physical exercise: "Well, I've got to get up early, good night," and he retired to his bedroom.

A short while later, Simona went to retire to her own.

"You were right, Don Cástulo," said Doña Rosita. "Really, that ninny is doltish to an extreme."

Urbano was now in bed and in the dark. He was reflecting. Simona's presence illuminated reality and brought forth the world from the void. She being absent, the world dissolved in darkness, returned to the void. It was necessary that he absorb Simona into his body, or that Simona absorb him into hers, by some subtle and delightful process in order to attain an indestructible union and so that all things, and he himself, might not suffer those alternatives of being and not being. He remembered that he had a glove of Simona's in the pocket of his jacket. He groped for it. Only with holding it in his hands and near his cheek like a charm did the world dawn, like the bud of a flower. He was surprised to see himself kissing the glove, with eagerness and at length. "A kiss, behold," he thought wordlessly, "the subtle and delightful process to absorb Simona into my body and for her to absorb me into her heart." In an instantaneous flash there appeared before his eyes the image of love in the kiss of the fisherman and the image of death in the drowned man. And now with words, of the mind and of the lips, he sighed, "A kiss from Simona and then death."

Monday, very early in the morning, Urbano went down the road to the quarry in an oxcart with the overseer, whose name was Antón de Munda. The oxdriver and three peasants came on foot. Urbano, with the voracious curiosity of a child, ceaselessly plied Antón with questions: What were all the various plants named and why? Why were the cherries already ripe, but not the mulberries on the hedges? Why did the cart have such large wheels and why did it squeak? Why were the oxen yoked together at the forehead, while horses were teamed at the neck? Why—he had observed it—when the resting cow stands up, does it first raise its hindquarters but a horse its front ones, and if it was a general rule . . . ? Poor Antón de Munda, very practical in several arts but not at all speculative, declared himself incapable of deciphering the greater part of these enigmas.

"Ay, Señorito!" he said, finally pushed to the limit. "All these things are as they are sometimes because men wished them so and almost always because God so disposed it. To us, what difference does the why of it make?"

"If the why of it didn't make any difference to us, we'd never leave off being children."

"Well if you ask me, only children are worried by the why of things, instead of knowing the what for. To look into the why is wasting time; to look into the what for is to use the time well. I call a child the one who wastes time, and a man the one who doesn't misuse it; for experience has taught him not to misuse it. I know that wine cheers you up. I know it by experience. What difference is the why of it to me? They'll tell me because it has spirits. And spirits, why does it cheer you up? If I set myself to stringing together whys, I get absolutely nothing out of it and wind up getting sad and losing the time I should've spent in drinking and cheering myself up. Begging pardon, and no offense meant; to me it figures that people who have nothing to do are like little children, though they put on airs; and in this case the señoritos are idle. And I'm not referring to you," he finished with a sarcastic wink, "who nowadays must be quite busy, with Señorita Simona, in the evenings. I cross myself at the señorito's courage in getting up so early."

Urbano was pained by all of Antón de Munda's words; but the last ones, singularly, made him feel deeply torn. As in the tree pruned of redundant branches the sap concentrates and builds up, so the phrases of Antón de Munda were the knife that clipped off from Urbano's mouth burgeoning curiosity, turning back toward the inside, exacerbated and in fermentation, the desire to know.

At the quarry, Urbano wanted to break stone and load it in the cart, like the peasants. After half an hour of work, he gave up. He was embarrassed. He had thought himself now a strong man. Out of consciousness of ridicule, having discovered an ironic smile in the looks of the overseer and of the peasants, his energies were rekindled. He went back to the job resolved to burst, before feeling humiliated.

"Don't get overheated, Señorito," said Antón de Munda ironically. "It's not a bit out of the ordinary these first days of being married that your kidneys and limbs give out."

These incomprehensible words stung Urbano's feelings, like the lance that touches the fine hide of a thoroughbred, pushing him blindly to physical exertion. The last stone on the cart was loaded by him.

Though aching in every bone, he had to return to Collado on foot. On the way he mused, "I'm making a man out of myself. Simona is making a man out of me. I've a long way to go, but I'm making a man out of myself. My mother didn't want me to make a man out of myself. Can it be the wish of all mothers that their sons not cease to be children? Not even physically did my mother consent in my becoming a man. For her, my body's health consisted in privation; that the sun not touch me, that I might not be caught in a draught of air, that I might not exercise my muscles, that I might not develop my strength. And my mental health, for her, privation of privations and shocking ignorance. To make myself a man physically I don't consider difficult. But to be a complete man, in soul and body, that is the difficult thing. Simona, my Simona, my happiness and my torment; I want to be a man, for myself and above all for you."

Urbano arrived home exhausted. After lunch, he said that he was going to rest.

"And after being away the whole morning," said Simona, with a touch of irritation, "you're leaving me alone again?"

Urbano's chest swelled, with pride.

"I'm as sorry as you," Urbano replied. "If you like, I'll stay with you, but I won't be able to keep from falling asleep, I'm so tired."

"Well, sleep in the hammock, under the trees."

"A magnificent idea," Doña Rosita interjected.

Urbano resisted, embarrassed.

"What's wrong with that, ninny?" said Doña Rosita, who was now starting to become impatient with the simplemindedness of that platonic husband.

Urbano fell right to sleep. Not far away were Doña Rosita and Simona, doing needlework. Don Cástulo, furtively, had slipped away.

"That Don Cástulo," said Doña Rosita, "runs away from me. As he's so wise and learned, he's gotten bored with my silly conversation."

Simona rested her eyes as much on the sleeping husband as on the needlework. She got up from time to time, to shoo away a fly that had settled on Urbano's nose, to intercept a sunbeam that was playing upon his eyelids, to straighten the pillow for him.

"He looks like a little angel," said Simona to her grandmother, with maternal rapture toward Urbano.

Just then, Urbano gave out a powerful snore.

"Little angel! He snores like a man," the grandmother exclaimed, laughingly. You're in for it, child, if your husband breaks out snoring with that enthusiasm in the evenings. He won't let you sleep."

"Why not? From my room you don't hear him."

"It's true. I don't know what I'm saying."

Urbano slept until seven in the evening. Afterward, he and Simona took a walk around the estate. With Urbano's absence during the morning and the other kind of absence, sleep, during the afternoon, Simona felt as if he was escaping her and that she was losing

94

influence over him; she now put into play by instinct her inborn, primeval feminine coquetry to attract him, to reclaim him, to subjugate him. She went and came running around Urbano; she looked at him with half-closed eyes, of supplicating languidity; she played at throwing leaves and flowers at him, showing, on laughing, her moist mouth, with turgescent and tremulous lips, and with the laughter her cheeks were splashed with dimples; she stretched, her head thrown back, her neck supported in her interlocked hands, the elbows high, whereby her torso was straightened and her breasts raised. She was another Simona. Urbano having abdicated the amorous initiative, which by nature corresponds to the male, Simona, under the species' imperative, took the initiative. Without design, with perfect innocence, feeling herself stirred in all her fibers upon contact with Urbano, modestly and as if by chance, she brushed his hands, his forehead, his eyes, his cheeks, his mouth on the pretext of whipping him with a flower; or she leaned on him, tired out after a race, so that her face might fall near his, so that her curls might tickle him, like live and naked nerves, and their bodies might touch on the broadest surface possible, guessing that Urbano would feel the same perturbation though anguished, irresistible, and desirable, and in this way she had him for her own, totally captivated. With what dignity and concealed pride Simona heard Urbano, taking both of her hands and looking into her eyes, say to her with passion, "How beautiful you look to me, Simona! Your beauty is growing within me, as the love I have for you grows, moment by moment. I adore you, Simona, I adore you."

He had never spoken thus to Simona. He felt satisfied with himself. Simona savored in her heart Urbano's words, "Your beauty within me." Urbano did not really know what he had said; the one who interpreted all its profound sense was Simona, who had just absorbed to the marrow the sensation and taste of her beauty.

That night, after supper, Urbano stayed longer in the dining room. Finally, as on previous nights, he went to roost in his olive tree, and Simona to hers. The tutor and the old woman remained.

"You aren't saying anything. You're withdrawn. Is Collado now tiresome to you?"

"Quite the contrary, I see with terror how rapidly the fatal date approaches when your invitation is up."

"Don't let that worry you. You're at home here. You can stay here until Urbano makes his move, or what's the same thing, *per secula seculorum,* as you always say."

"I'm infinitely grateful, kind Señora," said Don Cástulo, rising to bow in a sign of acknowledgment, in front of the old woman. He sat down and remained abstracted.

There was a pause.

"I see you these days spending a lot of time in the woods."

"Let us sing the woods' praises, says Virgil; may the woods always be worthy of a Consul. This some French author has interpreted in the sense that Virgil had prophesied the idea that presided in the creation of the park of Versailles: a domesticated wood, shaven and pomaded. Virgil had the prophetic gift. He prophesied as well the coming of Our Lord Jesus Christ. But I rather feel that Virgil saw in the woods the image of a patrician conscience, in whose serenity are engendered lofty meditations."

"Well those meditations aren't doing you a bit of good. I see you worn out and bleary eyed."

"*Minus afficit sensus fatigatio quam cogitatio;* words of Quintillian: fatigue is less wearing than thinking."

"And what about your new-fledged romanticism?"

"Not new fledged, but enslaving. Don't you see me worn out and bleary eyed? Don't you see me in perpetual adoration before the Holy Sacrament of me myself? Don't you see me with all the doleful air of an apostle of Desolation, as all the great romantics were? Ah, Señora! I too, like Chateaubriand, possess a soul of those the ancients called sacred sickness."

"Virgin of the Milk and of the Good Birth! You astound me.

What kind of meditations are those that have brought you to such a state? They can't be very Catholic."

"Meditation on woman. *Mille modi Veneris,* states Ovid: Venus plays with men in a thousand ways. Ovid, master of love, the same who advised, *Mulier cupido quod dicit amanti, in vento et rapida scribere aqua*: to write in the wind and in swift water the words of the woman who speaks of love, which Sophocles had already said."

"Do we women deserve such a bad reputation?"

"I say and will repeat to the last breath, *Mulier, hominis confusio*: woman, man's confusion. *Tes men kakes kakion oyti ginnetai gynaikos: esthles d'oyden eis hyperbolen pephyk ameinon.*"

"What's that, Basque?"

"It's a golden sentence of Euripides: 'There is no worse evil than a bad woman, nor has there ever been produced anything better than a good one.' But how to distinguish, beforehand, the bad from the good?"

"By trying them out, Don Cástulo, by trying them out; there's no other way."

Don Cástulo was going to continue with his anthology. Doña Rosita restrained him with a gesture of her hand: "Go to bed, Don Cástulo, and rest your head, which tonight you've got mixed up like a salad."

"Consoling sleep has divorced itself from my eyelids."

Neither could Urbano sleep that night. He tossed and turned in bed, restless. Thus passed some hours. Finally, he was pacing about distractedly, when there appeared before him, with a chill on the skin, the words of Antón de Munda: "Nowadays you must be quite busy with Señorita Simona in the evenings." With impulsive certitude, which was like a premonition or portentous hunch of the spirit, he said to himself, sitting up in the bed: "Simona is on the balcony, waiting for me. That's it; these evenings we should be busy in talking on the balcony." He dressed. He approached, feverish, breathless, the balcony, which he opened cautiously. Almost touching his, was Simona's balcony. Empty. Urbano leaned on the balustrade. Above, among the foliage, out of the dark background, some stars seemed to detach themselves from the branches and to fall with the nervous and brief fluttering of falling petals. The fireflies dotted the meadows below; they were like already fallen stars, and on resting upon terra firma took on a more ecstatic, more tranquil shine; stars in repose. Urbano, reliving in his senses and in his heart, more than in his mind, the afternoon's contacts with the pliant and warm body of Simona, longed for—in a great wave which surged up to then plummet in the depth of his being—a full appoggiatura, in which to fall, and to lie, and to repose, and to abandon himself to a happiness, which he conjectured, in the form of absolute laziness.

The voice of the nightingale sang out, transparent, sad, and gross, which, on just hearing it among the shadows, makes one imagine and almost see that the impassioned bird is swelling its throat, like an enormous sob. Urbano felt in his throat the song of the nightingale. Morning was breaking when Urbano returned to his bed.

Tuesday morning, Doña Rosita fashioned a plan. She had observed that on the previous nightfall Urbano and Simona for the first time looked at one another as lovers look at one another, with ardent and thirsting eyes. Doña Rosita attributed it to the short time that they had been able to be together that day. Privation is cause for appetite. The grandmother determined in consequence to have Simona with her all day on the pretext that she needed help in certain domestic tasks, and that Urbano might wander about by himself, like a soul in penance. "Without a short spell of purgatory," the old woman told herself, "one does not ascend to heaven."

"First obligation of the married woman, to be very much the woman of her house. It's high time for you to learn about domestic duties. I want to take out all the clothing from the chests and bureaus today so it may air; then we will put it in order again. You will do it for me, because I'm old for these jobs, and you'll make a list of the clothing and other articles and family heirlooms. In this way you'll find out what you have, since all of it will be yours from tomorrow on." Thus spoke Doña Rosita after breakfast.

"I'll keep you company," Urbano volunteered.

"Behold the mighty Hercules, weak before the force of love, wanting to take part in woman's work. Oh, eternity of symbols!" said Don Cástulo.

"We don't need this delicate Hercules; he'd be in our way. Let him go for a walk," Doña Rosita decreed.

"But what am I going to do by myself?" Urbano grumbled, mournful.

"I've already told you, go for a walk. You can hunt crickets."

Urbano sallied forth on the venture. His eyes were dull, like those of a sleeper who has been suddenly awakened. He found himself in a meadow where some saddle horses were grazing, under the care of a young shepherd. He sat down on the grass, next to the little herdsman.

"How fat that horse is! It's going to burst," Urbano exclaimed, for the sake of saying something.

"It's not a horse, it's a mare. It's not fat, it's pregnant," replied the young shepherd, with indifference.

"Some disease?"

"What?"

"What you said."

"I didn't say anything about disease."

"What you said about it not being fat."

"That it's pregnant."

"And what's that?"

"What questions, Lord! That it's going to have a colt."

"A colt?"

"Well, what else is it going to have? A calf? Don't you know what a colt is?"

"Sure I do; that over there is a colt."

"No, Señor; that over there is a filly."

"What difference is there between a colt and a filly?"

"Go on; according to that, there's no difference between a rooster and a hen. But, I never saw the likes of a rooster that lays eggs."

"Of course not; but is it that fillies lay eggs?"

The young shepherd doubled up with laughter, on the grass. Urbano, embarrassed, pleaded, "Don't laugh like that. I've always been in a city, without hardly going out of my house. It's not strange that I know nothing about these country things. Since you had compared colts and fillies to roosters and hens . . ."

The young shepherd continued writhing and, between snorts of laughter, he sputtered, "Christ-a-mighty! That'd be something to see, a filly laying eggs. They'd be like melons."

"That's enough, young fellow; it's not that funny. Tell me, in what way are colts distinguished from fillies?"

"Well in what way's it going to be, Señorito, if it's right before your eyes. Fillies, when they grow into mares, will have colts, and colts no."

"And where do they have them?"

The boy burst into laughter again. Urbano persisted, with persuasive calm, "Don't laugh and answer."

"Where? Where else? In the belly."

"That's why that mare sticks out so."

"That's why."

"It's curious."

With this, Urbano felt satisfied, and rewarded the young shepherd with a *peseta* for his information.

On the way back to the house, Urbano passed next to the cow barn. At that moment, a farmhand was leading them out to water.

"How come you leave that cow tied up in the barn?" Urbano asked the farmhand.

"It's not a cow, it's a bull."

"Ah, yes, there we go," Urbano replied, in a pedantic tone. "All these calves have been had by these cows, and none from that bull."

"No, Señorito. Every single one of these calves is from that bull."

As he was now talking to a grownup, Urbano was afraid to go on asking questions, not wanting to make a fool of himself. He thought, "The little shepherd or this grown farmhand have pulled my leg. Or else, it may be that both of them are telling the truth, except that I don't understand. Don Cástulo always assured me nature is enigmatic. Because it's enigmatic it's so interesting." He had lifted a tiny corner of the veil of the universe and it was now inevitable that, slowly or quickly, he might continue drawing it back. He returned homeward, slowly and deep in thought. By chance, Don Cástulo was reading in the garden. Urbano sat down beside the tutor and proposed to him the problem that had presented itself to him with the replies of the young shepherd and the farmhand.

"I see you making headway, Urbano. This book that I'm reading is called *Emile*. In it the new gospel is preached and argued: let us return to nature. Yes, beloved disciple, one must return to nature, the supreme doctress."

Urbano had nothing against returning to nature and indeed wished for it ardently; but first of all he wanted Don Cástulo to clear up his questions about what he had asked.

"Look, my boy, the first and foremost point this book expounds is that young people should not be instructed with any kind of verbal lesson; that they go about learning on their own account, by means of personal experience. So, then, God forbid my lecturing you on anything pertaining to colts and fillies and other irrational creatures. Observe for yourself and you'll learn. Don't even think of looking for knowledge in books. Here it is advised," striking the book with the index finger of his right hand, "that young people flee books—books, humanity's worst affliction. Submerge yourself in the water of the Styx, to invigorate your body and make yourself a robust animal; if you were to read this book, it would convince

101

you. A pity that at my age it's late to increase the small portion of libido that has fallen to my lot; besides, I'm quite washed out and not at all amenable to roughness. What are you laughing at?"

"I'm laughing because you give me all that advice basing yourself on what a book says, and on the authority of that book you add that one shouldn't read books. To me, this is as incomprehensible as that of the young shepherd and the farmhand."

"Not so much, child. Montesquieu says, referring to the Quixote, that the only good Spanish book is one wherein it is demonstrated that all the other Spanish books are bad. Paraphrasing said opinion, it stands to reason that the only good book in the world be this one, because it is proposed to do away with the rest of them, Spanish and non-Spanish."

"And what would you do without books? How would you suspect that we should return to nature? Do nature and the world and life exist for you outside of books?"

"I notice in you hidden critical and perceptive faculties. It's that you are making yourself a robust animal. Your skin has tanned and you've gotten brown like a sailor. Your jaw juts, like the cutwater of a ship, confident and aggressive. You speak with the penetration of a man of experience, all of a sudden, mixed in with the ingenuous chatter of a child, which you still are. Give me your hand that I may confide in you, like a bosom pal. Yes, my Urbano; books are my life, my world, my nature, and I couldn't live without them. Never mind if I abominate them. But for God's sake! don't read books. I mean, don't read books yet. Read them later, all you can, in good time; let them work with your reflections on your past life, but may they not precede your experiences, provoking in you intoxication with a fancied life that will leave you useless for real life. Books are like the elemental forces, like water, fire, air, earth, love— fatal if they dominate and enwrap you, the best gift of the heavens if you tame and limit them in the channel, in the hearth, in the sail, beneath the feet, in the heart. Hold on tight to life and love! Hear my words as the cry of distress of a man who wishes to save

himself. Your life preserver you have at hand. Hold on to life and
to love!"

"My life preserver is Simona. Do you mean to say embrace Simona?" mumbled Urbano, pale and quavering.

"Listen to the voice of nature."

"Nobody has taught me the rudiments of that language."

"Well, if the time comes that you need an interpreter, call on
me. I swear to you I won't lead you astray."

Urbano kissed Don Cástulo's hand, carried away with effusion.
Don Cástulo, sorry at the very instant of swearing, thought, "Poor
creature! A valiant go-between you're going to find in me!"

After lunch, Doña Rosita took Simona in her charge again,
despite Urbano's lamentations and protests.

The boy left to himself, killing time in the garden, recalled that
in a small room in the mansion there was a cabinet with books. He
felt, for the first time, attraction toward reading, his tutor having
put him on guard against it. Insubordination in the face of the warnings of a respectable person tempted him as an act of virility. All
books were now prohibited books for him; that is, seductive books,
occasions of danger. Besides, unsatisfied in his appetite for real life,
he sought to nourish himself on imaginary life. He went up to the
small room; he seized a book entitled *Norma's End*. He began to
read. This is a book of amorous adventures and extraordinary coincidences, so perfectly innocent and free of any sensual allusion
that its coincidences and adventures seem more to take place be
tween pure spirits than between beings of flesh and bone. From the
first lines, Urbano experienced a subtle metamorphosis; he ceased
to be himself and was successively each one of the characters of the
book. After a while, by a kind of polarization, he felt personified
only in some characters, the good and kind ones; and the other group
of characers, the unkind and bad ones, inspired a terrible aversion in
him. When he had to address himself to one of these odious characters, he read the passage in a loud and hoarse voice. In distressing
passages, he stopped his reading, to catch his breath and sigh. At the

end of a satisfying scene, he left the book and began to skip. Unsuccessful in relieving the excess of emotion, as he happened to see a piano in the living room, he opened it, and spent several moments raining blows on the keys and bellowing out an improvised and atrocious song.

When, upon nightfall, after searching and shouting for him all over, Simona came upon him reading, he sent her away, almost rudely.

He didn't present himself in the dining room till the book was finished, supper already half over.

"What were you reading that held you so?" Don Cástulo asked. "Some epic novel?"

"Yes, Señor, a novel."

"No doubt a corrupt novel," Don Cástulo went on.

"*Norma's End,*" Urbano declared.

"I've read it," Doña Rosita interrupted, "and it's pure pablum. I don't understand, child, how you've gotten wrapped up like that, reading it."

"It's that the reading of the first novel," Don Cástulo elucidated, "is a slight attack of insanity, a brief madness."

"Exactly so," Urbano assented, "since they say that madmen, once sane, remember nothing of what happened to them when mad, as if they had misplaced from memory that insensate period in their life. For, if you ask me what takes place in the book, I wouldn't know how to answer you. All I know is that I've been insensate. But nothing has remained within me. And what have you been doing, Simona, while I was reading?"

"Don't speak to me; I'm angry with you."

"But haven't you heard me confess that I've been mad? Aren't you going to forgive me? Come on, don't hold a grudge, give me your hand, and let's make up." Affectionate and supplicating, he squeezed Simona's hand, gazing at her face with those burning and thirsty eyes that Doña Rosita had noticed in him the previous afternoon.

Urbano asserted that nothing had remained within him from the reading; but there remained with him an effusive predisposition, a heightened tension. He ate little supper. Then, he paced, from one side to the other of the dining room, driven by a subconscious excitement.

"Please sit down, child, you're making me dizzy," pleaded Doña Rosita.

"I'm going to bed. Good night."

On saying good night to Simona, he released her hand with difficulty, longing for an inseparable attachment, to carry his wife with him, like a ramification of his body.

"Will we pass the time or won't we pass the time?" Doña Rosita said afterward to Don Cástulo.

"We will pass the time," radiantly replied the interpellated.

"You concede?"

"Yes, Señora, I knowingly and unreservedly concede; the more because it's not a question of me, but of Urbano."

Urbano had stretched out without undressing on the bed. After some time, he went out on the balcony. Simona was leaning out on hers.

"Ah, Simona!" Urbano exclaimed, extending his arms to grasp Simona's hands. "I came to wait for you, my love. Last night I waited for you until dawn."

"Last night, and the night before, and the other nights, I was waiting for you, right here."

"Dearest! And how come my heart hasn't told me that? Traitorous heart, I'm going to punish you." He began to pound on his chest, and at the same time said, "Heart, you're an imbecile. Heart, you're a fool."

"Hush, don't say that. You're mistreating me, because that, that, is my heart," and standing up on tiptoes, she covered Urbano's mouth with her hand.

Urbano hastened to retain over his mouth, with his hand, Simona's hand, which he kissed at silent length. It was as if he had swallowed an exquisite narcotic; he could have remained like that forever, above all because thus he could not speak, since he did not know what to say, on having his lips free.

"But how haven't we seen one another last night?" Simona said. "You must have come out very late. I was here many hours, an infinite time."

"I came out very late. I won't forgive myself for it." To reply, he had to let go Simona's hand. He repeated, irritatedly, "I won't forgive myself for it."

"Don't get irritated all over again. You hurt me before."

"When?"

"Before, in the heart."

"The fault is this brazen and stupid hand's. It I should have punished, for having wounded my heart, which is my Simona."

"What are you going to do, madman?"

"Bite it."

And he did feel, truly, impulses to bite something.

"That hand is mine, it belongs to me," Simona said, drawing Urbano's hand to her with her own. And as soon as it brushed over her cheeks affectionately she kissed it.

Urbano had present his entire consciousness in his hand, upon which Simona had reclined her head, cuddling and shrinking up instinctively, as if she might have liked to have reclined all of herself in the fleshy and warm nest that the palm formed.

Urbano began to feel a buzzing in his arm. The buzzing spread to his torso. His chest cavity seemed to him to be filled with a boiling liquid, from whose bottom rose infinite bubbles, crystalline and luminous like little globules.

"Simona, my life, my love," Urbano breathed, weakly, letting his spirit, all bubbly, find release through his breathing. And each "my life" or "my love" was one of those tiny globules which dissolved in the air.

He closed his eyelids. In the inner darkness, some phosphores-

106

cent spirals twisted about themselves, dizzying him. Then, with slow ease, the spirals went about uncurling, as if they were tracing out in letters and words: "hold on tight to life and to love." Urbano thought he read this which Don Cástulo had called the cry of distress of a man who wishes to save himself. It was like a momentary frenzy. Urbano embraced Simona and their mouths found their way together.

At this moment, the nightingale sang.

"I have a lump in my throat; it's choking me," Simona sobbed, barely parting her lips from her husband's.

"It's the nightingale's singing."

It was not the nightingale's singing. Simona knew what it was. It was the child, which she felt for the second time, risen in her throat, struggling to extricate itself and come forth.

"Now," she thought, "is when I must tell Urbano about it, in the dark and whispering in his ear, the way grandmother advised me."

But, as the anguish might lessen, Simona, overcome by timidity, decided to put off the revelation until the following night, if the same symptoms persisted. And she settled her lips back on Urbano's, until one and the other received, in their bodies and souls, a cold and ashy shower which fell with bitter sonority. And it was, who could say, the sweet song of the lark, dissolved in the rosy light of dawn.

Wednesday morning, after breakfast, Urbano and Simona sat in the shade of the garden to converse. Urbano thought that just as sorrow, in the space of a night, ages and turns the head white, so love, in no longer a time, makes the heart of man adult. Urbano spoke with the gravity and good sense of a mature man. Out of a kind of sacred respect, similar to the awe that the proximity of hallowed things inspires, neither he nor Simona dared to allude to the balcony scene, as if they had lived it in a state of hallucination and did not retain memory of it; but they were saturated with its memory, which they kept, that it might not evaporate, like perfume in a sealed flask.

Like Saint Paul, Urbano now felt two men within himself: an active man and an interior man. He was speaking, genteelly, of matters far removed from love. Of when and in what way they would set up and furnish the flat where they might settle; of how much the initial cost would be and then the monthly expenses; of how he could earn this money, since he didn't want to depend on his parents or on Simona's family. Going into business did not appeal to him; the career of lawyer was more to his liking. He recognized that, though he had his degree, he was ignorant, abysmally ignorant, of even the most elementary concepts of his profession. They had taught him by rote some few formulae whose meaning they had not allowed him to grasp, which he repeated from memory like a parrot, with which he passed the examinations, thanks to string pulling and bribery; formulae which he forgot from one course to another, and those from the last course he had totally forgotten, after receiving the degree. He needed to begin studying all over again, with discernment now, the laws and many other serious books. He would apprentice himself to an established lawyer. He would subscribe to good magazines. He was determined to know it all, through and through. They would travel too: there is nothing so broadening as traveling; it is an education from experience.

"You've made me into a man, Simona."

Thus spoke one of the two men now within Urbano—the practical and active man, the man in relation with external reality; man fit for the effort, which in his optimism he expected to overcome easily all outside opposition. At the same time as he was speaking, his attention, through his senses—eyes, ears, nose—played over the world about him with tranquil satisfaction: the aqueous shade of the trees, where spots of sun swam like goldfish; the sound of a string plucked by a pick, of the linnet, and the violin voice, of the redwing; the lazy essence of the rose and the heavy odor of the carnation. It was a sensation of original freshness, as on his first morning at Collado. He was rediscovering the world, and he found it ever more virginal. Like one recently operated on for cataracts, objects touched his retina, so close did they appear to him.

But besides this external man, whose attention dispersed over outside things and future deeds, there was another interior man, exceedingly recondite, who had his attention focussed on his own self, as with a lens. He thought, by free association, in an interval in speaking, "Well didn't I just say that I've forgotten all that I studied?" What happened was that, suddenly, there had flourished in the clear area of his consciousness some few words learned many, many years before, he being a child, when he was studying psychology. "Spinoza defines the soul: *idea sui corporis,* the idea of its body." The idea of the body of whom? Now that in another time indecipherable definition was illuminated with shining splendor. The night before, Urbano had acquired the idea of Simona's body; in other words, he had acquired a soul. Up till then, he had been a lifeless man; now he was a complete man, with the prerogatives of intimacy and a notion of how to conduct himself—interior man and active man, soul and body.

"You've made me into a man, Simona."

At the juncture formed by this phrase was introduced the interior man and the active man. For the rest of the conversation, one and the other man alternated and intertwined, disputing hegemony.

For the whole day, the active man conducted himself like a big, grown man, to the admiration and contentment of both Doña Rosita and Don Cástulo, hearing him at the table take part in the dialogue with unaccustomed incisiveness and good sense.

But the interior man went about tensed all upon himself, with an attention expectant toward his soul, which was none other than the idea of Simona's body, awaiting, with infinite anxiousness, to fortify and reconfirm that new found sweetest spirituality come the night. The emotion was swelling up by moments within his chest in ways that he himself, imaginatively, compared with a snowball.

As in midafternoon, Urbano happened to find himself alone with Don Cástulo, he asked him, "You promised to clear up my doubts when I might come to you. How is it that the calves are from the bull and the colts are from the mare?"

"Well, you see, . . ." began Don Cástulo, blushing and evasive.

"Why are you blushing? I suppose this has nothing to do with blushing."

"You know that I get all upset over nothing, which is why I've flunked all the examinations."

"Well, answer me."

"Well, you see, the bull is the father. All God's creatures have a father and a mother, as you have them."

"I don't see the similarity. According to that people are like animals."

"Up to a certain point, yes. Animals see and hear, breathe, and eat like us."

"You'd already advised me to be a robust animal. Fine. But seeing and hearing, breathing, and eating is not being a parent. Are animals and people parents both alike in the same manner?"

"Don't be silly! Don't even think of it!"

"Then, how are animals parents?"

"Well, you see . . . by having children."

"And people?"

"Also by having children, of course."

"Then, animals and people are parents in the same manner."

"In a certain material sense, yes."

"Then, there is a material way of being a parent, which is what I don't understand. What is that material way?"

"I can't answer you."

"Because you are ignorant of it or because you don't want to answer me?"

"Don't torture me, Urbano."

"You're blushing and avoiding answering me. I deduce that

110

you are not ignorant of it, but that it's something that causes blushing."

"It's nothing, I swear to you, that ought to cause blushing."

"Well, why are you blushing?"

"There's the absurdity; partly, because of my character, and in much greater part, because they've obliged me to blush since I was little, when these matters come up. There's the absurdity."

"What matters? Where's the absurdity?"

"The absurdity is in that we can't speak naturally about these natural matters."

"Not being able to speak naturally is not an obstacle to your answering me, even though it be without naturalness. Death is a natural thing. Let us suppose that Simona has died and I don't know it yet, but you do. You would have to tell me about it; avoiding, of course, telling me about it naturally, because such casualness wouldn't be natural now; but you'd have to tell me about it, since, in the end and after all I'd have to find it out, possibly with a great shock, which would be worse."

"You've spoken with singular perspicacity, seeking in the knowledge of death the simile for the knowledge you're asking of me."

"Death . . . of whom or of what?"

"The death of your innocence and perhaps of your illusions."

"Innocents is the name given to children and to madmen—deluded ones, to fools. You judge me foolish or insane; or else you still look on me as a child."

"If only you were a little child, then I would speak to you with naturalness and relative clarity."

"Why didn't you speak to me at the time?"

"I'm sorry about that; but I was obeying superior orders."

"From my mother. Is it that a mother's mission consists in stunting a man, her son, hindering him from growing from child to man?"

111

"Let us suppose so. Is there a more beautiful, more sublime mission that that? The devil, the world, and the flesh take charge of inevitably making a man of a child, which is like converting an illusion into a disillusionment. The devil, the world, and the flesh are three infanticidal monsters, worse than Herod, because Herod was satisfied with doing in whatever children happened to be at hand; but these other three constantly demand new innocents to destroy. And the mother, she alone against these cruel enemies of the soul, defends her child, so he may never cease to be a child, so he may conserve his infantile soul being a man, and thus life will be made tolerable for him. Because either the soul does not exist or it's an innocence of childhood. The man who doesn't have a child's soul is not human."

"If there's one person in the world who doesn't have a child's soul, that's my mother."

"Exactly. To say 'mother' is to say 'sacrifice.' Your mother, with heroic courage, has sacrificed whatever there was in her of the childlike, of innocent enjoyment of life, to cede it all to you."

"I don't thank her for it. Besides, I don't understand these gabblings."

"You'll understand them some day, in time; and then you'll thank her."

"Let's drop digressions, and come back to where we started. If I were now a small child, you've told me that you would speak to me with clarity. Is it that there are things that can be declared to a child but not to a man?"

"That's common sense, and that's what education is founded on. If a child's ears are crooked, from the habit of pulling his hat down too much, once he's a man it's too late to straighten them out for him."

"In other words, it's too late to straighten out my ears for me."

"It was an example. Your case doesn't refer to ears."

"Ears, or noses, or whatever you feel like. Do you think it's too late for me?"

"Try to understand me. It's too late for me to try to instruct you like a six-year-old child. But, on the other hand, it's the ideal opportunity, the best granted by the benevolent fates, for you by your own self to instruct yourself without having to be obligated to anyone."

"Let me embrace you and call you, for the first time, friend, as well as teacher. In these few days, I've come about educating myself with portentous celerity, to the point where at times I imagine being guided by the hand of a providential being, perhaps the Guardian Angel, as my mother says. During this talk with you, I felt, at times, like a going backward in time and that my education was retarded, if it wasn't a terrible failure. And, nothwithstanding, though without my realizing it, you've been making me advance at a rapid pace in the right direction, toward the highest good, which my heart seeks and you paternally hide from me in order to spur me on more. Your last words give the most precise expression to my vague feelings."

"Advice of a teacher and of a friend: *festina lente*, make haste slowly. Desire is usually father to the thought. Don't see in a vague feeling a consummated reality."

At night the second performance of the balcony scene was put on, with all the details. The nightingale sang. Simona again felt the child in her throat and again put off the confession for the following night. For Urbano, that ball of snow which, during the day, had been compressing in his breast, suddenly dissolved on the embers of Simona's lips and flooded through all his limbs, a most delicious numbing cold, like a death brought on by happiness. Until in the sphere of heaven, the first ray of dawn signaled the morningtime and the lark gave forth its reveille, which for Urbano and Simona was taps.

Urbano retired, inebriated still with vagueness and sentimentalism, the idea of Simona's body corroborated, but no more than the idea, when in his mind there reverberated an echo of Don Cástulo's voice: "Don't take a vague feeling for a consummated reality." And

113

in the taste of honey that anointed his lips was diluted the light aftertaste of gall.

Thursday morning, a good while after breakfast, Doña Rosita observed, "The children are late in getting up."

"Bad sleep; or what's the same thing, little sleep."

And on saying this, Don Cástulo put on a look of smug satisfaction.

"Eh?" inquired Doña Rosita, eager as a chick in the nest awaiting feeding, open mouthed, her elbows shaking, like half-feathered wings.

"Yes, you heard me correctly," Don Cástulo reiterated, still beaming merrily.

"Come on now, jughead. Is it guessing? Or is it factual? Spill what you know. Lord, what a slowpoke."

"That we spent the night on the balcony. That is, each on his own balcony."

"Bah! Taking the air."

"The balconies touch, and the lovers . . . well, we don't want to be outdone by the balconies."

"What a subtle phrase; I don't know what interpretation to give it."

"Hey, that we were mouth to mouth, without separating them, the whole night long."

"Kisses?"

"A single kiss, raised to the n'th power. I correct myself; two kisses. One, last night. Another, the night before."

"I don't believe it. Your head's a little tousled. You've dreamed it. How do you know?"

"Haven't you noticed, kind and lovable friend, that, whenever I speak of Urbanito's amours, I employ, without being able to help it, the first person plural, just as if I too were a protagonist?"

"I've noticed, and I've scolded you for it on occasion, pointing out to you that it had nothing to do with you, egoist."

"It's inevitable; and egoism isn't at issue in this. The thing started at the point of Urbanito and Simona's relations being formalized. I was his confidant and adviser; I collaborated, when I wasn't the sole responsible author, on his love letters. It was inevitable: I fell in love platonically."

"With Simona? You monster!" Doña Rosita exclaimed, with a mock grimace.

"Poor little Simona; she's hardly the one. I fell in love with an ideal and nonexistent creature, more beautiful than all the beauties and lovelier than all the princesses."

"Which corresponds to the measure of your desire. Too bad."

"What happened was that since then there was established a perfect parallelism between Urbano and I. In the crises in which Urbano finds himself, I find myself likewise, imaginatively. What he feels, I feel, with absolute identity. He is the mechanism of the clock; I am the dial, where the hands mark the hour. And vice versa; I am the column of mercury in the thermometer; he is the numbered scale. I expand, he expands; I contract, he contracts. I don't need to inform myself with my senses of Urbano's situation; I look into my heart and that's enough for me."

"Out of all that gibberish I make out only that you figure you can guess Urbano's conduct by virtue of certain hunches that you feel, as they commonly say."

"What hunches, or any such nonsense? I know it, with scientific certainty. Why this that happens to me is described in psychology as a phenomenon of the double—a phenomenon out of the ordinary, I'm proud to say. Didn't I assert to you that never in a million years would we dare to kiss so much as the little finger of our wife? Well now I tell you that, Oh miracle! without knowing how, for the breath of God has pushed us, our lips have joined to those of the ideal woman, and on them we have become drunk on an inexpressible liquor."

The lean Don Cástulo stood up, arms open, with the transported face of the mystics. Doña Rosita started to laugh and said,

"You have indigestion, and then have wild and obscene dreams."

Don Cástulo first smiled with desolate bitterness, then, by degrees, went about regaining his habitual expression: "No, Señora; there's not the slightest shadow of obscenity in my dreams. It's not the *Sapphic* and libidinous kiss that Saint Preux gave to Julia in the wood of Clarens, according to the way Rousseau makes us feel it, with all its carnal fire, in *The New Heloise*; it's the immaculate and pure kiss between spouses, spouses who are so before God, though not yet before nature. The kiss between spouses is chaste, though it may be fecund, chaste as the kiss of a child. More than a kiss it's an osculation. And what's an osculation? Now people will say that etymology is worthless; well etymology gets us to the bottom of words. Osculation, osculum—etymologically it means "small mouth." You will have observed that children, to kiss, compress and project the little mouth, in the shape of a chicken's behind. That's an osculation."

"Well, if that's an osculation, I don't see how anyone dares to give a kiss, same as I don't see how anyone eats an oyster."

"But you must some time have eaten the rump of the chicken, which is worse than kissing it."

"You make me laugh," said Doña Rosita, placing her hand in front of her mouth, "I don't know whether with your boldnesses or with your eruditions, which you just can't help showing off at every second word."

"Erudition, my Señora Doña Rosita, is like decorations of colored nonpareils which are put on a dessert; they're indigestible, but with them the sweet seems more appetizing, and without them perhaps it would seem to us repulsive."

"What it comes down to is that you've dreamt."

"What it comes down to is that we're at the turning point, and thus I've written today to Micaela. I'll bet that, tomorrow or the day after, Urbanito's mama orders a Te Deum sung in San Isidoro."

"Let's hope the Te Deum doesn't change into a Requiem mass."

"Tush, tush."

Doña Rosita was on tenterhooks all day, impatient to find out at night whether Don Cástulo was a madman or a medium.

After lunch, Urbano said to Don Cástulo, "Even though you have anathematized all books to me, I feel that they are indispensable to me in order to instruct myself seriously."

"Leave books alone for now, Urbano. Pay attention to what's most important to you. Don't be an idiot."

"There's time for everything. Neither you nor anyone else will divert me. I want to instruct myself seriously. I wanted you to tell me the books most appropriate to begin with. What should I read, then?"

"Urbano, don't pester me. I mean, don't pester yourself."

"What should I read, then?"

"Let me be."

"What should I read, then?"

"Read the Bible."

"Thanks."

Don Cástulo had said the Bible to get rid of Urbano. Urbano took it literally. To wit, in the book cabinet he had seen a Bible. He headed straight there and began to read Genesis. His efforts of attention bore him little fruit. He didn't understand it at all. He finally grew weary.

After supper, everybody already retired, Doña Rosita remained in the dining room until midnight, passing the time playing solitaire. When the cuckoo clock struck twelve, Doña Rosita stood up and on tiptoes went out the back of the house to the garden. She intended to ascertain for herself the amatory scene on the balcony, to go to the heart of the mystery. She carried a delicious emotion in her breast, puerile and senile. Her mouth became dry; her temples were pounding. In order not to make noise on the gravel paths, she walked on the grass of the lawns, already soaked with dew. The wetness soaked through to her feet. "A fine thing," she thought. "At my age and with satin slippers, on the wet grass. One minute of curiosity, ten months of rheumatism!"

117

On the ground floor in the servants' quarters, she saw a light in a window. "That window," she said to herself, "is from Conchona's room. What will that good for nothing be doing, wasting kerosene at this hour? I'll take care of you tomorrow, blockhead. Oh my goodness; I'm going to sneeze without fail. If the children are on the balcony, they'll hear me and the jig is up; an outing for nothing and rheumatism as a bonus." She buried her nose in her scarf and smothered half a dozen sneezes. Her ears buzzed. "Am I dreaming?" she asked herself, holding her breath. "What's this noise that's filling my ears, like the sound of a seashell? Is it fluttering of angels' wings or is it the murmur of kisses? It comes to the same; the two are both one thing, for when two innocent lovers kiss the angels flutter about, mad with rejoicing. It's the murmur of kisses, since the echo reverberates in my heart." The sound did not proceed from up above, but was located among the shrubbery. "Have the children come down into the garden? That makes perfect sense." Doña Rosita's weightless shadow wandered slowly toward the place where the murmur of kisses came from. By chance, a film of golden light filtered from Conchona's window to a circle of myrtles, which was the love nest. Beyond this fine luminous curtain, in the shadows, Doña Rosita made out the form of the two children merged into a single shape. One was seated upon a bench and had the other on his lap. Doña Rosita came closer. She could hear: "From the first I saw you, I said to myself: that gorgeous hunk of man is for me or not for anybody." And there exploded an ingenuous, quick, and resonant kiss. "What coarse words are those?" Doña Rosita said to herself, horrified. "And that gross kiss? Can my Simona speak in such a way, in moments of abandon? Lord, what are we coming to? Oh!" Her sight adjusted to the play of darkness and shadow, Doña Rosita discovered that it was Conchona herself who was holding Don Cástulo, sighing, on her lap, like a suckling child, and she was lavishing on him those endearments and those kisses that sounded like whip cracks. "Ah, scoundrel!" Doña Rosita muttered mentally at Don Cástulo. "Was that your phenomenon of the double, that your parallelism? You've taken me for a fool; you've had a good laugh on me, you old and lascivious monkey. So we're at the turning point? What do you call being at the turning point, satyr? And it's a good thing you've found a rustic nook, like the animals, and haven't profaned my gray hairs inside my home." And she interrupted herself in the midst of the silent harangue, to laugh, also silently. "We're all children of God. Poor Don Cástulo! In spite of everything, this idyll is as pure as that of my children, assuming that my children have come to the same point. But when Don Cástulo asserts it, the rascal, it's a sure sign he's seen it." Doña Rosita silently went round the house, until she was in front of the façade, from which the balconies of Urbano and Simona opened out. In the thick darkness, Doña Rosita was a while in making out, up above, a white image; Simona's form, there was no doubt. Down toward Doña Rosita's white head descended the murmur of kisses, the gentle beating of angels' wings. The nightingale sang. Doña Rosita thought of her frigate captain. Tears glistened in her eyes. "I'm not crying from sorrow, Dear Lord. If there is any sorrow in my soul's passage, you have arranged things, Lord, so that you crown with happiness the end of my life." And the weightless old shadow slipped away silently, to take refuge indoors. She was roused from her revery by the piercing cries of two cats, who were making love in their own fashion, scandalously. Doña Rosita stepped across her threshold, sneezing and saying to herself, "Curse it, atchoo! Get on with it. Atchoo! What a night. Even the cats want to get into the act. Atchoo!"

That night, Simona, because of the discomfort that her corset caused her on bending over the balcony rail toward Urbano, dressed herself before going out in a looser and more comfortable style. After stripping almost naked, she put on some clogs and wrapped her body in a light white dressing gown. In this succinct selection of attire, malice aforethought had played no part, nor had design figured hardly at all. It was a natural reaction of adaptation to her state of mind, which was abandon to the fullness of her feelings. The slightest annoyance with clothing distracts us from immersion in our most delicate thoughts and feelings, the kind that are not savored but in self-absorption. Complete freedom and forgetfulness of spirit must go hand in hand with forgetfulness and freedom of the physical body, which calls for solitude. For Simona, to be with Urbano in the middle of the night was to be more self-absorbed and alone than in the solitude of her room. But the result was that Urbano, despite himself, was acquiring a more complete and palpable idea of Simona's body. To Urbano, the freeness and openness of Simona's body caused a faint of cowardice. He felt her body so contiguous to himself that it seemed to him as if he, Urbano, were naked; and, without knowing why, he was ashamed. For Simona, on the other hand, she couldn't overcome the desire, which was consuming her, of being unreservedly one with Urbano. The sighed for and unguessed unity in love she felt painfully split into two halves, and as though imprisoned, each portion in a separate cell, barred behind the rail of each balcony. Simona was overwhelmed, because of this, by a kind of abandon or melancholia, to the point where from the very wantonness there arose some breezy gusts, in the way of impulsive desperation.

The more Urbano felt dismayed and frightened, the more Simona gathered the necessary courage—and it was not a little—to get where she proposed: to confess to Urbano that they were going to have a child. She put her mouth next to Urbano's ear, and on her moist tongue there already crackled the glowing coals of the revealing words, when the gelid demon of doubt took hold of her. And what if it were not true that she was going to have a child? From the nape of her neck through her spine and from her shoulders downward, ran a shiver, like a thin vesture of running water. An icy blast ran through the roots of her hair, standing it on end. The nightingale sang, and Simona did not feel the lump in her throat. The doubt was transmuted into black certitude. "I wasn't going to have a child. I'll never succeed in having a child." And, on reaching this point, thinking of words, she got tangled up in the prepositions; she didn't know how to express it, "a child by," "a child of," "a child with," or "a child for Urbano." The only thing she was sure of was her crushing sorrow. She drooped her wilted head on her husband's shoulder. She would have dissolved in tears and sobs were it not for fear of alarming Urbano. With heroic discipline, she decided to cry only in the secret of her heart. She concentrated on her inward crying, a real crying, with liquid and salty tears, which Simona felt welling and slipping within the walls of her chest, like the water that oozes in the depths of a cavern. The crying flowed endlessly, filling a pool and the level rose. After much time, that rising flood reached her throat. She felt as if she were choking. "Is it the crying or is it my child who was hidden and is calling me again, at the doors of my body, wanting to come out? It's my child. With his tiny hands, he's gently scratching my throat from inside and making me choke." Simona raised her head with the heightening of faith; then she placed her lips to Urbano's ear and, in the softest breath, sighed, "We're going to have a child."

Urbano did not understand. Simona's words had struck him hollow, concavely, and he returned them on the rebound, in an echo: "We're going to have a child?"

And Simona, with shortened breath, "I'm going to have a baby."

And Urbano, stupefied, dumbly, "I'm going to have a baby?"

And Simona, her voice thinner and thinner, more and more vacillating, "I'm going to have it . . . I'm going to have it by you . . . from you . . . for you . . . with you . . ."

Little by little, Urbano began withdrawing again into himself. His spiritual self, shortly before bloodless, now overflowed with bitterness, deceit, unpleasantness, and burdensomeness. With an arid tone he said, "Explain what you mean. What do you know, what do we know about what having a baby is, about how a child is had?" And suddenly changing tone, he exclaimed tremblingly, "Lightning!"

"There hasn't been any lightning. The sky is clear. The stars are shining through the trees."

"There's been a flash of lightning. I was listening to you, with my eyelids shut; but the lightning flash passed through to my pupils."

"You're seeing visions."

"If only you saw them too!"

"What visions do you want me to see?"

"If only it were a vision that you're going to have a child."

"It was a vision in the beginning."

"If only they were visions. Yours and mine. Mine more than yours. No. Yours more than mine. I don't know."

"Mine was a vision in the beginning. Now it's a real thing."

Urbano believed he had seen lightning or, better said, had a flash; but he didn't want to use this latter expression with Simona because it might have sounded vulgar. Urbano realized immediately that the flash he had seen was not a meteorological event of the heavens, since he had seen it with his eyes closed, but a mental flash, a radiant phenomenon in the dark night of the soul. He had suddenly comprehended, as though under a great burst of light, infuse and abrupt. What is it he had comprehended? The Bible, no less. In the afternoon he had been reading it without understanding a jot. Now everything unfolded neat and clear, like an open book with footnotes at the bottom. No detail was missing. He and Simona were Adam and Eve. The devil was also on the scene, though hidden in the darkness. He, Urbano, had heard the unmistakable hiss of the serpent and seen among the shadows a shadowier shadow, an infernal shadow (Doña Rosita's shadow); but he kept quiet, because telling Simona about it would surely make her faint from fright. The hunger for knowing everything which afflicted him, what was it but the temptation of eating the forbidden fruit; the apples from the tree of knowledge of Good and Evil? And who, if not the very devil himself, inspired in him that insatiable, sinful curiosity? Sinful, yes. He found himself in sin, or rather he had lost his innocence, for he had noticed for the first time that Simona's body and his own were naked; naked to his thinking, which in this case was the same thing. All this had to end in a bad way.

The archangel would come, with flaming sword. Goodbye, earthly paradise! Jehovah would come to expel them from Eden, saying to him, "You will earn bread with the sweat of your brow" (which, to Urbano, was not worrisome but pleased him: to earn bread for Simona!), and to her, "You will bear children in pain," which troubled Urbano doubly, first because of Simona's pain and then because he wanted to find out what bearing children was. All that delightful life was going to end because of Urbano's accursed curiosity. He had no doubt that the child which Simona had announced to him was also the result of his curiosity. And despite the imminent punishment, Urbano wanted to go on knowing; he persisted in nibbling, with a lessened appetite, the bitter apples of knowledge. Insistingly, he asked Simona, "Explain what you mean. What is that real thing?"

"A thing inside my body."

"A bulge?" Urbano interrogated, associating some of his recent memories and information.

"Yes, a bulge, inside me."

"Where? In what part?"

"In my throat."

"And lower down, right in your body?"

"It must be in my body when it's keeping still; but sometimes it comes up to my throat, as if it wanted to get out through my mouth. One day, without my being able to help it it will come out. What will we do then?"

Urbano kept silent. Suddenly, he said with sad seriousness, "Haven't you seen the devil? Haven't you felt him?"

"Are you out of your wits? What's the matter? You're shivering."

"The devil has been tempting us, spying on us, since a while ago, from the garden. I've seen him and I've heard him slither on

the grass. Our happiness has come to its end. We've lost our innocence. That's why I'm ashamed that we are naked."

"But, we're not naked."

"It's the same thing. I'm blushing, as if we were. That's why,
because we've lost our innocence, you're going to have a child, and
you will bear it in pain. But don't worry, my love; I'll suffer with
you and will earn bread for you with the sweat of my brow. Do you
hear? What's that noise? Is it the archangel who is thrashing his
sword about? Its terrible reflections are spread through the heavens."

"It's the roosters crowing, Urbano. It's morning dawning."

"The roosters crowing? In the past, the lark sang. Today the
roosters crow. It's reality which is awakening us. But don't be afraid.
I'll take care of you and our child. Good night. Good morning. A
goodbye kiss. After all is said and done, it's more than enough. A
kiss of yours, and then death."

"Goodbye, my silly. I don't know if I like you more silly or
sensible."

On retiring, Simona thought, with childlike seriousness, "These
men. Grandmother is quite right in saying that we women are the
ones with good sense. No sooner did I tell him we were going to
have a child than he's been on the verge of losing his mind." And the
line of her chaste mouth curved, vibrating, in a smile of charming
pride.

Friday morning, Doña Rosita had her chocolate alone, bored
with waiting so long for Don Cástulo. The old woman was burning
to find herself face to face with the tutor. "How will he get out of it,"
she thought, "that sanctimonious bumbler, when I let him have it?
Imagine letting himself be taken in by that crude beast, who belongs
not under any civil roof but who should be free to graze in the pas-
ture." The señora became so agitated that a cocoa-soaked biscuit
broke, from hand to mouth, and fell on the tablecloth. This Doña

Rosita took as an unpardonable breach of etiquette and, what was worse, a terrible omen.

Don Cástulo appeared finally, with the faded and draggy look of the no longer young man who has stolen the time for love from his hours of rest. Doña Rosita, licking her lips and eyeing her victim, like the cat the mouse, said, "If you want to send the daily letter to Doña Micaela, reporting the phase of the honeymoon, be quick about it, for the messenger is leaving in a minute."

With that kind of slowness with which sleepwalkers proceed, Don Cástulo wrote two or three cryptic words and then the envelope, which he handed silently to the old woman as if he were delivering to her a message from the other world.

"What are you writing today, if it's not noseyness?" the señora asked.

Don Cástulo did not reply.

"Hey! Wake up sleepyhead. Shake the sleep from your eyes," and Doña Rosita threatened to throw a crumb at his face in order to bring him to his wits. The señora reiterated the question.

"What I've written today? I've written 'short by a hair.' "

"A hair?"

"Yes, Señora. A hair, a capillary unity, a fiber, a filament—an angel hair, if you like."

"Did you know that angel hair is a kind of sweet?"

"I deduce that whatever is angelic is the archetype of sweetness."

"And don't you know where the sweetness of angel hair comes from? From the pumpkin."

"I didn't know it; it's not given to the limited human intelligence to know everything."

"But you learn new things every day."

"I try to; it's my chief vice, which, thank God, I'm beginning to cure myself of. I shouldn't want to know but very few things more."

"And you should like the rest of us not to know those things that you alone know. Well, little friend, the cat's out of the bag."

"I don't understand, my venerable friend."

"If I were you I might have put in today's letter: 'Not short by even a bristle.' "

"Now I understand less."

"Angel hair? What pretentious nonsense! What euphemisms. Bristles, tough bristles, authentic bristles."

"Am I still asleep? I don't know how to decipher those enigmatic phrases. What is this about angel hair now? And what are those bristles?"

"That Conchona's head is properly a perfect pumpkin for anyone who's not too myopic and romantic to notice." Don Cástulo stood up. "But it's not a sweet pumpkin, of those from which angel hair is made. It's a pumpkin with bristles." Don Cástulo paled. "Bristles the matting of her noodle. Bristles the handlebar mustache, that decorates her big mouth. Phooey! I'm horrified to think that you kiss that muzzle. What a stomach! You might just as well kiss the ox driver."

"Señora, though enamored of all things Hellenic, I abominate the ill-named Socratic love. Kissing the ox driver . . ."

"There you go, speaking in Greek. I knew you'd start that. You, like the squid, defend yourself covering yourself up in ink, printer's ink."

"I don't have anything to defend myself for, cruel mistress and Señora."

"But I speak the old Castilian of my ancestors. I'm going to set accounts straight for you, accounts clear and chocolate muddy. I call a spade a spade and you a libertine, a lecher." Don Cástulo raised his hand to his heart. "You've abused my hospitality. You've converted my house into a theater for performing lascivious scenes."

"I protest."

"All right; if not the house, the garden."

"I protest. Our love is immaculate. The heavens be my witness. We make love, yes, Señora: I declare it with forehead high and free of remorse. I have found the ideal woman, the Archetypal Woman. What was I to do with her? We mortals are a plaything of the gods, said the divine Plato."

"Chapters and verses like in sermons, no, by God. They vex me, even if they come from sacred authorities, like that one you just mentioned, calling him divine, by which I presume, he must be some theologian; but, get to the point, and enough erudite flowery sayings, if you don't want me to explode, and I'm about to do so." Doña Rosita was exploding, exploding with laughter.

"If you," continued Don Cástulo, "judge the fact of my having fallen in love, in desperation but honestly, with a woman humble not by her qualities but by employment and condition, appointed to the duty of servitude to these Penates, I say that if this constitutes, in your opinion, and you are within your rights, abuse of hospitality, I, on bended knee, if it is necessary, kissing the soles of your feet and even watering them with tears, will beg you to pardon me. Then I'll pack up my bag, and I'll go away from this pleasant asylum, where the happiest hours of my unhappy existence were spent; but not without first proclaiming, with all respect, that Conchita's head is not a pumpkin, no, but statuary canon of beauty, on the outside, and exemplar of moral beauty in the intimacy of her thoughts; that Conchita's hair puts envy in the hearts of the angels, however hairy they might be; that Conchita's mouth is a Castalian fountain, where princes, emperors, and popes would most gladly give their investitures to water, were it not that it fell to my good fortune to be its possessor and guardian, and no one will come forward to touch her without my launching a destruction the likes of Troy. And whoever may disagree with what I here sustain about Conchita's head, hair, and mouth does not know what he's getting into."

Doña Rosita gave herself up to laughter.

"What are you laughing at, Señora?" Don Cástulo asked, who

had let off through his mouth all the steam of his feelings and who was now drooping and trembling. "I've made myself very ridiculous, haven't I?"

"Blessed Don Cástulo! I'm laughing, first of all, at hearing you call that she-ass Conchita. Then, I'm laughing, not because you seem ridiculous to me, for you never seem so to me; but you make me laugh. A laughter mixed with pity; no, correction, with true sympathy; even more, with affection, why must I deny it?"

"Ah, my perspicacious friend! You speak well. I wanted to be a hero of serious romanticism; I am a character out of comic romanticism. I belong, it's some consolation to me, to the superior order of comedy, tragicomedy, which is laughable and inspires pity. You note it, with your great talent, and I subscribe to it."

"Not at all. I've expressed myself badly. It's not that you are pitiful."

"Yes, Señora, I'm pitiful to myself."

"What foolishness! Why?"

"Because I have fallen from your favor. You have expelled me from your house—I, who was planning to beg you to be bridesmaid at our forthcoming wedding. Without your participation, my hymeneal will be an incomplete hymeneal, since you've captured my most exquisite affections. Your absence that day will be like a little sprig of hemlock in the nectar of the nuptial amphora."

Before this unexpected announcement, Doña Rosita remained a good while thoughtful and severely regretful of her previous sallies and jests.

"You're going to get married?"

"My love does not admit delay."

"How was I to guess? I thought it was a question of a fling."

"I don't know if I would be capable of a fling; Conchita, never."

"It's all settled, then?"

"Settled."

"Well, I will be the bridesmaid."

Don Cástulo went down on his knees to kiss Doña Rosita's

hands, saying, "Oh, magnanimous soul; most high and kindest Señora! How will I ever repay you for this mercy with which you humble me? I'm unworthy of your longanimity. Your anger with me was just."

"Get up, good man. Now you do seem ridiculous to me. Really, you're crazy. What anger or any such stuff?"

"But weren't you angry with me?"

"Such a wise man and such a fool. Didn't you guess that everything I said to you was in jest?"

"You've split my heart from end to end."

"A bit annoyed with you yes I am, for your dissimulation. Instead of being frank with me at the right time, you spoke to me about parallelism, phenomenon of the double, and other fiddlefaddle. Phenomenon of the double—I'd have said duplicity, cunning duplicity."

"Was it in jest what you said to me about . . . ?"

"About Conchita? Why, of course. Certainly she's not a Virgin of Murillo, but I admit that she has a kind of rustic charm."

"Let's say a natural charm. I've embarked on a voyage of return to nature."

"Well, bon voyage. Certainly Conchita's mouth is surrounded by a down which isn't really bristly, it seems. And who knows but that that down may not be bristly but of pure silk. You would know about that."

"What do you mean, bristly? Venus' feathers."

"There's no argument with me. Are you satisfied with my explanations?"

"One worry remains with me."

"If it's within my power to dispose of it . . ."

"You've said something most cruel to me."

"Jests, dear Don Cástulo."

"Something about the kiss . . . and you used as a comparison the ox driver. I felt a deadly torture."

"I don't remember . . . Ah, yes, yes . . . now . . . now . . . ," Doña

Rosita vacillated; on her cheek showed the blush of confusion and the wrinkles of repentance. "It's an old theme of mine, a mania. I believe that love without kisses would be more perfect, more . . ."

"To love without kisses, Señora? Rabbit pie, without rabbit. So inseparable are the kiss and love that the Greeks (and sure enough if the Greeks weren't well versed and experienced in this) had not but a single word, *Phileo*, to express, alike, the act of loving or of falling in love and that of giving kisses, so that they're the same thing."

"Still, to join one's mouth to that of another person seems to me to always have to be something violent, something repugnant; well, not repugnant . . . distasteful, at least. The same whether it be a woman's mouth as a man's. This is what I meant. Does my explanation suit you?"

And as she spoke, Doña Rosita thought to herself, "There's no way of repairing the harm done by my stupid impertinence. There's no smoothing over the foolish thing I said to this poor fellow."

"It suits me, because I see clearly that you haven't meant to hurt me; but it doesn't suit me, as theory. On this point, I respect the infallible judgment of the *Manu Code*: 'All the apertures of the body, above the navel, are pure. All those below are impure. But in the young lady, the body, in its entirety, is pure.' "

Doña Rosita on hearing this was greatly scandalized and found a way out of the embarrassment she had been stuck in.

"Be quiet! How dare you! What an outrage! You're blemishing the apertures of my ears, which are pure, with impure words."

"They're not impure words, they're religious pronouncements."

"Don't insist or I'll get angry, and this time for real."

"There'd be no reason to. This admirable doctrine about the orifices of the human body I would successfully defend even in an Ecumenical Council. Let them set cardinals against me. I would crush them. But, what? It wouldn't be necessary. I would put this hand into the fire that all the Holy Roman College concurs in the aforesaid opinion."

"Well do me the favor of closing the orifice of your mouth, forever, on that subject, or I tell you, I'll provide you with some cardinal colored bruises for being foulmouthed. Tell me, now, when do you think to get married?"

"The sooner the better. If it can be in three days, better than in eight, and in eight, better than in fifteen."

"The spur of love."

"It's just that I'm already over forty and shouldn't wish to leave small children behind."

"Quite sensible. You're already worried about offspring. And of course, advancing the wedding three days, it's guaranteed that you'll see your children grown up. Say that you're in a hurry and don't be a hypocrite. To change the subject, how's it going with my youngsters? Are they in as much of a hurry as you? Is the ball still on the roof?"

"On the very edge of the eave, to fall or not to fall. Comes there not a gust to push it backward, imminent consummation. There remains but one tiny grain of sand in the hourglass. That is one slightly unfilled cell in the hive: pure honey."

"Gust? Where is the gust going to blow from? What nonsense!"

"Polycrakes, at the apex of his happiness, feared exciting envy in the gods. The gods, Señora, are jealous and vengeful."

"I know but one God, and that one is merciful. Tell me now, how do you speak with so much authority about the children? Is it that you spy on them during the night?"

"You're going to call me a seer. What I told you the other day about the phenomena of parallelism and of the double is true. It happens sometimes that Urbano says to me the very thing I'm thinking about. Apart from this, no night do I retire to my bedroom without first going up to the corner of the façade, and there I wait for awhile screwing up my eyes and stretching my ears to see if I catch something of what Urbano and Simona are doing and saying. I delight in their happiness as if it were a matter of a great triumph that I myself have achieved."

"Blessed Don Cástulo! Last night I too went out into the garden to see if it were true; and I discovered two truths, that of them and that of you. I too felt the greatest happiness of my life, a kind of drunkenness of triumph. Only I've caught a cold. If I raise this handkerchief to my face so often it's because my eyes are moistening with emotion and, on the other hand, because I've caught cold. Good fortune reigns in this household. God be praised! What have I done to merit so much generosity from the Supreme Creator? A misfortune, what's called a misfortune, I've never had, except for the death of my husband and that of my parents. My life has been the running of quiet water, under a gray but serene sky. And still God regales me with new favors, ever finer. For, believe me, my girlish love with the one who later was my husband didn't excite or move me as much as that of my Simona in this her marvelous and incredible honeymoon. And this when God should have punished me, many times over, because thinking proper a certain old-fashioned austerity I've expressed, foolishly and crazily, without feeling it, cruel judgments about life and love. Look at me, speaking ill of love and of life."

Simona came in. The virgin-wife, too, was wearing a look of triumph; her lips full, curved still in that proud and smiling arc with which at the early morning hour she had retired from the balcony. The grandmother observed Simona's expression; and interpreting it as overflowing happiness that shows on the face, she felt almost suffocated with tenderness.

Urbano was not long in appearing, with a downhearted look.

"Urbanín," said Doña Rosita, "for goodness' sake straighten up and put some sparkle in your eyes. The shadow of a willow seems to float upon your brow. All of us today are in jolly spirits, delirious with joy. Don't spoil the happiness for us."

"Why are you delirious with joy?"

"Because we are, for no reason. Cheer up, my boy."

"I'd certainly like to, but I'm worried."

"Why?"

132

"Because I am, for no reason, the way you're all content."

"Silly, silly, silly," said Simona, getting up to kiss his forehead over and over, forgetting herself, without paying any heed to the presence of Doña Rosita and Don Cástulo.

Urbano, likewise oblivious to those who were present, returned the kisses on Simona's cheek, with sad slowness. On separating, it was as if they took no notice of having kissed. Don Cástulo winked his eye at Doña Rosita and Doña Rosita was giddy and deliciously disturbed, as if she had received the kisses. She thought, "Well that about parallelism and phenomenon of the double isn't a tall tale."

At around eleven-thirty, the four still sitting together, a servant announced to Doña Rosita that two men needed to see her.

"Two men?" asked Doña Rosita, wrinkling up her nose, for comic effect. "Two men, no less, just for me?"

"Two men, or two señores, if the señora pleases, just for her or not."

"It's not the same thing, men and señores. What appearance do they present?"

"Spruced up, after a fashion; just like señores, in their ordinary dress, or else plain men in their Sunday best. One, seems to me to have a rash, which is a high class disease, a disease of señores, if it doesn't come from drinking; the other one's got a great big double chin hanging down, which to my knowledge is an ailment of only poor people. Ah! I was forgetting; they say they were sent by the judge."

"Well, bring them here; hurry it up, ninny; and you could have said that in the first place."

On the servant's going out, Doña Rosita said to Don Cástulo, "Some local affair that they're making the rounds with, and they stop in here in passing in search of information. It's not the first time, according to what my daughter told me."

The two individuals came in, looking more or less as the servant had described them. They remained standing, twisting their hats in their hands.

133

"Have a seat," the señora invited.

"Thank you very much; we're better off standing to carry out our duty," said the one with erysipelas.

"Do you wish to speak to me alone, or is it all right if my grandchildren and this friend are present?"

"It's all the same," the one with goiter murmured, with a great sigh.

"I'm not bad at remembering people's faces and I remember you from the other times. Pity that my daughter isn't here, who is the one who's informed of whatever goes on around these parts, and would tell you, certainly, whatever you want to know. I live with my head in the clouds, out of touch with everything. I'm afraid you may leave without knowing any more than when you came."

"Not at all," stated the one with erysipelas.

"I'm afraid so. Is it something similar to that of the other times, legal matters?"

"Unfortunately; but the case is more serious," moaned the one with goiter.

"You're a very sensitive person," said Doña Rosita to the one with goiter.

"We all have a soul hidden away," cut in the one with erysipelas; but to the case at hand, lady, duty is duty. In short, we came to discharge you."

"I didn't know I was sick. Are you quack healers? Have you stopped in, by chance, after having a few drinks?" Doña Rosita replied, with a disdainful smile of aristocratic elegance.

"Come to this moment, all are insulting, whether grand seigniors or lowlifes," Erysipelas affirmed, with a philosophic nod of his head. "Señora, we're not drunk, but very much in our place, heavy though it weigh on us. We are the voice of Justice, and we summon you to leave this house this very day.

"You invite me gallantly to go on a trip? A thousand thanks, gentlemen. My bones are weary now and, even if it were to visit

134

Dreamland or the land of El Dorado, no one will move me from my house," said Doña Rosita, with a serene and ironic countenance.

"Señora, enough fooling around and jokes," said Erysipelas scornfully. Doña Rosita sat bolt upright, reddening for an instant, with anger. "This house is not yours."

"Well, if not whose is it? Prester John of the Indies, maybe?" asked Doña Rosita, recovering her haughty serenity.

"Be quiet you, and don't be a boor. Who knows but that the señora may not know?" interrupted Goiter, facing his companion. "Señora, this house, actually, is no longer yours. It belongs since yesterday at twelve midnight to that moneylender, vampire of all these towns, villages, and hamlets, who has more than his weight in gold but which is of no use to him, since he's consumptive, from starvation, in order not to spend money, whom they nickname in jest Poor Dear." The señora made as if to speak. Goiter went on, "This house was recorded in the register as being, through inheritance, the señora's property; but the señora has assigned to her daughter, Doña Victoria Cerdeño, widow of Cea, absolute power of attorney, granting her management and free disposition over all the señora's possessions; unless the document is falsified and the señora's signature counterfeit." Doña Rosita denied this with a nod. On her brow, from the space between the eyebrows to the white hair, the creases of the mask of tragedy were being gathered. Goiter continued, "Doña Victoria mortgaged to Poor Dear this property of Collado, with all its appurtenances, including cattle, furnishings, and furniture, under the terms of I don't know what ungodly arrangements, in which that old crook is a master. All the provisions the law requires have been complied with. Doña Victoria was given notice. Some eight days ago, before going off on a trip, she stopped by the court, to say that she would send, before the time limit ran out, a few thousand *reales* that she had abroad, with which to stave off Poor Dear for the moment. From there she wrote that she hadn't been able to arrange to send that money and, that since it was inevitable, to proceed with the handing over of Collado to Poor Dear, and that she herself would prepare you for what you should do come this occasion. Doña Victoria is by now very well versed in this, and she doesn't give up just like that. Other times that we've had the pleasure, I mean the displeasure, of visiting her here, it was, as now, concerning certain foreclosed mortgages on various estates which fell into the hands, some of them, of the aforementioned Poor Dear and others to a banker in Pilares, Don Anacasis Forjador. Such is the sad and true story that much to my sorrow I've had the bitterness of relating, because, God is my witness, I'm not suited to be a court lackey. I'm always on the point of giving up the profession, but I'm not fit for anything decent, because with this bulge in the neck one is very badly looked upon. Courage, then, Señora. All you can do is resign yourself to leaving this house, in which, it's plain to me, you will also leave heart and soul."

Doña Rosita, after draining in silence this copious chalice of gall and vinegar, muttered, with lips of livid whiteness, "Heart, soul, and life."

There was a long pause. Doña Rosita then muttered, "I won't leave this house."

"Señora, forgive my reminding you that, if we are not but the weak voice of the law, the law also has a powerful arm against which there is no resistance that's valid," Erysipelas cut in sharply.

The lividness spread from the lips over Doña Rosita's whole face: "I won't leave this house, but for the way I came to it; from nothingness to return to nothingness. They'll carry me out dead. Don't be impatient, good man; it will be within a very brief time," and with the last word floating on her lips, Doña Rosita fell to the ground, lightly, like an autumn leaf, as her body was weightless.

The howl of tragedy was heard, when paltry human speech, so inexpressive for all that is transcendent, is nullified and the shriek is born; that howl that terrifies mortal flesh more surely than the very sight of death. It was Simona who flung herself upon the fallen body of the grandmother. There are two watersheds in emotion: one for love, the other for grief. Sometimes, old and forgotten sorrows suddenly cascade down the amorous slope, on the occasion of a new love, whose flow they enrich prodigiously. Or else an unfulfilled love finds perhaps no outlet but for the other slope, where a small sorrow leads it, which receives an apparent volume of copious, repressed, and blind love. Simona's emotional outbreak was grief over the inert grandmother and it was likewise adumbrated love, which for a week she had been wearing herself out in bringing to light—unsatisfied love, repressed and anguished love, which was coming out now in a terrible howl.

Urbano remained still, unmoved, his hands in his pockets, intent on the circumstances with which the catastrophe was developing. He had heard and seen it all with a kind of intellectual curiosity. The only thing that interested him was the form that events took, since he was advised of the outcome beforehand. He knew that they were going to be thrown out of Paradise. He was expecting it, from moment to moment, since he had gotten out of bed. The only remaining question in the disaster was how the expulsion would come about. The modern version of the biblical drama he did not adjudge as dignified and in as good taste as in the book of Genesis. The substitution for the Archangel by that erysipelatic and crude petty clerk came across as irritating and weakened the dramatic effect. And the other one, the one with the goiter, what was he doing there, with his legal and sentimental gobbledygook? Furthermore, the old woman's death wasn't called for. Urbano vituperated the author of the drama for that death, as superfluous and unjust. Urbano assigned to himself now a sublime role in the history of the world; he was, in his opinion, the first man who was going to earn his bread by the sweat of his brow, his bread and Simona's. He would not have found it a great problem to earn it as well for Doña Rosita, who was a small eater. Decidedly, killing off the grandmother was not right or even half right; or if she had to be killed, to have done it at a better time, before her having found out that her house was no longer hers. Urbano began to feel irritation before this injustice and a great pity for the grandmother, and, finally, an irrational desire to cry.

Goiter silently opened his arms, as if smitten with despair. Erysipelas shuffled a foot, and then pulled his companion's coattails, braying in his ear, "Hoist anchor, Bartolo, and let's shove off. This is really too much. First, a lot of doing just what they please; you give me the loan, I'll give you the pledge, notarized and all. That's it right there! Then, the loan ran out, the pledge belongs to me, I'm not giving it to you. Nobody wants to hand over the pledge. Us, swinish go-betweens; half-starved donkeys with saddle sores and a heavy burden. Back there, in the court, kicks and cudgelings; out here, insults, bad manners, and nasty words. Have you ever noticed any of them treat you to a glass of sweet wine? Dog, they all call you, with their eyes anyway if not out loud. They're the dogs, who steal a scrap and wish to bury the traces. But, what most gets to me is the fainting. Let them kick off once and for all, after we've pushed off. Still, if it were a pretty woman, down on the ground showing her legs . . . As for these, what most gets to me is the fainting."

"It's never going to be pleasant, Celedonio. I swear to you that I'm not made for these calamities and woes. This is the last time. I'm leaving the job and its meager rewards. Besides, it doesn't suit my health. My heart comes up to the goiter. May God protect me, with this heavy weight that He himself tied to my neck, like a cat they throw into the ocean to drown!" sighed the so-called Bartolo.

Don Cástulo, without losing presence of mind, went to separate Simona from the grandmother's body, to which she was clinging, trembling all over, her eyes burning and a light foam on the commissure of her lips.

"Easy, little one," advised Don Cástulo, with a thick and labored voice studded with diminutives. "It's a little fainting spell. This will be over right away. Calm down, calm down. Don't get excited; you're a little woman now, a little married woman."

But Simona continued with her lamentations. Hearing the cries, from outside, Conchona ran in, knelt down on the floor next to the señora and joining her hands, as if in prayer, wailed, "God's own saint! Older than the crow and more innocent than the dove." Suddenly she changed manner and tone to ask, looking at Don Cástulo, "What happened, Don Castulín my life? And what's everyone doing there, holding their breath, staring like owls, while my precious señora, who's just like a holy image, is sprawled out on the hard floor like a piece of garbage and nobody goes to pick her up?"

Conchona led Simona off to one side; she took in her arms, with consummate delicacy, Doña Rosita's light body and deposited it softly on a sofa.

"Is she dead?" queried Urbano.

"Dead? What's that you say? God in Heaven forbid," Conchona replied. "She's out cold. For a case of reviving the spirits there's nothing like giving an old shoe to smell, and this is what I'd do, with the señora, for I've seen that it's a remedy with a real kick."

"What nonsense!" Don Cástulo hastened to say, looking askance at Conchona.

"Beg pardon, Señores," Conchona mumbled embarrassedly, "I'm an ignorant country girl. I meant no harm by it, and only want to help the mistress in her need. Vinegar is also used in such cases and fainting spells, begging pardon, on the wrists and temples, and to smell under the nose." And she consulted, with a humble look, Don Cástulo, fearful of having made another blunder.

"That's all right," Don Cástulo approved.

Don Cástulo and Conchona at the same time started off for the sideboard in search of the vinegar bottle. Then Conchona caught sight of the two messengers and said, facing them, "You're the ones, you body snatchers, who brought the evil eye to this noble house and brewed up the poison for this saintly señora to drink. I know you well and your dirty deeds, you vultures." Celedonio, frightened, raised his hands to his goiter, which was where his heart was paining him. Bartolo smiled insolently. Conchona continued, "What're you doing here, gloating over your devastation? Get out of here, you're plaguing the house. Get out, or I'll kick you out myself, giving you a boot in the snout with an old shoe, which, if it was improper to think the señora might smell it, for you it would thus be a great honor."

"Be quiet and don't be insulting without cause. These men are sent here. They're obeying orders. It's not their fault but the law's, because law means injustice, brutality, and misery." Thus spoke Don Cástulo to Conchona, harshly. Conchona, head lowered, seemed to beg forgiveness with her attitude and with her sad and tearful look. Don Cástulo went on, "Look after the señora, while I run to catch those men and get them to put aside the anger you've caused them."

They met in the garden. Don Cástulo excused Conchona, explaining away her outburst as an unthinking reaction from concern over the señora.

"Tush, tush, tush. Don't worry about smoothing over what doesn't need smoothing over. I hear those tirades like someone who hears it raining. I'm used to it," said Erysipelas, showing at one end of his acid smile a greenish and triangular eyetooth.

"And I can't get used to it," sobbed his companion, leaning forward wearily and making his goiter wobble pendulantly, like the udder of a milk cow.

"Come into a little room here. Rest. You'll have a glass of Malaga wine. Let's talk. This can't remain as it is," pleaded Don Cástulo.

"That's a different story, which tempts me for a change," said Erysipelas, his smile spreading into affability, so that a new tooth stuck out, on the other side, to make a pair with the first one: "Let's talk."

They went into a small low-ceilinged room. Don Cástulo pulled the bell cord; a servant appeared to receive orders and returned shortly with Malaga wine and biscuits. Don Cástulo declared that that sudden misfortune was sure to bring down a long illness on the señora. She was quite old. What an inhumanity, to evict her from her house in that condition! The honored judge would take it into consideration. He had to grant some delay. What difficulty was there in that? Erysipelas, while swilling down his wine, ventured his opinion that there would be no problem, except that, in view of the fact that everything there, except for personal effects (clothes, jewels, and other small articles), no longer belonged to the señora, the new owner would be coming to take inventory or perhaps might settle in, in order to prevent their making off with not even a cobweb, for Poor Dear stooped so low! Don Cástulo objected to this intrusion. Perhaps everything could go back to the original situation. There had to be some inexplicable slipup back there. The señora's daughter would show up of necessity, at any minute, and would straighten it all out. The Cea widow was very rich.

"The widow? Ay, ay, ay, that fancy bird!" exclaimed Erysipelas, with a roguish glint. "That one's hardly got a canary seed left."

"What?" asked Don Cástulo, dumbfounded, becoming round-mouthed like a fish.

"But, don't you know anything? Why, everybody knows it. Look here; when even the court knows, which is where the news arrives last of all," said Erysipelas.

"I've heard that she spends a great deal; but she had such a fortune. What has she done with it? Where has that money gone to?"

"Into the hands of Poor Dear, of Señor Forjador, of Don Eleuterio Muñiz, . . ." said Erysipelas.

"The chaplain, her chaperon?" Don Cástulo asked, repositioning his glasses which, on arching his eyebrows, had slipped down on him.

"Her . . . watchamacallit," affirmed Erysipelas, with a clownish smack of his lips, partly from the wine he was enjoying and partly from the idea he was suggesting.

"Seven sisters he has," Goiter broke in; "Mummies and dried up old birds. He's the youngest in the family. The seven used to be seamstresses and went about bareheaded; now, all with a fancy bonnet and cloak."

"But whatever the chaplain may have gotten is a pittance, a

handful of sand, which doesn't ruin anybody. On what has Doña Victoria been able to spend the rest of the money?" insisted Don Cástulo.

"Psst!" whispered Goiter, coming up close to Don Cástulo. "On gambling! Señor Forjador has declared that Doña Victoria has borrowed money and then some from him from a place in a foreign country where there's nothing but an enormous casino, where you can't play with small change, *ochavos* nor *perras*, but with *pesetas* and up to *duros* they bet. A hangout for desperadoes from all the lands of Jews and Lutherans; and women, those of the world, but elegant ones, with fancy clothes, rouge, and lots of jewelry; and devil-may-care married ones; or errant wives; and widows, like the one in question. In short, that's the kingdom of Barabbas and the pernition of pernitions. They call it, and I think the name fits beautifully, the land of Monicaco." *

"Not Monicaco, but Monago†; don't be a dummy," Erysipelas corrected.

"Monaco," Don Cástulo concluded, sunk in his cogitations, without noticing the other two's assent.

A servant accompanied the messengers to the exit from the estate and on the way went about informing himself of what had happened.

Don Cástulo went back to the dining room.

Alone with her instinct, her good sense and her aggressiveness, without the anxious worry and fear of disgracing herself in something before Don Cástulo, Conchona, during the short absence of her respected lover, had asserted herself, proceeding always with dexterity. She had the señora propped up somewhat, so that she might breathe better; she had placed a cloth with vinegar around her forehead and mustard plasters on her feet; with an enormous fan, of the kind called "club fans," she gave her air. At the side of

* A conceited, thoughtless person.—Tr.
† An acolyte.—Tr.

the sofa were Simona, kneeling, with the grandmother's hands between her own, and Urbano, standing, looking at the invalid, who was beginning to take on color and show signs of life.

Conchona, without moving from her position or turning her head, said to Don Cástulo, "For the love of God, my lordyship, let me be and don't scold me, for I get flustered and I'm lost. If I do something stupid, don't let it slide, whatever I did, and I'll correct it; but if you bawl me out, I get all upset and do something even stupider. She's coming to! She's coming to! She's opening her eyes!"

Doña Rosita's eyes had acquired portentous clearness.

"With what clarity I see it all," whispered the señora wearily. "How I see into everything. You," she went on, looking at Conchona, "have helped me. You're very capable. You're an angel. Thank you Con . . . chita," and she offered, with her eyes, this diminutive, to Don Cástulo, who, understanding that the señora was going to say Conchona but had deftly corrected herself in the middle of the word, thanked her movingly, bowing, his hand on his chest.

Conchona brought a glass of water with brandy, which she made the señora drink: "Down the hatch, and never you mind if it's brandy. You're not the first lady to drink it. From my father I heard, as a tot, that Queen Isabella drank it all the time. Drink, drink it all; there's no tonic like this one for reviving the spirits."

After this speech, Conchona took the señora in her arms, weightless as a sheaf of dry grass and, without consulting anybody, followed by the other three, carried her upstairs to the bedroom and then to the old marriage bed, of sturdy mahogany and with a coverlet of knit and lace, where Doña Rosita had slept and dreamed and sighed for more than forty years.

"In the bed, no. I'm suffocating. Put me in an armchair next to the window, with the window wide open."

Conchona obeyed.

"Now, you off to look for the doctor and me for some hot water bottles for the señora's feet," said Conchona to Don Cástulo.

143

"Doctor? It's not necessary," said Doña Rosita.

But Don Cástulo and Conchona had already gone out. On the staircase, the tutor drew the serving maid toward him, hugged her, and kissed her forehead tenderly.

"You really are an angel. As well as a clever and efficient woman. You'll make a man happy."

"Hush up, hush up, you're making the blood rush to my cheeks! I am what I am, a simple brute; don't make fun of me, Sir," said Conchona modestly, trying to hide her powerful head on Don Cástulo's narrow thorax.

"But, Conchita, why shouldn't you address me familiarly?"

"I don't dare to; later on."

"Tell me, how do you think the señora is?"

"There's a bad sign in that she wants to be sitting, because of shortness of breath. That's how Marica died, Carbayo's wife."

"Hush, hush. The doctor will inform us. Let us trust in God."

Doña Rosita, alone with her grandchildren, had said to them, "Listen to me with calmness. You, Urbano, who are seemingly tranquil, are the one most upset. You, Simona, so ruffled in your features, have not lost your grip and inner strength. You're upset, Urbano, because you're thinking of the future. You're strong, Simona, because, with the shock of the moment, you don't suspect there is a tomorrow. Difficult days are on the way. I see it as if from a very high mountain, where not even the air gets in the way of seeing though it is in short supply for breathing. Days of trial are coming over you and it's necessary, in order to pass through them well, that you, Urbano, compose and fortify yourself and that you, Simona, foresee the danger and, once foreseen, not be alarmed. They will tear you from one another, as the woodsman cuts a shrub and splits it into two pieces of firewood. Separated, think that one day you will blaze in the same hearth. I intended to leave you rich; I leave you nothing in material goods. Let my words be my bequest. Listen to me carefully. Up yonder, they keep an account on each mortal being, entry by entry, with the plus and the minus in pleasure and suffering. Death is the closing of accounts. Always, on the account's being closed, the sum of pleasure and that of suffering are equal, since the contrary would not be divine justice. It would not be divine justice, because at the moment of death all would not be in the same conditions; for he who had enjoyed himself in this life, though until then considered favored, would come out disadvantaged in the next, which is the important one. A life interlarded with good fortune and misfortune can end at any point, because the plus entries and the minus are balanced. He who lives long years of enjoyment is guaranteed a long old age of misfortune; just as the slow pain of an unhappy youth leads to an extensive and happy old age. It comes to the same thing, with one difference, that there's no greater torment than remembering the happy days in the time of adversity, nor is there greater consolation in the dark hours than the certainty of future pleasure. A long life, tinged lightly by a tenuous sorrow, receives due compensation, on the closing of the account by means of a measureless and sudden joy, of the kind that kills. Just as a peaceful and smooth life, over which floats a lazy mist, amber color, of mild happiness," Doña Rosita said these words very measuredly, "is compensated for by a sudden pain of death. This pain, of an instant, immense and dizzying pain, equivalent to a lifetime of lesser sufferings, I have just undergone, and my weak body could not stand it. I ceased to live briefly, and I come back to life briefly, I believe only for the space of time needed to tell you my feelings. I've returned, transfigured now, to life to give you my cheerful farewell. A celestial happiness inundates me. I've paid my debt, and my soul feels so light that it wants to fly from my body, like the afternoon smoke. I've discovered that the legitimate father of happiness is sorrow. I see you as flowers from my aged trunk; the incarnation of my dreams. My vegetative and rooted life is transmitted to you as active and windblown life. As a youngster, I wanted to be a seagull and brave the storms, over the rigging of the frigate that my captain commanded. Oh, my captain, I'm coming to your side! But now is not the time to speak of myself, but of you. Each

anniversary of this day of my death, I pray you to consecrate a
memory to me. Not Requiem masses, nor funeral commemorations,
no; you will celebrate it with extraordinary happiness, with a day
of rejoicing, and, if possible, you will commit some unusual folly,
saying, 'This folly, to the memory and in suffrage of the many follies
that Grandma might have liked to have committed.' The world, my
children, is dying of boredom. Trouble is preferable to tedium. In
your forthcoming and terrible troubles (I see them, I see them
clearly), lose yourselves as in a battle and then celebrate with
frenzy, like victorious savages. Let no one crush you. Stop crying,
Simona, for there's nothing to cry about now. Soon you'll know
what it is to really cry. Get up from my feet. Come close to the window, the two of you together. Look at the garden, the park. Will
you say it's Paradise lost? No, only limbo. And if for you it was Paradise, which it truly was, it's due to your anxiousness and desire for
happiness, which you have not attained. Paradise is outside, beyond
these walls, in the struggles of life. And now I am going to rest. Let
us keep silent."

Simona huddled again at her grandmother's feet, crying
softly, without knowing why. Dread had left her numb, empty of
thought. The few particles of sense that had remained stuck to her,
like droplets, on the inner chambers of the mind, now flowed outward, in slow tears. She had listened to the grandmother, without
understanding a single word. This kind of spiritual torpor was not
fright in the expectation of death. Simona had never thought of,
or known, or glimpsed what death was. The sight of the grandmother inert on the ground had produced a mechanical reaction
in her, just as on the squeezing of a trigger the shotgun is dis-
charged. The charge, in Simona's soul, had been put there by love.
Thus she had been left numb and empty.

Urbano stood about. Impatience was gnawing at him, like a
person who reads a book of adventures, knowing beforehand the
outcome, and who hastens to skim over the pages getting a bird's-

eye view. He might have wished that all that move more quickly, more resolutely. When he believed the grandmother dead, he had rebelled against divine injustice. Now, the grandmother was not showing signs of dying. And Urbano was assailed by an irresistible desire that Doña Rosita die as soon as possible. He sought to avoid this infamous idea. He averted his eyes, which he had fixed on the old woman, and rested them by chance on a panoply of ferocious Tagala tribal arms, throwing weapons, brought back by the frigate captain on a return voyage from Manila, which were posed over a dresser, a short distance from a Sorrowful Virgin under a lamp. The criminal idea pursued him. He did not dare to look back at the grandmother, fearing that his evil wish might fly out in the glance and actually kill. He wished to justify himself in his conscience, saying that he did not desire Doña Rosita's death, but to get it over with quickly. Time was pressing; it was necessary to get out of the house as soon as possible. And by an unexpected association of causal ideas, Urbano furtively left for his room to pack his suitcase.

Don Arcadio Ontañón, old village doctor and friend of the family, arrived, with his mustard-colored cape, which he did not take off winter or summer, and his chartreuse parasol, which he used as well for rain. He belonged to the school of hearty doctors, who encourage the patient to make out of his aches and pains and even his very death a joke. "First," he explained "because being in good spirits is the best medicine. Second, because you have to gild the pill, and the most difficult pill of all to swallow is the one that you've got to kick the bucket." Actually, with his sallies and witticisms he made the most melancholy patients laugh. His great comic effect was due to the fact that he was very timid and loving. Furthermore, he used to quote Hippocrates, Galen, and Avicena in Latin. "Those were doctors," he exclaimed. "When Christianity came in medical science was lost. Christianity, enemy of nudity and therefore of anatomy, isn't interested in anything more than graduating, or ordaining, doctors of the soul, confessors. The good doctor must be pagan or heretic. The progress of medicine is in inverse proportion to the progress of Christianity. When the faiths weaken, pathology and above all hygiene will prosper. I'm such a bungling doctor because I'm Catholic, Apostolic, Roman, thanks to God."

Don Cástulo had recounted everything to the doctor. "The chit chat," replied Don Arcadio, "came to me that this once upon a time beautiful body of the Cerdeño fortune was cancerous with mortgages; and of the merry widow's frivolities. That merry widow! Look here, Señor, in my long years of practice I've discovered that, just as the sensory world is reduced to three dimensions, the universe of pathology is reduced to three diseases, two of women and one of man. The two illnesses of woman are spinsterhood and widowhood. Man's illness is . . . woman, that is to say, marriage. Marriage is a woman's health, who even in this has to contradict us. Celibacy is man's health."

"I protest, I protest," Don Cástulo had replied.

Don Arcadio entered Doña Rosita's bedroom making jokes. Since for him the biggest joke of all was marriage, he said, "I always predicted that you and I would end up united in the same hymeneal. A thousand times I begged your hand. Do you decide to accept me, at last? Have you called me for that? Hosannah!"

"I haven't called you for that or for anything else," Doña Rosita replied, smiling weakly. "Here, your science is not of any use."

"I come not as a doctor; I come as a suitor."

"I feel very well, very well, very well. I feel a well-being as never before. So much well-being that it almost suffocates me."

"That well-being is originated by my presence. It's what faithful lovers feel on receiving the beloved. And I, as lover, am not content with anything less than listening with my own ear to the beats of your heart."

And, with delicacy, he leaned forward to listen to the heartbeat of Doña Rosita, who continued murmuring, with a thin voice,

"What are you going to tell me that I don't know, that I don't feel? Oh, gentle death! And there are those who fear thee."

"I'm satisfied, completely satisfied; this heart beats only for me," Don Arcadio said, with a saddened joviality, while he palpated the swollen hands of the señora on pretext of caressing them.

From the door of the bedroom, the doctor turned to say, "It's up to me to set the date of the great event."

"The great event is already set," replied Doña Rosita, with her eyes open wide.

"I'm referring to the date of our wedding."

"You won't be long in seeing me dressed in white, in a wedding dress."

Outside the room, Don Cástulo inquired anxiously:

"What?"

"*Exitus fatalis.*"

"Imminent?"

"In a week, in two days, this very day: I can't foretell with certainty. Imagine a cup of finest crystal, all cracked, which miraculously remains standing; an emotion, a touch, a breath, the most imperceptible, will break it into pieces. That's her heart. How long will it be able to remain in this condition?" Don Arcadio shrugged his shoulders. "I'm saddened. Doña Rosita was worthy of love and of respect. I've taken care of her for the past three decades. We're leaves of the same spring and the wind that carries her off seems to me as if it were sighing already in my ears."

The doctor and the tutor said goodbye in the garden (Don Arcadio already in his wagonette), when a carriage appeared at the foot of the avenue.

Don Cástulo waited.

From the running board leaped Doña Micaela; she ran toward Don Cástulo; she took him by the lapels of his jacket; she shook him; and, with a voice rough and broken, she asked him, "Consummated?"

Don Cástulo saw, almost touching his face, the dry physiognomy of Doña Micaela, more haggard than ever, the eyes protruding from their sockets, delirious, the hair in clumps, the bonnet awry. Don Cástulo was struck dumb.

"Answer. Are we in time? Has it been consummated?"

Don Cástulo did not reply. He was unable to gather his thoughts. He could only think and speak in fragments, "Very serious . . . A cup standing, miraculously . . . It can as easily be tonight as in a week . . . And the mortgage due . . . If only you could, let you be rich . . . "

"What are you blathering about there? Don't you see my mortal anguish? Answer: Is it consummated? Do you have some idea of where it stands?"

"What, Micaela? Calm down, daughter; speak clearly."

"What do you think I'm talking about? Urbano's marriage."

"Oh, yes! We're at the turning point. Short by a hair. With the recent shocks, my brain became a little scrambled. I thought that you were speaking of the señora."

"Are you quite certain that it's not been consummated? For sure? Swear it, on your salvation."

"Well, why shouldn't I be sure, Micaela? As sure as I'm seeing you. More; since I doubt that this is you, in reality, and not some hallucination of my spirit, overstrained by such rough and unaccustomed hard knocks."

Doña Micaela released Don Cástulo; she leaned her head backward, raised her arms to heaven, stood up on tiptoe, and, with restrained abandon, exclaimed, "God, your anger begins to abate; in the black unleavened bread of chastisement that you've given me to taste you put at the end a pinch of sweet leaven. Although belatedly, I read at last your ineluctable design. If the marriage is not consummated, then there is no marriage. If it has not been consummated it's because you, Lord, have stood in the way of it. You spoke, Lord, through the tongue of Leoncio, and I, a fool, having ears, did not hear you. You, Lord, have taken my heart between your hands and have given it a spin, as you do with the earth on which we walk, changing night into day and day into night. What before was dark has become illuminated in my soul; and the old clarity has been swallowed up in darkness. I hate what I loved and I despise what I adored. Pardon, my Leoncio; I am yours from today onward; I will be your slave. And for you, Urbano, my son, I feel the same bitter repugnance as for that blind part of myself from which you were the product, because I wished it. I must kill off this present Urbano, as the Micaela of before is dead." The last words were the transition from the broad biblical accent to the commanding and tyrannical manner, habitual in Doña Micaela. Bringing once more her haggard face up to the face, increasingly frightened, of Don Cástulo, she continued, "I've consulted with Señor Palomo, the theologian. If it's not consummated, there's no marriage, there's no marriage, there's no marriage. Hurrah! I've started divorce proceedings. Nothing has happened. Sweet liberty! Go, Cástulo, in search of Urbano. Bring him to me, any way you're able. Without wasting a second. Let's flee from here. Let's fly to Leoncio's side, not sparing the horses."

Don Cástulo, in his desperate effort of insubordination, said, "Neither Urbano nor I can flee in that way. Well, I don't speak for Urbano. You're his mother, and he a minor. I am my own master and a man of conscience. Micaela, respect my character."

"Character, you? Since when?"

"In these eight days my character has grown strong, I tell you."

"So much the better. We need you by our side, for your advice more than for your character. But if besides you can come to our assistance with decisive character, which I didn't suspect of you, we need you twice as much."

Before Doña Micaela, Don Cástulo felt disarmed, helpless, as before the will of Destiny or under a cosmic force. Nevertheless, he tried a last evasive stratagem, by moral persuasion, which was his one forte against Doña Micaela: "Public conscience, and what is more serious, our intimate conscience which, though mute,

151

sigillus magnus, never keeps still, will revile us for this dastardly running away. Yes, dastardly. We abandon Doña Rosita, dying; Simona, deserted; we propose to thwart the marriage. And what decent grounds will you cite? That this unhappy family doesn't suit you now because it has come to ruin? Think it over again, Micaela."

"As for the ruination, I was expecting it, but I didn't know of it. The ones who have come to ruin are us. Who's going to support the new couple? Yesterday Leoncio declared himself bankrupt. He wanted to kill himself, cutting his throat with a shaving razor. Luckily, it was a German razor, from the store, one of those very flashy ones but which don't cut, as a clerk explained to me. Paolo Boscoso—what a friend!—is with him constantly, so that he doesn't repeat the attempt. Let us fly to his side, fly to his side. If a misfortune occurs, you'll be the one to blame. Look out for you, I'll make you pay for it!"

In Doña Micaela's eyes, Don Cástulo saw a lamp of dementia light up. They were serpent's eyes. Upon catching that look, Don Cástulo felt that his own face was freezing into an immobile and flat mask. He was now perfectly under the control and at the mercy of Doña Micaela. He went in search of Urbano. On ascending the staircase, he caught a whiff of stew, by virtue of which his face, still flat and stony, began to relax. He sniffed and smacked his lips, mechanically. Mechanically, he took out his watch and said to himself, "Four o'clock. And we haven't eaten. How the time flies. How the time flies. Have eight days gone by?" Without knowing what he was doing, he came into Urbano's room, and it did not surprise him to see him seated on his suitcase, waiting.

"Your mother is downstairs in a coach. Let's hurry."

Urbano, after the continuous extreme tension, had had all the stuffing go out of him. His spirit wilted, he rested in absolute laziness. The strain of being a protagonist in a long dramatic situation had beaten him, too much for his nerves' flexibility. He needed a rest, an intermission, before resumption of the action. Or better, that the skein might go on unraveling, without his intervention, and that they might not need him again except after the denouement, to tell him what had happened.

Urbano, with his suitcase, followed Don Cástulo. In the corridor, they ran into one of the servants, Winker by nickname, from an everted eyelid he had, showing the bright lining, like crimson percale. Winker carried in his arms a pile of pieces of white bedding and, way up on top, a bronze chimney clock with dancing shepherds. Upon seeing the masters, he hid his head behind the clock, but through the space between the legs of one of the shepherds, one could see the crafty eye, with the crimson eyelid that twitched. Don Cástulo came up to him to say in his ear, "You will tell Conchita . . . well, you know, Conchona, that we have to go."

"Escaping from the blaze," said Winker with a sigh, as if he would rest from the load he carried in his arms.

Don Cástulo, without hearing him, continued, "Misfortunes never come singly. The señorito's father, in dire straits, from an accidental wound in the neck. Urgent case. We can't say goodbye to anyone. Such an emergency, you understand . . . Doña Rosita, dying as well. Tell Conchita, serenity, serenity. She's a jewel, she's worth a silver mine. She'll know how to look after herself. Perhaps tomorrow even I may be able to return. I'll write as soon as I arrive. Goodbye."

"Have a good trip," said Winker, with another sigh, or gasp.

Doña Micaela said nothing on seeing Urbano but, "Get in!" pointing to the door of the coach.

Then, the three of them in the carriage, in the inside the dry and authoritative voice of Dona Micaela resounded, "Giddyup!"

The coach rolled on the gravel, with a sound of water falling on embers. The last thing that was heard was a whipcrack, which exploded in the air; softened by the distance, it sounded like a great forest-born kiss, among the song of the birds.

Shortly after bidding goodbye to Don Cástulo, Winker met— providentially, thought he—Conchona, each of them loaded down and headed in opposite directions, Winker, with his two dozen Holland sheets and his bronze clock and Conchona with four filled hot water bottles with which to replace the other ones, now tepid, at Doña Rosita's feet. Winker stretched his neck and peeked up and over the pastoral group, his reddish eye now atwinkle.

"Providence brought you, bold Conchona. I've good news for you. We're alone. The señoritos went off. There remains the old lady, who's heading for the next world, long are the days that await us there, and the sweet little one, which is as if nobody remained. The señoritos didn't amount to anything either, but they did wear pants, and even a broomstick with pants is a scarecrow and always throws a little bit of a scare. Our coast is clear. Grab what you're able, as we're all doing. Stuff your trunk full, for you'll never get another chance like this one. Every man for himself. It's all over here. Whatever you don't carry away, the thief of a moneylender has got to sweep off. Steal from the thief, even if only for the pardon the proverb promises you. Dump those clay treasures you're carrying in your arms and turn them in for more substantial items. I'm making for the linen closet. There are still some articles fit for a bishop, with their palm-sized lacework. Don't miss the boat, now that Providence brought you this way."

"Providence did bring me; well said, Winker," Conchona muttered, ambiguously. To providence she attributed that encounter and the circumstance of finding herself with the hot water bottles in arms, which hindered her from involuntarily placing them akimbo, threatening and provocative, thus giving away her angry feelings and her righteous, though still unclear, intentions. Then hearing the other, she thought that the providential role of those hot water bottles consisted in their being smashed over the back of Winker's head and scalding him from head to toe. In the end providence advised self-restraint, while for the time being she informed herself of what most was incumbent upon her, getting ready for all eventualities. She said, "The señoritos went off? When? Where to?"

154

Winker related what he knew, repeating in his own words Don Cástulo's words. He commented in conclusion, "The old fox and the whelp, tail between legs, feet headed I don't know where, go dashing off, because in the coop the hens are gone and they smell the cudgel. And the little snotnose, do you think he'll leave the señorita in such a way, as they say, with a belly, no shoes, and in the middle of the street? You know, it makes me mad. I'm an honest man. That's a lowdown trick. Oof, my arms are falling asleep from this load. Hurry up, Conchona, and don't be stupid."

"Me, stupid? You'll soon see about that. I'm going to hurry up with a will all right."

Conchona, firstly, went into Don Cástulo's bedroom. There was the carpetbag, some articles of clothing hung from the rack, toilet articles in the washbasin, on the nighttable an open book, on whose pages were marked, clearly, prints of Don Cástulo's thumbs. All of this signified that Don Cástulo had gone off in a rush, to return right away. How Conchona might have liked to be able to read the book. Conchona bent forward to kiss it with religious respect and out of love for Don Cástulo. From there she went to Doña Rosita's bedroom and placed the hot water bottles at the old woman's feet.

"Thanks, woman," said the señora, tender and childlike. "Though it seems like a warm day, my hands and feet are frozen."

Simona, huddled on the floor, next to the grandmother, asked, "And Urbano? Where is he? Why doesn't he come in to keep us company? What time is it?"

Conchona wavered a second. Then she replied naturally, "The señoritos have gone to Regium, for medicine and other matters."

"I understand. I see clearly," said the grandmother, opening wide her somewhat cloudy eyes. "Simona, leave Urbano to himself. In these cases, men are in the way. We're better off the two of us alone. Don't leave me. I'd like to rest and I can't, because of the suffocation, so I hold my head backward."

"I'll show you a posture in which to rest," said Conchona, coming forward. She drew up a table; she spread on it two pillows and advised, "Lean forward and rest your arms and head on the pillow. Aha. How is it?"

"I'm very comfortable, very comfortable. Where have you learned this? You're an encyclopedia, Conchita."

"For me, never mind nicknames, for I don't understand, though I presume it will be a compliment from the señora. I'm a simple brute, but with more heart than a bull; and if you don't think so, just wait."

Without Rosita's or Simona's catching sight, silently Conchona took down from the panoply a serrated iron lance adorned with feathers and the frigate captain's revolver, which hung below the panoply.

She stole away to hide them in her room.

She headed for the kitchen. All the servants of the estate, some fourteen people, were crowded together in a hallway, whispering passionately.

"Made your harvest?"

"Filled the granary already?"

"Brought in a good crop?"

"Blessed Saint Peter, you won't have been asleep! The girl's missing."

"She's topping us all in stashing things away."

"And she was in on the secrets of the house. That advantage, where does it leave me?"

"The crannies where the old silver's hidden away, she knows them."

"The biggest slice of all you got, Conchona; I swear it."

"For us, some common everyday silverware and gleaned carefully, so the loss not be noticed."

Thus spoke, jumbling together, several voices, no sooner than Conchona had entered. The new arrival imposed silence; stretching forth her hands she said, "Tell me now, doesn't your conscience bother you?"

"Does it bother you?"

"I asked you first."

"We're taking what's ours."

"Did you buy it then; did they take it from you first?"

"They took our wages."

"Me, they owe since last summer."

"Me, it's going on three years."

"I lose track."

"I have extra money in, for paying a bill, because of the señora's not having any cash on hand at the moment."

"And that money, where did you get it from?"

"Come on now and be sensible."

"We're not stealing, we're collecting back."

"We'd find ourselves out in the cold and without a *maravedi* in our pocket."

"This ship's sinking. Everybody grab hold of the nearest spar to keep afloat."

After a pause, Conchona declared, "I'm with you; I just wanted to hear you out and find out the tack you were taking. You're not being very bright. You're lost. The moneylender'll come, hand in hand with the judge and the guard dogs. Do you think to leave without them searching your trunk? You'll land in the jug, bones broken and hands empty."

Hush of consternation. Some rustic hand scratched the back of a curly head.

Conchona went on, "I come to get you out of the quicksand, dummies. Carry your booty to the cows' hayloft. We'll hide it all in the hay. Not a soul will go there to search. There it's quite safe; the windows with bars and the door with a lock. At night, we take it out; if not today, it will be tomorrow. Get going, get going quickly, for I've got to keep up a show, at the señora's side. In half an hour you'll make the move. Wait for me, and I'll be along with mine. I don't have to miss out."

"God bless you, Conchona, you're sharper than the cuckoo."

"A cuckoo, sure enough, who lays its egg in another's nest."

157

Conchona waited, hidden, listening to the cautious movements and syping on the servants, one after the other, with a bag of booty en route from the hiding place. Half an hour elapsing, Conchona, making sure of carrying in her apron pocket the key to the hayloft, requisitioned the lance and revolver and set forth gallantly to carry out her plans. A bellicose expression exalted her face.

She planted herself in the doorway of the hayloft, her silhouette against the light and, with the harsh voice of an owl, shouted, "There you stay, in the rattrap, like the filthy rats you are. I can take care of the whole lot of you by myself, for though a woman I've got hair on my face. If anybody disobeys, by the bones of my ancestors I'll kill him with one shot or sink in his belly the teeth of this poisoned spike."

Nobody made a sound between the amazement and the fright. Conchona locked the door with the key. When she returned to the house, some servants had pressed to the bars, muttering insults, imprecations, curses, and making threatening or obscene gestures with fists and arms at her. Conchona, without deigning to look, continued triumphant, deified, the lance aloft. Don Cástulo might have compared her with Pallas Athena. In her arrogant virility, she was almost beautiful. Her yellow hair could pass—the sun burnished it from the side—for a golden helmet.

Before going to bed, Conchona went to look for the old family mastiff, Cerezo by name, wild boar-like hair, corpulent as an ass, meek as a lamb, brave as a lion, and brought him with her to the house, which she barred from inside. Cerezo knew his way. By habit, he went straight up to Doña Rosita's room. Under his weight the chestnut planks groaned, and with his nails, he made on the floor a dry and timid noise like a child who raps with his knuckles at a closed door. He entered the señora's room, contemplated for a moment the silent tableau of the old woman and the young girl, and curled up gently next to Simona.

Later Conchona entered with a cup of broth for Simona. Doña

Rosita seemed to be sleeping. Her difficult, rapid, and shallow breathing was heard.

"Pssst! Drink this broth," Conchona said to Simona, touching her on the shoulder and whispering.

"I'm not hungry. We've just had breakfast. What time is it? Isn't Urbano coming?"

"Urbano will be a while in returning. Take this broth and don't fret, child."

"My head's in a spin."

"That's from weakness."

"I don't know if I've been asleep or been awake. I don't know if a century has gone by or a minute has gone by."

Simona swallowed the broth, absentmindedly. Conchona went out.

Doña Rosita sat up, her strength almost gone. She fell back on the back of the sofa.

"How the odor of roses rises! Don't you see it, Simona, rising in puffs, like a censer? How the birds' song flies! Don't you see it, Simona? Each note is a little angel's head, without body, with two little wings on the neck. Stand up, Simona. Come close. Take off this miniature I wear on my breast. You put it on. So. It's your great grandmother; no, it's your picture. Open the chest of drawers. The little left column of the central arch is a secret. Pull on it. Take out a silver key with the sky-blue ribbon. Open the large drawer below, on the right. There are several boxes and a little package of silk paper. Bring it all over to this table. So. Open the large box. Give it to me here. This is the necklace in which I was married; beaten gold, red diamonds, emeralds, and rubies. Come close that I may put it on you. Is it heavy? This was how the collar was long ago which was placed on the necks of brides. Open the other box, the amethyst-colored one. It's the bracelet in which I was married. Come close that I may put it on you. How broad it is, how heavy, how solid; a slave bracelet, because the wife will always belong to

159

her husband, and there will be nobody who may break that servitude. Open the round box, the one of black leather. Come close that I may put this diadem in which I was married on you, for the wife will be the husband's sovereign and there will be nobody who may destroy this sovereignty. Open those small boxes. Come close that I may put all those rings on you, as with an image of Our Lady, for the wife will always be a Virgin for her husband, and there will be nobody who may cool this adoration."

Doña Rosita spoke solemnly and breathlessly, gasping for air at times. Simona listened and obeyed. On hearing the last words, she began to cry softly.

"Don't be frightened. Don't go and get me frightened. Why are you crying, Simona?"

"I'm crying from emotion, Grandmother. I forgot to tell you. Now I really am going to have a child. I'm sure. I confessed it to Urbano, at night and in his ear, as you told me to. Urbano, on learning it, answered me, very sad, very sad, that we had lost our innocence. Grandmother, why did the Virgin have Jesus without losing her innocence, while I have lost my innocence?"

A tumultuous wave of tender affection stirred the grandmother's heart. She wanted to smile, but a sudden cough prevented it. Cerezo raised his head to look at his mistress, with humble, loving, and moist eyes. The señora continued, "You'll have a child, of course you will. Your innocence, my Simona, you've not lost nor will you lose it. Those are Urbano's apprehensions."

"I want you to tell it to him. Why isn't Urbano here? How come he's so long in returning?"

"Let him be long; even if he takes days, weeks, months. Don't be impatient. Slave, sovereign, goddess; nobody will break your servitude; nobody will destroy your sovereignty; nobody will cool your adoration. Are you there, Cerezo? God bless you for being at my side now. Yes, God bless you; you too are a creature of God. Go to sleep. And you, Simona, go to the bureau. Open the lowest drawer. Take out the bundle of Chinese silk. It smells of pepper, right? And of sandalwood and of lavender? The spice that preserves; the perfumed wood that conserves; the flower that purifies. Put the bundle on my bed. Open it. Spread out those things in which I went to my nuptial altar. The dress of white silk brocade, embroidered with pearls. Imitation pearls, don't you believe it. The fitted veil. That veil is worth a fortune. I should really like to leave it to you. But, no. Pardon; it's a sacred promise. Tomorrow, for my second nuptials, you will dress me in that gown, that veil. Swear it to me."

"Tomorrow, Grandmother?"

"Swear it to me. You don't understand. You will understand soon."

"Grandmother, I swear it."

"Now give me that little package of silk paper which is on the table. Come up close. Look. This that looks like dust is a rose. The rose that he gave me the day of the first kiss. Do you see? Dust. Well, I kiss these ashes now. God bless them! Look at this other in the dust; the orange blossom, symbol of pure matrimony, of the rightful union between two. Look at this blossom; it's as the first day. The love, the mad love passed. This remains. Place this blossom on your breast. Keep it all your life. Leave it to your daughter, if you have one. And this blossom will always be the same, while the generations of roses pass. Now, help me to lie forward on the pillows. I'm going to pray, before resting."

Simona, without taking off the jewels, sat down on the floor, leaning on Cerezo's back.

An indefinite time went by. The grandmother sighed, in the softest thinnest voice: "Captain, now it is you who waits for me in the port . . . The church bells are tolling . . . Who's that old man, with a white beard who . . . is stretching out to me his hand . . . to disembark . . . ?"

"She's dreaming," thought Simona, who remained dozing. Another unmeasured time passed. Simona opened her eyes. "My sight is blurry. I can't see well," she said to herself, rubbing her eyes. She leaned out the window. The sun had set.

"Is it going to be night already?" Simona exclaimed. "Grandmother, Grandmother!"

Upon Simona's coming close, she found the grandmother rigid, cold to the touch.

"Grandmother! Grandmother!" she repeated, with a great trembling, which made the heavy old jewelry tinkle on her head, on her neck, on her hands.

Cerezo had gotten up on his feet and was earnestly resting his strong jaw on the señora's knee. Hearing Simona, he lifted an ear without moving and gave a low, mournful howl.

Simona, stumbling in the darkness, ran to the door of the bedroom. Her shouts filled the deserted house. Conchona came in with a light, in whose glare Simona was covered with sparkles and scintillations. Conchona set the light on the floor and embraced Simona, kissing her tenderly.

"Rest on me, child," Conchona stammered. "I'm rough and crude like a stone wall; strong, like a castle. Under my protection, you're safe and sound."

Knocks on the door sounded and then a voice:

"Open in the name of justice!"

Conchona leaned out the window, screeching in her owl's voice, "Justice, from God. Go to the Devil, or I'll pour boiling oil on you and sic the dog."

Cerezo, stretching up toward the window ledge, barked with ferocity, in the night.

THE TRIALS OF
URBANO AND SIMONA

[Los trabajos de Urbano y Simona]

NEW MOON

First, from Collado to Regium in a hired gig, then from Regium to Pilares in the stagecoach went Doña Micaela, Don Cástulo, and Urbano without speaking or even looking at one another.

Don Cástulo mentally analyzed the situation, sorting out its elements. "Primordial element, force which dominates all the others: Doña Micaela. Extraordinary woman. Rectilinear, dominant, ambitious. Of low birth, she wanted to elevate herself. She climbed, she climbed, her step sure, her head erect, without looking back. Now she had one foot on the peak. She thought herself rich. She had become related, through her son, to a family of lineage and extensive property. Suddenly, all comes crashing down, and she spins toward the bottom. But she falls with the same courage and ferocity with which she previously elevated herself. A creature of one piece, sculpted in strong material: she does not bend, nor break; she will never be askew, she will never be curved; she will be turned completely around and she will remain straight; the first or the last, wherever she may be will be the extreme of the possible. More than in her success, I admire her fallen. Too close, in her childhood, to the terrible secrets of life, she, she alone, a weak woman, declared war on life, on life just as it is, and sought to impose on it a new law. I remember her words: *I knew it all at the age of eight; my son will marry without knowing anything, pure as an angel.* She proposed it, and she carried it out. I was her accomplice, as tutor of the child. We made an angel of Urbano, which is to say, a monster. A married angel is a monster. I have read in Saint Thomas Aquinas, if I'm not mistaken, that angels do not marry because they are her-

165

maphrodites, like lilies. Whatever the case may be, a human angel is a monster, a castrate of the bestial element, no less divine than the angelic element; man is a composite of angel and beast. We made an angel of Urbano and conducted him to the bridal chamber to be united with an angel, Simona. This was tragic and it was comic. Xenophon warns that eating new honey turns one crazy. Poor Urbano, the first night of his honeymoon, was almost demented, with only the odor of honey, which in his innocence and ignorance affected him with terror. He wanted to commit suicide. He fled from the virgin bride to the paternal household. And I come in by the inexorable will of Micaela, as erotic initiator, poor me!, dragging the angel anew toward his angel. Everything seemed to be heading on a happy course. We were on a beautiful country estate of affecting bucolic character. We were: the newlywed angels, Simona's grandmother (Doña Rosita, old lady–girl, or girl–old lady), and I. Nature would be the experienced matron who, by degrees and with care, might go about instructing Urbano and Simona in the cult and mysteries of love. The affair promised a rapid and delightful outcome. The two angelic spouses were already kissing secretly, from balcony to balcony, in the middle of the night, like two lovers not yet joined by the marital bond. Urbano was becoming a man in appearance and in his thinking, and Simona was maturing for love, day by day, hour by hour. All this was a trick and a stratagem of life, malicious and merciless life, on which Micaela sought to impose a new law. Life was preparing its revenge and its victory. No more than a quarter of the moon had gone by. Another grain, that of a single day, in the hourglass; just one more early morning dawn or the complicity of another night and the hymeneal of Urbano and Simona might have been consummated. And nothing, in the heavens or on the earth, would be strong enough to untie the carnal knot established. On mixing wine with water, neither God no mixing. All of a sudden, Doña Rosita is informed that she is nor the devil can return them to their original state. But there was ruined. The court summons her to abandon the estate where we were living, expectant before the connubial idyll. For this disaster Doña Victoria was culpable, the merry widow, mother of Simona and daughter of Doña Rosita. Who would have imagined it? Doña Victoria, such a friend of clergymen, of one in particular, with whom she now is traveling far away, turned out for us to be one fine fancy bird, as the messenger from the tribunal put it. Doña Rosita, before the unexpected blow, though she now has no place in which to fall dead, falls as if dead. Simona becomes insensate. Urbano becomes dull again. I don't know where I am. At this point Micaela supervenes, beside herself. Don Leoncio, her husband, has just declared himself bankrupt. They've been left without an *ochavo*. Now we have Micaela turned completely around; but it is the same Micaela of always, a cosmic force, the center of universal gravity. To Urbano, whom she adored before, she asserts that she abhors him; that she had formed him with the bad half of herself; that she is going to destroy him; and that she is going to form him anew, with the other good half that has been revealed to her in the pain of the catastrophe. To her husband, the miserable Don Leoncio whom she always martyred, she declares that she now adores him, because he, inspired by God and without her paying him heed, had foreseen the gloomy consequences of Urbano's marriage. We will see how far this sudden adoration goes, when Micaela finds that Don Leoncio is maintaining a liaison with Barranco, that scandalous hussy, who must surely have contributed with her dissipations to the present ruination. Surely this courtesan will now lose Don Leoncio everything. So that Micaela has dragged off Urbano and me clandestinely, without permitting us to make a peep or say adieu, leaving on the estate the moribund old woman and the girl in abandonment. Why this villainy? For the same reason that the hurricane levels a district. Micaela is a blind force. But perhaps the hurricane is unleashed wilfully? The bag of winds is under the rule of Zeus; well, of Jehovah; well, of the Eternal Father. What interest does any of these three gentlemen have in afflicting mortals with irremediable harms? Where did we come from? Where are we going? For the time being we are going to Pilares to join Don Leoncio, who in a moment of confusion has attempted to commit suicide, giving himself a cut in the neck, fortunately, as Micaela says, with a German razor. Then, Micaela intends to annul the marriage of Urbano and Simona, as it is only interim. And the Catholic Church, will it lend itself to sanction this crime? Urbano and Simona idolize one another; they are hungering one for the other; separated, they will die of sadness and starvation. Of course, together they would also die of starvation; they don't have a *maravedi* and Urbano is incapable of earning one for some time, though he has received the title of doctor of laws. Horror! Pity! Tragedy! Yes, a true classical tragedy. You, miserable and plebian rabble who are traveling with us in this infernal vehicle; you, the one who is next to the door with your wooly and dirty head, your suspicious look, on your knees what one would take for your son, he looks so much like you! and it's a dog who has plagued us with fleas; and you, the fat lady over there with an abbot's face, who have made the coach stop three times because you are sick, and then from the culvert you turn our stomach with the gurgle of your vomiting; and you, the one with the earmuff cap and the Zamoran blanket spread out for hours en route and in spite of the heat, as if you were crossing Siberia; and you, I put you down to be a notary!, with your pointed nose and hawkeyes, under your armpit your leather case, pregnant with imbroglios and larcenies; and you, the one who's said that you are a surgeon and that you are going to bleed I don't know how many, and saying it made your mouth water; and you, who's in front, bumping me with your knees and treading on my corns, country priest of the mass and the dinnerpot, fat as a hog, who since we have left have not done anything but snore and eat bread and sausage, spit, take filthy snuff and tickle my nostrils—all of you, what would you reply to me if I were to give you the word that right here, brushing you, you had tragedy, authentic tragedy? I can see you laugh, with your thick laughter. You laugh at tragedy, as you laugh at mythology. You consider myths improbable and characterize them as old wives' tales.

What you don't understand, you declare doesn't exist. If you knew of Antigone, you would say that she isn't probable, and that therefore she didn't exist. If you knew of Micaela, of Urbano, of Simona, you would say that they are improbable and that therefore they don't exist. I, the most improbable of all, am the one who least exists. But, yes, in spite of the common opinion, in spite of you, I exist. Here you have me, against all logic and verisimilitude. What am I doing here, not being a personage of the tragedy? All my life sighing for love; all my life dreaming of woman; all my life as far from the feminine skin, from the feminine breath, from the feminine voice, as the autumn is from the spring; all my life, such a coward in gallant initiative that before wooing a maid, I might have preferred to take castor oil or an enema, and to the enema I prefer death. Well, in my forty years of age, at the last limit of my timidity and shadow of my desperation, I inspire a perfect passion in an ideal girl; we kiss, I faint. I determine to marry as soon as possible. Improbable? An ideal creature, although a serving maid. Improbable? Fairy tales and histories abound in examples of fallen princesses and illustrious scrubwomen. But the most improbable, and not even I understand it, is, Why have I left my Conchita there on the estate? Why have I separated myself from her on the eve of marriage and when she most has need of me, alone with Doña Rosita dying and Simona abandoned? Micaela said that they, she and Don Leoncio, need my presence and advice. My sweetheart needs them more in this terrible time. And nevertheless, Micaela dragged me off. Am I not a creature adorned with the prerogative of free will? Well here I am, against my will and by my will. What will my Conchita have thought of me on discovering my shameful flight? Will Doña Rosita have died by now? Maybe the moneylender showed up, accompanied by armed force, and threw the dwellers off the estate, including the cadaver of the old señora. I am seeing with my mind's eye the frightful scene: the dead body, which lies in the open countryside under the light of the stars; the prostrate servants, who are sobbing; the family dogs, who are howling; Simona, virginal like Antigone, robbed like Antigone of the legitimate hymeneal, who breaks into a heart rending lament. My insides quake at this spectacle. And all those oafs who are traveling with me, so fresh, as if nothing were up, the case being that we should all join in a sorrowing clamor, like a tragic chorus. And Zeus, Jehovah, and the Eternal Father, so fresh, as if nothing were up. My will rebels. As soon as I arrive at Pilares, I'm going back, I will run and help Conchita, Simona, and the sad remains of Doña Rosita. This matter of going right back as soon as arriving, psst! it's a bit difficult: Micaela is going to stand in my way. If not today, tomorrow or the next day, or later on. What I will do today will be to write to Conchita. Oh heavens! My heart is paralyzed; my strength is ebbing away. How am I going to write to Conchita if I don't know her last name. Improbable, right, country priest? Right, pettifogging bird of prey? Right, abbess and stomachy señorona? Right, canine gentleman? It is improbable. I can't write to my sweetheart. Every one there knows her as Conchona. But how can I put on the envelope of an epistle to my loved one, 'For Conchona'? Never. When I return, she won't be there any more. How will I find her? I'm lost. Let a thousand lightning bolts fall and pulverize us. Let the stagecoach fall over a precipice and all of us perish. I too am a tragic character. I invoke liberating death. Ay! Ay! Ay! God, you're breaking my shin."

Under the vivid suggestion of his troubled thoughts, Don Cástulo had begun to jump about in his seat, flailing his arms and legs around. The last words of his mental colloquy he said aloud and choleric, facing the fat priest, who replied aggressively, "Like it or lump it; before you gave me a kick in the lower stomach, waking me from a pleasant dream. I receive nothing I don't return. In the pulpit and in the confessional I preach restitution. Outside of the temple, I preach by example."

He cleared his throat, took snuff, sneezed, took out some bread and sausage from his sack, and set to devouring them, looking with watchful and furious eyes at the insignificant Don Cástulo.

All the other passengers laughed up their sleeves, except the man with the dog, who gave out a cackle, and the dog three barks.

Neither Doña Micaela nor Urbano noticed the incident. Doña Micaela, with the heavy rancor that suddenly had risen up in her soul, was molding, behind her compressed brow, a future to her design, a future inexorably vindictive. Her rancor was concentrated against Doña Victoria, Simona's mother. She considered herself the victim of an infamous deceit. She had believed Doña Victoria to be, with her little body and her innocent little doll's face, an honest woman, possessor of millions; and she was a corrupt woman, concubine of a bad priest with whom she had squandered the patrimony, which was not hers but Simona's, and which therefore should have been Urbano's. The day of Urbano and Simona's wedding, Doña Victoria already knew that she had no means to support the couple. With what shrewdness she hid it! She wanted Urbano's parents to be burdened with the girl. Ah, shameless woman! Doña Micaela was pleased with their own ruin; in this way she could proclaim, with her head high, "I break up this recent marriage, not because the bride may have ceased to have money, but because we have lost everything. I would break it up just the same, even though she might be rich. For propriety's sake. I still didn't know when I went in search of Urbano that Doña Victoria had already met her downfall. God is my witness! God, who though irritated with my errors, has favored me with the greatest mercy, having prevented the marriage from being consummated, which is what I begged of him yesterday from the depths of my anguish. It is clearly apparent that my wish to annul the marriage is the will of God." Doña Micaela determined the will of God by consulting her own will beforehand, and she found that they always coincided. That she might not know that Doña Victoria had met her downfall was true in a literal sense. At the moment of going in search of Urbano, Doña Micaela did not know of the downfall as an accomplished fact, but she knew it as a fated and imminent occurrence. For the past year, Don Leoncio had

171

been predicting it and she did not believe him. The day before, a short while after having declared himself bankrupt, on arriving home bloodied in the arms of the clerks he had repeated it, "My love, make yourself strong. As serious as all this is, the worst is still to come. They will foreclose Doña Victoria at any moment. She has escaped far away to preserve her health. Doña Rosita and Simona will be thrown out of Collado. Everyone in the street. As I am good for nothing, I didn't want to be a burden on anyone. That's why I tried to take the easy way out. You won't lack being taken care of by charity. Nor Doña Rosita either for the short time there remains for her to live. But Urbano and Simona? Urbano is not a man; he's a newborn babe. What will become of them?" And Don Leoncio had burst out crying. Seeing that lean and aged head, that stoic head ever patient under conjugal vexations and wrongs, seeing it now dissolved in tears, at that instant was the conversion of the hard Doña Micaela. She flung herself at her husband's feet, embracing his legs, begging his pardon and telling him that she adored him and that in the future she would be his servant. A little afterward, Don Leoncio told Doña Micaela something he had never dared to even insinuate: the story that was whispered about of the priest and Doña Victoria. Concluding her conversion and hearing her husband, Doña Micaela suddenly traced out her plan of action, rectilinear as before, but in the opposite direction. Once assured that Don Leoncio's wound was not dangerous, she went to visit a prebendary priest, Don Hermógenes Palomo, an acquaintance of hers and a man of much canonical learning, reputedly, and she asked him how the ecclesiastical marriage could be annulled. The priest replied that only if the marriage were not consummated. Doña Micaela was informed by the daily missives from Don Cástulo that the marriage had not been consummated, and she rushed off to frustrate the consummation, separating Urbano from his wife.

Urbano went along as though in a daze in the stagecoach. Through his semiconscious and diffuse spirit wandered airy fantasies. He saw himself, with Simona in hand, roaming over a rough

landscape. Now, they were living in a hut; they had domesticated a
wolf; they had flocks of sheep, which Simona tended, and he tilled
the land. The agricultural implements, and the very ideas of plow-
ing, sowing, and harvesting, all had been invented by him. Simona
went about almost naked. He, seeing her, felt a fearful trembling.
The strange thing is that he did not see her with his eyes, he saw her
with the skin of his hands, of his arms, of his chest, as if in each one
of the goose bumps which he got on seeing her a diminutive pupil
were hidden, with which would not be perceived line nor color, but
solidity, volume, form, smoothness, gentle warmth. He saw her by
touch. He saw her like a blind man with no eyes, who miraculously
may see by another manner. Now he had to separate from Simona
for a long ocean voyage, in a kind of boat that he himself had invented and constructed. Simona said goodbye from the balcony of
Collado, he from the boat. The boat was joined by a cable to Simona's balcony. The cable was of rubber, very elastic; it stretched, it
stretched more and more, and the wind redoubled its force to overcome the resistance. If the wind were to cease for a second, Urbano
saw that he would be hurled against Simona's balcony. He recalled
the urchins who shot garbanzos with slingshots. The balcony had
now been lost from view. Urbano felt the countertension of the wind
and of the cable. He let himself be carried along, waiting without
impatience. He stretched out on the boat to sleep, face to the sun.
Though torn from Simona, the forced separation had not harmed
him. He had his entire skin impregnated with Simona and it was as
if he carried her clasped to himself. With his eyes closed, to sleep, he
saw her—solid, smooth and warm—with his skin. He was a man
now, and he had to put the world through its paces, to earn his bread
and Simona's. Two fascines of the same log, you will wind up by
blazing in a common fire; so said an unreal voice, echoing in the
wind. It was Doña Rosita's voice. Oh, how Urbano loved Simona,
now, in the enforced separation! Simona was the ideal. She pulled
on one end of the cable. The wind pushed in the opposite direction.
Urbano looked toward that place from whence the wind was com-

ing, and he saw, among clouds, a monstrous and petrified head, like
the gargoyles of fountains, the eyes irascible, the cheeks puffed, blowing. Though somewhat deformed, Urbano recognized at once his
mother; and in the middle of everything, it made him laugh. "Before, I feared you," thought Urbano; "then, I hated you; now, I pity
you. You think you dominate me, but you don't see the cable, un-
breakable and elastic."

"Wake up, sluggard," said Doña Micaela, seizing an arm of her
son and obliging him to stand up. "We're already in Pilares."

Night had fallen. At a good pace, the three headed for home.

Don Leoncio and Paolo were playing cards. Below Don Leoncio's noble head—pessimistic and metaphysical expression, olive
complexion, sunken cheeks, steely-colored hair—the huge white
bandage around his neck looked like a muffler. Paolo, old friend of
the family, with his gallic grayish forelock and moustache; with his
drawn face, childish, cheerful; with his inevitable riding boots.

Urbano was moved on embracing and kissing his father.

"Careful, don't be an oaf and hurt his wound," cut in Doña
Micaela, solicitous toward her husband, severe with her son.

"Don't, Micaela. What wound, if it's only a scratch? Paolo, who
has seen it, says so. Embrace me again, Urbano. My poor boy. You're
the one we have harmed. You forgive us, don't you? Don't worry.
God will set things right. I am looking at you and I don't believe my
eyes. You're a different man; I say that now you are a man. In just
eight days. You're tanned, stronger; your look is serious. And Simona? Poor widowed little turtle dove. How have you left her? There
must have been a dreadful scene. Write her, write her immediately,
and God will set things right."

The taciturn Don Leoncio spilled forth now in pathetic ver-
bosity. Doña Micaela, who had seen with horror the flow of blood
from his neck, now listened enviously to the effusive flow of words.
More than Urbano, she needed Don Leoncio's loving words. With
a hidden feeling of hatred, she separated Urbano from his father,
saying, "Calm yourself, my Leoncio. You've lost a lot of blood and

you're weak. Get too excited and you'll harm yourself. Don't upset yourself over the troubles of Urbano, who, thank God, is very tranquil. He's been sleeping in the coach on the way here. Young lads don't have so much feeling."

"Micaela," put in Don Leoncio, "I've been a young lad and . . ."

"You yes," interrupted Doña Micaela. "But don't compare yourself with anyone else. You're an exception."

The vehement and humble affection of his mother toward his father caused Urbano a new kind of happiness, deep and bracing, never before experienced. Don Cástulo admired the apparent change in Doña Micaela's spirit and celebrated it. The bad times she had put him through, trampling verbally in his presence on the most patient Don Leoncio . . . Don Cástulo said, permitting himself for the first time to contradict, after a fashion, Doña Micaela, "That the young lad has no feelings, I deny. It is an absolute proposition, and therefore false. But, let's recognize that man's true fullness of heart, for love and for all sorts of sentiments, delicate or passionate, is not acquired until between the years of forty and fifty. Furthermore, at this age man is more seductive than at any other." Here Don Cástulo puffed himself up. "I imagine Don Juan Tenorio a man of forty to forty-five years old. And from that point of forty-five on, I would guess that, for a long period yet, the heart gains in amorous capacity. What do you think, Paolo?"

Paolo, who was going on sixty and had a platonic sweetheart since around twenty, assented tacitly, paling.

"For woman, I testify that she does not know how to love until past forty," Micaela said, sententiously.

"I disagree," replied Don Cástulo. The young lass is the passionate woman. Nature has it so. For of what use to nature and to life is the amorous ardor of an old woman?"

This innocent rhetorical question of Don Cástulo wounded Doña Micaela in her deepest and most sensitive part. In the emotional whirl of those two days, in which she trembled at times for fear of going crazy, she had thought dimly, without daring to face her own thought, that perhaps she might have another child by Don Leoncio.

"Cástulo, you're a great imbecile," said Doña Micaela. The strange glint in her eyes caused everyone uneasiness.

"Forgive me, Micaela. Perhaps I am mistaken; certainly I am mistaken. It was a manner of speaking," stuttered Don Cástulo, cowed.

"I shouldn't have taken your opinion seriously," Doña Micaela corrected, smiling sarcastically. "It's public knowledge and well known that you lack discretion. Let's drop it. It's time to dine, on what there is. Paolo, would you like to share our poverty? We will eat cold cuts, leftovers from our bygone time of well-being. You are rich and have no reason to submit yourself to want. We are not fit friends now for you. We will seek our acquaintances now among our equals, the poor who pray and go begging at back doors."

Paolo made movements and gestures, which were meant as protests of fidelity. From pallid, he had turned red, remembering how his mother, Doña Encomienda, had said to him on learning of the bankruptcy of the Fanos, "They were rabble in their origins; once again they are what they were; from the mire they sprang, in the mire they sink; they are finished for me. Besides, it turns out that Don Leoncio, with his inquisitor's face, is lover of that misbegotten Barranco."

"It's not so bad as all that, Dear," said Don Leoncio. "I don't have money, but I have arms and strength to work."

"Not a bit of it," interjected Doña Micaela, exalted. "You have worked enough for us. Now I will work for you. I will enter some house as a servant. I will take in sewing. I will do ironing. You need not go without anything. And let Urbano work, let him kill himself to support us, now that we have supported him for twenty years, a layabout like an odalisque."

"Of course Urbano will go to work too; he's now a man. But he has to work for himself—and for Simona."

"Don't mention that family, Leoncio, if you don't want to make

176

me lose my mind. Let Simona be supported by that bitch of her mother."

"Micaela, I've never heard that word from you, my love," admonished Don Leoncio, with mild sadness.

"Because I always took special care to keep away from dealing with that kind of woman. And the biggest . . . that, of all, I had at my side. And I became related to her. I didn't know it before. Now I know it, and I say it. God will not want this shameful relationship to prevail."

"Fine, let's not talk about that; there's time later on. Let's dine, if you like. Don Cástulo, will you please ring the bell, so the servant will come?" said Don Leoncio.

"What do you mean, the servant?" asked Doña Micaela, vexed. "But haven't the servant and the cook gone, as I ordered? Having servants, when we ought to be servants ourselves?"

"The servant," answered Don Leoncio, "does not want to leave us in these circumstances. He says he won't collect his pay."

"But he eats," cut in Doña Micaela. "And above all, it is indecent that people in the deepest poverty, but not invalids, allow themselves to be served by others."

"Insofar as the cook," continued Don Leoncio, timidly, "I have told her to stay. I cannot resign myself to seeing you in the kitchen."

"We are poor, we are poor, poorer than the birds of the forest and the worms of the earth. I am not ashamed. On the contrary. I will flaunt my poverty. I will dress again in the humble clothing of the workwomen, as I dressed as a child. I will look the part; I will wash the dishes, I will attend the fire, I will scrub the floors. And I will do it with pleasure; for you, for you, my Leoncio."

Don Cástulo thought, "Woman of one piece. She doesn't bend nor break. They've turned her upside down and she's the same as before; always rigid. Now she wants to be poor with the same haughtiness, showiness, conscientiousness, and scrupulosity which she applied before in conducting herself as a señora."

"I'll explain to you later. Hush, for I hear the servant coming," said Don Leoncio, placing a hand on his wife's shoulder, to pacify her.

During the supper, in the intervals when the servant was out, Don Leoncio went about explaining: "The situation is not so difficult. From yesterday to today new developments have taken place. The accountants, examining my books with care, have declared that I have proceeded with perfect honesty and irreproachable good faith. Several entries that I gave up as lost and credits I considered uncollectable they consider easy to make good, among them the lump sum of thousands of *duros* that Doña Victoria owes me, since those who are in a position to know affirm that, though in quite difficult straits, the widow still has finances to clear her debts and then some. The main thing is that none of my creditors will go without being paid off."

"I never thought that would happen. If they didn't collect now, I and Urbano would work until it was all paid off and no one might say anything about you," exclaimed Doña Micaela.

"It's not necessary," Don Leoncio went on saying. "Nobody doubts my honesty."

"Who would dare to doubt it, Leoncio? I would be capable of spitting in the face of whomever doubted it," Doña Micaela commented, ardently.

"We are left without a *real* of cash, it's true," continued Don Leoncio; "but honesty is a capital. I know that I have inspired compassion."

"Compassion, for what?"

"For our misfortune."

"I don't consider it such."

"But the others do. This very day they've come to offer me a position. Antidio Velasco, the one from the hardware store, says that he'll give me a job with pleasure."

"Velasco has always been lower than you; he envied you. You say he will give you a job with pleasure? I can believe it. You, an employee of his? No, Leoncio, no. He shall not have that pleasure."

178

"It's not as an employee, Dear. Antidio is old now, tired; he cannot attend to the business. I would take his place as head of the store. He spoke to me of a considerable salary, which would permit us to live with decorum."

Doña Micaela was not renouncing her new ideal of heroic privations, so fervently embraced. She said, "I prefer poverty. Poverty a thousand times over. Poverty is my pride for now. I will not tolerate your humiliating yourself, Leoncio; I will not tolerate it."

"There are others who are ready to hire me. So that we don't have to go without the necessities. Ah, we were forgetting! Your *pesetillas*, Don Cástulo, whose custody you've given me, are safe and nobody will be able to touch them."

"I'm not concerned about that trifle," mumbled Don Cástulo, lowering his eyes.

"I am. Besides, it's not such a trifle," replied Don Leoncio. "It won't come in badly for you, to begin with, if from here, as I suppose and lament, you part ways from us."

"I too lament it, dear friend," answered Don Cástulo, trying to put on a very remorseful face. "What are we going to do? Black destiny disposes. I, in this household, now would be nothing more than a burden without any reciprocal advantage."

"You're not going," decreed Doña Micaela. "You will work and help us. It is your duty."

"No, Micaela. My work is worth nothing to you. I will not remain as a parasite. I too have my pride."

"What are you going to have, if you're a creampuff? How are you going to make out alone in the world?" said Doña Micaela, half harsh and half pitying.

"Alone or in company. That is my affair," assured Don Cástulo, trembling at his own daring.

"Let's leave that, for now," said Don Leoncio. "We'll settle it later, after thinking it over. Don Cástulo will neither be thrown out abruptly nor forced to stay. He will decide. I would be well pleased to have him with us always, but one has no right to limit a man's liberty. Thinking it over well, the best thing for Don Cástulo would be to get married, don't you think so, Paolo?"

Don Cástulo blushed to the roots of his hair. Paolo, who bore around forty years of unaccomplished matrimonial desires, assented silently. They said he had a facial resemblance to the celebrated orator Castelar, except that nobody could get a word out of him. Doña Micaela muttered, "Marriage? This is not the time to contract one; it's the time to dissolve another one, to the devil with it! How few happy marriages there are, how few spouses who are congenial, like you and I, Leoncio!"

After Urbano retired to his room, Doña Micaela relapsed into the theme which obsessed her: "I tell you, Leoncio, that Urbano is as unconcerned about Simona as I am about the emperor of China. It's been a childish whim, which he's now over. It even seems to me that he wanted to leave the person who is his wife and is still not his wife. He had his suitcase packed before I arrived. I said nothing to him; he left without even saying goodbye to Simona. Cástulo will confirm it; speak, Cástulo."

"Love," Don Cástulo said meditatively, "is like explosives; their power cannot be calculated or their effects measured until after they have exploded. Our explosion is coming. Wait till then and see." Paolo assented mutely.

On the following day, at nine in the morning, Doña Micaela took Urbano with her to the house of Don Hermógenes Palomo. On the way, the mother had said, "We are going to consult with a learned theologian over the matter of your union with Simona. I recognize that we have done it badly; we have done everything badly. One must set mistakes right, undo what's done and begin again in a different way. What do you say?"

"I say," replied the son, "that you are right, Mama. From the very instant you married me I understood that you had done it badly and that it had to begin again in a different way."

"Your agreement pleases me. And that when you, because of

your age and your ignorance, do not understand completely the full meaning of your words."

"I understand it better than you, since I have suffered the consequences of that mistake. I am the victim."

"Victim? Of whom? Of what? Victim of your own self, you mean," muttered Doña Micaela, hoarsely.

"You've said it yourself; victim of my ignorance. Now then, am I perhaps to be blamed for my ignorance?"

"Hush, hush, bad son. You throw up to me having kept you innocent and ignorant? Well that blessed ignorance is what has saved you, what has saved us. But now the hour has struck for you to know; for you to know everything. You will acquire the knowledge, not from me, but from more authoritative lips. When you discover the terrible face of the truth, then we will see if you vituperate me or thank me for having hidden it from you for the longest time possible."

"Mama, I don't vituperate you at all. Nor does the truth have to frighten me. I want to know, I want to know as soon as possible, in order to go back as soon as possible with Simona, this time as a man."

"You will not go back with Simona. I am opposed. God is opposed."

"Don't get angry, Mama; but when you, backing yourself up with the will of God, wanted to unite me with Simona, I guessed that it could not be. Now, you want to disunite me from Simona, and I guess that it cannot be either."

"If you go against my will in this, it will be the same as if you stab me with daggers, physically."

"It will not be I who goes against you; it will be the force of events. Calm down, Mama. I don't want to make you upset."

They arrived at Señor Palomo's residence. A large-bellied maid conducted them to the large and deep office of Don Hermógenes. The room contained scant and mediocre furniture: half a dozen walnut chairs covered in red satin; a set of bookshelves where some large dusty books lay in abandon; an untidy office table. On the walls hung some lithographs and an accordion, which produced a certain surprise in Urbano. In the thick wall, a window opened, which gave onto a garden, bathed in sun and sprinkled with the chattering of birds. On the sill of leaden and mossy stone was spread a handful of bread crumbs; and the sparrows perched to peck at them. The room communicated with Don Hermógenes' bedroom by a double door, the upper half of glass, with little green curtains. Through one of the leaves, half open, was seen a dark room, unventilated, and an unmade bed; a penetrating epicene odor came out from there, of sweat, tobacco, sandalwood, and uric acid. Don Hermógenes was tall, thin, hairy, and gloomy. He wore a greasy dressing gown of gray *vichi* that reached to his feet and buttoned down the front, goatskin slippers, and calotte. He was behind the table; in front of him, a little box of cut tobacco and booklets of cigarette paper, another with butts of fine cigars, another with rolled cigarettes, and a mended dish, with bread crumbs. Don Hermógenes excused himself, on account of the heat, for his attire. He indicated to the visitors that they be seated and, sitting down himself, continued making cigarettes while he spoke.

"It's necessary," said Doña Micaela, "that you express yourself with absolute clarity. My son is in the same state of perfect innocence as when he was born. Though a little belatedly, I recognize that it is contrary to nature and contrary to religion that an infant such as this be married. Our Holy Mother Church will have foreseen this case."

"Yes, Señora; the Church has foreseen everything. For all opinions, even the most opposite ones, you will find corroborative authorities in the exceedingly rich doctrinal repertory of the Church. For the Church, each moral conflict is like the tongues of Aesop. And since you ask me to express myself with absolute clarity, I will do so in what is pertinent to the present case. With an infant, as you maintain your son is, is there a true marriage, even though a minister of the Church may have established the sacramental tie? *Sub uno respecto, cedo; sub altero, nego.* Maybe yes; maybe no. It's a most subtle matter. We must avoid the danger of rushing toward a rash solution. To which side shall we incline, before the dictamens encountered that the theologians offer us? *Primum: Quisnam esse debet matrimonii finis?* What should be the end of marriage? Before all, *prolis susceptio, juxta illud; crescite et multiplicamini*; that is, offspring, according to the text of grow and multiply. And I ask, is your son fit for this end?"

"Actually, no, Señor," Doña Micaela hastened to answer.

Urbano listened with thirsting eyes.

"Easy, easy, Señora. Even thus and so, the discrepant rulings of the authorities make us vacillate. If we listen to Crisostome: *matrimonium non facit coitus, sed voluntad*—which means more or less, the will, and not coitus, is what makes the marriage. But, on the other hand, in Liguori we read: *quia copulae tantum capacitas ad esentiam matrimonii requiritur; unde sicut nullum est matrimonium inter eos qui nequeunt consumare eo actu, ex quo de se esset possibilis generatio; ita validum est inter eos qui possunt copulari, esto per acidens nequeant generari*—in our language, that copulation is the most essential thing in marriage, from whence, just as marriage is null between those who cannot consummate the act, although they not be sterile, so is it valid between those who can carry out copulation, although by accident they cannot engender. Do you follow me?" Don Hermógenes asked Urbano.

"No, Señor, not a word."

"But it's crystal clear."

"You use a number of words that I am hearing for the first time, for example, coitus."

"But you are a lawyer and must have studied in civil law things similar to those which I am now telling you."

"No Señor, I have not studied it. My books were always missing pages and chapters, which Don Cástulo and my mother cut out. This to which you are referring would be in the cut out pages."

"I have educated my son," put in Doña Micaela, "in such a

manner that there might not reach him the remotest insinuation of sin."

"Marriage, my Señora, is not a sin; it is a sacrament instituted by God."

"But at his age," insisted Doña Micaela, without giving in, "he didn't have any reason to penetrate certain mysteries, which might have bothered him and made him get into trouble. Let's leave that. It's water over the dam. Let's come to what's important. Urbano is ignorant of everything; he is impotent; his marriage is null."

"I know nothing; I want to know everything," Urbano affirmed wholeheartedly.

"Behold two propositions that go beyond the bounds of human possibility. A cigarette," said the theologian, offering Urbano a fat and overflowing cigarette, which he had just sealed by means of saliva.

"No, Señor, thank you."

"It's Havana tobacco, the kind the bishop smokes. Our prelate has fancy taste; he smokes the best cuts. I've bribed a palace intimate, he collects for me the butts His Highness throws away, some almost unsmoked. I myself pick them apart then. The consequence, that I am the one who smokes the best in town; after our pastor, of course. Here, try this cigarette."

"Thanks, I don't smoke."

"I've already told you," Doña Micaela intervened, "that my son has been brought up in innocence."

"My dear Señora; the tree of knowledge of good and evil, the one which produced the forbidden fruit, was not a tobacco plant," Don Hermógenes expostulated bitingly, getting up to spread bread crumbs on the window sill. On sitting down again, he went on, "To the point, what were you saying before, young fellow? If I don't remember incorrectly, you said, 'I want to know everything.' Behold there the temptation to original sin; behold there, the stupid desire of nibbling the forbidden fruit."

"Just so. I too, like Adam, want to eat the forbidden fruit; I want to know it all," insisted Urbano in a singsong of infantile stubbornness.

"Aha! You will nibble, little friend, and you will remain as ignorant as before. No, don't listen to the deceitful satanic inducement. You will never be like God. You will never know it all. That exceeds the bounds of human limitation. The other thing you've said, that about your not knowing anything, also rests beyond human nature; in this instance, not as too much, but as too little. You know something, something and then some. You've spoken to me of Adam. Do you know what happened to Adam?"

"Yes, Señor," replied Urbano.

"Well, well!" exclaimed the theologian, with an insinuating and leering grimace.

"And who has taught you that? It certainly wasn't I, Don Hermógenes," said Doña Micaela, irritated with Urbano.

"It's unimportant," declared Señor Palomo, disdainful toward the Señora, fixing his inquisitorial and crafty little eyes on the youngster. "In the matter that concerns us the only one who knows sufficient is you. Answer honestly. What happened to Adam?"

"They threw him out of the earthly Paradise."

"Why?"

"For losing his innocence."

"Why or how did he lose it?"

"Seeing his wife naked, and seeing himself naked too."

"And what's strange about that? Weren't they man and wife?"

Doña Micaela heard these questions of the theologian with the pained gratification with which the fervent penitent suffers physical torment. Urbano lowered his head blushingly. Don Hermógenes insisted, "What's strange about it? Haven't you seen your wife naked? Answer honestly."

"Yes, Señor."

"And you were naked too."

Doña Micaela looked furiously at Urbano and clenched her fists under the black tulle cloak. Urbano answered, vacillating, "Yes, Señor . . . that is to say, I saw her and I did not see her naked. I was naked and I was not naked."

"Clarify that for me," ordered Don Hermógenes, whose little eyes were shining with more liveliness by moments.

"I didn't see her with my eyes; I saw her with my hands, with my chest, with my skin."

"Oho! You were in the dark. You saw her by touch." The sparks in the theologian's little eyes danced.

"I was not naked, but I felt I was naked."

"Yes, yes I understand; in underclothes. All that took place in bed, right?" inquired the theologian lowering his eyelids and swallowing air, with a very dry gulp. During the last interrogation he had not glued any cigarettes.

"What do you mean, in bed?" Urbano bellowed dumbly, stand-up, colorless, his jaw thrust out, his head lowered, in a stance of making a charge against the theologian.

"Green and juicy," said Don Hermógenes, uneasily. "Señora, you've been fooled, and you've fooled me, involuntarily. This child has nothing to learn now."

"It's not possible, it's not possible. There is some confusion here. Speak to him more clearly, alone, if necessary. The child knows nothing. I'm not mistaken. The child knows nothing," said Doña Micaela, with a shaken and hoarse voice, looking back and forth, first supplicant at the theologian, then fuming at her son.

"I know nothing. I will not leave here until I know it all." Urbano asserted gloomily, without modifying his charging stance.

"To learn, it's best to go to Salamanca," Don Hermógenes replied, shifting. "What had to be known, in this case, we've got perfectly well known. That is, the marriage is consummated. Isn't that so, little man?"

"Consummated, unfortunately," replied Urbano, still in butting posture.

"Ah, the pure lamb converted into a filthy ram! No, no, no. A thousand times no. He is like an idiot. He doesn't know what he is saying. Ask him, Don Hermógenes, what he understands by consummated marriage, and you will be convinced that he doesn't know what he is saying," shouted Doña Micaela, twisting from side to side and finally leaning over the office table toward the theologian.

"Our first marriage is consummated," added Urbano, "because now it is finished; Simona there, me here, far from one another."

"Oh!" shouted Doña Micaela triumphally. "Didn't I tell you?"

"God save me with the overgrown infant," Don Hermógenes muttered through his teeth. And then, aloud, "But do you really not know what consummated marriage is?"

"If it's not what I just said, no, Señor."

"Do you know what love is?"

"What I feel," said Urbano, with childlike simple purity. He appeared childlike again.

"And to consummate love?"

"Well to conclude . . ."

"Or to begin. Look out the window."

On the sill, two sparrows, inebriated with sun and with life, were making love, with humorous impudence among the smell of fresh mountain mint and peppermint which rose from the garden.

The theologian added, "Do you know what those two sparrows are doing?"

"They're playing," replied Urbano, with sweet serenity.

"It's unbelievable, Señora!" said Señor Palomo, "excuse us, we cannot go on speaking in your presence. I have to communicate with your son in private—not in confessional privacy, since what comes out of our confidential talk we must use in the divorce proceedings, if it comes to that."

Don Hermógenes took Urbano by an arm, and together they disappeared through a small false door, disguised behind the theologian's easy chair.

Doña Micaela, alone, wrapped in the shadow of her cloak,

meditated: "Religion, salve of all wounds, remedy for all illnesses, reliever of all afflictions, shield in all contrarieties, solution of all troubles; and there are unbelievers who deny you. You used to hang them! Holy Mother Church, whose sublime wisdom there is no difficulty you do not unravel, nor burden you do not lighten, nor mountainous obstacle you do not flatten; and there are heretics who persecute you. They should be burned, as in the old days! And to think that there are unworthy ministers who seduce widows and waste the heritage of orphans. Flayed alive I would like to see them, or garroted, with their tongues two palms out! And concerning tongues, what will Don Hermógenes have meant with that about the Church is like the tongues of Aesop. I must ask Don Cástulo about it, that know-it-all."

Doña Micaela's thoughts were drifting when she heard, from behind the false door, a small choked cry, a cry almost animal-like and urgent. Why did there suddenly spring to mind from the depths of the past an indecorous and ridiculous phrase, which as soon as she heard it many years back she had forgotten? By what malignant association did that phrase now make an echo in her memory? Micaela was a child, just becoming a woman; a traveling gypsy girl bade her hello and said, "Ay, blushing little rose; a splendid gentleman will deflower you; you'll shriek like a rabbit; but then you'll be at ease and very pleased." It wasn't as if she thought it, but rather as if she heard another person—though inside, a stranger—apply that phrase of gypsy cant to the cry that she had heard from behind the false door. Urbano had just lost his soul's virginity, that rarest treasure which she, in a sublime undertaking, had succeeded in preserving intact, fighting alone against the world, nature, and the devil, conquering them. Her heart flew into thumping, like a little bird that flutters, caught in a fist of steel. A heavy, cold sweat broke out on her. She felt her eyes clouded, as if swollen. She shivered. "What will Urbano think of me?" she wondered, with a wan spirit. She felt temptations of violating that false door; running in search of her son; shouting at him, "It's a lie, a lie; what this man has told you is a monstrous lie; you yourself will understand that that cannot be, that that is against the natural order." And on seeing in his child's eyes the conviction and the relief, to kill him herself, so that there might never more torment his innocent conscience even one sinful doubt. But Doña Micaela remained immobile, without will and without strength. She quickly recovered from this momentary weakness and regained her unruffled and rigid character. "So it will be and so it must be," she articulated, with her lips.

The small door was opened. There appeared Urbano, who ran to embrace his mother, pressing her against himself, between convulsive sobs.

"Mama! Mama! Mama! Oh Mother!" stammered Urbano, and his tone was like that of eternal farewells.

"Hey, hey; get control of yourself, Urbano. No more childishness. You are a man now," admonished the mother severely.

"I don't want to be a man. Let them give back my childhood," the boy cried desolately.

"Sit down, son; compose yourself," advised Señor Palomo. "You're not going to go out in the street with that face. You're exaggerating. One would say that you've lost your soul."

"I did lose my soul. If that is love, how am I going to love Simona from now on?" sighed Urbano, hiding his tearful face with his hands.

"What do you mean, lost your soul, you fool!" said Don Hermógenes. "On the contrary, you've acquired it. God has flooded your spirit with light and now you are in a position, as not before, to resolve whether you have the will to marriage, as Crisostome says, or you don't have it." The theologian went on, directing himself to Doña Micaela, "The Church has always observed the most prudent parsimony in the granting of divorces. I must warn you that an ecclesiastical divorce is a long drawn out business and of uncertain outcome. Clear cut and quite evident reasons are demanded. The proof is exceedingly disagreeable."

"I don't need reasons, or proofs, or divorce, since I am not married. I am not married, because I, in my heart, do not consider myself married, nor do I want to marry Simona, nor have I ever wanted it, now that I know what marriage is—and love. Oh, no! Love is not that, even though the Church affirms it, even though the Pope orders it," said Urbano, as if in a trance.

"Don't interrupt, madman," shrieked Doña Micaela, turning to her son, with an imposing countenance.

The theologian made a conciliatory gesture and resumed his speech: "If we were living centuries ago and this boy were a king or the señorita a queen, the Roman pontifice probably would consider it well to grant the divorce without much ado. But this is not the case. I cannot see but two possibilities for divorce. First, through impotence of the huband: *Judicium de impotencia non ad Parochum neque. Confessarium spectat, sed ad judicem eclesiasticum, qui audire debet medicos et obstectrices*—the judgment of impotence does not fall to the parson nor to the confessor, but to the ecclesiastical judge, who must hear doctors and obstetricians. Impotence declared, the Church is still not satisfied, but obliges the couple to a cohabitation of three years, in order to gain the certainty that the impotence is absolute and perpetual. During this period, the aforesaid doctors and obstetricians must try certain methods and prescriptions, *praescripcionibus laborantibus,* to overcome the impotence, always such curative procedures not being painful or dangerous, *dolorosae ac gravisimae.* It is necessary likewise to make certain, beyond the shadow of doubt, of the virginity of the woman, which we do not know if the mother of the girl will be disposed to. In sum the difficulties are innumerable, supposing you adduce the motive of impotence, which I don't think, well hope, since I like Urbanito, that there is any reason for, *non est hic locus.* The second possibility rests on religious profession. Religious profession dissolves marriage *quo ad vinculum,* according to Tridentino's doctrine: *Si quis dixerit matrimonium ratum et non consumatum per solemnem. Religionis profesionem alterius conjugum non dirimi, anathema sit*—if someone were to say that interim and unconsum-

190

mated marriage is not dissolved by the solemn religious profession
of one of the two spouses, be it anathema."

Urbano, who had heard with a shudder in the marrow of his
spine, that about putting to the test the virginity of Simona, came
forward to say movingly, "Before you spoke, Señor Palomo, I was
already feeling the awakening of the religious vocation. I will retire
from the world. What am I doing in the world?"

"I will not be opposed, blessed be God! If He calls you, heed his
divine voice. It need not be hard for you," exclaimed Doña Micaela,
with a long sigh. A celestial contentment possessed her, a sudden
spiritualization, a kind of lightness or weightlessness of the body.
She could not contain her emotion. "What joy you give me, my angel! The worries, discouragements, and sorrows I went through over
you were worthwhile."   . .

"That, you will now think over calmly," intervened Don Hermógenes. "In my opinion, it would be better that Simona enter a
convent. The daughter of a widow needs protection in these times.
Besides, man is more useful to society than woman. Urbano should
remain free."

"Simona, no; Simona, no," corrected Urbano, with fervid bitterness. "Simona still doesn't know; perhaps she may never know.
Let her enjoy the world, the blue sky, the flowers. I am the one who
must shut himself in a convent. To forget what I have learned."

They said farewell.

In the street Doña Micaela said, "Give me your arm, Son, so I
can lean on it, as on a staff. I'm already seeing you in your habit and
dressed up in regalia to celebrate mass; and even with your beautiful miter and your stately cardinal's hat, why not? And they will
even exalt you at the altars. Oh, sinner that I am; mother of Saint
Urbano, confessor and virgin! I'm seeing it."

Doña Micaela did see all of this, true; but she saw it fuzzily,
vaguely, as though painted on a transparent tulle, behind which was
perceived the desired reality, which in vain Doña Micaela struggled
to hide from herself, calling up these whimsical and fleeting visions.

The hoped for reality, which forced itself on Doña Micaela's heart, stirring it with various and contradictory feelings—awe, anxiety, enthusiasm, cowardice—was that, Urbano professed in religion, she and Don Leoncio remained alone, like newlyweds. The other time, because of her coldness, her stupid pride, they had not had a honeymoon. Now they would have it. Why not? It was still time. That imbecile Cástulo had said the day before that an older woman does not know how to be passionate. When will a young girl know how to love like a woman of forty-five? She was not old yet, though she might look it, with that black corset cover and the black clothing and toques of a holy woman. Off with this attire, which did not suit her now! Like a pauper, she would go without corset; she would dress again in the plebeian and showy finery, in which she was so pretty as a fifteen year old and which makes town women, even the already older ones, so handsome and elegant.

Urbano had not even heard his mother. On arriving home he locked himself in his room, closed the shutters, threw himself on the bed in the dark. He despised the light. Thus he remained two days, without wishing to eat. The world and life, from which he wanted to isolate himself, followed and oppressed him in the retreat of his thinking, causing him anguished repugnance, not only moral but of a physical order. He recalled his devout transport in the village church of Pendueles during the mass. In those moments of mystical speculation he had thought he had penetrated the meaning and use of religion. "However much I may come to know," he had thought on that occasion, "I will always encounter on all sides the frontiers of mystery. There where the shadow of the mystery begins, religion takes us by the hand and dissipates our terror. However often I may see myself in that shadow, woeful me, helpless and terrified, I will lift up my heart to the Father who is in the heavens, with renunciation of my intelligence, and I will feel consoled." But now, terrified and helpless as he never might have conceived of it, he wasn't successful in lifting up his heart to the heavenly Father nor renouncing his intelligence. Now he knew it all, for what did the rest come to compared with the Great Secret which he had just learned? Religion was not showing itself to him as guardian of the mystery, but rather as its revealer. How was he going, then, to renounce his intelligence? He confronted the Father of man, creator of the world; and, like an offended and righteous son, demanded of him strict accounting in a sort of blasphemous mental prayer: "Whatever is, is because you have wished it, and as you wished it. You have decreed—your caprice, law—that love, the most beautiful thing in the world, not have its end in itself, but that it is an illusion, a pretext, a trap, into which poor mortals fall and, thinking to love, are not doing anything but dumbly obeying your design for propagating and conserving the human species. This is in substance what Señor Palomo has come about saying. In other words—why must we cover up the truth, if we are alone face to face?—you have fun laughing at us, your creatures, your dolls—your children. The joke might be passed over if cruelty didn't accompany teasing. You are omnipotent, you could mold us to your design of propagating the species by means of a noble and beautiful act, accessible only to the chosen and authentic lovers. This being in your power, you have invented—you have invented it—the dirtiest procedure, for which, as for all the other dirty needs, men hide themselves, and are loathe to dirty their lips speaking of it; moreover, much worse than dirty, monstrous. Now I understand many things. The only pure love, they say, is that which is consecrated to you; the only pure betrothals, those which are celebrated with you, in religious profession. Now I understand the reason. But, then, if we follow the path of purity, your design that the human species propagate itself will not be fulfilled, and very soon the earth will be deserted, barren of these unfortunate creatures of yours who love you and fear you (I have observed that it pleases you more to inspire fear than love), and if we bend to your design that the species be preserved, of necessity we must degrade ourselves and lose, in our own eyes, the dignity of the soul. You have arranged it so; you have established that perfidious and painful contradiction wherein in the act of obeying you

193

we feel ourselves filthy and ashamed. And in case there were any doubt, you haven't been able to allow that your only son—the rest of us are stepchildren—be born by the same filthy procedure that gives origin to the rest of mankind; the Chosen One had to be born of a virgin. He was God, that is sure; but he also was a man, and inasmuch a man, he should be identical with all other men. In everything he was equal, save in this; a sign that all the other functions of human nature need not shame us, since the man-god exercised them like us. But in this you did not want him to be equal; you did not consent that his mother be like all other mothers, a sign that you considered disgusting your procedure for propagation of man; and to save one from shame you have condemned the rest to opprobrium, in the unappealable ruling of a dogma. If the mother of your chosen Son had faced the common destiny, she might have saved all other mothers; by her having been an exception in maternity, all other mothers must experience an intimate shame, like a forgiven but not forgotten disgrace. Now I understand, Mother dear, why you took pains to keep me ignorant, until the moment in which, by my having incurred the same shame, I might not have a right to be ashamed of you and of my origin. Now I remember and understand —at that time I didn't understand it—what a Jesuit said to me, with whom I was doing spiritual exercises: the only woman worthy of love is the Virgin Mary; that is our true mother; we must free ourselves of the weakness of loving to excess the other mother, here below on earth. Quite clearly the voice of God advises it: abandon your father and your mother, as meaning, forget that you come from an impure man and woman. And he cited a monstrous phrase— now its monstrosity sinks in—from Saint Ambrose: *every married woman knows that she has something for which to blush.* But I'm not ashamed of you, Mother dear; now I love you more than ever, because before I feared you and now I pity you with an infinite compassion. You have nothing for which to blush, no. If the will of God consists in degrading and humiliating you, I raise you up and exalt you and declare you worthy of adoration. If the Father who is in

194

Heaven incites me to deprecate you, my father on earth, all sweetness and kindness, from whom I never received anything but demonstrations of abnegation and affection, has taught me to respect you and love you, above all things. I'm a good son, to him and to you. I am so without trying, because my heart overflows with sorrow and with love. And if I am not a good son to the other Father, the Father of all, it's not lack of obedience but his harshness. Who murmurs in my ear: *Blind man, is the earth the center of souls?* I answer yes, yes, yes. What kind of religion is that which persecutes natural feelings, covering them with ignominy? But who has proven to me that religion actually imposes that aberration of sentiments; that that is what the heavenly Father has wanted and that is what the Holy Spirit has revealed. Will it not rather be stupidity and misinterpretation by the ministers of the Lord, called to interpret the message of the divine dove? I believe in God the Father; I believe in God the Son; I believe in God the Holy Spirit. But I also believe that between the dove of the holy Trinity and Señor Palomo* there is an immeasurable difference."

Thus, insensibly, by imperceptible gradations of thinking and feeling, no different than the blinding heat of the sun's changing through purple twilight into melancholy clear moonlight, Urbano's soul, burned from then on by the light of the Great Mystery, had gone about being transported to a mood of resigned semidarkness, of poetic sadness and vague dreaming. But the light returned to blind him and burn him, as in a new dawn; and this time, it was no longer resentment against the world and its maker, but with himself; it was sharp despair. As those amputated of one member continue to feel its presence and bitterly realize the deception on going to verify it by touch, Urbano, Simona having been pruned from him, felt still her form, resistant and flexible between his arms, and her sweet warmth on his epidermis. In the darkness he sought her exquisite lips and crushed her with eagerness to his breast; at that

* Dove.—Tr.

very moment the hallucination vanished, and Urbano cried with rage. Seven days and seven nights he had had her for his own, her supplicating head, her avid arms, her delicious torso, her unseen legs. All of her was dedicated to him, in amorous and innocent expectation, there within the virginal chamber. And he didn't understand. He could have had her by his side in the bed, asleep in a happy dream, and he wouldn't have tired of contemplating her, watching over her. But he didn't understand. A curse on his mother, on Don Cástulo, who, keeping him in abominable ignorance, had robbed him of happiness! When, when would he recover his Simona?

Urbano spent very nearly twenty-four hours in these cogitations, fluctuations, and anguishes. At the end of this time, he fell exhausted on the bed. He had erotic and absurd dreams. After a long soporiferous rest, he was awakened by a sharp pain in the stomach. "I've got a hunger like a bear's," he said to himself; and as it was just dinnertime, he headed for the dining room.

"Lazarus reborn," said Don Leoncio. "You had me upset and worried. Eat, eat, my son, and regain your strength, for hunger is a bad counselor."

Urbano devoured a loaf of bread. He paused to ask, "And Don Cástulo?"

"He has left our house, for good," said Don Leoncio.

"Ingrate; we'll see him in the streets, hounded by stonings, like an ownerless dog," commented Doña Micaela; and in a changed tone, "Has God been kind to you, Urbano, in these two days of recovery? Has he clearly manifested to you his divine will? Toward which of the religious orders does he call you: Franciscan, Dominican, Hieronyman?"

"Either I'm much mistaken or God wants this one to become a monk of the two-in-a-cell kind," said Don Leoncio maliciously.

Urbano, with his mouth full, broke out laughing, with a noisy mirth, like a drunk's.

Doña Micaela, lowering her eyes, mumbled, meek and stricken, "You are torturing me."

196

Urbano raised his eyes to look at his mother. In those two days of his absence, she had been transformed. Among her hairs, black and hard like coal, some locks were streaked with dull whiteness. Doña Micaela's skin, which had always been of a firm nature and cordovan colored was still more darkened, as though mottled, with wavy splotches, like shadows. Doña Micaela had deep set eyes. As a boy, it seemed to Urbano that his mother's pupils, hard and round, shone in the bottom of a basin, like a cricket's head in the shadow of his hole. Now, below the drooped eyelids, the globes of the eyes jutted forth. Urbano's heart tightened, in a confused foreboding. He hastened immediately to look at his father. Don Leoncio's habitual expression was one of sadness; a resigned and nostalgic sadness. Now too he was sad, but his sadness disclosed a secret satisfaction.

Doña Rosita had just died, quietly, in her favorite armchair, leaning forward on a little table not far from the open window, through which entered the chill of the century old forest and the aroma of jalap. There was Simona, almost out of her wits, covered with the ancient and heavy jewelry adornments—the diadem, the necklace, the earrings, the bracelets, the chains, the heavy rings— that the grandmother had placed on her a short while before dying. With the young girl's trembling, the jewels tinkled, and by the light of the oil lamp on the ground they glowed like coals and gave off fleeting phosphorescent exhalations. There was Conchona, the strong and loyal servant, solid as a castle, as she herself had portrayed herself; the only column left standing within that ancient, noble house, suddenly demolished; the only composed heart, in those moments of grief and desolation. There was Cerezo, the corpulent mastiff, with his great head stretched out on the dead woman's lap, his eyes moist and blinking. There, on the broad nuptial bed of old, were the white silk brocade gown and the white veil embroidered in threads of silver, in which Doña Rosita went to the altar and had asked to wear to the grave.

That same morning all was well in the noble mansion. Simona, newly married, and her husband. Don Cástulo, Urbano's tutor, a gentleman of quality, handsome and well mannered like a colonist. This gentleman had fallen in love with Conchona and wanted to make her his, in matrimony, as soon as possible. Of this Conchona believed that nobody was aware, but she and her admirable fiancé. What might the dead woman have said on learning of it? The house, well provided with everything, the necessities and the superfluous, the useful and the beautiful. Fourteen servants, in waiting. A herd of cows; horses and foaling mares; dovecote, rabbit hutch, hen house with more than two hundred hens. Surrounding the palace—the house could be called a palace—was a park like a forest; beyond the forest, meadows, orchards, fruit groves, and all kinds of fruit trees, cornfields, rye fields, all enclosed by a solid stone wall, set on top in a sawtooth shape. Over so much abundance and beauty there presided, like an image in an altar full of offerings, the aged Doña Rosita, with her ever-saintly face and smile of benediction. Only missing was the merry widow, Doña Rosita's daughter and Simona's mother; but the latter was not missed, as she was always going off someplace distant, accompanied by a clerical friend, chaplain of the house. If there were an earthly paradise, it was on that sheltered estate. All of a sudden, that accursed midday, there fell upon the paradise the birds of bad tidings from the court. The merry widow —who might have guessed it?—has squandered her fortune. The estate now belongs to a usurious moneylender. All those who dwell on it must leave on the fly as in a fire. The sad news and the shock mortally wounded Doña Rosita. Don Cástulo—what a smooth talker!—convinces those from the court to stay the execution. The servants catch a whiff of what is taking place. Fear spreads; greed and selfishness awaken. Without saying boo, Don Cástulo and Urbano leave hastily to give aid in another disaster, in the groom's family. The old woman prostrate, the girl aswoon, the servants make themselves masters of the field. Like bold pillagers in a fire, they poke into the corners, stir the ashes, to steal what they can. But there is she, Conchona, with her virile courage, who has hair on her face for something, a thing which doesn't matter to her—since it doesn't matter to Don Cástulo—and on this occasion she brags of it. By means of a subtle trick, she imprisons the servants in the hayloft, out there, next to the cow barn, and returns to lock herself in the mansion, as in a fortress, with the moribund old woman, the afflicted girl, and the guardian mastiff. It is nighttime now. Great shrieks of anguish break the silence of the dwelling. Conchona comes running, with an oil lamp. In the grandmother's shadow, is Simona, rigid like a statue, adorned with resplendent jewels. Ay, those eyes of a madwoman—burning embers—on the milk white skin; and the fiery red hair! The grandmother has just died. At this moment heavy knocks resound. It is the justice, with the usurer, who come to take possession of the house. Conchona, in shouts from the window, replies that she will not open up. There is no human soul there, but the cadaver of a saint, an angel delirious with grief and fear, a mastiff, and a tiger, which is she, Conchona. The house's goods are safe; the plundering of the servants, confounded; in the distance they are heard to shout and blaspheme, prisoners. Let the justice return another day, when the señora is buried. Now, Conchona will not consent to the profanation; she would defend herself with a poisoned lance from the Philippines. This reasoning convinces the usurer and the constables. Behold her, Conchona, confronted with grim reality, she alone, arbitrator and determiner of the consequences. What to do?

Conchona did not let herself get easily frightened, as it were not a matter of love life (the fear of seeming stupid or boorish before her lordyship, appelative of intimacy on referring to Don Cástulo); but love, now, gave her animal forces and keenness of judgment—love for her mistresses and above all the certitude of meriting admiration and applause from her beloved.

"Sit down, little one; sit down and pray, if you can, for the grandma's soul, though it's not necessary. She flew direct to the kingdom of God and right over the bald head of Saint Peter she passed, without stopping, like an arrow. Sit down and sleep, little one; and if you're not sleepy, close your eyes, so as not to see the sad business that with these unworthy hands I must carry out, as God commands in the duties of misercorde." Simona sat down. The strong servant continued, "Or don't close your eyes, for deeds of mercy don't instill fear, but console. She weighs less than a suckling babe; no flesh, and not like we sinners; her bones the tiny and delicate ones of a little bird; she was just soul, and her soul flew to heaven. I kiss these hands, like relics of the Church. Conchona lifted up the weightless body of the dead woman, who kept her curled up position, with which, being already small, she was reduced in size. "The señora passed to the other life without suffering, joyful as the blessed. What a tranquil face; it's smiling! More beautiful now than ever before. The wrinkles are gone; the color is high. She's changed from a tea rose to an Alexandrian rose. I feel reverent carrying this body. An obedient servant am I, as God commands." Conchona raised her voice, so that the girl might not hear the creaking of the dead woman's bones, as she, gently, went about straightening out the bent arms and legs.

Simona, with her pupils widened, looked without seeing; she heard without listening. Cerezo stood by, remaining unmoving.

Then, Conchona undressed Doña Rosita; she washed, combed and perfumed her; she redressed her in her virgin bridal outfit; she deposited her in the nuptial bed, crossing her hands, as in prayer, and covered her head with a lace cloth. Cerezo jumped up on the bed, to lie at the Señora's feet. Conchona went to shoo him. Simona said, and it was the only thing she said all night long, "Leave him!"

Cerezo stretched out at his mistress's feet, as in the Castillian crypt stones.

Conchona knelt to mutter prayers. Her thoughts drifted to her beloved lordyship.

The trembling silence of the night was heard.

There arrived at times, undulating like hellish torn banners, vile shouts from the captive servants. And once more the black water of the silence flowed, a drone in the ears.

The nightingale sang.

Simona raised her hands to her throat and broke into a sob, prolonged in musical modulations. Then she cried quietly.

Conchona saw that Simona had fallen asleep. In her arms she led the girl to her room without Simona's being aware, exhausted by sleepiness and sorrow.

It was still dark night. "At the least, the very least, the señorita will sleep for three hours, at a stretch. I have more than enough time," thought Conchona.

She left the house. She walked across country, at a good pace, toward the residence of Don Arcadio Ontañón, the old family doctor. The cocks were rustling in the roosts. An Asturian cart creaked; it was like a formidable insect awakening. It was dawning.

The façade of the doctor's residence was covered with a mesh of bluebells, which chimed soundlessly in the auroral breeze, and instead of sound, they gave off perfume. Conchona knocked at the door. After a while they asked from within, "Who's there? Some birth?"

"In the name of God!" replied Conchona, shouting. "A death."

"Well, what are you knocking for? There's no thaumaturgist living here who brings back from the dead."

"Open up, Don Arcadio. It's Conchona, the maid from Collado. Doña Rosita has died. We're in the greatest difficulty."

A half-dressed overgrown boy opened the door and conducted Conchona to the bed of the doctor, to whom the servant related everything.

"And what am I going to do for you woman? Do you want me, by some enchantment, to make the wandering merry widow come? Do you want me to suspend the laws and raise the mortgage which has made the estate change ownership? Do you want me to kill the usurer? Look, that I could certainly do. All there is to it is that he come to consult me. Convince him to."

"Jesus what a man, without an ounce of brains. And he's a doctor. What you have to take care of is sending the carpenter's box right away, notifying the priest and everything that's needed for the burial, which you'll know better than I, from the many people you've killed. I'm running back to the mansion, before the child wakes up. You too, should come later, in case the child becomes ill, which wouldn't be surprising."

"I will do all that, Conchona, most willingly, from friendship and affection for the deceased as much as out of duty of conscience. Go ahead, go ahead, Conchona. You are big and look as clumsy as an elephant; at the proper time, agile and industrious as a weasel."

"The last I understood; the first, I didn't."

"I didn't say it for you to understand. Run along home. The **absurd** thing about conjugal selection: if the lads looked for more qualities in the lasses than a pretty face, you would now have had a beau, and the best of them all."

"Who told you I don't?"

"Run along home."

Conchona returned to the estate. On going by the hayloft, the servants, behind the bars, howled with hunger.

"Cursed bitch, who stole it all for yourself; give us something to eat at least."

"Eat hay, swine."

She went into the house. The señora was sleeping the irrevocable sleep. Simona lay in a temporary death. When the doctor arrived midway through the morning, the girl had not awakened. A short while later they brought the box. Between the doctor and Conchona they placed Doña Rosita in the coffin, which they left open. Then, Conchona covered it with flowers from the garden.

"Goodbye, my friend," said Don Arcadio, kissing the dead woman's hands devoutly.

Conchona cried, and between sobs said, "But aren't you crying, Señor doctor, now that Simona cannot see us? Jesus, what a man of flint!"

"You clearly show your good-hearted and loyal character with that phrase: to cry now that the girl does not see us. Almost everyone cries so that they may be seen crying. I too would like you to see me cry. My tears are dry, child; much more burning than liquid tears. And inasmuch as my heart being of flint, you are right; but I note that in the innards of flint is hid fire."

And Don Arcadio sadly shook his head, from which his fleshy nose stuck out, cylindrical and shiny on the tip, like a candle. He sat down in the armchair next to the window without taking off his inevitable mustard-colored cape, his green parasol between his legs.

Still crying, Conchona sighed, "Let me relieve you of that horse-blanket, which I'm suffocating just seeing you under. Beg pardon; I meant the cape."

"Never mind, woman. The cape doesn't weigh on me as it wouldn't weigh on Doña Rosita if it were placed over her. You see me as alive and kicking. Well, I am half dead, three-quarters dead, five-sixths dead; every day a part of myself dies. Do you believe that only Doña Rosita has died? With her have died, forever, forty years of my life. Oh, death, death! You understand nothing of this, woman."

"I understand it only too well, ay!" the servant exclaimed with an explosive sob.

"You're wrong, Conchona, for I am the one who says it and I don't understand it; nor has anyone ever understood it; nor will human intelligence ever penetrate the mystery of death."

"I understand, and it's enough for me that the señora died and that sorrow runs me through and through."

"It's better this way, that she has died."

"Don't say that."

"God recalled her at a good time. She had always lived in her house, without leaving it, like a pearl in a nacre shell. Who knows where the pearl would come to rest, torn from its shell? God has taken her to augment his heavenly treasures. Now, in the nacre shell there will rest a filthy slug."

Simona made her appearance, white and with an inaudible step. She threw herself upon the bier to kiss the grandmother. Conchona wanted to remove her; but the old doctor, with a sign, restrained the serving maid. Thus the girl remained, until a short while later the undertakers arrived.

Downstairs the priest from Pendueles was waiting, in his black silk priest's cope and yellow braids, accompanied by the acolyte in scarlet.

Simona declared her desire to go to the burial. Conchona tried to dissuade her. Don Arcadio decided that the child's wish be granted.

"We can wait until the señorita and the maid put on mourning."

"Why black? My grandmother is in white," replied Simona.

At the front door was Don Arcadio's coach.

"Wait here until we return," said the doctor to the boy who was holding the horse by the reins.

A panting villager ran up, his cap under his arm.

"Señor doctor, my Felisa is having labor pains, to let the nipper out any minute."

"Tell her not to let it out until around three in the afternoon, when I'll be able to come."

"And if she lets it out right away?"

"A sign that I'm not needed by her."

The humble cortège got under way; four men with the coffin on their shoulders; the priest and the acolyte; the granddaughter in white; Conchona in a multicolored dress; and Don Arcadio with his mustard-colored cape and his green parasol open. Behind, Cerezo, head lowered, his tail between his legs. They went along the country paths, bordered by flowering blackberries and wild laurels. In the distance sounded a chorus of stone cutters and the rhythm of the hammer on the cold chisel that polishes the stone.

In the cemetery of Pendueles there was not but one mausoleum, that of the Cerdeño family. It was an austere edifice, of blackish granite, oriental style, similar to hypogeum entrances. It did not have a door; an iron gate, between two stubby columns. One descended to the crypt, in the front an altar; in the walls niches with inscriptions. Within, the murmuring of the sea was heard, as if it arrived rolling through subterranean galleries. They deposited Doña Rosita on the flagstones on the ground at the foot of the altar. Simona wanted to remain there, sitting up over the grandmother until they closed her up in the niche. Don Arcadio forbade it.

On returning to the estate, they found the usurer, with some scribes, installed in the house making note of everything. The usurer tried to search Simona's trunk and Conchona's box, before they might remove them. The doctor intervened.

"You must understand that the honesty of this woman is clearly proven, after what she has done to avoid the rest of the servants robbing you; a matter which in the final analysis didn't matter to her a jot, and I doubt if it's appreciated. But you should show her your gratitude with a gift of worth. For me, I don't care a fig whether the world be honest or cease being so; what concerns me is that the world be plump, cheerful, and healthy. For my part, insofar as the matter of honesty and pillage, I am of the opinion that pillage ought to be prescribed better, and that the great excess of it that some few monopolize be shared among the majority of men, unfortunates who sin from not knowing how to be pillagers at the right time. But to you, the moneylenders, the bankers, the rich, the men of law and order, it is to your advantage, even if it be from an instinct of self-preservation, that the breed of honest people not die out, for which it is not sufficient, as you think, to soundly punish the petty pillaging and to protect juridically high class pillaging; it is necessary, above all, to truly recompense those who uphold honesty."

"Just so. That is the Bible, and I observe that chapter, without forgetting the morrow, when anything might happen, for there're more days than sausages. I intend to reward this maid with two meters of percale for a blouse," said the usurer, clearing his throat before coming out with each sentence.

"Wretch," thought the old doctor, "I pity your provisions for the morrow and your sausages. You're incurably consumptive."

"The blouse percale you can use for handkerchiefs, which you well have need of with that cold," said Conchona. "What I did, I didn't do it for you, may you go to blazes; I did it because this house is the señorita's and, if there's any true justice, to the señorita it will return."

"Don't count on it, lizard."

They tied the baggage to the back of the coach, and then Simona, Conchona, and the doctor, who took the reins, mounted. To the rear, followed Cerezo, with his donkey lope. In the middle of the field, the doctor stopped the horse and said, "Now, we must decide where we are going."

"To look for Urbano," replied Simona.

"Long trip for my puny nag," objected the doctor.

"Señorito Urbano will come by himself right away. I'm amazed that they're not here already, he and the lordyship—assuming his father may not have gotten worse. Don't worry, my queen, soon we will all be together," said Conchona.

"Well then take me to catch the coach to Pilares. I'll go alone. I'm not afraid. I want to be with Urbano. He's all I have left."

"And your mama, Señorita," corrected the doctor.

"It's true, I was forgetting. I'm not myself. Have pity on me."

"Let's take it easy," added the doctor. "You're coming to my house for the time being. There you're making yourselves comfortable; there you'll have something to eat; there you're resting. Tomorrow, God will say."

"Or to my house," Conchona suggested excitedly. "A country house; poverty and cleanliness; luxuries where you find them; cornbread and milk aplenty; and hearty stew, with beans and sausage. Ten little nephews I have, from a sister that God carried off, all corn colored, cheerful as linnets, the oldest ten; father, mother, and grandma. If the señorita were to honor us, we would receive her like the empress of the heavens."

"It's up to Simona," concluded the doctor.

Simona kept still. Don Arcadio went on: "As an old man, wise in tricks and guiles, I read more in silence than in deceitful words. Hey then, to Conchona's house. Giddyup, Charles the Fifth." The doctor had given this name to his nag because, with his prognathous and slack jawbone, he found in him a great resemblance to the emperor and his whole royal line. He continued, "Your choice doesn't offend me, Simona. I consider it natural that to the hole of an owl long on in years you might prefer a nest full with the happiness of baby birds. Giddyup, giddyup, Charles the Fifth."

"But, you will have to write to Urbano immediately, telling him where I am. Let him run to find me."

Conchona's family received the señorita with suspicious respect. The little children, fingers in noses, standing together off at a distance, gaped openmouthed at Simona and the big dog. All had the clear and bright eyes of little mountain animals.

Simona was offered the only bedroom in the house, in which there were two beds. Conchona slept on the ground in the ramshackle shed-covered hovel, which actually was heart and stomach of the household—hearth, kitchen, dining room, living room— midway between the room with the two beds and the cattle stable, and set off from both by some sort of partitions of unplaned boards, through whose cracks there penetrated at times the murky smell of a mother cow and the tender cry of a sucking lamb. The rest of the family slept, as by custom, in the granary, all thrown together without undressing on cornleaf sacks.

Simona was interested in and attracted by all of that for its picturesque novelty. She buried herself in the noisy sack, as if for a game she were to tumble on the floor of an autumnal forest, piled high with dry leaves. At the slightest movement, there arose from the sack mattress a great murmur, like the wind blowing dead leaves. She heard Conchona snoring in the kitchen, the cows ruminating in the stable, the pigs grunting phlegmatically in the pen; outside the melodious song of the toads, that of the crickets, like a tiny and timid horsebell. The birds woke her early in the morning.

In the closed planks of the window shutter the pine knots shone round and purple like wet cherries.

During the day, Simona established acquaintanceship with the ways and people of the house, above all with the junior contingent.

Underneath the granary, Conchona's mother was spinning flax on the archaic spinning wheel. To Simona that simple and ingenious artifact and that venerable and immemorial industry seemed a little game. She tried, for fun, to wind the spindle and thread the fiber. Then she made them show her the linens which they wove with those skeins. They brought out to her some rolls of strong and brown hand-loomed cloth. Simona fancied that the cloth had the color of rye bread and that it smelled like hot bread too. She asked what that cloth was used for. They answered her, for dress shirts and fine sheets. Simona expressed surprise that they might stand so much roughness against the skin. They replied to her that she had slept the night before between those sheets, and Simona, who remembered nothing but the sensation of pleasant freshness, did not want to believe it.

The little children offered Simona San Juan figs picked from the fig tree, still moist with dew.

The afternoon meal—country stew and the cornbread soaked in warm milk—she enjoyed immensely, after two days without eating hardly a bite.

Everything around Simona stimulated her healthfully to come out of herself, as if in a counsel to peace of mind and to oblivion. But Simona was sad and disconsolate. Conchona and the little children tried to distract her. Simona, from time to time, said, "Falín, Xuanín, Xuaco; from the side of the shack there, go up to the hill and from the highest tree see if in the distance a coach is coming, or a gentleman on his horse, or even a fast-walking lad."

"If they're not coming, they will come," predicted Conchona. "Don't torment yourself, my queen. They will come, Señorito Urbano and the lordship. Don't lose confidence. The unconfident woman is not a woman nor is she anything at all. Remember that the day of the wedding, the señorito disappeared, as if lost. All the next day you were waiting for him in the tower; you were ready to despair and the señorito returned."

"I wasn't despairing then. My grandmother had told me that Urbano would return. Now I am despairing. My grandmother, before dying, told us, Urbano and me, that someone, I don't know who, was going to separate us from one another for a long time, a long time."

"She said that?"

"She said that; some of her words are still echoing in my ears; just an odd word or two; several of them meaningless."

"God's own Saint; it's quite clear that she was delirious."

"No, she wasn't delirious. I'm the one who at times am beginning to be delirious. Listen. My grandmother spoke and spoke. I was on the ground at her feet, full of fear. I heard the grandmother, but her voice was only a noise. I couldn't decipher a single word of what I was hearing. And nevertheless, I noticed that her words were filling me up and remained inside me, shut away as if asleep and in the dark. Then everything that took place outside of me crushed me, oppressed me; and my grandmother's words and the others that we all carry in our hearts and heads, to know what we feel and think, got darker and darker and more confused, piled up roughly against one another. I couldn't talk. From being so full, I was as if empty. Here, in your house, I have stopped noticing the oppression from outside. On the contrary. It's as if little cracks were opening in me little by little. Those words of my grandmother, set in the deepest and most hidden part of my soul are now coming out through the cracks, here and there, in lines that join and separate, like little ants. They almost make me dizzy. I don't know if I'm delirious. They are odd phrases. Each one by itself says something; together, I cannot make sense of them. I only know that my grandmother predicted Urbano's separation and mine. And my grandmother couldn't be mistaken, because she was seeing things from the other world already, like the spirits that are in heaven."

"Anxieties from weakness; you think all that because you're run down from eating little, from not sleeping, and from fears. Your hands are still shaking a little bit. Don't be anxious, queen; the anxious woman is not living nor does she let anyone else live."

"I'm not living, no. And I'm more troubled because I don't know the reason. I forgot it. I forgot it on seeing the grandmother dead. It was something that I carried inside; I still have the memory of a most sweet burden. What was it, my God, what was it? All of a sudden, that pleasant weight evaporated; it was converted into a bitter emptiness."

"Coral of the seas, pearl of the Orient, cinnamon of the Indies, my queen; many sorrows trouble you, much you lost, but you still enjoy the greatest fortune and you still have the most precious thing on earth: a husband in love."

"And missing."

On recovering from the recent great sorrow, in its violence unconsciously felt, there was germinating in Simona a new consciousness, sorrowful and resigned, of life. It was as if her personality had been changed. That little girl of three days before, innocent, ignorant, and trusting, had been reformed into a sad, fearful woman, belabored within by an insidious remorse. "I don't know of what to accuse myself," she thought, "but without any doubt I have sinned. Misfortunes do not happen by chance; they are punishments that God sends. I have been a bad daughter, a bad granddaughter, a bad wife without knowing it. If not, my grandmother would be alive, my mother might have come at the dreadful hours, Urbano would not have abandoned me." That night she couldn't sleep. The roughness and scratchiness of the sheets chafed her. Later she dreamt that they were carrying her to be buried in a sack made from tree bark.

The next morning, Conchona was outside the shack shelling corncobs for the chickens, when, at the far end of the apple orchard, there appeared Don Cástulo, his hat in one hand, his head burned by the sun and pouring sweat, the collar of his shirt unbuttoned. Conchona ran to squeeze him between her robust arms and cover him with kisses.

"A pitcher of water, a bucket of water, please," gasped Don Cástulo, collapsing on the opiparous breast of his beloved.

"Water? God in heaven forbid; so a pain in the side can lay you low and that's all for me. Here I was just saying that my own lordyship had to return to me, and right soon. Now it's so, and Señorito Urbano?"

"Let me catch my breath. We've got to have a talk before Simona sees me."

They sat on the grass in the shade of an apple tree. Don Cástulo opened his mouth to breathe; he began his story in a rush of words; he got out of breath again. The chickens came up to Conchona's skirt to pick at the cobs. Don Cástulo, in stages, went about completing the story. He had arrived the evening before, in the night stagecoach. Then in the morning, he went to the old doctor's house, perspicaciously calculating that nobody so well as he could fill him in on where his fiancée and Simona were stopping. Then, asking here and there, getting lost, coming back perhaps to the same place and retracing maybe his steps, his brains melting under the sun, there he was at last, at the side of his adored Conchita.

"Very cleverly," interrupted Conchona. "But, Señorito Urbano? Señorito Urbano's return matters more to me than anything else."

"Ingratitude, you wear the face of woman," exclaimed Don Cástulo jokingly.

"It matters to me for gratitude toward my masters. If the señorito does not return, the señorita will die on us."

Don Cástulo explained to his fiancée the present situation of the amours of Urbano and Simona. Simona's mother had been left without a *real*; Urbano's parents, ditto. On what were the newlyweds going to live? Conchona demolished all objections, resting her case on one supreme argument: "They're in love."

"If they have nothing to live on, let the señorito go to work," said Conchona.

"He has to learn to work, which is a long apprenticeship."

"Well, let them eat bread and onions, or let them live on charity. We don't have an *ochavín* either."

"In that you're mistaken. I have a few *pesetillas.*"

"Like how many?"

"Around forty thousand *reales.*"

"Jesus, Jesus, Jesus! That's a regular fortune. An idea occurs to me. Why don't we give that cash to Señorito Urbano and Señorita Simona? And everything's fixed up."

Don Cástulo, perplexed before this disconcerting proposition, didn't dare to look Conchona in the face. It wasn't a question solely of money. Urbano's mother, a señora who always got her way, was now resolved to unmake the marriage. Conchona was scandalized. She had never heard of such a thing, that married couples might get unmarried. Don Cástulo indicated that the two of them were married, but that, strictly speaking, they still hadn't been completely married. Despite the embarrassed circumlocutions of the narrator, Conchona caught on. She didn't want to give credence to Don Cástulo. By the spirits in purgatory; had they not spent eight days living together! Don Cástulo answered that they had lived as children, because they were innocents and didn't know. Conchona was not convinced; that, even the animals know, who also are innocents. Don Cástulo retorted that animals know how to swim and men don't if they are not taught. "In any event," concluded Conchona, "a parson married them, and married they were. Who would unmarry them? The Holy Mother Church wasn't going to permit an infamy of such magnitude."

"What a priest does the bishop undoes; what a bishop does the Pope undoes. I don't say always, but with enough frequency. Don't trust priests, Conchita, go they dressed in black, in purple, in red, or in white."

"But do priests go dressed in those colors?"

"High priests do, yes. Priests, all in all. I'm instructing you, Conchita: don't trust priests. A priest is a man beaten in life, a failure; from whence, in spite of themselves, they hate, because they envy it, all that is love and happiness. The poor man hates the rich man, the stupid one the intelligent one, the fool the wise man, the ugly the handsome, the sick the robust, the eunuch the lover, the priest the man. Why does the priest hate the man? For the same reason as the poor man the rich man, the ugly the handsome, and the suffering the sound; because others possess what they love and cannot possess. The priest loves woman, and therefore hates man. I won't consent to your even making confession, to keep you and me safe from the clergymen. Through confession, the priest is converted into spiritual husband of the woman. *Cocuage mystique*, as if we were to say mystical cuckolding, a French author calls confession. *Hoc est magnum sacramentum.* I beg God, Conchita, that you never come to Vulcanize me with a priest."

Don Cástulo felt himself awesome, saying these things, and he believed that in his fiancée they would produce the kind of admiration he most coveted, scandalous admiration. So it was. Conchona, who saw in the expatriates from America, in the colonists, the archetype of manly superiority, had observed that they did not go to church and that they boasted of impiety. From the first, she fell in love with Don Cástulo for his outward resemblance—in her eyes—to the colonists. This last touch of similarity, of near identity, filled her with pride.

"Virgin of the Rosary! What blasphemy! You're going to damn yourself. Ay! I have to convert you, so we're not separated in the next world," said Conchona, affrighted and happy.

"You will convert me into whatever you want, my love, Parthenis, my little virgin; you will convert me into a hog, if you so desire, like the charmer Circe to Odysseus' companions," exclaimed Don Cástulo, in a transport of sentimentality, smacking on Conchona's cheek a peck that startled the chickens. He murmered supplicatingly, "When are you going to addess me familiarly?"

"After we marry. I still don't dare."

"Angel of modesty!"

Now Conchona took the lead and told, with sobriety character-ized as sublime by Don Cástulo, of her firmness and determination on that lugubrious night of the death of Doña Rosita. Don Cástulo, becoming touched, made the posthumous panegyric of the deceased. He concluded, "In only seven days we had come to know and esteem one another with a friendship seemingly lifelong. We were twin spirits, strange rarity in this vale of discord. Two separate bodies and a single mind, like those tapers that accidentally come out stuck together by the top. It seemed to me that she burned with my light and I with hers, such was the oneness of our feelings."

Don Cástulo told Conchona that Doña Rosita, the very morn-ing of the attack, had promised him to be wedding bridesmaid. Con-chona broke into a convulsive sobbing, which agitated stormily the surface of her oceanic bosom, to Don Cástulo's no small curiosity and disquietude. When she calmed down, Don Cástulo said, "Time is short. We must get on. Two matters, of the utmost seriousness, I've got to resolve as soon as possible: to break the news to Simona gently; to ask you of your parents."

Conchona did not understand what that was about asking some-thing of her parents. Best not to ask anything of them, since they had nothing; and even when they might have it, they wouldn't give it away. It was to ask her hand in matrimony, to ask for the paternal consent, elucidated Don Cástulo. This Conchona understood still less. It was she who had to consent, and she had already consented. For the rest, her parents happy as could be, even if she were to marry a mere villager: one mouth less. Marrying a señor, what were they going to reply but good and glory be to God? Even thus and so, Don Cástulo didn't want to omit that ceremonious solemnity.

Insofar as telling Simona, Conchona, "even if taken for an ass," expressed her feeling of speaking clearly to the girl.

"A few tears, because crying relieves us women so much! . . . and then the world may drown, and that doesn't scare us," said Con-

214

chona. She added, looking mischievously at Don Cástulo, "We women are more courageous than you."

Don Cástulo caught the allusion. In the courting of Conchona, she was the one who had made all the advances with singular daring and so much tact that modesty suffered no injury. Don Cástulo replied, blushing, "More courageous? In love yes. That is, that is: not in love even. Are you courageous?"

"You know that."

"Go on; as courageous as you are, you still won't dare to . . . ?"

"To what?"

"To address me familiarly."

"Because respect is as great as love. Wait till we marry. Then maybe I may address you familiarly, and I'll even give you little beatings, not like with grownups, like with children, playing."

Don Cástulo was again carried away by sentimental excess: "Let me kiss these lily hands, these hands that are going to beat me; when they beat me I will die of pleasure," and he kissed, greedily, those two honest and industrious hands, in another way fleshy and red as two prime sirloins.

Conchona took charge of speaking with the señorita. With all her courage, her voice choked. Simona did not allow her to finish.

"Your kind efforts are not necessary, Conchona. Last night I've thought a great deal; and I haven't thought with my words, the ones each of us carries within, but with the words my grandmother introduced into my soul before dying. All those run-together and obscure words have been coming out, spilling, bubbling. And my grandmother's voice made itself heard in my heart. She said, 'I intended to leave you rich; I leave you nothing in material goods. Let my words be my bequest. It is necessary that you, Simona, not lose your head in adversity. They will tear you from one another, as the woodsman cuts a shrub and splits it into two pieces of firewood. Separated, keep in mind that one day you will blaze in the same hearth.' I don't wish to know anything more. Who the woodsman may be doesn't matter to me. If I knew it, perhaps I wouldn't think well of him, and one shouldn't think evil of anyone. I'll await, with certain hope, the day on which the hearth may blaze. I'm not losing my head in adversity. I say: to be far from Urbano, knowing that we must come together, is a sorrow; but it's a pleasurable sorrow, because thus I will merit his love better. I wouldn't call this adversity. And my grandmother forecast adversity. Let it come. I'm ready. Grandmother also said, 'Even if Urbano may take days, weeks, months, do not be impatient. He is your slave, he is your master, he is your worshipper. You are his mistress, his slave, his goddess. Nobody will break your servitude; nobody will destroy your sovereignty; nobody will cool your adoration.' Now you are seeing if I can be confident and tranquil. Besides, there's something else, a divine thing, which infuses me with superhuman warmth. Yesterday I had forgotten it, and this caused me an anguished emptiness. I told you already. But it has come back again, flooding me with emotion. I will whisper it to you. I'm going to have a child."

"A child! Blow me down." In the fullness of the surprise none but this vernacular and unpoetic though perhaps quite eloquent expression occurred to Conchona.

"Our having just been married," continued Simona, with simple earnestness, "as we were going along in the coach, the archangel appeared to me, and I, on the spot, felt the child in my throat. Oh, Conchona, my heart melted!"

"Glorious Jesus! Then it was like the Most Holy Virgin Mary."

"Of course, woman, and like with all other women. You're a single girl and cannot guess what this is."

"Ay, my little one, white as milk and snow and ermine!" sighed Conchona, embracing and kissing Simona; at the same time she was thinking, "My lordyship is right. What innocence. I hear her and I don't believe it."

Another bit of news remained for Conchona to communicate to the señorita, and here her credited courage weakened further— the news of her wedding. Not being very adept in subtle phrase making, she decided to let fly the news in one burst, "as someone

216

who might throw a stone at a cat," she thought inside herself. The cat was her own timidity, which she wanted to scare off. She said, puffing up her cheeks, "A single girl I am; I will soon cease to be one. I'm getting married. Doña Rosita was to be the bridesmaid."

"I will be it, Conchona, if you permit me to."

"Permit? Are you asking me if I'll permit the sun to shine on my wedding?"

"I have nothing to give you, unless it be one of the ancient jewels that the grandmother left me. Her wish was that I keep them; but the rings are a lot for me. I can give you one."

Conchona refused. Simona insisted.

"We'll see later," concluded the serving maid, going out of the shack.

"Hold on. You haven't told me who the fiancé is."

Conchona was already outside the gate. Without turning her head, she shouted, "Don Cástulo," and went off running, as if chased, among the fruit trees.

Simona didn't know if that was an answer or that Conchona was calling the tutor. Without doubt it was the latter. How was it going to be the former? Absurd.

Don Cástulo and Conchona presented themselves. After a brief scene, of condolence and affection, with Simona, Don Cástulo, who felt constrained with the girl, "initiated his relations, so longed for, with Conchona's family and with the humble homestead where his beloved had seen the light of day and grown to reach the present ripeness of succulent and unblemished fruit." This was what Don Cástulo said in a low voice to Conchona. And looking around at everything, he exclaimed in a loud, emotional voice, "Idyllic! Enchanting! One imagines himself transported to the ages of authentic poetry. The muse comes haltingly to me and stirs me, like Apollo with his favorites. Oh Jean Jacques, I revere your saving admonition; I will return to nature!"

On seeing Conchona's mother at the wheel, he called forth to shine anew the gynaeceums and the Hellenic wife, model of wives,

217

weaving in the shade, with a pensive air, white wool for her husband and her offspring.

When Conchona showed him her sister's ten orphans, Don Cástulo commented, "The never-in-vain frequented bed of the poor, as the poet said."

All listened to him openmouthed. Conchona overflowed pride.

Although Don Cástulo tried hard with erudite and philosophic observations to put it off, the crisis of the petitioning of the hand arrived. Directing himself to Conchona's grandmother and parents, he said in a declamatory tone, "Venerable old woman, esteemed of the gods, who have gratified you with the good fortune of preserving yourself in possession of the fine human body to the plentitude of your days and seeing yourself flower and reflower three times over in three rubicund and jovial generations; hardworking father and virtuous mother, once, twice, thrice over, happy, since you have engendered the most beautiful maiden, best endowed with gifts of cordiality and of ingenuity, delight of your eyes and of each who looks upon her. What man is there worthy of appropriating for himself this treasure, embracing her to him in the gentle deliriums of sacrosanct Hymeneal? None. Nevertheless, your charity and generosity, not my merits, have commissioned me, the most wretched of men, to conduct her to the nuptial altar as legitimate husband and señor, which I will not do if first you do not grant me the indispensable blessing, as being the procreators."

On concluding, Don Cástulo bent from the waist in a ritual reverence. Don Cástulo's interior monologues were always in this flowery and high-sounding style, just as his spoken language was frequently stumbling and clipped. He always became frightened in front of people. He was never able to get through some oral examinations, because they made him faint. Only with Doña Rosita, in the cozy morning chats, had he begun to feel himself fluent and eloquent. (Fluent and eloquent were the words he employed mentally, analyzing this phenomenon.) Oh, if he might be able to speak aloud as he spoke inaudibly in the hermetic retreat of his cranium! By this time he would now be a professor, university rector, minister, a big shot. Dismal destiny that of mortals! The most noble inborn faculties bring paired at birth to a brake that holds them back or destroys them. He, a great silent orator, lacked nerve for speaking in public. On the other hand, the bold of tongue lack Minerva's wisdom and even common sense, as happens with almost all orators. But now, before the progenitors of his fiancée, he expanded in a honeyed flow, similar to the eloquence that is attributed to Plato. Why? Because he had there a proper audience. This audience was composed of a single person: his sweetheart. Looking at her out of the corner of his eye, he had observed that Conchona was swooning with enthusiasm and admiration.

All these things and many more Don Cástulo thought dizzily, bent from the waist, awaiting the reply of the country people. The wait stretched out. Conchona's grandmother and parents could not reply, for they had not understood a word. At last, Conchona, who hadn't understood either but who had guessed, clarified the situation.

"It means, speaking in Christian, that the lordyship is marrying me."

There was a stunned silence. Conchona's father, a taciturn peasant, imagined that if the señorito wanted to marry a serving girl, it was for a good reason; he was up to something. Just as it was, disinterestedly, the matter didn't seem very clear to him. Scratching the ground with a hazel rod, his brow lowered and suspicious, he muttered, "I warn you that we have nothing here. Not the clipping of a fingernail can we give the lass. The homestead we have on lease; with hard work, we make enough to eat."

Don Cástulo, arching his eybrows in a smile of commiseration and superiority, replied, "By God! You offend me, Señor Bernardo. I want Conchita without a stitch. Well, that's a saying. I meant to make it understood that when I take Conchita for mine, I will take her without a stitch, as her virtuous mother gave birth to her. I still haven't explained myself. I say that not even the clothes she has on will I accept as a gift. She will leave from this house, if she leaves, with the clothes I buy her."

"Does the señor say 'if she leaves'? The married man needs a house. If Conchona marries, I imagine she'll leave this house for her own," said Señor Bernardo.

"Well here comes the good part," said Don Cástulo trying out an enigmatic smile. "I have a sum of money, around forty thousand *reales*. This money I will place in your hands, Señor Bernardo, so that together we may undertake some agricultural enterprise. It follows that Conchita and I will stay on to live with you. I have already told you that I want to follow the advice of Jean Jacques: let us return to nature."

"Do you have something to say, Father? Because if not, now it's my turn to declare my wish," intervened Conchona.

"Two men in one house, be they not father and son, and even thus and so, don't team up well," said the peasant, scratching the earth. "Each one pulls to his side. The both want to be in charge. Who would be in charge here? One poor, the other with cash, brings me the conclusion . . . "

"Hey, my turn," interrupted Conchona. "After we're married, Father, have no fear; we don't have to disturb you. You will continue as much master of your house as the king in his palaces. You needn't see hide nor hair of us, if not on a visit. We will go to the city. What we must do with my husband's money, I have it already worked out, to the *maravedí*, to get us a whole lot more. And now, we all ought to be happy as mummers, if there were no trouble: that Señorita Simona is sad. "Let's eat; our heads in the clouds, we've forgotten our stomachs."

All went into the country kitchen. They sat around the fireside. Conchona distributed the food. Don Cástulo watched her graceful movements bewitched. The little children surrounded her, while she, standing, cut slices in the cornbread, of golden crumbs and stony crust.

"What a picture of ineffable beauty! The tears come to my

eyes," sighed Don Cástulo, with his bowl full of stew between his knees, a boxwood spoon in his right hand.

"Tears? It's the smoke from the furze," corrected Conchona, laughing.

"It's from emotion, Conchita," insisted Don Cástulo. "You look the picture of perfect motherhood. The blue and silvery smoke from the hearth surrounds you like a halo. Patriarchal ideas take hold of me. I fancy that those ten tender infants are our sons. When will it come to be true?"

"That depends on you. I've more than enough oomph to bring up ten and twenty too, if you've the drive for so many."

"I'm a wholehearted believer in your abilities. You'll be mother of a magnificent race. And I will transmit my spirit to it."

"Leave that tune now and eat the stew. A bad year for the devil if as soon as we marry I don't fatten you up."

After eating, Don Cástulo asked his fiancée in what she had figured to employ the matrimonial capital. Conchona outlined her proposal. The best thing was to found in Pilares an academy preparatory for the institute and the university, a boarding academy. Of the administration she would take charge. Don Cástulo would be the director and would seek other professors and assistants, among them Urbano, to whom ought to be given the best salary. They would have to give the academy a very pretty and very unusual name, the more unusual the better. Don Cástulo was amazed.

"But who's told you about all these fripperies of academies, institutes, and universities?"

"What I tell you is that an academy would do for earning mountains of cash; to sweep in *centenes*. I swear I don't know what *centenes* are; but that was the way Señor Noriega expressed himself, and I didn't forget."

"*Centenes* are gold coins. Who is Señor Noriega?"

Conchona cleared up that most strange riddle. Before Doña Rosita, Conchona had served in the house of a rich colonist, named Noriega, who had two sons; one studied at the institute and another at the university as independent students with private tutors, precisely because the father didn't want them to be independent on their own.

"This, like that of the *centenes*," said Conchona, "I never succeeded in understanding; but I remember it well, that the father had them studying as independents because he didn't want them to be independent. You will unravel the mystery for me."

"Yes, I will. Now, go on."

Frequently, Señor Noriega lamented that there might not be in the province a single academy where the lads might be boarded and supervised with good professors. Conchona listened to him with curiosity; she had always been curious to learn and to find things out. She still kept in her memory the sentences of the colonist: "This is an old, tired country, without initiative. So overly well lettered and not one academy, which could be set up with very little money and then bring in cash and sweep in *centenes*." So that as Conchona heard from Don Cástulo about the small amount of capital, at the same moment there sprang to her mind the idea of the academy. Don Cástulo rewarded Conchona's happy and promising idea with a broad embrace and several concentrated kisses on the cheeks. He still did not dare to try the saporific kiss, on the lips, of which Rousseau speaks, because he was afraid to faint with happiness. After the honorific osculation, Don Cástulo indicated that they had to get married right off in order to go about setting up the academy together so that it might open at the beginnings of the term, in the coming autumn. There now ran all through Don Cástulo's body a conjugal tickle or itch. He stood up (they were, as in the morning, seated on the grass under an apple tree).

"What are you going to do?" asked Conchona.

"I am going straight to Pilares to arrange affairs, to see if the wedding can be in a week."

"Are you going to go on foot? It's nine leagues."

"I am going to Don Arcadio's, who will lend me his gig to Regium. There I'm taking the afternoon coach."

222

"A little bit of calmness. What about me?"

"You?"

"What if I don't want to get married in a week?"

"Conchita!"

"While Señorita Simona is like this, abandoned, I'm not getting married."

"And what difficulty is there in our getting married? We take her with us."

"In that case, all right. Now you may go ahead. No, no. Wait. Señorita Simona will want to write to her husband. You can carry the letter."

In the house there was neither paper nor pen. Don Cástulo had a lead pencil; but all the paper he had in his pocket consisted of various sheets filled with notes in a tiny hand and placed in a wrinkled and filthy envelope. Don Cástulo, with a splendid gesture, brought himself to the sacrifice of rubbing out the notes from one of the sheets. There was no eraser. Simona suggested the soft part of the bread, which they used in the Salesas convent in the drawing class, for erasing. There was no bread. They tried to use cornbread crumbs, with disastrous results, for though the notes disappeared well enough, the sheet remained black and useless. Then the ingenious Conchona, ever-resourceful, suggested that the back of the envelope could be written on. Simona, with pensive serenity, inscribed some lines.

Don Cástulo said goodbye. Conchona went out to the top of the orchard to see him leave. The sun was setting. Don Cástulo, now distant, turned his head toward his beloved, the yellow Conchona, who, wrapped in the saffron light of the afternoon, seemed to him a massive mountain of gold.

Simona's letter said:

"My love: They have taken me far from you, but do not think I love you less. I am not a bad woman. If I am separated from my husband it is not by my will. I suffer much, and in the suffering I find gladness, thinking of you. I understand that you will not be able to be mine, because before I had not suffered to deserve you. Now I do deserve you. I ask God that all the misfortunes I must suffer before having you happen together, all in a single minute, and, that minute passing, that you embrace and kiss me. My God, a minute is an eternity! A second is enough, even though in that second I be the most unhappy of women. The most unhappy of women I am, in the eternity of the minutes, and of the hours and of the days. Your love, my Urbano, is my consolation and my torment. I want to console myself loving you more and my torment increases. Remember what I whispered in your ear the last night. When will you return to kiss me?"

Don Cástulo sent this letter along to Urbano by a messenger. Urbano answered by mail:

"Simona of my heart, Simona idolized, my soul, my life; I have just read your lines and I am writing nervously, as in a frenzy, so that you may receive my reply as soon as possible. If you knew what I've gone through these past days! Everything, everything, everything of before has ceased to be. Our marriage has ceased to be; better said, it never has been. Don't think of what you whispered in my ear the last night: it's an illusion. We are not married. Now they will reveal it to you too, as to me they have revealed it; and they will show it to you brutally, without your leaving room for doubts. Oh, no; never, never will I consent in your seeing yourself in that mortal anguish and mortal shame! Nobody can reveal that to you but I myself. Just in thinking that you may learn the truth from other lips, perhaps from the lips of another man, even though he be a man with skirts, the blood rushes to my head and I feel murderous. You cannot understand me; you will think I have gone crazy. What I tell you—if you love me, keep it in mind always, like an indestructible truth, as my truth, the truth of your Urbano, and let nobody make you waver, not even the most authoritative persons, though they assert to you the contrary—what I tell you is that I am glad that we are not married; that now I love you more, infinitely more than ever; that for that very reason that I love you, I don't want to be

224

married to you; that I will not allow anyone to reveal to you the reason we are not married; and lastly, that to avoid that infamy, this very day, tomorrow, as soon as I can, I will abduct you. I have no money. My father has no money. I don't know how I will come by it. I'll steal it if necessary. I'll steal it, and I'll steal you. We'll go along the roads, we'll fly far away, we'll live on the fruits of the countryside, we'll beg alms, I'll take a job in a faraway city. Whatever. I'll abduct you. We'll sleep in a forest. By my side you won't be afraid. There then, I'll tell you . . . and you'll understand what now you cannot understand in this letter. And you'll say I am right. How much I want to kiss you, now."

Urbano did not know how to come by money. A day went by, another day, many days. And he did not receive a reply from Simona. "Will she have become offended?" wondered Urbano. "I don't know what I wrote. It was a moment of delirium. I certainly said some monstrous thing to her, which caused her terror and repugnance toward me. She has stopped loving me. I am absolutely certain she has stopped loving me. It's better. Thus I will begin from the beginning, like all other men, I will begin by making her fall in love, and not as before, when from early childhood, we knew that as grownups we were going to (they were going to have us) marry and we found ourselves in love by familial decree. Now it is for real. I will do it all, on my own. *Finis.* I make a cross. This cross is on the tomb of the past. There is no yesterday. There is only a tomorrow. And the tomorrow is called, *Simona of flesh and bone.*"

Two weeks after the writing of the letter to Simona, a street rogue knocked at Don Leoncio's door and said that he had to speak with Señorito Urbano.

"What errand brings you?" asked Urbano.

"Some people who wish to see you," replied the lad.

"What does anyone matter to me nor what do I matter to anyone? Is it one or several people? Men or women? Haven't they told you the name?"

"To me they said only to come to find you and they warned me at length, threatening that if I didn't do it, they weren't going to give me a *peseta,* that I be silent about whether it were one or more, men or women. So that, if you please, come with me."

"Where to?"

"To the Avilesino rooming house."

Urbano went out with the rogue to the rooming house. They went up; they went through a dimly lit hallway. The escort rapped on a door with his fist. Loud barks sounded within. They opened up. In the ashy shadow was made out the thin silhouette of Don Cástulo, who took the visitor by the hand and brought him in, saying, "Come in, my dearly beloved son. This miserable inn room is a sumptuous temple of immortal and omnipotent Eros. It will seem dark to you, because the light that the torches of the Hymeneal give off is invisible; none sees it save he who sacrifices on the altar of the god. I present you to my wife Concha Carruégano, united with me by the seamless bond of wedlock, since yesterday morning. I have called you, oh most beloved disciple!, so that you, before anyone, be witness to my happiness. I am drunk. Conchita intoxicates me. She is a barrel from which inexhaustibly flows the liquor of love. I don't say barrel because of her corpulence, which I repute a perfect canon of monumental beauty, but because of her copious amorous capacity. I very profoundly lament seeing you sunk in sadness when I am soaring in the spheres of Aphrodite Uranus. Don't be discouraged. I assure you that your day will come. As older, it is only right that I go ahead of you. Now I can truly serve you as teacher. Anyway, Urbano," embracing him, "pardon me my happiness, when I tell you how much your misfortune pains me."

Urbano made a show of his happiness effusively. What he didn't forgive Don Cástulo was the previous secrecy and not having invited him to the wedding. Don Cástulo excused himself; he had not dared to approach Don Leoncio's house out of fear of Doña Micaela. Urbano protested; his mother was so dejected that she did not inspire fear, but pity and love. But couldn't they tell him anything of

Simona? He had written her and was still waiting for the reply.

"When I wrote her," confessed Urbano, "I was a little upset. I put down many stupidities and impertinences. It's clear she got angry; and she broke off with me. I'm glad. Since in strict truth we were not married, I will begin anew. She is a stranger and I a lover who has first proposed to be her boy friend and then to make her his. Time will tell, and everything comes to pass; there's no rein that holds back time."

Conchona replied to Urbano that he was mistaken. The señor-ita had not written him because she had not been able to. Having just received and read her husband's letter—which to be sure she had kissed, crying and laughing with happiness, as she read it—, there appeared, like two ugly phantoms, the two oldest sisters of the roving Don Eleuterio Muñiz, the priest who accompanied Simona's mother on her rambles. (Here Don Cástulo started in: "Filthy Levite! Execrable presbyter!") They came with a written order from the mother to take Simona away. How the unhappy girl cried! But what was she going to do but follow them, like a lamb? They must have been holding her incommunicado and a prisoner. You only had to see the witch-like faces of the two old maids. They let some-thing slip about their going to shut Simona away in a convent.

Hearing this tale and of the death of the grandmother, Urbano was very shaken. To comfort him, Conchona could think of nothing better than to say: "Here is Cerezo. I couldn't bear to separate from him. He loved the mistresses very much. He's the only thing that's left us from those days on the estate of Collado."

"Those days!" sighed Urbano, patting the large head of the mastiff. The dog sniffed his hands, as if he still perceived a scent of his mistress, and then kissed them in his fashion, licking them.

"Those days! Ay!" sighed Conchona, with a kind of sigh that only she could sigh, and which was something like the veil of the firmament being torn asunder.

"Imbecile, an imbecile was I, those seven days," moaned Ur-bano dumbly, his hands locked together and clutching at his skull.

"Come on, lad, calm down," advised Don Cástulo, with a trembling voice, patting him on the cheeks. "Nothing is lost. You've put it well before, and very philosophically: there's no rein that holds back time. At the hour of triumph you will look back and it will seem to you that you haven't walked any distance at all, or that you have walked too quickly. More than forty years in pilgrimage toward my Conchita have I used up. I might have to feel fatigue, signs of old age. Not at all. I am like an adolescent. It seems to me that I am just starting out in life. Well, let's talk of something else."

"Ay, my lordyship," exclaimed Conchona, "listening to you, I drool."

"But, Conchita, when are you going to address me familiarly?"

"I don't dare to. You are my God."

"Precisely God everyone addresses familiarly."

They confided to Urbano the project of the academy and promised to make him a professor; as wages, whatever he might need. Don Cástulo suggested to Urbano that he might go over the lessons for the September examinations with certain boys from rich families, who had failed in the June ones; in this way, he would be practicing for his post in the academy and at the same time earn some money. If he was thinking of winning Simona, it was indispensable that he have charge of his own money. Urbano agreed to this idea; he would look for pupils; he asked Don Cástulo to look for them for him too.

Returning home along the streets, it seemed to Urbano that his body trod more solidly on the earth and that his step was firmer and more manly. It was that the last redoubt of the mystery had surrendered to him, to his thinking. A few days before, putting a *Finis* to his previous life, he had been up in the air, since he did not know where Simona was or the reason for her silence. Now truly a stage of his life had come to a close and another was beginning, long perhaps, maybe tedious, possibly combative; but he was going to be, and not outside design, the maker of his own life. On the atrium of the future he inscribed cheerfully: *Incipit*. Not a little proud would

228

he be to scale a convent wall and abduct a nun! How delicious Simona had to be as a nun! Just thinking of it, there spread over his face a beatific and foolish smile. Some seamstresses passed by his side, who shrieked between giggles, "A señorito who laughs to himself. He's batty."

At supper hour, Urbano told his parents that Don Cástulo had gotten married.

"Either my mind is beginning to go crazy or it's the world has gone mad and natural laws no longer rule," commented Doña Micaela. In another time her eyes were authoritarian and hostile to external reality. Recently they had changed to an expression of fright, combined with a shifting of melancholic anxiety. "The world is coming apart. Everything is going backward. Had you told me that oxen fly, that asses sing melodiously, that fish pull carriages, that the sun freezes, that the sea boils, that mountains are valleys, that wells are towers, that it rains up, that snow is black—well, I might believe it. Nothing surprises me now. But you told me that Don Cástulo got married, and with a big servant girl reputedly much younger than he and quite fat; he so tiny; he a wise Merlin, she a beast; and this I find hard to believe, it's beyond my comprehension. True enough with all his wisdom I always took him for something of an idiot and even a great deal of one."

"Micaela, you're unfair," said Leoncio, with affection in his voice. "I find Don Cástulo's marriage logical and praiseworthy in all its details. Insofar as the difference in age, I approve of it. What are twenty years of difference? Keep in mind that few are the men who at sixty are not as young as at forty, and very few the women who at forty are not as old as at sixty. In my opinion, the rule for figuring the right proportion between husband and wife should not be applied at the moment of concerting matrimony, but by calculating and looking at the years to come, the more the better; because matrimony is not the fact of the wedding, but a long life in common."

"I understand you, Leoncio. Your words martyr me, but I can do no less than subscribe to them. You and I are almost of the same age. You still are young; I, soon, will turn old," said Doña Micaela bitterly.

Urbano looked at his mother and observed that the white hairs of a few days ago had disappeared.

"I wasn't referring to our case, Dear," corrected Don Leoncio, confused. "There are exceptions. I was speaking of Don Cástulo. Don Cástulo, because of the life that he has always led, is like a young boy; he has conserved his youth. Besides, I am older than he."

"How good you are, Leoncio. You seek to smooth it over, so as not to offend me. Let's leave that aside. I accept that there is no disproportion in age between Cástulo and that extraordinary thing he has taken for a wife. But how about the difference in education, in background?"

"On that point, his good judgment in selecting her is still more obvious. He will have an ignorant wife, sure enough. What could be better? A woman who doesn't pretend to know more than he, who doesn't try to alter him, who listens to him as to an oracle. A woman of no education, without a doubt. What more can he ask for? A modest woman, without airs nor ambitions, faithful, submissive, whom he will be able to educate as it best pleases him."

"Don't throw it up to me! By God! Don't condemn me! The opposite of that ideal of wives that you picture have I been. That's what you mean. A presumptuous woman, domineering, prideful, insupportable. But, don't you condemn me. That woman has died. I myself have condemned her. Don't you see, Leoncio, that it's true what I tell you?" Doña Micaela's face reddened as it paled. Her voice broke. She broke into desolate crying.

"Little one, don't torture yourself with unfounded apprehensions," stuttered Don Leoncio, affected, getting up to caress Doña Micaela. "Do you think me so barbarous and gross that I might allude to you in that offensive manner?"

"No, Leoncio, you didn't mean to allude to me, I know that. You were carried away describing the model wife, just as you imagine it. You didn't intend to offend me, nor were you even thinking of me; I mean you weren't thinking of me with your head. But with your heart, without your wishing it, without your knowing it, you were shaping the longed-for woman (the one you might have wanted), as a type of woman in everything opposite to what I have been for you."

Don Leoncio stayed a moment, dumbstruck, mute. He was thinking, "Micaela has the gift of divination. She penetrates not only into my thoughts and even my intentions, but deeper, into crevices of my soul that I wasn't aware of until she shows them to me. Perhaps this is a gift of all woman. My mother was the same. And Don Leoncio felt himself filled with a kind of filial tenderness, of admiration and of remorse, toward his wife. He said, embracing her with gentle violence, "No, Micaela, no. From the day I met you I loved you, I admired you, and I put you on a high pedestal above all women. You are my wife and the mother of my son: a self-denying and faultless wife; a mother like no other ever was. No one surpasses you, nor has any husband ever felt for his wife an affection as pure as I feel for you. You must believe me, because I speak from the heart. I swear it." Don Leoncio considered himself perfectly sincere in his protests.

Doña Micaela also considered him sincere. But she did not feel satisfied with that so pure affection. This was what was making her unhappy at present. This is what she might have confessed to him now, drawing her face near to his own, had not Urbano been right there, in the way, like a dummy. Oh, what a son; he had not served for anything but to bring her griefs, including the excuse by which sometimes his father, taking his side, might oppose her! Now, hearing him chew, she became nervous and irritated.

Those tendernesses and endearments of his parents, a beautiful novelty in the home, caused Urbano, for his part, a very intimate and somewhat ambiguous pride. With a placid smile he said, "You have nothing to complain of, Mama."

"Who told you to stick your nose in? You're to blame for everything," Doña Micaela turned to say, shriveled and bitter. "While

231

we're on the subject; the days go by and there I see you, wool suit, thirty *real* boots, stupid and lazy, eating and sleeping, without making up your mind."

"Mama, I will begin to work right away. I've already hit on an occupation."

"I'm not speaking of that. I mean making up your mind on the religious order you must join. You said it; no one forced you; you gave your word. A man, if he's a man, keeps his word. As you know, matters have not been pursued, counting on your professing. If you go back on your word, like a little woman, I will be the one who sees myself pushed to carry forward the divorce proceeding."

Urbano lowered his head over the plate. During the rest of the evening, in the atmosphere there weighed a silence charged with magnetism.

The next morning, Doña Micaela being at mass, Don Leoncio, before leaving for work, called Urbano: "Come with me and we will talk along the way."

They went out together.

"You don't intend to become a monk, clearly," said Don Leoncio. Urbano assented with a nod. "It's not that I don't respect religious profession. I respect it too much. That's why I wouldn't like to have to respect a son like a venerable person. Now, if my father were alive and as an old man were to take a fancy to enter monkhood, I think I wouldn't mind it too much. But you . . . Don't think either that your mother especially insists on that. Your mother is very reasonable. By not contradicting her abruptly and persuading her with gentleness, she is won over and gives in to good sense. You'll remember how she was opposed in the beginning to my accepting a job in Velasco's store; three days later she herself advised me to accept it. She is all heart. I didn't know her, really know her, until now. I accept our catastrophe as providential, because after it your mother has showed herself just as she is. I explain it like this: the people most sensitive to the cold are the ones who put on the most clothing; well, in the same way, the most loving people, those

whose souls are most sensitive to the cold of unloving, are the ones
who most cover and wrap up and hide their feelings for fear of
falling ill from them. I know it from myself. Now then, there comes
a great catastrophe, a shipwreck, a bankruptcy, a fire, and all, down
to the most thin blooded escape without dressing; they are left without clothing and show themselves just as they are, forgetful of their
own selves—which is what has happened to your mother. Your
mother had formed for herself that rigid exterior as a defense, because she has a heart so very gentle and tender. With the blow the
poor woman has suffered, the hard crust broke open, and now all of
her comes spilling out in so much abundance that at times it makes
me worry." Urbano agreed with a nod. "You've noticed it too? I
hope that it may be a passing thing. Recently opened wounds bleed
copiously; then comes the slackening, a peaceful debility, and later
on convalescence. The poor woman is in a state that demands all our
love and also our tolerance. For example, at times she treats you
with abruptness. It is an involuntary reaction for which you must
pardon her. I'm sure you won't attribute it to lack of affection." Urbano nodded denial. "It's as impossible for a mother to stop loving
her son, not being crazy," here, Don Leoncio took a breath for a
brief instant; unexpectedly, a chill ran over his skin and he felt
weakness and as if the arm with which he was gesticulating dropped,
"as for fire to cease giving warmth and burning. What's happening
is that your mother has concentrated in you her whole life and all
her dreams. I don't know if those dreams were capricious and excessive; her highest intentions I answer for. The dreams have vanished. Perhaps at times, when your mother looks at you she sees not
you, she sees her failure, her pain is renewed, and she gives an in-
stinctive cry, like a wounded creature."

"Father, in that same way I explained it to myself, though not
as clearly as you have explained it to me."

"Your duty is to make her understand gently, sweetly, that no
such failure exists. It's not a question of deceiving her. No such

failure does exist. For her to have failed it would be necessary for you to have failed. And you have not failed, in anything, do you hear? in anything. Simona will be yours, in good time."

"I think that same thing."

"I am in my fifties, getting on, and I am beginning to live, in every sense of the word, my son, in every sense. Look at you at twenty. I want us to be friends, you and I, that you may confide your hopes and fears to me."

"Father, I've always taken you for a friend."

"And I, you; but we were silent friends. Let's be communicative friends. Tell me, concerning your marital situation, what do you think, what do you feel?"

"I feel as if all that went before was a chimera and that now I am in reality. I've just fallen in love with Simona, since my love is a quite new and different thing from the love of before. The new Urbano is a man unkown to her. I have to woo her, win her, and take her."

"I always said your marriage was premature. Of course your mother's project was perfect, marvelous; so marvelous and perfect that to be realized it would be necessary that the world and society be perfect, as your mother is so in her ideas. You mustn't nurse anger at your mother."

"I suffered a lot; much remains for me to suffer, but I recognize that all has occurred for the best."

"It seems that with my blood you've inherited some of my feelings and my beliefs, though I've always kept them to myself. That's my maxim: everything that occurs always redounds to our own good. Many times it becomes most uncomfortable to accommodate oneself to the veracity of this maxim. I say this for you, recalling your private interview with Señor Palomo, of which your mother informed me. On learning of it, my blood froze. When you were locked in your room, I wanted to enter, to embrace you, and to beg your forgiveness."

"Forgiveness, for what?"

"I don't know myself; but I felt that necessity. I was ashamed, with a spiritual shame; and I tortured myself imagining what you would think of your mother and of your father. You would despise us, with disgust perhaps." Urbano, very red, was going to speak. His father grasped his hand, squeezing it, and went on. "We're speaking as friends. Dissimulation eats away at and spoils friendship; it's like a worm inside a beautiful fruit. All of us, even those who have learned those things very young, gradually, unconsciously, in a way that they might not have to shock us or repel us more than any other act of life, nevertheless, on reaching the full knowledge of them, first off we've thought of our parents, with blushing and disenchantment. What will you not have felt, a full grown man, and, this notwithstanding, pure as an angel, when they placed you suddenly and without consideration before that fearful mystery, which is all the mystery of life? All right, even thus and all, it was the best thing that could happen."

"Yes, Father."

"I am of the opinion that men should learn those things from their father's mouth and women from their mother. I hold for my part, from intuition or presentiment (maybe I am in error), that even though women are generally held to be more modest than men, which is true—for if women do not protect themselves with modesty they are lost—in spite of this it seems to me that women, on learning the intimate secrets of love and of maternity, do not suffer the grave crisis of surprise, confusion, and shame that the news of this knowledge produces in man, or they suffer it in much lesser degree."

"Do you believe that, Father?"

"Women are born almost taught. Then, everything in them is like a preparation for love and maternity. Since girlhood, the very development of her body instructs her. A girl cannot become a woman without finding out, without losing in some manner her innocence. A man, on the other hand, become a man without his body proclaiming it scandalously; that's why a man with full beard and innocent as a suckling babe is not altogether improbable. But I don't conceive of a woman full grown and at the same time absolutely innocent."

"I don't understand you, Father."

"We will speak of this on another occasion, for here we are coming to the store. As to what I was saying, it's been terrible that you had to learn from a strange man that grave secret. Terrible that you mightn't have learned until now. Even so, that has been not for the worst, but for the best. Insofar as learning it with so much tardiness, doubtless your maturity of judgment will help you to understand it better and give it its true place in life. Unlettered though I am, I sustain that the standard and the manner of education in what pertains to love that, as much the Church as society, oblige us to accept, are bad, they are bad, they are bad. I wouldn't know how to tell you in what the badness consists or in what sense it could be reformed; but they are bad, they are bad, they are bad. They mention love to us, the Church the same as society, as the most beautiful, the most holy, the most sublime thing in life. What is love? we ask, fascinated. Nobody wants to tell us. Love, they reply evasively, is Love, as everyone knows. Then, one day we too come to know what love is. But we have to learn it secretly, whispering, with our heart pinched and our cheeks burning; because it turns out that love is a shameful, indecent, bestial act, which the Church and society reprove and persecute. How do we get out of this tangle? Love, word, empty word, is the highest. Love, act, incarnate love is the lowest. The Church and society only tolerate the hidden act of love, cloaked in sacrament and contract: matrimony. Only in this way is love clean and legitimate; any other way it is sin and crime. But the love act, the fact of love, is the same with matrimony as without matrimony. If a man is most purely in love with his girl friend, does he incur mortal sin and find himself outside the law as long as he does not marry? Come now, the Church and society do not take for love pure love but the fact of love. Now then, if a man and a woman make love in fact, without being married, the Church and society call her a prostitute, him a libertine. Notwithstanding, not by any other

236

manner do the husband and the wife make love. The Church and society wish that that very act, toward which they try by all means to inspire aversion and blushing in the worshippers and the citizens, they wish that these same citizens and worshippers not be repelled or be ashamed when it is made object of a sacrament and contract for them. Like one who says: to kill a man is criminal; but if the murderer has gone beforehand to declare before a notary and a priest that he has decided to murder, now that's different. In such a case the murder is a sworn oath before the Church and an agreement before the law; it is holy and it is legal. For let's not fool ourselves; the Church and society understand for matrimony that same act of love that without matrimony they characterize as the most vile and nauseating."

"Yes, Father; Señor Palomo said that that act is the essence of matrimony."

"Well, that is bad, that is bad, that is bad."

"It is bad."

"If some brew is an emetic, it will continue being emetic even though they serve it to me in a rock crystal glass which is engraved with the cross of the Redeemer and the arms of the king. I think, in my small understanding and limited knowledge, that, if from childhood the Church and society had suggested to us the idea that eating is a disgusting thing, we would wind up by not being able to support seeing others eat without our stomach turning over, and each one would eat alone in a private room. Now let us suppose that the Church and society were to add: exception, eating is a ceremonious act, devotional and civil, when a banquet is celebrated which the parson and the mayor attend. If we sat down at one of these banquets, we would avoid looking at the others eat, and on doing it we wouldn't be able to avoid having an intimate feeling of shame and uneasiness come over us. Is perhaps eating more shameful than making love? That will depend on who the one is who is eating and how he eats, or who the one is who makes love and how he makes love. Would you secretly revile your father if you saw him, once in a great while, on special occasions, drink and relish a good Bordeaux wine at a meal or a small glass of old cognac after dessert? Another thing entirely if your father were to fortify himself daily with strong tavern wine and aguardiente; this would then be vice and weakness."

"Of course."

"I can't make out why the Church and society make of love a dirty act, correcting the work of God almighty. God has wished that animals and rational beings be alike in the simple act of love. If animals are innocent, men will be innocent. Is there something ugly or repulsive in the love of two birds? For God's sake; it might be called a funny little game!"

"That's the way it seemed to me."

"True, in men love is not reduced to the senses, but is a divine feeling of the soul; and therefore it is sublime. But this does not mean that the love of the senses is indecent. I make a distinction, of course; it's one thing to say that the love of the senses in itself is not indecent and another thing to say that it cannot be abusive, vicious, vituperable, and disgusting, as is excess and lack of propriety in all human acts; eating with gluttony or eating rotten or bad-smelling things. God has disposed that the human species be preserved by means of the act of love; let us praise his will, with high and cheerful countenance, and not with bowed head and averted eyes, like guilty ones. But must we undertake to carry out strictly the will of God and not make love except to propagate the species, so that whatever isn't this we condemn and avoid as vicious love? In my opinion, just as in spite of the fact that we eat to live we also eat to eat, to enjoy a pleasure, and this, within moderate limits, no one is condemned for, so with love we can, with prudence, love love itself, the delight of disinterested love. Because in the final analysis, what purpose does God have in preserving the human species or would men have in propagating themselves if life were forlorn of all inoffensive delight? This is what is rational and not what the Church and society insist on imposing on us, whose dictates (let it be said between parentheses), except in this, in all else I praise and revere. Let them not come to me with 'it's always been so and so it will always be.' I once heard from Don Cástulo that the Greeks of old were not frightened of the act of love, but rather had, as celestial protectors of this act, nothing less than a god and a goddess, with numerous temples. Those Greeks might have been as pagan as you please, but no doubt among them matrimony would have more value, more spiritual value, than amongst us, and with no dregs of baseness, their considering in that society the act of love, even though without sacrament nor contract, as a beautiful action that the gods protected; with what praise and honor would not be crowned the fervent abnegation of a man and a woman who promised to each other, and were to carry it out: my love toward you is so great and in such a way grips all my person and powers that I surrender my will to you and will love no one but you for life! It becomes like the giving of alms in relation to the divesting yourself completely of all worldly goods. If giving alms is meritorious, to give away your entire fortune will be sainthood. But if you force me to characterize alms giving as immoral, how will you convince me then that total generosity with riches is not much more immoral and therefore monstrous? That makes no sense. No, it has not always been as now. It cannot continue being as now. Without going further into the Greeks, of whom I know extremely little and that by hearsay, let's look at what was taking place in our Spain in the epoch of her greatness, when, according to what they say, there was more religion than at present. In my boyhood I was very fond of the theater; I saw put on many works of Lope, Guillén de Castro, Calderón, Moreto, Tirso de Molina. Well my impression is that the Spanish men and women of that time made love outside of marriage with enough liberty. They used at times a most shocking language. For them the act of love was not a nefarious mystery, but a sweet and desirable thing, and the lads were not shy in proclaiming it, with frank detail, to the ladies. So you see . . . "

"Ay, Father! Why haven't we talked many times like this, friend to friend, before, since years ago?"

"Son, years ago I probably wouldn't have spoken thus, among

239

other reasons because I myself hadn't discovered most of the things that I've just told you. I repeat to you that everything happens for the best. In fifteen days, fifteen days of apparent misfortune, when I've inspired pity in everyone, I've acquired more experience and more understanding of life than in fifty years. I'm beginning to live, in all acceptations, my son, in all acceptations. I'm happier than ever. The only black cloud was you. Now, with the certitude that you do not feel despairing, but that in adversity you have found yourself, as I have done so, now I am totally happy. Well, goodbye. Give me a kiss."

The father kissed the son on the forehead and went in to work. The store clerks greeted him with respectful solicitude, moved by the sympathy communicated by the man who knows how to descend in position with equanimity and dignity; they asked after his wife, after his son, after the state of his health and feeling. When he was owner of his own business, the subordinates did not used to show him such respect and affection. From this angle he had come out ahead. To feel himself in a benevolent atmosphere was for Don Leoncio one of the elements of happiness. Another element, more important, consisted in having freed himself from worry about the morrow and from the sense of responsibility which used to torture and gnaw at him when he was owner of a business and the prosperity or decline of profits, as well as the well-being or privation of his family, depended exclusively on his business acumen and dealings. "We Castilians," he used to think, "are not great businessmen. We're no good at great enterprises, moneylending, ventures, and high finance. First of all, because we're too honest, if one can be too honest. Secondly, because the only thing that frightens us is responsibility." He preferred that the owner assume the responsibility of the business; he was more at ease as follower of orders, giving, in the carrying out of the orders and vigilance of the execution, all his care and honesty. Of course, he now earned much less than before, but he earned more than enough, now that Micaela had been taken by the fancy of enlisting in the ranks of the poorest of the poor, and *the other one*—what wonders life presents us with!—was refusing to take money from him; on the contrary, she was adamant that she had to give it to him. These two (Micaela and the other one) constituted the two prime factors in the present ventures of Don Leoncio. After a whole long conjugal life under the heel of a haughty, despotic, contemptuous, and insulting woman, when adverse circumstances had conjured to topple him in the dust of defeat, a worthless and washed up man, that woman, suddenly is changed into the most submissive, meek, sweet, and loving creature. Too loving perhaps. Don Leoncio, in spite of the daily diet of vexations chewed over in the shadowy silence of his heart, never had ceased loving his wife and admiring her; but owing to the absence over many years of amorous intercourse, because she declined (they slept in separate rooms), Don Leoncio had gone about distilling his affection toward his wife until he arrived at loving her as a father loves an unloving and insolent son, like a being of his flesh but not with an affection of the flesh—with a disembodied affection, the more constant when the more pained. Micaela herself dressed scrupulously to annul the external trace of sex, with austere, almost sacerdotal clothing, a flat hairdo and some girdles or corsets which flattened her bust. To where she had acquired a masculine countenance. Don Cástulo said that her profile was reminiscent of an Italian gentleman named Dante. The love which had been awakened in Micaela could not be —Don Leoncio tried to think—but a spiritual love, a passion of the soul. It was quite true that lately she had removed the harsh corset and, in spite of plainly weakening, her bosom, notwithstanding, stuck out in an inadmissible manner, as if it were artificial. Could such unexpected prominence be due to some malicious intention, to an attempt at seduction on Micaela's part? How gross! It was, evidently, that she had taken to dressing poor, without corset, and the long-compressed flesh was spreading out. Besides, in fifteen days of grief and great loss, Micaela had aged fifteen years. In the home

241

picture all was fine and dandy for Don Leoncio, though his wife's spontaneous amorous impetuosity did put him off a bit. Because his wife, since long ago, was not a woman, but wife and mother of his son, Don Leoncio had seen himself impelled to find another woman, a real and palpable woman. A woman who is not the legitimate wife, it is well known, does not accept an older man unless it not be for convenience's sake; and this class of women society brands inconvenient women. Don Leoncio protested against this mischaracterization: they are convenient and even necessary. Don Leoncio gave the other one all the money she asked him for in exchange for a little affection, though it might be feigned, on the very rare occasions when he could escape to visit her. Her name was María Egipciaca. Don Leoncio had had relations with her for several years. He did not delude himself that his lover loved him, but for self-interest. In his visits María Egipciaca showed herself amorous but without real fire. Don Leoncio satisfied himself with that cold erotic simulachre. Crushed continuously by the arrogant nearness of Micaela, dried and yellowed, he ceaselessly longed for the opportunity of enjoying himself in the presence of María Egipciaca, with her white plumpness of middle-age, which bewitched Don Leoncio, and her light and airy laughter, of a free and uninhibited female. Don Leoncio, one day, had discovered that María Egipciaca looked like Simona. A remote resemblance, hardly exact, and for this very reason disquieting. At first, this caused him a kind of moral repugnance. Then, his scruples quietened, thinking, "What's so strange about it? It's natural that preferences be inherited." At the time of the bankruptcy, Don Leoncio thought, "Now that I cannot give her money, María Egipciaca will not want anything to do with me. Those women are like that. They do rightly. They've not joined the Sisters of Charity." And this thought was one of the stimuli that put in his hand the suicidal Teutonic razor. Micaela being off on a trip in search of Urbano, María Egipciaca presented herself in the house of Don Leoncio. God, if some day Micaela found out about it! On the day following the dramatic scene of the wife prostrated

242

before the martyr husband, a second edition of the same—this time, the lover prostrated. But was it supposable that that abounding mountain of snow might enclose within itself a volcano? María Egipciaca's looks, gestures, and words had been volcanic. She swore eternal fidelity to Don Leoncio, "the best of men, and the most decent of lovers"; she insisted on giving him some thousands of *duros* that she had saved, since they were his—that is to say, they proceeded from his generosity. No little eloquence and even annoyance did Don Leoncio have to expend until getting her to keep the money again. After that day he had seen María Egipciaca a few times, and she kept up the same sweet tune. All of this was why Don Leoncio had declared to Urbano that he was beginning to live and that in fifteen days he had acquired more experience of life and more understanding of life than in fifty years. And what remained for him to experience and learn directly in those two living texts, the one of lean parchment folio—his wife—the other, massive oversized volume lined with white and silky velvet—María Egipciaca!

"The kernel of the fruit of happiness is of bitter taste," thought Don Leoncio, when, a short while after biting into and enjoying this fruit, he had already come across the accursed kernel. Doña Micaela worried him more and more. Don Leoncio couldn't quite decide if his wife was becoming seriously ill or if what she asserted she felt were apprehensions and quirks of imagination, disturbed by the shock and violence of the recently suffered emotions. Sometimes she said that her body had ceased having any weight and that she felt herself rising, like the reflection of the Argand lamp, toward the clear sky; other times, that her legs were sacks of sand and that she couldn't lift her foot from the ground. Now, she was suffocating, she reddened, she was becoming asphyxiated, she sweated; then, she paled, wrapped herself in a blanket, shivered, with a chattering of teeth. Somewhat unusual forms of pain attacked her which she described always with images from the Inquisition, associating her tortures with memories from a book, *The Dungeons of the Holy Inquisition*, which as a child she had read. "It's as if some executioners were tearing at my entrails with burning hooks." "It's as if they were pouring molten lead on my neck." "It's as if they were driving reeds between my fingernails and the flesh." "It's as if they were putting me on the rack; my bones are breaking, especially my hips. You can hear them crackle."

"They're not crackling, Micaela, nor do you hear anything. You're just imagining it. You must distract yourself," advised Don Leoncio, to whom the relating of those refined tortures made his skin like that of a plucked goose.

He won his wife away from her imaginings, encouraging her to distract herself, and the remedy was worse than the disease, because Doña Micaela, gazing at him with doleful and moistened eyes, replied, "My distraction is you, you, my medicine."

Don Leoncio's soul fell to his heels. In vain he closed his eyes to the truth. His wife loved him not as he had figured, with the heatless fire of ideal love, but with the combined spiritual and carnal love of a new bride for her husband. A debilitating and sorrowful pity overcame Don Leoncio; he held back the tears. He felt impulses toward pressing her closely against his breast, crying, like a lost child who is once again found. But this might have been dangerous; she would interpret it in accord with her desire. How could he make her understand and feel that he cared for her, yes, cared for her, but that he couldn't see her as a woman, but only as a lifelong companion, as mother of his son, as faithful and inseparable friend; further still, that if he were to see her as a woman, he would cease to care for her? Don Leoncio hid it from himself; but, before the idea that his wife might again become his wife, in the bridal chamber and all, he felt a physical repugnance. This repugnance, repressed to the dark regions of the spirit sometimes came out to the surface, transmuted into other kinds of sensations. On occasions, hearing the complaining of his wife, her voice sounded to him like stridencies of a metallic instrument; it scratched his ears and set his teeth on edge. But what most disconcerted and depressed him were the affectionate endearments of Doña Micaela. She had taken to gazing at the ruffled and curled hair of Don Leoncio, dedicating to it sweet conceits, lyrical blandishments, and voluptuous manipulations.

"I'd never appreciated your hair," sighed Doña Micaela. "How obtuse of me. I had a little veil over my eyes. Your shiny hair, capricious and curly, which seems to have a playful will of its own. Your hair, multiplied in a thousand curls, like the sea in a thousand waves, or like the hair of the Divine Shepherd in the church images. No; like the sea, like the sea; these silver threads are sea foam. Your hair gives off an aroma that goes right through me, like at the beach."

And Doña Micaela cautiously, affectionately insinuated her pointed fingertips into the roots of Don Leoncio's hair.

Don Leoncio bounded in his seat and groaned, "By the nails of Christ, little one! You know that I hate to go to the barber and at times my hair hangs down, like a Hottentot, because nothing terrifies me so much as their messing with my scalp, which gives me the willies."

"You don't love me! You don't love me!" muttered Doña Micaela, as if to herself, huddling up and retracting her slow, elastic, and tentacular hands inside her bulging shawl, in the manner of a snail.

"Yes, I love you, Micaela. You don't understand how much I love you."

"You love me and you don't love me. You don't love me as I want you to love me."

A shiver of the supernatural passed through Don Leoncio. He thought, "My wife sees inside me as if my ribs were the bars of a cage and my heart a frightened bird inside. And, nevertheless, she doesn't understand. Can it be that women have been granted the gift of loving, of loving more than us, but the gift of understanding has been denied them?"

"How I suffer! How I suffer!" monologued Doña Micaela, as if to avoid and at the same time secure that her husband hear her.

"First was hell. Long years of matrimonial life, in which this house was hell. It was hell, because I was the devil; I made the hell. And I found it to my liking, like the devil in hell, because I was the devil. God almighty has permitted that the devil save herself, not without passing through a long purgatory. I am in purgatory, which torments me more than hell itself, if it weren't for hope. I will ascend to paradise, I will ascend. The arms of my beloved await me, which is the light of the universe." She hardly moved her lips. Her voice drifted off, like a halo, about her Dantesque profile.

How she suffered! Her fixed obsession was centered on regaining Don Leoncio's sexual interest. Her repentance for her past life did not assuage her to the point where her conjugal life might not be restored in a renascence of the nuptials. She needed another child. A daughter perhaps; they would baptize her Angeles, symbol of those other angels that will revive the dead with their trumpets for the final judgment and will rescue souls from purgatory. But would there not now have faded for her the incentive with which woman attracts man? What she had never done, one night she examined herself in the mirror nude from the waist up. Her breasts, compressed so many years beneath the ferreous corset, had almost disappeared. And another detail more horrifying still: a cluster of rough hairs were standing out over her breastbone. Hair was also growing down from her jaws, in whiskers. Her bone structure showed under her skin. She went to a pharmacy on the outskirts of town to order some pills to enlarge her bosom and others to put on weight, whose advertisement she had read in the *Pilares Echo*. In the meantime, she repudiated the corset and stuffed her blouse with rags, confident that in a short while her own abundance would supply the fullness without Leoncio catching on to the temporary deception. The pills did not produce the advertised swelling. She blackened her white hairs, more and more numerous, with burnt cork in order to hide the whiteness. Doña Micaela began to have stomach pains. They gave her dizzy spells, during which the world of the invisible materialized for her. Many nights she forgot

herself, her naked torso staring in the mirror. She squeezed her
breasts distractedly from instinct, as if her body were a plastic mass
and she might model them, erect and mellow. One time that she
carried out this operation, she noticed that, on squeezing them, a
rosy liquor oozed out. She wanted to roll up her eyelids, in a gesture
of amorous ecstasy, thinking of her Leoncio; but the upper eyelid
did not obey, but stayed down and the eyeball almost exposed. Seeing herself in the mirror, she was terrified. She was fainting, and the
subtle phantoms, dissolved in the air, thickening, taking shape. She
saw before her her own self, but as a youngster, just married, and
she heard that the apparition was saying to her, "What are we dismayed for? You have not ceased to be I myself. You're as much a
woman as I am; you know that. That aurora of rose that flows from
your breasts announces the brightness of the day white and luminous as milk. You will have a child." Though a sickly timidity, accompanied by dizzying palpitations, took hold of her every time she
tried to come into the open with Don Leoncio, not as it were by
means of gestures, looks, and silent actions, she resolved that from
the next day on her husband would surrender to her. She tightened
the trap of seduction, with volleys of words, still not open, but
inflammatory enough.

Don Leoncio, intimidated, took the refuge of retreat to a second line of defense. This defensive position was found situated in
the domicile of María Egipciaca. Just as the bitter voice of Micaela
sounded to Don Leoncio of the stridence of metal, that of María
Egipciaca sounded to him of a tremulous and velvety stringed instrument. It seemed to him that it was a light, clear, and sweet voice,
like resin or caramel. It did his heart good, like putting your hands
in very hot water, when in winter you return home with them
frozen. But that fleshy and snow-white fruit hid its bitter kernel too.
It was a bitterness precisely opposite to that of Micaela; bitterness,
nonetheless. Micaela was thinning rapidly, and she was already thin;
María Egipciaca was putting on weight by the minute, and certainly she was fleshy. María Egipciaca's appearance was changing, losing

its feminine lines and coming to resemble an obese and effeminate man. Micaela had lost her appetite; María Egipciaca was ravenous. Don Leoncio feared that she was drinking. She excused herself, saying, "I'm not drinking, for I'm a high-born lady. Don't forget that my father was a magistrate. But unless I drink something and stuff my head a bit, I don't shut an eye all night long. Still, if you were at my side, what would not being able to sleep matter to me? But alone, I get sad and tearful." Doña Micaela's skin darkened. María Egipciaca's was no less white than the whitewash on the walls. Doña Micaela's hands were stringy and inflamed; María Egipciaca's plump, soft, cool, and moist. The thing in which the both were identical was in passion, contained and concealed in one, overflowing in the other. Don Leoncio loved Micaela more and more (or pitied her) as a wife, growing farther away from her at the same time as a woman. With María Egipciaca he became more and more fired up, and at the same time thought less of her with his heart. María Egipciaca's transports, progressively more frequent and extreme, were reaching the limit in Don Leoncio, with secret and serious worry, on his part, over his strength and health. "I didn't know what love is until now," sighed María Egipciaca to Don Leoncio with the softest breath, squeezing to the point of drowning him in her oscillating fatness. Don Leoncio kissed her mouth and throat, losing himself in a penetrating delight, which he had never dreamed of nor hoped for. Once, after kissing with unaccustomed ardor María Egipciaca's neck and all around her mouth, they were left scarlet colored; the coating of cream and rice powders with which her skin was plastered had become messed.

"But, little one," exclaimed Don Leoncio, put out, "why do you wear those oils and junk? What need do you have of them? Your skin is smooth and delicate as silk paper."

"Glutton!" replied María Egipciaca with ill-suited girlish modesty. "It's your fault, for gobbling me. I wear this (and I never wore it before, you know?) because around my lips and gorge I have a redness like from a rash."

Some of María Egipciaca's words (glutton, gorge, rash) grated most sharply on Don Leoncio. Why couldn't María Egipciaca speak the refined and beautiful language of Micaela?

"Woman, that bright red suits you. Now it can truly be said of your lips that they are like petals of fragrant pink."

"You mean that I have a snout like a tomato."

This of the snout and the tomato grated even worse on Don Leoncio. He thought, "How simple, how common; in spite of her being a magistrate's daughter. But I can't live without her. Why couldn't María Egipciaca and Micaela be fused in a single woman; the soul of the one and the exterior of the other? The fact is I cannot live without them, nor can I live with them."

María Egipciaca's assiduity was weakening Don Leoncio's body, especially in the knee joints. Micaela's assiduity was weakening his spirit and will. He had to put an end to that tension or he would wind up by falling to pieces exhausted. It was not a question now of a second retreat, but of a decororous flight, disengaging from the field until he might consider it well to return, from time to time. A decisive episode with Doña Micaela was what finally provided him with energy to free himself.

The cycle of summer was coming to a close. It was in the middle part of September. Sunday. Don Leoncio and Doña Micaela had lunched alone. (Urbano dined out often; sometimes with Paolo, sometimes with his tutor of old.) Doña Micaela was dressed as a workwoman, with varicolored sequins—an eccentricity that Don Leoncio respected as long as she didn't take it into her head to go out in the street in that costume.

"I have a plan, Leoncio. If you love me at all, you will do me this favor. I want us to go out for a walk together, to the village."

"All right, woman. That's a pleasure for me."

"Well let's go."

"But aren't you changing clothes?"

Doña Micaela went down on her knees, crying; for God's sake, let him grant her the pleasure of going out with him, dressed so.

They could go following solitary streets and get out into the country without anyone seeing them. If Don Leoncio didn't give in, she wasn't answering for what might happen; she wanted to distract herself; she could no longer hold back a secret anxiety; she feared she was going crazy. Don Leoncio, looking in her eyes, caviled, in his heart, suddenly pale: "Crazy? Micaela crazy?" He made his wife rise up, caressed her trembling; without speaking they went out together, arm in arm. Doña Micaela led. Don Leoncio let himself be taken, his body enervated, his will suppressed. As an old Castilian, Don Leoncio did not see in the country any more than the earth that gives us bread while we live, and gives us a grave when dead. Doña Micaela, who had always been cold and insensitive to the beauty of the world, found herself excited that day.

"I don't know, my Leoncio, how they can sing of and praise the spring so with its clashing green of growth and its insolence of shapes. The autumn truly is beautiful. How serene! How peaceful, how sad! Spring is a frivolous and brainless little girl. Autumn is a woman in love and unrequited. Her bones now show, which are the trees, almost bare. Certainly their showy leaves of youth have fallen; but in place of them they have fruits, fruits of gold. All is golden. The vessel of heaven seems full of intoxicating sherry wine. Let's sit here on the grass."

"Won't we catch a chill, Micaela?"

"You don't remember this place."

"No, to tell the truth."

"It's almost thirty years ago. It was also in September. I went dressed as now. Nothing has changed. Look all around. Nothing has changed. Do you see those spotted cows? They were right there thirty years ago. That bluish smoke which is rising from a roof is the smoke of then. Nothing has changed? Yes, something has changed; but it has been for the best."

"That's my maxim, Micaela: everything occurs for the best. That's why you should never get overexcited, nor lose faith in your-

250

self. Let the days go by. Time is the best ally. You'll soon see how everything occurs for the best."

"Something has changed," continued Doña Micaela, with her eyes very open, projected upon the infinite. "Then I was a frivolous and brainless little girl. Now I am a woman in love and unrequited. Then—do you remember?—you gave me the first kiss, which I, fool, did not want to return. You said, 'You're bad, Micaela. May God not punish you and one day you want to kiss me and I refuse.' Do you remember?"

"I don't remember, Micaela," stuttered Don Leoncio, dreading what he saw coming. What was Micaela thinking of doing? "If I said it, that would be childishness and joking. Forget that now, it's ages ago."

"Ages ago, God had readied for me the day of expiation. I do not flee from it; I desire it. Leoncio, I want to give you a kiss on the mouth!"

Don Leoncio felt as if his body was made of rag or of dry sponge. For some moments he couldn't articulate a word. He had his eyelids down, and, this notwithstanding, the flaming eyes of Micaela transpierced them; he felt them fixed on him. A panic came over him. From the very terror he gained strength to say, "Yes, Micaela dear; why shouldn't you kiss me? Why shouldn't I kiss you? Aren't you my wife? My sacred wife . . . "

"On the lips I say."

"Of course, of course, dear wife." And the muscles of his face tightened up in an agonized grimace, which he feigned to be a smile, like obedient children when they take a purgative.

Doña Micaela, thirsting, feverish, applied her lips, thin and tremulous, to the lips of Don Leoncio, enfolding him at the same time in her funereal arms.

"Leoncio, Leoncio," sighed Doña Micaela, "on your lips I perceive the taste of another woman's lips. Leoncio, you have kissed another woman. It doesn't matter, Leoncio. I want you to kiss me, I want you to kiss me, anyway; even if it be, if you can't any other way, closing your eyes and thinking of the other one."

Don Leoncio brusquely repelled his wife. Blessed God! He was going to offer a candle to the Christ of Succour as a sign of gratitude. At the bend of a road, a group of villagers appeared.

"Will they have seen us?" mumbled Don Leoncio, now serene. "Woman, those scenes should not be played in the open air. Pull yourself together and calm down. This is finished."

"I'm afraid so," replied Doña Micaela, in a gloomy cadence. And coming close to her husband, she whispered, "During the nights, alone, I see ghosts. My hair stands on end. An invisible hand strangles me. I get very afraid. One morning you'll find me dead from fright. I don't want to go on sleeping alone."

Don Leoncio, who understood, came forward to reply, "My poor Micaela. Why haven't you told me it before? That must be fixed up right away. From tonight on, the maid will sleep in your room."

"And why not you?"

"Woman, at this stage . . . What would Urbano think?"

"You're right. This is finished. It's my expiation. I don't reject it; nor do I receive it with disrespect. I'll drain the chalice to the dregs. I'll sweat blood. But you won't hear a complaint from me. Let nobody suffer for me. Simon, I forbid you to cut off the centurion's ears."

"Crazywoman!" thought Don Leoncio, and his own reason wavered.

That was when the liberating idea came into his head. The very next day, he would say to Antidio Velasco that he wanted to be a traveling salesman, even with half the salary, and in so doing, with the boxes of samples, wander through the towns of the province, to forget, to recompose himself."

"I was forgetting to tell you," said Don Leonico, feigning naturalness, "that now I am a traveling salesman; anyway, provisional traveling salesman. Sales are not satisfactory. Tomorrow itself, I'm undertaking a long inspection of our clientele."

Doña Micaela commented, "And you're leaving me alone with Urbano."

"With whom better than with your son?"

They returned in silence. Don Leoncio justified the flight to his own conscience, reflecting, "Is she crazy? I won't say completely, but she has symptoms. Am I to blame for this breakdown, for refusing to correspond to her love in the way she desires? Lord, this does not depend on my will. Most probably it seems that that kind of love, so extemporaneous, proceeds from the craziness. If we take away from her the cause of the excitation, the craziness will leave her; she will love me in the right way, and we will be happy again. The best thing is that I absent myself for long periods. I wish in my heart to see another twenty years gone by; she and I two little old people, with a warm ember in the heart but well covered over with ashes. By then we'll have already grown grandchildren. Lord, lord; what life is; an impatience for the morrow, a constant desiring of death."

Two days later, Don Leoncio went off on a trip, with his boxes of samples. Doña Micaela and Urbano remained alone in the house.

One day, at Simona's side (in the virginal septenary of his moon of gall honeymoon), Urbano, like those extraordinary twin fruits that are born and grow inside a single skin, had seen himself as split into two men, without detriment to the unity of his person— one, the external man, active and practical; the other the spiritual man, discursive and analytical. Both men had now found incessant occupation. The practical man was constantly on the go. Urbano had several lessons daily. His students were boys little younger than he. To give them the lessons, he had to study them beforehand himself—to study them, scrutinizing their meaning, and not in the previous manner, when he learned them mechanically and then recited them by rote, as if they were paragraphs in Coptic or in Salmuk. What joy, to go about learning and informing himself of the present and the past—to relate things with concepts and concepts between one another; to correct a maladjusted or rather, unjust, concept, trying to accommodate it to reality; and to correct a noxious and blind reality inscribing it in a precise concept! "Truly," Urbano would declaim, "men ought not to begin their academic studies until the age of twenty, for not until then do love of study and comprehension come into play." Urbano did not study only in treatises; these provided him only with suggestions and concepts, geometric notions, the profile of things; he studied life with his students, who by virtue of the parallelism of age with the young teacher had not been slow in making themselves his friends and confided to him all their eagerness and experiences. Each hour that went by was for Urbano like the rapid turning of the pages of a Cabalistic book.

Aside from those of his disciples, two other closer friendships occupied Urbano—one that of Don Cástulo, the other that of the centaur Paolo. Don Cástulo had been his teacher and had not taught him anything—that is to say, that is what Urbano had believed until now, that Don Cástulo had not taught him anything but superfluities, poetic quotes, classical phrases, episodes of faraway and long, long ago, worthless scraps. How wrong Urbano had been! Now that he was going about feeling with impatient hands the muscular and untamed body of daily reality and that he realized its tumultuous dynamism and its ugly and cruel movements (Urbano compared reality with a tough colt that everyone vaingloriously hoped to be able to mount; quickly the savage creature hurls them down and drags them, their foot stuck in the stirrup, until breaking their necks; few are those who maintain themselves some time on her back), now was when Urbano understood the high mastery of Don Cástulo and his incomparable teachings: delicate sentiments, purity of intentions, love of beauty, disinterestedness in thoughts, cult of intelligence, elegance of spirit. Perhaps these teachings—more exemplary than expressed—of Don Cástulo were not worth anything in themselves; but neither was daily reality in its own right worth anything, but on the contrary was, though fascinating, odious. The problem consisted in applying those norms of Don Cástulo's to the exercise of integral and crisp daily reality. Here, Urbano employed another metaphor: "as they say, to dominate the tough colt and ride with head held high." These metaphors of equitation were due to the friendly contagion of Paolo. Paolo was a most vigorous horseman. He never spoke, unless it was of horses and schools of riding. As much as from the scholarly texts, from his pupils' confidences, and from the example of Don Cástulo, Urbano learned from Paolo's silence. He learned from him patience and hope. Paolo was a submissive son. His mother was still alive; she always called him "little one" (and Paolo was now going on sixty). For nearly forty years he had had a girl friend, whom he had loved imperturbably. The mother had opposed marriage, because the girl was from a humble background. And Paolo was waiting with patience, without his love wearing thin. "If you lose patience," said Paolo to Urbano, "you dominate neither a horse nor do you dominate your own feelings; they dominate you. If you lose patience, you break your head, you mistrust yourself; a lost man." This is where Urbano's equestrian images came from. Urbano did not lose patience. Much the reverse; the days went by and Urbano was astounded by their rapid course, thinking, "As these days have gone by months and years could go by, and one day I may be surprised to find that I have stopped loving Simona. That, no. Simona is in me, is my soul." And at this border of feeling began the hegemony of the interior man. He recalled the phrase from Spinoza which had affected him so much when for the first time he trembled on touching Simona's body: "soul, idea of its body." His own soul was the unforgettable idea of Simona's body. There still remained on his skin the indelible impregnation of Simona's body; he still felt her forming part of himself, as amputees feel the missing member present. And he waited without losing patience.

In Urbano's relations with his mother, the interior man had started out by getting into a comfortable posture; then he had straightened up into a noble and abnegated attitude. All those who acquire a new faculty tend to abuse it. The faculty of interior analysis recently manifested in Urbano, he subtilized and twisted it according to his inclination, in a kind of egoistic casuistry, thinking to himself, "When my mother loved me excessively she succeeded only in vexing me, belittling me, and making me suffer. Now that she doesn't love me—it's clearly apparent—it seems that she provokes me so that by reaction I feel master of my own self, and this makes me feel good. There's a kind of psychological law of compensation. But analyzing it more deeply, this hidden and hypocritical good feeling, will it not be a vindictive feeling, an instinct of reprisal? She made me suffer, I make her suffer; eye for eye, tooth for tooth. Will that supposed psychological law of compensation be simply the old and brutal Talion law? Do we still carry in the cavern of our breast the primitive, stupid, and sanguinary man? Evidently. Oh, what happiness to discover him, to know him! For inasmuch as a thing is known, it is likewise dominated. The only thing not dominated is mystery. Now I have you, bound and immobile, cavern-dwelling beast, father of base feelings. I will not let myself be dominated by these feelings. I will dominate them, since I know them. And with what simplicity I have triumphed. It seems to me that if we might always verify how the mechanism of the loom functions with which our soul weaves its dreams, its illusions, its greeds, its hates, its insults, its envies, its vanities, its jealousies, and its fears —the greater part of conflicts of conscience would disappear. The soul weaves deceitful tapestries, with figures that seem real, and they astonish us or frighten us; if we might see them from behind, the astonishment and the fright would cease."

And he began to love his mother with a new love, refined and conscious, love from the heart and love from the intellect. "What is the greatest treasure in life?" he reflected. "Life itself. I'm alive; I'm a living creature. What a treasure! What a proud thing! What a marvelous enthusiasm to feel and know oneself to be alive! Even pain itself, the most intense pain, is a frenetic trumpet call with which man proclaims his victory and prerogatives over dead nature, which does not feel, and brute nature, which does not know. Never

256

is man more lofty or more alive than when he feels and knows he
suffers; when he experiences a live pain. And who has granted me
this treasure par excellence, treasure of treasures, treasure unique
in the universe, life? You, Mother dear. If I were full of sores and
diseases, hated by women, abhorred by men, in a prison without
light with a black crust for food and a jug of putrid water for drink;
even thus and so, for being alive—and he who says life, says hope—
I would undo myself in love, tenderness and gratitude toward you,
Mother dear, who gave me life. Though you were the vilest woman,
infamous to good people, run through the streets and stoned by the
wicked, condemned by justice to garrote as a criminal, I would
love you the same; I would love you more, infinitely more, in shame
and in disgrace; and I would offer my life to the judges in exchange
for yours, telling them, with pride and vainglory: there is no other
woman on earth like this one; this woman is my mother; I want to
die for her; my action has no special merit; I'm not doing anything
but returning to her what she has given me—life. Though you
might hate me and mistreat me, in word and deed, I would bow my
head, I would kiss your hand and would murmur in my heart:
thanks, Mother dear, thinking of the life that you have given me.
Before, when you loved me and made me suffer, I rebelled silently
against you. Now, I want you to make me suffer more, more, more,
in exchange for the ceasing of your sufferings; I don't know what
they are, but I clearly see that they are killing you."

In spite of these vehement sentiments, when Don Leoncio told
him that he was remaining alone in the house with his mother, Urbano couldn't help feeling terrified. At their first meal together,
Doña Micaela said, "Urbano, are you afraid of me? The day before
yesterday I said to your father, let nobody suffer for me. And I am
one of those people who keep their word. Fine; without wanting to,
now I am making you suffer. You will think it's been an allusion to
some remark you made to me out of turn. I haven't meant badly.
The phrase escaped inadvertently. I've been born gifted with a rare
talent, you know, the talent of knowing how to annoy people. I

assure you that this is a very rare talent. How men might wish for it! Then, I exercised this talent so much even without noticing and against my will, I put it into practice, as out of habit. But, as I've already told your father: It's finished, let's be friends."

"Yes, Mother," replied Urbano, kissing Doña Micaela's hand at length.

In meditation one morning in the church of Pendueles (three days married; Simona, on her knees, was not far from him), Urbano had verified a discovery about the world and men; all grownups grow old without ceasing to be children; the only person (he had thought then) without admixture or touch of childishness, who was so perfectly—unfortunately!—was his mother; she didn't seem to have ever been a little girl. He followed his train of thought: Will there not be perhaps reserved for her a complete and late childhood?"

Urbano remembered those thoughts now, observing his mother sinking by moments into puerility, at the same time as by moments she grew old. From the middle to the end of September, she was transformed. Her hair turned absolutely white; her skin, almost black, furrowed in innumerable wrinkles; her neck, swollen; her eyes exalted and staring. Dressed as a workwoman, her hands behind her back, she walked all day long the length of the corridor with great strides. Entire days, she did not open her lips; other days, from dawn until going to bed, there came from her throat a stifled and burbling noise, like the warble of a rather unmusical bird; and from time to time, she broke into an innocent smile. To Urbano she said, "Ay, little bouquet from my womb, little bouquet of sweet-smelling plants! Where are your flowers? Flower, flower. Thyme and rosemary; sage and lavender; chamomile and mallows; *yerba-luisa* and laurel. Lord, I want it; Lord, I beg it; Lord, let them bring the rose bush; Lord, the rose bush beneath the laurel. With my tears I will water the garden. My life I offer up in holocaust; Simon, do not cut off the centurion's ears."

Before her son, Doña Micaela kept up a blissful smile. Urbano's heart was lacerated. Only the certainty that his mother was living now in a state of happy beatitude consoled him. She had ascended to paradise, finding herself still in mortal flesh. He caressed her like a little girl.

"This is my little girl, my beloved little girl," murmured Urbano, kissing his mother's white head.

"Ah, silly one! Little girl, you say to me; the little girl is you. The little bouquet flowered. They brought the rose. The angels brought it. They ingrafted it in the laurel. Angeles the angels said I should call you. The trumpets of judgment are playing a *muñeira.** I danced so much with the priest's housewife."

From that time on, Doña Micaela asserted that Urbano was a little girl, Angeles by name.

Urbano couldn't keep his mother company very often. He was very occupied with his students' examinations and the final arrangements of Don Cástulo's academy, which would open at the beginning of October under the rubric of "The Grove of Athena." The real goddess who presided over the destinies of this incipient grove was not the daughter of Zeus, but Conchona, ever resourceful. She had directed and disposed it all, with insuperable economic thriftiness, comfort, cleanliness, and simple good taste. The academy was installed in a large old house, most majestic and well suited to the purpose; in the rear, a beautiful garden for recreation. They were already counting on twenty boarding students, at a fee of twenty *duros* per month, and more than forty nonresidents. Don Cástulo had wanted to adorn the refectory and the classrooms with classical plaster casts of nude Venuses. But the subtle Conchona made him face this practical dilemma: either to have the academy full of statues in the raw and without one student or to have it full of students and without one statue. Don Cástulo had replied, "You're right, my sharp Conchita. It makes me ashamed to live in these times; but, you're right. We will exile immortal beauty from this grove. Never-

* A lively Galician dance.—Tr.

theless, let us avoid extremes, which are vicious always. You've said without one statue; that, no. One I will have, in my office: the Aphrodite of Melos. And if the priggish papas of my pupils are scandalized and withdraw their favor from me, off with them. I prefer not having a single student to living without a single conviction."

Urbano desired that Don Cástulo might return to visit Doña Micaela: "Inform her of the forthcoming opening of the academy. She will be distracted, listening to you. She will be cheered up by your good fortune. She has always loved you. She had a mania for you."

"And I have loved her, and I do love her. Look, Urbano, your mother is the most admirable and extraordinary woman that I have known; more even than Conchita (who is present here), and it is as much as I can say. Conjugal love does not blind me. Conchita possesses in the highest degree all the common, homely virtues; for proper woman, an archetype. But the qualities and talents of your mother, her character above all, are of such that appear on exception in fragile human clay. In other ages, your mother might have become a queen, an empress, a popess. And not to speak of if she were born a man. For all of which your mother frightens me. After so many years of being like one of the family, I have escaped selfishly; I haven't given you any part in the wedding, I haven't gone back there. If she sees me now . . . I don't want to think about it."

"My mother is not the woman you have known. You are going to be startled by and feel sorry for the sad condition to which she has descended. She's an innocent creature, all sweetness and timidity."

"Go, lordyship, go; it's an act of charity," pleaded Conchona, passing her hand over the back of Don Cástulo's head.

"Let's go, Urbano. Conchita, give me my hat."

"But are you going to go out like that?" asked Conchona, arms akimbo.

"Like what? What's the matter with me?"

"Without buttoning up your pants," mumbled Conchona, very red.

"Heavens!" cried Don Cástulo, extremely embarrassed, repairing the carelessness. "It's an absentmindedness (unsociable, low, I know it) into which I have slipped frequently since I was a little boy. As I grant so little importance to dress and to good appearance . . . .Urbano can tell you that this used to happen to me frequently.

Micaela reproached me for it and Don Leoncio laughed. I also wore my tie twisted and the cuffs of my shirt without links, which, thanks to your provident and solicitous hands, no longer happens to me now."

"It's true, Concha," confirmed Urbano.

"Don't I know it. Didn't I myself, though it may be wrong for me to say it," lowering her eyes, "notice that carelessness on several days, when you came to Doña Rosita's house. But, now, married, it's different. What will people think? And if the students see him like that? They would lose respect for him."

"I will correct myself, Conchita. Well, goodbye. Give me a kiss and excuse me."

Doña Micaela received Don Cástulo with manifestations of infantile happiness.

"Cástulo, Cástulo," said Doña Micaela, laughing brightly. "You return, as the years come round. How many years, how many years. Do you remember? We were children. We used to play under the arches in the market square. Did you know that I've had a little girl? Angelines; here she is. Now you will stay with us. You'll be my daughter's nursemaid. We'll put an apron and cowl on you. You've always been a little bit of a ladybird. Good, let them prepare your room for you. You're staying here; I won't let you leave."

Don Cástulo listened to her with mourning in his spirit. His tongue hardly obeyed him, on replying, "Micaela; I will come to see you often. I cannot stay, you know? because . . . Forgive me that I haven't told you about it beforehand . . . I am married."

"Ah, yes! I was forgetting. And who is your husband?"

"What do you mean, my husband? You mean my wife Micaela."

"I don't mean your wife, but your husband."

Don Cástulo kept silent. His heart gave a wrench. He had always been sincere and courageous inside himself, in his cogitations and examinations of conscience (the only way in which he wasn't a coward). He thought now, "Exceptional woman; even in her madness and unreason a prophetic breath inspires her. Coming right down to it, is Conchita not the husband and I the wife?" To not contradict Doña Micaela, Don Cástulo replied, "My husband, Micaela, is an almost perfect man."

"I don't doubt it; it's easier to find a perfect man—look at my Leoncio!—than a perfect woman. Don't think that men, as a general rule, are more perfect than us in what's pertinent to the soul, no. We, in soul, are more perfect, as more limited. The imperfection is of the body. That which men call our perfection, having a woman's body, and all the servitudes with which the body of woman is marred; that is our imperfection, to such a point that at times the imperfection of our body spoils the perfection of our soul. How badly made is the body of woman. Just look at birth, what a mess. Are you going to give birth, Cástulo? When are you giving birth?"

Don Cástulo listened to her half fascinated and half appalled, as if she were a creature beyond the ordinary realms of the spirit, whom he reputed insane and genial at the same time. It was too hard for him, even if it were following the whim of a crazywoman, to answer the last question, allusive to what for him represented the greatest emotion of his life.

"Answer me," Doña Micaela insisted, supplicatingly, almost tearfully.

"Within eight months," responded Don Cástulo, dizzied, with an imperceptible gasp. Oh, God! That secret emotion of becoming a father, which he conceptualized as the most sublime ("a father's heart is the masterwork of Nature," he remembered having read, someplace), a petty thing it was compared to the continual emotion, growing, intimate, wearying, and painful in which the mother is totally absorbed over the long period from when she conceives until she gives birth to the child. This Doña Micaela had made him feel, more than understand, by virtue of her mental aberration, now, in a kind of physical suggestion. Don Cástulo added in a steady and sad voice, "Don't talk that way, Micaela; the body of woman is not imperfect except when one wants to employ it in that for which it has not been created. There are no things on earth that man mistreats so much as wheat, the grape, flax, and woman. Man uproots them from the place where they are born and grow, drags them on the ground, deprecates and humiliates them, steps on and cudgels them, shreds and annihilates them in order to adorn his house and enjoy them in the form of bread, wine, clothing, and children, as all the sensual blessings of existence are circumscribed in eating, drinking, making love, dressing up, and lying down. Man makes sons, makes cloth of thread, makes wine, and makes bread; but bread goes on being flesh of the wheat, wine blood of the grape, the purity of thread purity of flax, the son flesh, blood and purity of the mother. What has the father put into him? Bread is holy and consecrated. Holy and consecrated let woman be, above all things. In the sacrifice man celebrates, as homage of gratitude to the gods, paying them selfish homage, because they preserve for him the happiness of living, the altar is dressed up with cloth, wine is libated, bread is blessed; and woman is the propitiatory victim. A saintly destiny, that of the woman!"

"Did you take me for a crazywoman, Cástulo? Way off. I'm not crazy. I listen to you openmouthed. You speak the truth, as if Solomon were whispering in your ear. A saintly destiny that of the woman! Cursed is the woman who makes an enemy of her destiny. I applaud everything you say minus your speaking of God in the plural, an old and funny mania of yours. The gods . . . as if they were kidney beans or chestnuts, which never are used in the singular (I

263

love kidney bean; I'll take chestnut), because in the singular they have different meanings. But, anyway, don't cut off the centurion's ears, Simon."

All of this chat had been peripatetic, Doña Micaela and Don Cástulo pacing up and down the corridor, as interlocutors; Urbano, as listener, was filled now with an urge to laugh, now with pathetic emotion, now with bewilderment, now with meditative preoccupation.

At the end of the dialogue, Doña Micaela did not forget to pronounce the obligatory invectives against riches. Don Cástulo left very removed from his old feelings. He promised to return to visit his childhood friend frequently.

FULL MOON

Fairy tales are half truth and half falsehood. The sad part of fairy tales contains a truth of everyday experience, a vulgar truth; the marvelous part, we all know, is a falsehood, but it is a sweet falsehood, more beautiful and salutary and, in short, more true than truth itself.

One bumps into sad fairy tales at every turn, in wood-cutters' huts, in sailors' cabins, in lighthouse-keepers' lodgings, on pilgrims' pathways, in the atriums of churches, in the garrets of cities, in the cellars of palaces, all over.

That house, off away from the others, at the end of the street, surounded by a garden uncared for and full of refuse, painted in a bile or wormwood green color, held within a sad fairy tale under way. From the windows there always hung out to dry blouses of scandalous colors, petticoats and ribbons; on occasion, some large women, tall and skinny, leaned out with frowning witch-like countenances, their faces very painted up, their hair very spongy and full of little bows; often, from within were heard broken and quarrelsome cries, bickering. Along the roof there sometimes glided a cat black and shiny, as of tar, and a cat white and fluffy, as of cotton. The smoke that rose from the chimney was almost reddish, like sulfur smoke, weaved in a subtle plume and traced oracular signs on the blue atmosphere.

In that little house Simona was locked away. Her guardians were the seven old maids, sisters of the clergyman who constantly accompanied, as chaplain, Simona's mother. In Regium, where they lived, it was whispered, as a most certain thing, that the clergyman had gotten a great deal of money out of the widow and that he was one of those most responsible for her ruin. The seven sisters had been menials; now they dressed like belles. They lived previously in a poor nook, now their own house. Fewer and fewer people had anything to do with them, since, because of all of this, they were highly discredited. Because of all of this, but above all because they were ugly, antipathetic, presumptuous, testy, and envious, though they might not be to blame for having been born thus nor for the deeds of their younger brother. It seemed that the very devil had baptized them, with Christian names, because this was unavoidable, but selecting from among them the most unfortunate in the calendar of saints; three which stand, alike, for a male as for a female, Práxedes, Leónidas, and Onofre; two, which sounded like drugstore poison, Arsenia, and Sulforiana; one, which sounded like a torture, Trifona; one which sounded like a crime, Degollación. Beginning right from consecration and baptism, the seven sisters were furious with all that happened to them. A thousand times they attempted to make some arrangement in their names, as they did with dresses, shawls, and bonnets, and adopt a gentile diminutive; but those cursed personal labels had no possible correction. They were indelible; they were the evil eye. They couldn't figure out if people laughed at them because of the name or if the name seemed queer because they bore it. "Because," said Arsenia, who was the most rationalistic one, "is there a more funny sounding name than Cleopatra? And nevertheless they say it's very pretty, very poetic and I don't know what else. All because when you hear Cleopatra you think of a very beautiful woman, queen besides, and above all, harlot. If Cleopatra had been called Trifona or Práxedes they would find it pretty too. If we were happy grand princesses, they would put our names in verse. If I were named Simona, they would laugh at my name all the same. That sniveling brat is so named and all account it a sweet and beautiful name. Believe me, sisters, men are idiots."

Upon the widow's ordering them to collect Simona, they were happy, calculating that she would pay them a good fee to keep the daughter as a guest and take care to have her well guarded. Doña Victoria had written to Práxedes, the eldest: "By a telegram from a close friend I am informed that Simona's husband has abandoned her, as soon as he learned of certain financial setbacks that have befallen me, thinking me without doubt ruined and out in the street. He and his family are rabble, ill-begotten, shameless creatures and swindlers, who passed themselves off as rich and laughed at me with lying promises. When they find out that I am not about to go begging—thank God!—that thankless and lazy boy will want to live with Simona once again and that I support them. By no means. I trust in your knowing how to avoid this danger. There are seven of you to keep an eye on her." Of money with which to pay for this service, the widow said nothing. The old maids considered that it was superfluous to make mention; as understood, it was not discussed. They were not going to accept a charge and a responsibility for free.

They went for Simona. They made every effort to bestow endearments on her and to say sweet things to her; but these were simulated endearments and hypocritical sweet things, as in the fable of the wolf who wanted to seduce the lamb in order to devour it. Their hearts were embittered with jealousies and hatred. They, so dried out and bony; Simona, so white. They, thistles; Simona, a violet. They, getting on, and still without boy friends; Simona already married, a mere child. "Heaven," "precious one," "dawn of spring," "garden in bloom," "moss rose," "valley of Eden," "work of art," the seven old maids, Práxedes, Leónidas, Onofre, Arsenia, Sulforiana, Trifona, and Degollación said to her, with a twisted grimace, running over her head and back, as in a caress, their hands, which hooked nervously with impulses of scratching and wishing, in the shadow of their hearts, that they might give her smallpox. They did not even have the consolation that Simona despair over Urbano's abandonment and absence, try as they ceaselessly did to bring it about with perfidious words. "Poor martyr," they sighed, counterfeiting gestures of compassion and feeling pleasure deep inside, "sacrificed to a villainous and most cruel man. A two-legged hyena, that one is. He was just after your money. Believing you poor, he escaped tail between his legs. You do well in hating him. He causes you much pain; you want to forget him and you can't. You will be a long time in uprooting his memory from your soul; a sharp thorn. Patience, precious one, patience. If only he might die. You would be free. You needn't lack for another husband; if not now, after some years. You're too young. The best thing happened to you. What were you doing, married to a man like that? Good fortune that he showed his hand. Like a robber dove, he'd be bold enough to return, if he knows that your mother still has cash. You'd hide yourself from him and despise him, right, my dove? And if you were to weaken, since, as so young you perhaps are credulous and simple, remember what your mother says. Read again these lines in her letter. She empowers us as your guardians. If he comes like a hawk, here we are, seven hawks. Just in case, it's as well that you don't go out of the house. Sad for you; how sorry we are for you. What are we going to do? Don't stop crying on our account. Cry as much as you want, for crying is a salve." And they were gnawed at and enraged inwardly, seeing that Simona far from crying smiled angelically. Simona was not afraid of them or of anyone. Against all malignant enemies she knew some words that destroyed witchcraft, and she carried in her breast a talisman—the words of her grandmother ("you will blaze again in the same hearth") and Urbano's letter. Simona smiled, and the old maids, raging within, thought up new poisonous phrases in order to irritate her in some way. "We aren't putting a mirror in your bedroom, lest you be frightened. For the same reason, we have our rooms well locked. Ay, heavenly one, we don't want you to despair or be alarmed! You're wasting away. You're growing almost ugly. What is called pretty, you never were; but youth and healthy colors supply beauty. You've lost your good color. We can tell you and it's not necessary that you look in the mirror and frighten yourself." In truth, closed up without going out in the air, Simona's complexion grew daily more milky, her lips more scarlet, her coppery hair a more polished tone, her jet black eyes more shining: she was more beautiful. The seven old maids went on exasperated: "How you will miss the days of wedlock! Tell us, marriage, is it something rich? Did he used to kiss you a lot? Ah, scoundrel! What do kisses taste like? How was your tongue left, sweet or bitter? When he embraced you, what did he say to you? Did it give you a tickle when he took you? I bet it did. And now, sleeping alone, like a widow. And still you complain, you who had a taste of it?"

These questions wounded and disconcerted Simona; but she didn't let it show. She smiled always. The seven old maids then whispered, in conventicle: "She's a sluggard. Cool as a cucumber. Don't you believe it. She expresses one thing, hides another. Trickiness, much trickiness that little one has in her noggin. Didn't you see the perverse smile, the mocking eye? In that she takes after her sly lizard of a mother, whom I could never fathom, in spite of our brother. She's laughing at us, it's plain to see. She'll get back at us later." The seven old maids, who always had been at loggerheads before Simona's arrival, had united now in a common feeling of aversion and of envy toward their prisoner. All their preoccupation, during their whole life, had consisted in hunting for a boy friend; with the presence of Simona, this preoccupation was exacerbated to the extreme of frenzy. They had a Catalan San Antonio de Padua (because the image was manufactured in Barcelona), advocate of single women without boy friends, at whose feet they burned night and day seven little oil lamps, one for each sister; then the little lamps were fourteen, then twenty-eight, and so on in geometric progression, as if, in a blind desire of making up for lost time, the seven old maids unconsciously aspired to polyandry. When not some, then the others, spent long hours in church, making vows and offerings to the Virgin, to Saint Joseph, and to the Child, so that he might grant them a boy friend, even if he were third rate. Apart from this attempt at mystical bribery, they gave themselves up to other superstitious practices—consulting cards, making auguries with birds and particularly guessing the future according to the behavior of the two cats. The black cat was named Barrabás; the white one, Lohengrín. When Barrabás went out on the roof to howl amorously, he predicted "dark man"; if Lohengrín, "blond man." The first lap the cat jumped into after his prediction signified that that was the one predestined for the "blond man" or for the "dark man." All the seven old maids competed in feasting Lohengrín and Barrabás, in winning their favor, so that, returning from the roof, he might jump first into their lap. When this happened, the chosen one for a month would devour with her eyes as many blond or dark men, according to the oracle, as she saw in the street or in church. To no avail. But the old maids did not despair. From the time Simona came into the house, Barrabás and Lohengrín took a fancy to her and the two fought to cuddle up purring in the girl's skirts. This was all that was lacking to fill the seven old maids to the brim with ire. "What is your husband like?" they asked Simona. "Blond or dark?" Simona replied, "Neither blond nor dark." "He must be like a zebra," commented Trifona, who was the one who dominated all the others through her despotic character and her talent for sarcasm.

A month went by and Doña Victoria did not send any money. And then a second month, also of nothingness. The seven old maids joined in conventicle, whispering, "It's plain that the widow's not parting with a red cent. She must imagine that it's our duty to take in and warm to our bosom that viper. She thinks perhaps, though she doesn't say it, that our money is hers. Hers? To me it doesn't matter where my money proceeds from. My brother gave it to me, who's a priest, and he wasn't going to steal it. A little or a lot, the money is ours and ours sure enough. Don't fume. Who will dare to say otherwise? I'd put my hand in the fire that now the widow freeloads and at our brother's expense. He's a Milquetoast and so loses out. Don't be critical; let's come to the point. A pretty predicament befell us with the young girl. The lesser of two evils; let her work and she'll earn what she eats. We'll save on a maid." From that day on, Simona worked for the seven old maids. They hoped that she might rebel or at least lament her fate. Simona, with smiling sweetness, said, "My pleasure is to work. Teach me to do things right; correct me if I don't get the knack. I want to learn to be very much woman of my own house."

It was rumored in Regium that the seven old maids shamelessly took advantage of money not their own, garnered sacrilegiously by their brother, and that, of still greater abomination, they kept imprisoned and starving the one who ought to be the legitimate possessor of that money. Everyone left off having anything to do with the old maids. Even the sexton of the church of San Tirso turned his head and made as if he did not hear them when they spoke to him—an understandable phenomenon, because coming out of the aforesaid candle extinguisher's ears were thickets hairy as hanks of horsehair. Life was made impossible for them in Regium. One morning they found that during the night the facade of their house had been pelted with cow dung. Other days, there appeared defamatory signs, written in brushstrokes with indelible tar that ran. The old maids avenged themselves for these affronts by discharging their fury on Simona. They insulted her with wrath. In this situation a stranger presented himself, who sought to rent the house. Degollación, who was the most astute and had ideas of oriental fiendishness, proposed: "God, who will not suffer seeing innocence persecuted, is our ally. Let's rent the house. Shall we not take the encumbrance of Simona with us? Let the widow help us by pitching in. Nobody cares much for us here. Let's go to a big town, where we aren't known. Pilares is just the place. There are some houses there, belonging to the widow, in Calvario Street. One of the flats, vacant. This flat they had destined for Simona, on marrying. Married she is; let her live in it—and us too. Let's set sail and find ourselves there, in a wink. The husband lives in Pilares, with his parents. Better and better. The widow will begin to worry, lest the turtle doves see one another and become inflamed once more. That this not be so depends on us—as if we didn't have enough headaches. But let the widow be frightened. In this way we'll have her at our mercy. Whatever we may ask for she'll do, because we'll be keeping the girl safe. And insofar as the girl . . . Heavenly one, lovely, pretty little one, the things you're going to go through with your little husband so near! Just like someone they give salty *bacalao* to eat and then place crystalline water within hand's reach, but don't let him taste it. Our recompense: her punishment. There's a God of justice. What do you say?" The other six said nothing, because the joy had filled their mouths with viscous saliva and they couldn't speak.

At the beginning of November, the seven old maids, Simona, and the two cats came to live in Pilares, in that flat in Calvario Street where Urbano and Simona thought that they were going to live the second and perpetual phase of their honeymoon. The previously dreamt of nest of love, a nest of vipers presently.

Urbano was not long in learning that Simona was in Pilares. Several days he strolled up and down the street in front of the house, his gaze fixed on the balcony. The old maids were leaning out. They didn't go in even to eat, imagining that that gallant was the suitor of some one of them. All seven made seductive eyes at him and sent him spasmodic smiles; each one in the illusion of being the favorite. "What a happy hunting ground, this Pilares," they said, excitedly. "Right off the bat, there's action. And what action!" Urbano, without knowing what to think of that ridiculous and desperate game, continued, with the hope of seeing Simona, strolling up and down, his gaze fixed on the balcony, which seemed to him like a cage full of puppeteer's monkeys, dressed ludicrously—until the old maids realized that the gallant was Simona's husband. Furious, they closed up balcony and windows, with shutters and all. Now, seen from outside, one might say that the flat was uninhabited.

Urbano went to unburden himself to his two great friends, Don Cástulo and Paolo. He feared, he told them, as much as that those seven furies might be capable of inflicting tortures on Simona.

Paolo disagreed, wagging his head vehemently, his eyes horrified—it was his style of wordless elegance. A pure and inoffensive soul, he couldn't accept that evil might exist in the world.

Don Cástulo stated, with his fine distinctions and subtleties of thought, "That they might inflict torture on her, I don't believe for many reasons. Now, that they might not be capable of inflicting it on her, that's another story. If they don't do so it is because they don't dare or because it does not suit them; but not for not wanting to or because they might not be capable. They are old maids and they are devout people. Celibacy is enough to make a monster of a woman. The abuse of religious practices is enough likewise to make a monster of a woman. Celibacy and devoutness put together, those two agents of corporal and psychological deformation, the result is a type of monstrosity much more monstrous than as much as the pusillanimous imagination of simple men has conceived. The sea monster, the gorgon, the vampire, the harpy, the basilisk, the dragon, the black widow are like caged canaries or lap dogs if they are compared with the perversity and ugliness of a devout old maid."

"Some consolation you offer me!" exclaimed Urbano.

"My son, truth is the only consolation of strong men." It sounded somewhat comical to hear Don Cástulo, so feeble, assert this hard aphorism.

"You, what do you advise me?"

"What would you advise him, Paolo?" Don Cástulo asked, in turn.

Paolo, with an unequivocal gesture of his hands, advised waiting, waiting . . .

"But Simona is suffering," replied Urbano, heating up. "I could wait. What I cannot do is say to Simona: suffer, my love, suffer and wait."

"First of all, who told you that Simona is suffering," countered Don Cástulo. The ones who suffer, surely, and suffer sorely, are the others, the old maids. If Simona were to contain in her soul some particles of ill will (which is useful, since it gives seasoning to life like salt to tidbits), the envious fury of the old maids would give her occasion to take pleasure. It's not that I deny to you, in the absolute, that Simona suffers. By nature, by divine curse, by whatever reason, love in woman always goes accompanied by suffering. If woman wishes to emancipate herself from suffering, let her emancipate herself from love, which is the case of the prostitute. In all remaining cases, man makes woman suffer only by the fact of loving her. You make Simona suffer; right now you are making her suffer; but I swear to you that, of all the forms of suffering that necessarily you must cause Simona, the suffering that you are now producing in her, obliging her to wait, is the lightest, the most bearable, the most pleasant. She will tell you so many years from now, looking back on these days."

There was a pause. Urbano said, "Have you finished now? Well I'm still right where I was. You've told me nothing practical."

"Forgive me, Urbano. Did you want something practical? Well, here you go. Go from here to the court and reclaim Simona before the judge as your legitimate wife."

"What you propose is absurd."

"On the contrary, all will say that the absurd thing is what is happening to you."

"All but you. I'm not married."

"Married you surely are, before God and before the law. Still, three months ago, although also married, perhaps out of respect and fear of your mother, who was bent on unmaking the marriage, it was possible that you might consider yourself half married and on the eve of divorce. Now, unfortunately, your poor mother can neither make nor unmake anything, and from you I have not heard that you might be thinking of going through with the process of divorce."

"Because it's not necessary; because I'm not married. Neither before God nor before the law, since I'm not so before my conscience. Nor have I any intention of feeling myself married within half an hour. I recognize that I'm not a full grown man, to foolishly accept that responsibility, like the last time."

"Well then . . ."

"Well then, your idea of reclaiming Simona before the judge is preposterous. Even admitting that I might consider myself married, what would we live on? Where do I get the money?"

Here the taciturn Paolo broke into speech with stuttering lips: "I'm rich. My money is yours."

"That would be living on charity."

Paolo blushed. Don Cástulo said, "You get a small salary from the academy, which we will increase when you have need. You could begin by living modestly."

"Another charity. Besides, I don't want to live modestly, and much less to oblige Simona to want. I'm ambitious."

"A maternal inheritance," commented Don Cástulo.

"And wilful; also a maternal inheritance," affirmed Urbano with a frown, thrusting his strong jaw forward. "I have my plans."

"Why, then, do you consult us?" inquired Don Cástulo with a round mouth, like a fish, a gesture he was wont to make to express surprise.

"I consult only about what is happening to me with Simona."

"But what is it you are asking? Let us know, with clarity."

Paolo and Don Cástulo meditated over this grave problem as if it were a question of a personal affair of theirs.

"The one who can give a solution to the conflict is Pentameter. In stratagems of love that rogue knows more than Ovid," suggested Paolo.

Urbano clapped one hand against the other in a show of jubilation, applauding the idea.

"I was thinking," whispered Don Cástulo as if speaking to himself, "that you can see her the day after tomorrow. Today is Friday. Sunday, very early, you set yourself on guard in the street. They've got to take her to mass."

Urbano clapped hands anew. At this, Conchona came out, followed by Cerezo, watchdog, now, of the Grove of Athena. (The three interlocutors were to be found in Don Cástulo's office before the supper hour, accustomed place and time to meet three days a week.) Conchona, after a brief hello, faced Don Cástulo, arms akimbo, saying, "Will you button up your pants? Ay, what a simpleton! I'm in despair. My blood boils every time I see him like that. He's going to make me sick. I tell you, look at him, tomorrow I'm sending him to Virolo, the tailor, for him to make him some pants that button up behind, like women's skirts. At least, that way the jacket will cover the opening."

"Whatever you wish, adored little woman," said Don Cástulo, patting Conchona on the cheeks; "but, for God's sake, don't excite or upset yourself. Now you need a regimen of tranquility, lots of food and good wine."

"Ay, what a lordyship!" sighed Conchona, her eyes turned up, widening her already wide mouth, which possessed an unexpected elasticity. "With one word, you calm me down. To me it doesn't matter that you forget to button up, as if you were going about in underdrawers. I say it for the others, above all for the students of the academy, who are young boys and scalawags. Do you know what I mean?"

"But Conchita, when are you going to address me familiarly?"

"I still don't dare. I'm getting there. I'm getting there."

Paolo, though taciturn, didn't want to forego giving his opinion concerning the pants. It was a point of self pride.

"If I were you, Don Cástulo, I would make myself some knickers like these," and he stood up, with his belted, side-zipped pants and his high boots. "Everyone laughs at my pants; but I have found that they are the most comfortable for going amount and for going afoot. With them you don't have that carelessness that your wife laments so much." Paolo never said ride horseback or go walking; he said go amount and go afoot, knight and footman.

Conchona asked Paolo for a pair of pants as a model, and they broke up the session.

Sunday, very early, Urbano was already on sentry duty on the corner of the street. At six in the morning, Simona came out among the seven old maids, who escorted her, surrounding her. Day was dawning weakly in a grayish mist. Urbano followed his girl friend (his girl friend he called her mentally) at a distance. The women entered the church of Santo Domingo. Urbano, behind. The seven old maids with their captive knelt near the presbitery, which was where there was more light. Urbano went to locate himself next to an oil lamp so that Simona might be able to see him. With his heart, he called to her in shouts, "Look at me, my Simona! Look at me for God's sake I beg of you!" As if she had heard these silent shouts, Simona turned to look at him, directly, without moving her eyes from place to place, and looking at him she remained at length, smiling. And now Urbano truly felt a kind of undeniable need to give an enormous shout. He had to contain himself; and the shout, which could not escape freely, brilliant and cutting like Saint Michael's sword, pierced his side on being turned back inward, causing him a most intense pain. Simona continued looking at him, and he drowning in a delicious agony. If he sought to breathe, the pain increased. He remained breathless, ecstatic. He turned up his eyes, taking root in his emotion. He relived again, instant by instant, the seven days of innocent nuptials with Simona at Collado.

But Sulforiana, who was the most alert and suspicious of the seven old maids, observing that Simona had her head turned, looked in that direction and saw Urbano in his withdrawn and devout attitude, his eyes lowered, the great hypocrite! She hissed to the other sisters cautiously and pointed out Urbano to them with her finger. Several of them seized Simona by the arms and, hardly touching the pavement stones as they flew nor making any rustle, like bats they fled from there.

Urbano opened his eyes. Simona was no longer there. Had he been dreaming? Had he remained asleep in bed without waking, dreaming that he saw her and was he still asleep? Urbano ran out. He trampled on a coughing old woman, who shook her fist and screeched at him: *Satana fugite*. Not a trace of Simona in the street. The house in Calvario Street, still shut up as if nobody had gone out. Was he dreaming?

He wasn't dreaming, as attested the persistent, tenacious pain in his side, which forced him to return home, get into bed, and kept him in bed more than a week. Doña Micaela kept him company, many hours, seated by the head of the bed. The señora was now going through a period of half-lucidity. Mother and son spoke amicably. "How sweet," thought Urbano, "to have one's mother at his side when he is ill. How sweet it would be to have one's wife at his side. Though . . . a mother is a woman consecrated to the care of the ill, nothing more than to that; for what are children but invalids? The mother loves her children as much because they are hers as for their dependence and not for any special worth. The wife loves her husband for his strength. A woman who had to constantly care for an invalid husband would tire in the end; a mother, no. In strict logic, a woman must be put out by her husband's infirmity as if he were deceiving her or were unfaithful to her; and vice versa, the husband with a sick wife." And Urbano continued meditating, his thought lightened by a slight fever, as in an alcholic intoxication.

He didn't dare speak of Simona with his mother. Doña Micaela brought up the subject: "When are you intending to get married?" for neither for Doña Micaela was Urbano married. "Get married, get married. We need a young woman in this house."

"When I'm rich, Mama, and I will be so soon."

"That no, that no. I don't want to see you rich. Leprous first. Riches, a precipice that drops to hell. Money, the most harmful invention, root of all evils. Lucifer, Lucifer himself invented money. With gold he forged his weapons, and brandishing them toward God's throne, he shouted proudly, 'I will conquer you.' And God lowered his head, for he saw himself lost. Justice, right, beauty, truth, charity, strength, valor, which God was proud of having invented and which He thought to be able to dispense kindly from his throne, for all eternity, were at the tips of his fingers. 'Your gifts and graces are my merchandise,' said Lucifer to him, with a great laugh of triumph, an endless laugh, which is resounding everywhere, if you know how to hear. Listen, Son, to the victorious hymn of Lucifer: 'Justice, the magistrates administer it for a salary. Right, granted to the highest bidder. Beauty, deluxe article for fat purses. Truth, weighed and measured by boss gold, which is the only truth. Charity, a copper coin. Strength, at my service for a wage. Valor, only as money values it. Jehovah, old dotard, I have corrupted you; I have prostituted you; you don't move if it's not for my money. You wanted to redeem men; you sent your son to earth, but you needed me. You sold yourselves, and I bought you for thirty coins. What might you have been able to obtain if I didn't buy you? You obtained nothing anyway. Your Christianity is mine before yours; it is the grand prostitution; all the homage that is paid you is venal, because I wished it. Then the homage is to me and not to you. To admit a new Christian to baptism, you asked for money; in order to give burial to a Christian, you asked for money; even to kneel in the temple, you asked for money. You are my tributaries, my vassals; the money you handled bears my effigy. No one, save I, coins money. Money is my invention and my handiwork. All coined currency is my coinage, with my coat of arms and likeness, which takes on infinite forms. The medallions which hang from the necks of our servants and ministers, the pastoral crosses of gold and gems, even the ring of the Fisherman, are my money, with my coat of arms and likeness. I have prostituted all of it for you. What more, if I have prostituted Love, which by nature seems inalienable? Men go about debased and blind with thirst for gold. I am the owner of the world. Remove that thirst from men, if such is your power. Only then will you have subjugated me. I laugh with a laugh of thunder. You've got to slake that thirst! Have I perhaps given gold to men as a generous benefice? No, but as a scourge. Gold is fear, envy, cruelty, treason, bloodletting, crime, premature death. In my just designs I have paired illness, infamy, stupidity, and misfortune as inseparable companions of riches. Men see it, in the example of all times; and their thirst for gold does not lessen. Who has made them so? The blame is yours. Annihilate the world and make it anew. Jehovah, I will finish off by putting you in hell.' Thus sings Lucifer, my son. Strip yourself of ambitions and Lucifer will not have sway over you."

Urbano, after hearing this impassioned invective against riches, remained meditative and melancholy.

In the evenings, the family of three gathered together; father, mother, and son. Don Leoncio enjoyed having his hands clasped one hand on his son and the other on his wife, as a result of which, his arms quite open and his head turned to one side, he seemed to be bound on a cross. "A blessed cross," he meditated in his heart; "I moor myself to it, in the undertow of life, as to an anchor." The coming and going of the business trips had ended now. His wife's madness had worn him greatly. His love for her had ascended to the most diaphanous sphere of sublimation, the sphere of the fire that burns without burning. Now he truly could hug and kiss Micaela like an adored and grieving child, a child possessed by that supernatural and irremediable grief which is a living death or a dead life. And on hugging her and kissing her, there came into his heart tears of lustral fire. The more this pure love dominated him, the more he was wearied of the profane love toward María Egipciaca. That was the word, weariness, physical weariness. Before he believed the two loves separate and compatible, like parallel lines. Now he began to fear that they didn't go together, that they opposed one another. María Egipciaca continued as extreme in her amorous manifestations and demands. In spite of this, Don Leoncio suspected—he was almost sure—that she was deceiving him, with a beardless and ruddy young boy. But Don Leoncio, playing the fool, did not leave off visiting her from time to time. In part from routine; in part, from gravitation of the weak flesh; signally, because thanks to her clamors, exaggerations, horse laughs, and flatteries, she broke, with a crude rent, the monotonous tonic chord, not devoid of happiness, though an oppressive and sad happiness, to which the present life of Don Leoncio was attuned.

One of those nights on which Micaela was working in the kitchen, father and son alone, Urbano said, smiling in a too-knowing manner, with which he tried to express complicated feelings: "On a certain occasion, Papa, you compared love with food to me. Some excesses in love, you said—or rather certain kinds of physical love between people who are not married to one another—are like small excesses or caprices in food and in drink, not at all repulsive if repulsive things aren't eaten or eaten gluttonously. I remember your words: 'Do you revile me because you see me on some special occasion relish a good Bordeaux or a good Cognac? It would be another thing,' you added, 'if your father fortified himself daily with strong tavern wine and aguardiente.' "

"It's possible that I may have said it to you," replied Don Leoncio, evasive and disquieted.

Urbano defined his smile further, into a sign of benevolent irony and affection: "Now, are you sure, Papa, that that small excess or caprice of yours is with Bordeaux and Cognac? I don't know anything about strong drinks, but on the surface I would say that what you regale yourself with is with strong tavern wine and aguardiente."

"But, do you know?" asked Don Leoncio, now tranquil, seeing Urbano's face. "Well tell me, what would you call in such a case Bordeaux and Cognac?"

"A beautiful and young woman."

"Which is as much as to define, by exclusion, the poor María Egipciaca, an ugly old woman."

"I haven't seen her. They tell me she's not very good looking."

"It depends on who may have said it to you. If a youngster of your age, he was right and he said what he felt. If a man of thirty to thirty-five, he was much less right and, though he may say what he feels, his feelings are not very humane nor gentlemanly. If a man of more than forty-five, either he lacked honesty or he doesn't know what he's saying; or he's a scoundrel or buffoon. The age of women does not exist in itself, my son; it is the most relative and mysterious thing that there is in the world, even for they themselves. Well then, following the comparison, slight excesses and pleasures in food are relative, that is, they are in relation to each one's means. A *perrona's* worth of roasted chestnuts is a poor man's pleasure. A rich man pays a good fistfull of silver *reales* for what they call *marrón glacé*. Result, chestnuts. What would we say if a poor man were to spend a week's pay in eating a dozen of those *marrones*? A madman. Well, apply it to excesses and caprices of love. In love, youth is prodigal riches; middle age, a well-administered moderate means; old age, sordid poverty. I conform to those amorous attractions my mediocrity permits me. If I had, at my age, fallen for a young vixen, that would be folly or something worse. I might perhaps come to disgrace myself, to lose my dignity. People would make me an object of derision. While now, all that they can think is, psst . . . , that I am being somewhat ridiculous."

Urbano broke out laughing, affably. Don Leoncio went on, "Which is what you think. Well, and so what? All amours are ridiculous."

"Papa . . . "

"You haven't let me finish. They are ridiculous for those who don't partake of the love. It's like seeing dancing without hearing the music—an extravagant and comic thing. Therefore, all lovers make the others laugh."

"I once heard something similar from Don Cástulo, though in a more intellectual style: the light that the torches of the hymeneal give off is invisible for he who does not sacrifice on the altar of the god."

"It's a truth of all times. Don't be angry with me, Urbano. Your amours, would they not seem ridiculous here, there, and everywhere if they were to become known?"

"My amours, Papa, have been truly ridiculous. I am the first to recognize it."

"Have been?"

"Yes; nowadays they are ordinary amours. A boy who has a girl friend and her mother is opposed. That's all."

"More ridiculous now than ever to outside opinion. To be playing the bear, up the street, down the street, in front of the house, not of your girl friend but of your lawful wife . . . "

"Pfah; for me, she's still not my wife."

"There's the most surprising, the most incredible thing of all. Happily for you, events are developing providentially in conformity to your caprice. You have insisted that Simona cease to be your lawful wife? You'll have your way. I have satisfactory news."

"Eh?" Urbano opened his mouth with such anxiety that the fumes from the eucalyptus vaporizer which was near the headboard, choked him and made him cough a good while.

"Your mother-in-law, according to my information, has found out that your mother consulted with Señor Palomo over the question of your divorce. It is known that that Palomo wrote at once to the other dove, the dove that always wanders with your dove of a mother-in-law. These kinds of black-hooded doves are always crows of the same brood, crows disguised as doves. They tell me that your mother-in-law became furious, that she insulted us, that she threatened us, and, in sum, she resolved to get one step ahead of us and carry out on her own the divorce proceedings, the ecclesiastical and the civil. She has great influence with the bishop, and the cleric considers her one of the family. Whatever she may propose, she will get. Moreover, she has entrusted the affair to a pettifogging obfuscator and rogue, Castañeda, for the civil end of it. So then, now you know. Now, your wife is prohibited to you. Religion and society interpose themselves between you and her."

"What happiness, Papa! What happiness!"

"My son, you amaze me. Ah! Don't let it slip my mind to tell

you two things that occurred to me a while back. First, that María Egipciaca—you know who I mean?" Urbano assented tacitly,
"though somewhat plump, is not at all ugly. You wouldn't find her
ugly. Somewhat exaggerated in features, somewhat in caricature,
she looks like . . . she looks like other young and pretty women.
Secondly, that I am going to break off with her. It's finished."

"Let it not be for what I've said to you, Papa."

"And even if it were so, I'd have to thank you for that."

Urbano, recovered now from his brief attack, resumed his
strolls in front of Simona's house. He waited two Sundays, from
dawn. All in vain. They had the girl hidden away, as in a galley.
Not even to mass did they take her out. Then it was necessary to resort to the tricks and strategems of Pentameter, as Paolo had suggested. Pentameter was Paolo's footman. All of Paolo's movements from
place to place in public were on horseback. He was never seen in the
streets but riding a slow nag, his footman to the rear, some six
meters back, riding another nag, more of a nag still. When Paolo
entered a house on a visit, the footman remained at the entrance-
way guarding the master's horses, or he went off with the two animals wherever he might please, with the provision of being back
at the hour specified by Paolo. Among his friends and relations on
the other side of the tracks, kindergarten where he had been
brought up, Paolo's footman answered to the nickname of Casín.
But Urbano, Paolo, and Don Cástulo had rebaptized him with the
alias of Pentameter. Don Cástulo used to say, lauding Greek poetry,
"There is nothing so beautiful as a hexameter escorted by a pentameter, after the fashion of a knight with his footman in pursuit; nor
anything nobler than a nobleman followed by his footman, in the
manner of a hexameter with a rearguard pentameter." Such was
the history of the alias. Pentameter, archive of venial buffooneries,
had his master bewitched. Nobody celebrated the sprightliness,
roguishness, and wit of his footman like Paolo. He was a lad of
twenty-five, dark and vivacious, gamin faced, as much from his na-

ture as studied, a winking eye, hair down over his ears, a pinched and crooked mouth, a curled mole on his chin, which was his greatest vanity. Peering out from between the two locks over his ears, the footman's face was an incisive commentary between parentheses. He spoke in front of his master, Urbano, and Don Cástulo with unheard of pertness, for the three encouraged him, delighted in listening to him. "Golden key, which opens all doors?" said Pentameter, with a crafty grin. "Ha! Love. The padlock for opening doors. Love's a picklock. Love's worth more than gold. Love's not bought with gold, if it's not faked love. With love you can make away with and extort copper, silver, and gold. Let women love me; I won't lack for anything. I've got twenty on the string, who are dying for me. There are all kinds in my orchard, as in the vineyard of the Lord: kitchen girls, innocent lasses (it's a manner of speaking), nursemaids, housekeepers, vegetable sellers, stallkeepers, butchers, innkeepers; single girls, married ones, and widows. This one a pair of reddish socks; the other, a yellow tie; that one, embroidered handkerchiefs; tobacco by the tons, which is the gift of kitchen maids, and I have six; the best stuffed sausage is for me; for me the first glass from the barrel that's tapped; and the ripest fruit for me to sink my teeth into; and plenty of money, which I make myself ask for before taking it. In short, I feel almost ashamed to collect my salary from my master." In all the streets he went along on horseback he had more than one lover, who came out to see him, on windows and balconies; and he, very gentlemanly, solemn and flashy, winked his eye evilly at them. "To deceive women," said Pentameter, "is not deceit; it is to give them pleasure, for they all wish to be deceived. Like robbing the rich is not robbery, but a work of charity, because it takes away cares from them; as long as one doesn't rob for himself, but to help the needy."

"Your psychology," commented Don Cástulo, "is that of the generous bandit."

"And your deeds," added Paolo, with a tone of conviction, be-

285

cause Pentameter, with his master's knowledge, stole all he could—and it was not a little—from Doña Encomienda, Paolo's mother, an old miser. Part of this money they shared, sometimes Paolo, sometimes Pentameter, with the poor. The old woman and her son lived on a large summer estate, six kilometers from Pilares. Ever since the master's and young lad's gift giving began, hordes of beggars swarmed to the estate, with whom Pentameter liked to converse, as many of them were vagabond, accomplished rogues, from whose lips were learned humorous knaveries, useful tricks, advantageous opportunities, and instructive stories. The other part of the money taken from the old woman passed into the hands of her son Paolo, to whom she gave not an *ochavo* for pocket money, limiting herself to paying his bills, because she sustained that "money is the perdition of inexperienced youthfulness." (The inexperienced youthfulness was Paolo's, with more than fifty years behind him.)

After consultation with Pentameter over Urbano's difficulty, the rogue replied, "Give me a space of two days to sound it out."

Exactly two days later Pentameter said, "I sounded it out; I can swing it. Within three days the señorito will be able to see the senorita, write to her and receive letters. Within a week the señorito will speak from the street to the balcony. Later on, that's no longer up to me."

Urbano and Don Cástulo showed themselves skeptical. They asked him to explain in less recondite terms.

"It's very simple," replied Pentameter. In these two days I've informed myself of all that I needed to know. I've seen the seven old maids in the street. After a few moments of following them, all of them turned their heads looking at me in a manner that I know well. All of them are dying for a boy friend. Nothing easier than to be the boy friend of one of them. And now I have in hand the key to the door—I mean, love, which opens all doors and batters down all walls."

"Some objection occurs to me," said Don Cástulo. The other six, from jealousy, will pick quarrels with the one selected by you.

They will make life impossible for her, as for Simona. They will lock her up. You will gain nothing."

"Bosh! I know how things go. Everyplace where there are several people joined together, one, because it's just so, because they've been born with that power, dominates the rest. Among the seven old maids there's one who commands, one of whom the others are afraid. That one will be my girl friend. Already she almost, almost, is so."

"But, how do you know which is the one who commands, my boy?" exclaimed Don Cástulo, arching his brows, with a gesture of commiseration.

"Aren't I telling you that I've followed them in the street? Why? To inform myself. How? Examining them. One of them has a short neck. That one commands the others. I've observed it and I've verified it; the woman who has a short neck, and particularly somewhat of a thick neck, commands; there's no need to belabor it. That's why I don't like short-necked or thick-necked girl friends. Except in this case, when it's a question of a joke. My new girl friend has a name that gives the shivers. She's called Trifona."

Paolo and Don Cástulo broke out laughing. Urbano was excited and thoughtful. Disconnected thoughts lumped together in his mind: "Can it be true that I will see Simona? How will Penta-meter manage to feign love toward such a repulsive woman? Will I come to speak to Simona soon? My mother has a short neck."

In three days Urbano was able to see Simona, for a few moments, behind the windows of the balcony; he could write to her and receive letters from her. Fifteen days later he spoke to Simona, at night; he in the street, she leaning out.

It was Christmas eve. Six of the old maids had gone to midnight mass, which is an occasion for a lot of jollity and promiscuity, in which the men customarily allow themselves great daring with the women under cover of the ecclesiastical darkness. Trifona had sacrificed herself for her sisters, offering to remain at home in the care of the captive. But hardly did the others absent themselves than she let Simona go out to the balcony, and admitted Pentameter into the kitchen, where she feasted him with a copious Christmas eve refection.

The sky was clear. One could divine behind the detached stars a background of infinite profundity. It was a sharp and dry cold; but Urbano, on speaking with Simona, felt inflamed with a hot enthusiasm, which rose to his cheeks and forehead, making them burn. He had forgotten Simona's voice by now. It sounded of the nightingale's song, of forest whisper; it smelled of jalap, of hay, honeysuckle; it shone in an infinity of bluish and trembling dots, like fireflies; it was like—what was Simona's voice like?—like summer, like golden light. And in Simona's voice Urbano tasted all together all of the memories and emotions of those seven days as a newlywed. His memory had forgotten them, but not his senses or his soul.

Groups of men and women passed by playing timbrels and drums, *zambombas*, hornpipes, bandores; beating pans, brass mortars, cans; shouting, singing, jumping, tumbling, and cutting capers. It was a jubilant delirium, a contagious frenzy, a victorious inebriation, a happy madness. Above that boiling sea of good cheer there hung in the air the amplified refrain: "This eve is Christmas eve." Urbano imagined that it was his Christmas eve, his own, which men were celebrating with so much fiesta and rejoicing. For a moment he had impulses to mix with the hubbub, to shout to the point of shrieking, and to give thinks to those good people for taking so much to heart his, Urbano's, good fortune. In the sapphire firmament, too, there reigned a great excitement among the stars, all dancing; and each star sent forth a shout, sharpened and transparent.

Pentameter took him by an arm, dragging him by force.

"Retreat call, Señorito. Pirates in sight. Head for the hills. And now, how was it? With this other party we didn't do badly. Every mother's son searches out in the carnival what best suits him. You supped on sighs; I, almond soup, seabream, and capon."

Sadness now oppressed Urbano. The street tumult and the ce-

288

lestial fiesta of the stars irritated him, as irrational and stupid. He entered a church, almost empty, where they had concluded the services. There, the happiness filled the cup of his heart anew, and he gave thanks to God.

A few other times he joined Simona to talk, but infrequently and always with danger. They wrote daily. Pentameter was the messenger. Urbano drafted long epistles wherein he noted down all his ideas and dreams. Simona's letters enchanted him with their candor. And so the days were passing. Urbano, in spite of Paolo's silent teaching, began to be impatient.

He frequented Paolo's friendship more and more, because of daily needing his footman, because Paolo's example infused him with resignation and serenity, and because of certain projects which he was maturing in the back of his head, counting on Paolo's co-operation.

Many afternoons he went out to Paolo's house on foot. Just crossing the threshhold it seemed to him as if he drank a cup of lime tea; his nerves were calmed down; the preoccupations that goaded him lost their urgency. From the outside wall to the large open space that was made at the front of the mansion, bored through purple ivy, there stretched an avenue, a tunnel under gigantic lime trees. Urbano thought on entering: "The shade that falls from those lime trees seeps into my soul. Truly, it's as if one were to swallow an infusion of lime tea. But it's just that around here everything is at ease. The trees do not move; the water in the trenches and in the fountains is still; the clouds remain immobile against the sky on reaching here. Is all still? Or is it the spirit of the owner which, keeping still, quietens everything about itself?" Urbano walked along the avenue, to the open spaces. There was Paolo, with his inevitable riding boots and his equestrian habit, seated in an armchair braced with logs country style. On the back of the chair there perched a crow, which Paolo had domesticated and who answered to the name of Don Periquito. This crow followed him all about the estate in little hops.

"Don Periquito, come here," he ordered, and the jackdaw jumped up to his hand, which Paolo extended in falconer mode. "You must have heard, Urbano, that a fifty-year-old crow is a nestling and at one hundred is but a youngster. How old will Don Periquito be? A century, two centuries; try to find out. I, at my fifty years or so, I am a tyke next to Don Periquito."

Just as Micaela with Don Cástulo, Paolo loved and admired Urbano. He had seen him transform himself, suddenly, from a gangling child into an independent and original man. Paolo believed he perceived in Urbano such a wealth of delicate sentiments and at the same time such an accumulation of repressed forces, latent energies, and personal ideas that, if they came into full play, would make of him a man out of the ordinary. When he saw him thrust out his jaw, with that hostile and willful gesture, Paolo experienced a kind of paternal tenderness. He was astounded at Urbano's capacity for action.

"The things you do by the end of the day, child, you who before used to spend your life like a groundhog. You come and go on foot out to this estate, some days two times; you give your classes in the academy; you court Simona in the street; you write prolix letters; you study languages; you daily ingest several books and digest them. The amount and how well you have learned in these few months amazes me, and in the most disparate fields. I'm a good judge of your progress, for I've always been given to reading. There's not a library like mine in the province; and of old books, national and foreign, on equitation and treatises on horsemanship and bridlery, there exists no collection in Spain like the one I possess. And, notwithstanding, nobody knows how to appreciate my treasures but Don Cástulo and you, you more than Don Cástulo. It's now over a hundred the volumes that you've borrowed to read, and of the choicest. Of course, I wouldn't let just anyone borrow them; only you."

Urbano constituted an exception for Paolo. To him alone he spoke confidentially of his loves or of his weaknesses, since the two

290

terms he employed alike, as synonyms. He spoke to him and he
spoke to him at length, because Urbano, to Paolo's thinking, listened to him with intelligent attention and with sympathy, as a
kindred spirit. Paolo's first love or weakness was his fiancée; but of
this he spoke only vaguely. His other loves were antiquities, books
of long ago, and horses. As it happened that his fiancée was old and
his horses chanced to be always old, Urbano thought that the loves
of his friend Paolo all fell under the epigraph of "antiquities." But,
for Paolo, antiquities never lost their youthful virtue, the freshness
and surprise of present-day things. His fiancée, at the threshold of
old age, continued for him changeless, at the springlike and just
pubescent age. The fiancée did not change, because Paolo's heart
was changeless. And when he rode those peaceful and barely mobile
nags, fit for señoritas or infantry officials, he gave himself the illusion of breaking in a wild colt. He fitted his horses with luxurious
archaic or exotic harnesses: Moorish saddles, bridle mountings, and
Mexican trappings. He showed his artistic antiquities to Urbano
with the same gesture of precise reality with which he took out his
hunting-case watch and said, "eight o'clock sharp." For him, an
Egyptian papyrus was a letter he might just have received in the
mail; a Syracusan coin was money which could be given to the kitch-
en maid to go shopping; he turned the folios of a Carolingian codex
with a light touch of the hands so that the miniatures, still wet,
might not be smudged; an edition of the *Rimas* of Lope, that of
Alonso Martín, of 1609, smelled to him still of printer's ink; he
characterized two bombards he had at the door of the mansion as an
extraordinary novelty in the art of the siege. In short, Paolo had lost
the notion of time. He himself confessed it to Urbano.

"I pity the world and its frantic desires. For me time does not
pass. With their silly hurries, men have left behind, forgotten, the
most noble and beautiful in life, which I, thanks to God, preserve
as a current and delightful thing: the cult of arms and that of
letters."

He possessed a splendid arsenal of arms of all sorts; from the quartz axe and the barbed arrow to the slingshot and the mailed fist.

He initiated Urbano into the cult and practice of arms, following the treatise of Pacheco and Narváez. He taught him fencing in its two styles; how one has to fight in single combat, honorably, with a gentleman, and how one must disarm and punish, with tricks and skills, the treacherous attack of villains and highwaymen. Urbano was very quickly an agile and strong fencer. Pentameter intervened at times, with his notions and experiences from plebian pugilism, favoring "the trip" as the most efficacious recourse in hand-to-hand fighting. Paolo was repelled by that vulgarity, but Urbano felt that it was good to try it just in case and, to test it out, grappled with the footman to see who would throw whom. Urbano came to always dominate Pentameter.

"Child, your muscles are like steel," exclaimed Paolo full of pride.

He also practiced at target shooting with dueling pistols, muzzle loaded, damasked, the breech incrusted with mother of pearl.

"Where you put your eye, there you put the bullet, child. Woe to him who might cross your path!" said Paolo with excitement.

"Woe! Woe! Woe!" replied Urbano in jest, laughing like a little boy.

Equitation was another entertainment, the one Urbano liked most. The apprenticeship was brief. Pentameter, in the center, held the halter and cracked the whip; one of the slow horses, Urbano on its back, ran around, on the circuit, in a dog trot or a circus gallop; outside the ring, Paolo instructed the green cowboy in the use of the rein and the spur, the handling of the wrist, the angle of the knee, the direction of the feet, the carriage of the torso, the posture of the head. Don Periquito jumped and cackled or perhaps fluttered, from one side to the other, going around, making his own circuit through the air. Shortly, Urbano had nothing left to learn from Paolo. Then, the teacher referred him to prowesses of Spanish horsemen, of ancient horses, although Paolo spoke of them as of friends and acquaintances by sight, distant in space but not in time, as if by chance they might be living in another city. One of them had a horse so well handled that he rode with him on top of a wall, and right up there turned him about, pirouetting on the hind legs. Another, resting his hands on the croup, jumped clear up, to land behind the ears; and it was a sumpter seven fingers' breadth over average height.

"That and the other one I will do," affirmed Urbano.

Urbano scrambled up a wall and walked a distance, his arms extended, like a funambulist.

"If today I do it on foot," he said, "another day it will be on a donkey, and then on horseback, when I myself train my horses. Hey, now to jump from tail to head."

Paolo did not agree to his trying it. His horses were bony and misshapen as dromedaries. Urbano thrust out his jaw and placed himself behind the horse, which was off to one side, unharnessed, bored and scraggly. He took a run, jumped, and came down on the base of the spine, which gave with elasticity, softening the blow.

"I've miscalculated the force," said Urbano, biting his lips.

He jumped once again and came down on the cross, over the prominent and sharp shoulderblades of the bony animal. From the intense pain his eyes clouded up for an instant and inside his head a sort of mist spread. He went white. He recovered quickly, and undertook the third try, pulling away brusquely from Paolo, who wanted to hold him back. He jumped, and fell on the horse's neck, and from there to the ground head first, not having been able to sustain himself with his legs on such a meagre support. On the fourth time he landed with gentle ease, behind the nag's ears. He still was somewhat pale; in his temples, two serpentine and bluish veins.

"Tenacity of steel, tenacity of steel," murmured Paolo. "Whatever you desire you'll achieve."

"That's what I'm after," assented Urbano, with a hidden intention.

What he was after was to persuade Paolo that, with an act of independence and virility before his mother, now doting, he might decide to mobilize a part of the fortune (paralytic and as though narcoticized in a banking house, that of Don Anacarsis Forjador, who was the one who profited from that money), and employ it in industrial enterprises. He, Urbano, would be the working partner; Paolo, the capitalistic partner. Urbano had read certain geological studies by a German engineer about that region and was subscribing to a French scientific magazine, *Nature*. He described his projects, before Paolo, in swift and soaring terms, impelled by ambition and lightened by the vanity of freshly acquired knowledge.

"My feet rest on a base of several kilometers in thickness and all of it solid gold—black gold, yes, but gold more valuable than yellow gold. And nevertheless I am poor. This province will become fabulously rich as soon as they go about extracting to the surface the black gold that's hidden in its bowels—coal. Why shouldn't we be the first ourselves to open this treasure chest which belongs to no one and belongs to everyone; run our arms up to the elbows into this forgotten riches, which will belong to the first who gets there? A little decisiveness on your part, friend Paolo; on my part, a little initiative. And that's not all. If coal is black gold and is worth more than gold, there is a crystalline coal that's worth as much more than black coal, as the diamond. This crystalline coal is running water. Each one of our rivers, so strongly rushing toward the sea, is a diamond mine; each drop of water a diamond. The coal of tomorrow, a tomorrow of years, will be anthracite; this magazine proves it. Our compatriots don't even suspect it. Let's forget all about mining claims; let's buy for four *maravedies*, the right to utilize waterfalls."

Urbano had traced out the scheme of the presumed enterprises. He himself would go to Madrid, and even abroad, to perfect the plan and to look for good technical personnel. They would give Pentameter a post of importance, since for prosperity in any business it is postulated indispensable to grant participation in councils and dealings to a certified scoundrel. Paolo judged all of Urbano's ideas admirable and self-evident, but he couldn't decide to take part

on his own account, emancipating himself from his mother's tute-
lage. If he had been capable of this, he now would have been married for many years. And as long as Paolo mightn't decide, neither
could Urbano decide to make Simona his. It was an agreement with
himself: "First I build myself a firm position; then right away, I
abduct Simona. Just so, abducted. Neither sacrament, nor contract.
Our love is a thing unique in the world and, as such, is beyond and
above the law."

But time passed and Urbano's impatience grew. Those scant
visual and epistolary satisfactions were not sufficient nutrition for
his great appetite for love. The month of February was now drawing to a close. Now almost never did an opportunity present itself to
Urbano for speaking with Simona from the street to the balcony.
He plaintively beseeched Pentameter. He could succeed in getting
Trifona to arrange for them—Simona and Urbano—a secret meeting.

"Ask me for the kingdom of Peru, Señorito, or ask me for the
moon, cut up in slices, like a melon. All that, maybe, maybe, I
would place in your hand, honestly or by trickery; but not what you
ask of this miserable sinner," Pentameter had replied. Your love
affairs, Señorito, are my penance and perdition. They've got me in
pain, and even without any appetite. For each letter of yours or of
the Señorita Simona, which I deliver or receive, I have to pay the
most toilsome and disgusting tribute—a kiss or two, which I must
give Trifona. Before it was here or there, wherever it might land on
her face, as I forced myself to kiss her like someone touches red hot
iron, exhaling and salivating. Making the best of it. Now she wants
them on the mouth. My mouth is petrified, Señorito, from abusing
that grace. Some smell of violets; but, others of onion, of garlic, and
even aguardiente. Well, I don't mind: tongue stew. This one,
Christ! She's too much for me. Her mouth smells of the cemetery, of
church and of hell; forgive me, but so it is. Though the señorito
might give me five *pesos* for each letter, they wouldn't be well paid
for. Try kissing my Trifona; you'll be convinced. And now the

señorito asks that I wheedle a rendezvous for him alone with the señorita? I cross myself a thousand times. What wouldn"t the evil-minded Trifona not want from me! I'd be feathered first."

Urbano kept begging him, suborning him: "Pentameter was very sly; if he showed interest in the cares of the señorito, he would find a way of resolving the difficulty." The footman, flattered by Urbano's phrases, responded—brushing aside a lock with one hand and with the other his curly mole—that he dimly saw a way. It was necessary, for this goal, that Pentameter add another to his collection of girl friends, a maid in the house next to where Simona was staying. Then, that the maid provide him with the key to the attic and to see if there was a way of slipping down from there onto the windowed gallery at the back of Simona's house; for he knew for a fact that the señorita slept in that part and the old maids in the best rooms, toward the façade.

Fifteen days after this conversation, Pentameter confided to Urbano that he already had in his command the key to the attic. The señorito would have to go out on the roof, slip down by a rope to a wall, run along atop it, jump to a little patio, lastly toss the rope up to Simona's gallery and shinny up it—all difficult enough for anyone, less so for the señorito, who was properly a gymnast. Urbano wrote to Simona that that very night she might await him in the gallery. At twelve midnight in the company of Pentameter, Urbano went forth, well provided with a long hemp rope, with a hook at the end, which he carried rolled in his belt underneath his cape. When he went out onto the roof, Pentameter said, "While I wait for you, I'll pass the time with Manuela, who's stupid but has a good breast, of turkey stuffed with nuts."

The tiles rattled under Urbano's feet, slippery with moss. He hooked the hook on the gutter; he slid down to the wall. In the little patio, to which he had to jump, a large dog threatened him with barks, which shattered the stillness of the night. By the light of the stars, he saw the white form of Simona, awaiting him. The dog barked with indefatigable boldness. A few moments more, the neighbors would wake up, the old maids would see him there. He was almost tearful, from disgust and from rage. He climbed up by the rope again, to the attic, interrupting, in its initial downbeats, the duet of Pentameter and Manuela.

"What am I going to do?" he moaned, frightened and irate.

"For tonight, nothing," replied Pentameter. "Tomorrow, you bring sugar and sausage, for a choice. If that damned dog doesn't shut up with the sugar, the sausage is in fine favor."

The next night on Urbano's jumping to the little patio, the large dog came up to him tail wagging, as if begging more sugar from him.

And Urbano, after so much time of painful separation, had Simona once again in his arms. An instant later—it seemed to him —dawn breaking, Urbano heard a whistle. It was Pentameter who was calling him, awakening him to reality. When they were together, Pentameter said, "What a great thing sugar is! It domesticates wild beasts. Let them not tell me about music. Men and animals look for what sweetens our existence. While we taste the greatest sweetness, it's only fair that the poor dog have his ration of sugar. Ay, that Manuela is bacon from heaven!"

Now, every night, Urbano and Simona shared love till the dawn. Almost always, on returning home, Urbano found his mother, pacing in the dark up and down the corridor, afflicted with incessant insomnia. Early in the morning, it was when the señora raved most, especially on moonlit nights. Sometimes, hearing the cocks, she gave out with cockadoodledos, hoarse and sinister. Urbano, before going to bed, embraced and kissed his mother, with a broken heart. One night—already into April, the happiest night of his life!—Urbano came home as though transported by so much good fortune, and on embracing and kissing his mother he experienced the most bitter sorrow. He burst out crying, blubbering.

"Cockadoodledo!" screeched Doña Micaela, rigid, frozen by

the dawn's cold. "Cockadoodledo! My sharp cry is the squeak of some silver scissors. Cockadoodledo! My cry rips the black vesture of night; the white body of dawn is left naked. Cockadoodledo! For you I do it, scamp, so that you may embrace her. Don't be afraid. I am your sentinel, the sentinel of darkness. With the silver scissors, I will cut the centurion's ears."

"Mother! Mother!" sobbed Urbano, and in his troubled heart he thought, "Mother dear, in the sharpest sorrow, without light and in shackles, mistreated and miserable, I would give thanks to you for this gift of life that you have given me. With what words, with what gratitude, Mother, with what renunciation, must I not prostrate myself before you today, when Simona has been mine, at last; the most happy of men, only for you, only for you, who have given me life? And you cannot hear me or understand me, because you've lost your reason. I feel almost out of my mind from good fortune and misfortune. Let me lose the little reason I still have, so you may recover yours, Mother dear, for today, for the first time, I embrace you knowing what a mother is." Alone in his bed, he was long in falling asleep. He was feverish. Then, he dreamt he saw himself suspended in the air, like a pendulum, and he was oscillating dizzily from a diaphanous and luminous region, which was paradise, toward a black and dreadful zone, which was hell; back and forth, without a moment's rest.

The next day he said to Pentameter, "You've been very good, sacrificing yourself for me. Now I will shift for myself. You can shake off the yoke of the old maid. I raise the penance."

"At your orders, Señorito, and long live Pepa! That is, Manuela."

As there was now no need for his mediations, Pentameter broke with Trifona, letting her understand, mischievously, with broad hints, that he had been playing with her. The poor wretch got such a shock that she took sick. She cursed endlessly from that mouth, spewing blackish foam. She fell down with fainting fits and fiendish contortions. The other six old maids took revenge for their own failure in the failure, more dramatic and lamentable, of Trifona; they let loose at her venomous wisecracks in order to inflame for her and make smart the feeling of her shame. Trifona's greatest martyrdoms were at night, shut in by darkness, alone in her virginal bed with the memories of her deceitful past happiness. She scratched the wall and ground her teeth. One night that martyrdom became insupportable and she got up to get a breath of air on the balcony. The other six old maids raised shouts of protest: "Do you want to kill us with pneumonia? Spiteful one, what fault is it of ours? You go ahead and die, but we're getting along very nicely in life, thanks to our modesty." The unhappy Trifona fled crestfallen, toward the gallery.

Shortly, the other six sisters heard great clamors, crying for help. They arose and ran out in nightshirts with a candle. On the gallery, with Trifona, was Simona, scantily enough dressed, her hands over her face. Trifona, with her eyes and mouth wide open, breathless and voiceless, pointed away from the gallery, toward the ground. The six pressed forward headlong to look. A man was slipping down a rope; then he jumped on a wall; then, he shinnied up the rope to a roof; and he disappeared. When the old maids recovered from the surprise, and their outrage allowed, they began to vociferate in the night.

"Whore! Whore! Whore!"

"We've been keeping under our honest roof a debased and dishonest woman!"

"Watch out for still water! You turned out for us to be a street bitch!"

"The mother a bitch, the daughter a bitch!"

"We should throw you out on the street just as you are, for all the world to point you out and spit on you. Whore!"

"How long have you been besmirching us with your obscenities?"

"Tomorrow, let the exorcist from Santo Domingo come with urgency, to sprinkle and clean these walls and these floors with holy water."

"And the other one, thief of honor, highwayman, footpad. If there's any justice, we'll see you in fetters."

Leaning out from the waist up, like seven deformed gargoyles, they vomited contemptuous reproaches in the quiet night.

Meanwhile, Urbano, in the attic, bellowed, beating himself with his fists on his forehead and on his cheeks: "Woe is me! Coward! Ah, pusillanimous and hateful heart! I got scared. I ran away, like a panicked animal, without knowing what I was doing. I should have stayed and strangled all seven of them with these hands."

"Whoa!" commented Pentameter. "Don't you see, Señorito, that all that which you're saying was impossible? There was no other way than to run off. Don't get all mixed up. Everyone knows them; no one will pay any mind to what they say."

The vociferations of the offended vestals were still heard.

"What a scandal! My poor Simona!" groaned Urbano; his breathing was a swirling, inarticulate noise. "I can't stand it! It's more than I can bear," and he made a move to hurl himself, in his desperation, from the attic to the ground.

Pentameter held him back by his jacket.

"You'll break the top of your skull, and it's hard to fix. Look here, your head is something that you're going to need at every step; you've got to take good care of it. Desperation is cowardice."

Urbano spent the rest of the night in stupidly rushing about the silent streets, fearful of his own thoughts. Pentameter had remained behind to inform himself of the course of events of the following day and to come to Urbano with the news. Early in the afternoon, Pentameter already had a lot to recount. Very early, three of the old maids had left with Simona in a closed coach; they carried a trunk on the coach box. Scarcely two hours later, they were back, without the trunk and without Simona. *Ergo,* deduced Pentameter, "Simona was still in the same city. In another house? Unlikely. Where, then? In a convent. In which of the forty convents of Pilares? Guess the riddle. There was nothing for it but to go asking, convent by convent."

The seven old maids "entered" Simona in the Derelicts convent, by another name "Shelter for Wayward Girls." Up to thirty fallen young girls were cloistered in that pious asylum. A small community of older nuns dedicated themselves to correcting failings and imperfections in the pupils, submitting them to a methodical religious practice, moral and practical, until they returned to tread the straight and narrow. Of the internees, some had committed a slight slip, seduced and then betrayed by the man whom they loved; others had linked the first slip to a chain of posterior slips, incipient prostitutes, free-lancers, undercover; others, finally, existed on professional and institutionalized prostitution, though still neophytes and not hardened in that manner of life. While the others had lost their liberty, these latter, on being transplanted to the convent, merely changed the mode and circumstances of confinement from an evil grotto, dark and infected, ill-fed and mistreated, to a spacious place, peaceful, clean and sunlit, with abundant sustenance, under a mild and courteous, though inflexible, government; and nevertheless, these were the ones who were least resigned to the work habits and to the chronometric regularity of the existence. Though that asylum was titled "shelter," none had gone there to seek shelter spontaneously; but they "sheltered them," they "entered them," sometimes by deceptions, others with intimidation, others with violence, now by some charitable madam, now by some Catonian gentleman—all for love of one's fellow creatures and devotion to good manners. The inmates belonged to the lowest social class, country or servant lasses. In the convent, they trained them in what is pertinent to housework, sewing, cooking, and confectioning. When they were well corrected of their past destructiveness and dissipation, wineskins with plugs, and well versed in the work, they placed them as maids with a devout and severe family, with a miserable salary, since those señores were full charitable enough compromising their security and even their good name by accepting a servant with a bad past.

Surely, none came up to that door with an appearance so propitious, manner more serene, or disposition so affable as Simona. The three horrible and dessicated scarecrows who accompanied her told the mother superior that she was dealing with a young girl refinedly libidinous and vicious, no less hypocritical and astute, mired in corruption, under guise of silliness; that the sisters should tread very carefully, so that she might not fool them; that that ingenous smile was a mask for ugly habits; that they had brought her without her mother's consent, because the extreme of the child's dishonesty did not admit delay, but that certainly the mother would very soon send her approval. Actually, Doña Victoria did write in a few days, congratulating the old maids on the idea of placing Simona in the Derelicts convent and thanking them. Far away from the provincial milieu, narrow and tedious, where all knew her and none looked on her with favor, the widow gadded about where she pleased, diverting herself roaming through varied countries without the least desire of returning to her native land. Her only tie with her place of birth was her daughter. Simona tucked away in a convent, the widow felt lightened of that preoccupation. She had thought that Simona might leave this convent to profess in another, for life, once the divorce was decreed, whose conclusion, though certain, was dragging out, since even though all roads lead to Rome, Rome is far enough away.

They dressed Simona in the regular uniform, a kind of penitentiary gown, of Nazarene fustian, with a saffron yellow cord at the waist; wool stockings and high shoes. A nun, especially experienced in analysis of conscience, the mother confessor, examined her. Accustomed to the suspicion, distrust, and cunning of the other inmates, who only after many conversations half confessed their sins, the mother confessor heard Simona with amazement, as she tranquilly related to her her story. It was an unusual case; it exceeded the spiritual know-how of the mother confessor.

"My daughter," murmured the nun, wringing her brain and her hands, "I don't understand why they have brought you here."

"Well it's very simple," responded Simona, arching her brows. "Because, before Urbano and I rejoin one another forever, we have to pass through many trials. My grandmother foretold it before dying."

"But, my daughter, that young gentleman and you are married. As you have not sinned, you have nothing to repent of."

"I don't know whether I have something to repent of; what I do know is that I am not sorry for anything. Inasmuch as our being married, Urbano says no. I've already told you that they're going to divorce us."

"My daughter, if they are going to divorce you, it's because they suppose that you don't love one another nor can you love one another. The error cleared up, who can want to divorce you?"

"My mother, for one. And Urbano wants to be divorced. And I, since Urbano wants it."

"You confuse me. That is to say that your boy friend wants you to be his, but without matrimony."

"Of course."

"And you?"

"What am I to want, since he wants it?"

"In other words, you haven't sinned in fact, but you have the intention of sinning."

"No, Señora; I'm not speaking of sinning."

"Well, what else is it, but sin and the most odious, to make love like irrational beings? Does it seem right to you?"

"Señora, to my thinking, the irrational thing would be that I might pretend to know more than Urbano or try to make my ignorant will prevail against his. When he says it and when he wants it."

"My daughter, I don't know what to reply to you. If God has

made woman as man's companion and that she love him with an
ideal and perfect love, that love is yours. I have been taught that
making love outside of marriage is gravest sin. But if God heard you
a moment ago—and he did hear you, for he hears everything—I
don't know why I imagine myself to be seeing his approving of you
with a nod of the head, smiling paternally and sweetly stroking his
long snowy beard. And may He forgive me if I have just said a great
foolishness."

Simona was more at ease, without any comparison, in the the-
ocracy of the Derelicts than under the heptarchy of the old maids.
The nuns, by virtue of her being the only señorita, for her gift of
sympathy and affectionateness, and signally because they had se-
questered her there without motive nor purpose, surrounded Simona with the greatest attention. They wanted to place her in a
position of favoritism and exempt her from the regulatory duties;
but she rejected all privilege.

"If love is sin," Simona said, "I'm as much a sinner as my companions. If it's not sin but rather is a generous sentiment, some are
more advanced than I and I must learn from them, for their having
loved so much and having known how to sacrifice reputation for
love. Others, certainly, have lost faith in love and have profaned it,
or better said, they've permitted that love be profaned in them; but
the profaners were the ones, the ones who made those unfortunate
ones lose faith in love, the ones who should be the punished and reformed ones."

With the friendly intimacy of the inmates, in one month Simona learned directly more truths about life and love than any
other woman in the course of an ordered and normal existence.
None of them seemed to her deserving of opprobium. To all of
them she dedicated fraternal affection. She thought at times, "If
Urbano were not as he is, who is to say that I wouldn't become as
some of them have been?" When some of the most fallen narrated
their pasts to her, Simona marveled on observing how events had

combined fatally to pervert them and drag them along without free will.

"Poor creature!" Simona would gloss over. "It's not your fault. You have nothing to repent of or to be ashamed of."

Simona was a little saint. The nuns began to become uneasy; because the little saint, with so much evangelical benignity and redemptive feelings, was subverting the reformees and impeding the reform.

Upon Simona's being in the convent a month, the gatekeeper sister, with surreptitious nunish subtlety, handed over to her a letter from Urbano. Simona went to read it in the garden, seated on the grass at the foot of an ascetic cypress, which trembled with emotion under the infinite and soft caress of a rose bush clasped to it. It was florid May. The swallows chirped under the blue sky. The hand of the breeze combed over the meadow, furry and lustrous like the skin of a young animal; the hand was invisible, but its passage over the grasses was seen. After reading the letter, Simona remained awhile in that place, alone, her gaze roving about, perceiving vaguely that, at the same time as she was becoming detached from herself, all things were becoming animated, were coming alive, were communicating among one another, with indecipherable signs and smiles of unanimity.

The convent bell tolled for the service of Flores. Simona went along to the chapel. From the altar, covered with lilies, there flowed a thick torrent of voluptuous aroma. That dense perfume was like balm; Simona felt herself anointed with it, as in a rite preparatory to love. Then the spring songs intoned by young voices, wherein trembled checked passion and nostalgia for the lover.

The following day, another letter. And another, the next day. A letter daily. Simona lived now as though transported. She went about deciphering the mysterious signs and the smile of things. All, though veiledly, announced to her a great coming event. Likewise Urbano in his letters, but he didn't tell her what it was going to be.

The tension of her spirit affected her body. She began to feel ill. A companion, acquainted with the symptoms that afflicted Simona, told her that she was pregnant.

Now she was pregnant, without apparition of the archangel, or celestial stage machinery, or a lump in the throat. She was pregnant, like any other woman; now she was a woman; she was going to be a mother.

She retired to the garden, beneath the cypress betrothed to the rose bush, and cried, with dry and tranquil tears. Would that be the great event announced by the mute things and in Urbano's letters? Simona smiled between the tears, laughing at herself. How was Urbano going to announce that? She was the one who had to announce it to him. In what form? By letter, she did not dare. But what, Lord, was the other great event? She couldn't stand the wait. She went about distracted; she lost her appetite; she did not talk to anybody.

A sad duty came to snap her out of her self-absorption. Typhus had made an appearance in the convent. Three inmates had died already. Daily a new one fell ill. The healthy, prisoners of terror, did not want to attend the suffering. Simona offered herself as volunteer, as a nurse, to assist the nuns. She was not afraid of sickness or of death, since she was destined for a great event. She did not even take the precaution of sprinkling herself with foul-smelling carbolic acid, a sure preventative against the contagion, according to the nuns' doctor. Now, given up to the work of charity, her hurry had passed off from her. She was disposed to wait until the sick might be cured. It almost annoyed her that Urbano (in those daily epistles which the gatekeeper sister, with ever fresh nunish intrigues, managed to hand over to her without anybody's perceiving nor suspecting) might allude to the great event as imminent. "It's approaching," wrote Urbano; "it's approaching by seconds. It's already dawning on the horizon. Our trials are now reaching their end. If you knew of my struggles (the ultimate effort), since when I learned where they had imprisoned you!"

Urbano had learned it from the mouth of the sleuthing Pentameter a week after Simona's disappearance. "Just what I was missing, a nun on the list," added the footman. "To win the heart of a nun must be as simple as getting wet when rain comes down. The difficult thing is to get to her. The doorkeeper nun it will have to be. With incense I am going to perfume myself, to make her nose tickle. Hold on! How dumb of me. The smell of sulfur and not incense will fascinate her. For a nun, is there anything more seductive than the devil? Go ahead writing the letter, Señorito; I promise that the señorita will have it soon in her possession. Then, the seeing her and speaking to her, it will likewise be arranged with all due speed."

Urbano sought alleviation from his suffering in the friendly support of Paolo. He set before him, in pathetic lights, the critical conflict in which he found himself. Simona imprisoned like a woman of the street, shut away in the company of other infamous women! He, meanwhile, inactive, arms folded, consenting passively that his beloved suffer public dishonor. Simona there, with her dainty soul, sunk in a cesspool, which would not corrupt her—no, because a pearl is a pearl, even among filth—but which was staining her.

"Don't talk that way, child," corrected Paolo, trembling. His eyes were at the point of brimming over. "The Derelicts is not a cesspool; it is a garden of flowers of repentance, glory to God. Jesus was a great friend of prostitutes. Those young girls are not properly prostitutes; they are in disgrace because they have sinned for love or from ignorance. For their guilt there is always another guilty party outside of the convent. Simona, among them, is not in the presence of sin but of the sorrow to which sin leads. Perhaps for Simona this is a sublime experience."

Urbano, inside himself, discovered a new spiritual perspective on hearing the penetrating and noble words of Paolo. But for tactical convenience and for his ends, he rebutted him. Paolo's considerations—he said—could not provide him any consolation. The idea of Simona finding herself locked away among dissolute young women was making itself intolerable. If he couldn't remove her from there immediately, immediately, he was going to kill himself. Only Paolo could save him and save Simona. "Let us organize our company!" Urbano concluded. Paolo, in desperation, repeated his eternal excuses. Although the greater part of the fortune was his to freely dispose of he wouldn't touch it without the maternal consent, and this couldn't be counted on. Urbano replied that he didn't need money, but Paolo's word, a solemn agreement between honest men. Given the promise, he would then contrive to amass some money with which to establish the bases of future operations. Paolo asked him what he would do in such eventuality to save Simona. Urbano replied to abduct her; and he described an abduction full of poetry and of dramatic developments by the light of the moon. Paolo listened avidly, and interrupted the description to collaborate in it, rectifying some of the details which could prejudice or frustrate the adventure, suggesting others and retouching the whole with beautiful and sensational brush strokes. Then they kept silent, dreamers. Urbano thought, "You will be mine, Paolo my friend, kind Paolo. Now I have the lever which shifts your remiss and timorous will. You love me a great deal; but neither the affection nor the pity which you feel for me are stimuli that conquer the dead weight of the fear of and respect for your mother. Imagination, your infantile and exalted imagination, which has suppressed time for you, granting you an unlimited world of illusions in exchange for the abdication of a few realities which the rest of men enjoy; your imagination will subtly take hold of your will, and you will want, as something of your own, what I want; with more violence than I perhaps. Tomorrow, the day after, in a month; I don't know when, but it will come about."

From that time on, Urbano spoke of the abduction every day to Paolo, and he observed how the idea was taking hold of his friend in the form of an obsession. When Urbano did not speak of it, Paolo initiated the conversation, always thus: "Last night I was reflecting that the best thing would be to . . . " Paolo, every night, was perfecting the plan in his imagination. But his will to cooperate in its realization continued inhibited, it seemed, or it was awakening with plenty of slowness.

Urbano had not forgotten that perspective opened in his spirit by virtue of a sober phrase of Paolo's: "Simona is now before a sublime experience"—An experience that he lacked. "Was Simona any day now going to learn, by direct knowledge, of certain clandestine profundities of life which he laboriously imagined? That wasn't so good. Was Simona, she alone, in advance of him to drink to the lees in the chalice of experience? That was not correct. To experience is to know; to know is to understand; to understand is to forgive. Was Simona going to be more understanding and tolerant than he? If it were thus he would cease to love her some day; then it couldn't be."

Urbano invited Paolo to go with him on a visit to the houses of ill-repute or, as the local newspapers called them, "dovecotes for wild doves." Paolo was horrified. Urbano made explanations: It wasn't a matter of trying the consummation of the vice—what did Paolo think of him?—but of approaching to examine it from up close. Not even that; Paolo recoiled, still perturbed: "What time would we go? How would we call? For whom would we ask? What kind of expression would we wear? Just on thinking of it my pulse is paralyzed. And if my mother were to find out about it?" Paolo's panic caused Urbano to wonder and smile. Then he had recourse to another young friend, famed as a rake and reveler, of whom he had been tutor the past summer; the perfect Virgil for the excursion to the subterranean circles of social life. Every night they visited one of those houses. Urbano sat down and was hours without speaking, drinking in through his eyes all that he saw or caught a glimpse of, savoring on the palate of his conscience an indecisive taste which he couldn't quite define. Was it disgust? Was it the pleasure of a drug that produced nausea? Was it pitying tenderness? Was it incitement, the beginning of liking? For his withdrawal and silence, the cheerful girls disdained him; they behaved in his presence with spontaneity and pertness, as if he did not exist, and he observed them with serenity. At times they produced in him an impression of monstrous grotesqueness; other times indignation, and he understood that some men beat them; ultimately, infinite sorrow, and his indignation, in this way, turned against society. He remembered some phrases of his mother, invectives against money: "The first man who minted a coin introduced prostitution into the world. Money prostitutes everything, even love, which by nature cannot be bought nor sold. We call prostitution nothing more than love corrupted by money, because it is the worst of the infamies of gold. That word applied to power, to justice, or to truth doesn't cause us so much consternation and uneasiness, as applied to love, because we can never convince ourselves that gold may prostitute love." And he, Urbano, had a hunger for gold, *auri sacra fames,* as Don Cástulo said. Wouldn't it be best to rid himself of ambition, that vesture which rubs and martyrs the soul, like the tunic of Nessus, and to go to live with Simona, humbly, in a quiet nook in the country, far from all the prostitutions of gold?

Thus caviled Urbano through "his sublime experience," spectator and transitory guest in the dark circles, brought by a duty of love, now that Simona was going through the same experience. What would Simona think?

Not knowing what Simona thought, Urbano accommodated himself with inquiring after Don Cástulo's opinion in the habitual sundown gatherings at the academy.

"Oh, prostitution!" exclaimed Don Cástulo, raising his skeletal arms, with a gesture of an orator of panegyrics. "I have always paid homage to prostitution. I long for the ages in which prostitution was an esthetic and sacred exercise under the auspices of friendly gods. Yes, little one, yes; don't be scandalized," he said, turning toward Conchona.

Conchona, in the latter stages of gestation, displayed a cyclopean pregnancy, which had Don Cástulo dizzied with vainglory. When she heard that about prostitution, Conchona thought that they were going to get involved in political polemic as on other afternoons. To her prostitution and constitution sounded the same. She retired, for that subject bored her.

Then Don Cástulo made the elegy of prostitution in the times of Pericles. He said that there had been no feminine callings as delicate as those of courtesan and hetaera; courtesan, courteous woman; hetaera, companion. He asserted that he had had many courtesan lovers from Athens, from Corinth and even Boetians, and enumerated their names. He told of the delights they afforded him and how on occasions they made him rage, leaving him out in the cold on the portico the whole night. After a long oratorical effusion, Don Cástulo in a low voice and with much, much difficulty, admitted that all that had been in dreams. He then got out from the shelves an edition of Lucian, and showed them, Paolo and Urbano, on the cover, the "Colloquies of Prostitutes," those *small living cameos of immortal grace*. These were Don Cástulo's words. He added, "They are eternal figures, like the human condition. Love is a bittersweet fruit; sweet first, bitter afterward; momentary delight and laborious servitude. There will always be women and men who love ephemeral love, lucrative and sterile, separating thus the bitter from the sweet. I am not familiar with the houses of present-day courtesans (that you are familiar with, Urbano), but surely in those houses, though with different attire, these same figures move." And he went about modeling, with light touches, the personages of Lucian. Urbano admitted the similarity, except that Lucian's figures produced a beautiful and pleasant effect for being remote, and the figures that he was familiar with caused bitter preoccupation. Don Cástulo blamed it on the difference in the times and on the influence of Christianity. He concluded, "Since it is inevitable, let us estheticize prostitution anew." Urbano and Paolo laughed, hearing those daring propositions, so incompatible with the figure, character, ideas, and customs of Don Cástulo.

One afternoon Urbano arrived at the gathering upset, livid. He came from seeing, dead and stiff, Perico Prendes, a law student, who had been his pupil. There he was, in the boardinghouse, stretched out on the floor on a spread sheet, dressed as a Franciscan, his face full of purple pustules, like Toro grapes. Perico was a regular at the houses of ill-repute. He had contracted syphilis. The vacation imminent, he was terrified to return to his parents' home in such a state. He went to see a doctor so that he might cure him in a month if only of the external signs of the repugnant disease. The doctor forewarned him of the danger; but he wanted the doctor to try, at all risks. In twenty days he burst, like a rotten and fermented apple. He was an intelligent boy, cheerful, kind, and generous.

"Now," exclaimed Urbano, sarcastically, "let us estheticize prostitution."

"There you have something that was not known in Athens nor in Syracuse, that disease. Truly, you leave me perplexed," responded Don Cástulo, putting his index finger between his brows. He concluded, "The blame belonged to the mercenary Columbus and Isabella, the Catholic, that señora who didn't change clothes for months."

Urbano did not return to the houses of ill-repute. For two days, he went about haunted by the vision of the dead student and tortured with transcendental and tragic preoccupations. Blinded and unfree, defying death, human beings run toward love, which is none but the triumph and conquest of life over death. Fatally, man gravitates toward woman and woman attracts man, and there is no obstacle that may stand between. And not only humanity, but nature entire is split into two elements—the eternal feminine, which attracts, and the eternal masculine, which is inevitably attracted. And not only nature, but its mirror, rational language; there are masculine words and feminine words, which seek for and unite with one another by means of the verb, the copulative, the act of love; all the rest in language is incidental. The universe used to be represented as an infinite and absolute struggle of sexes, as though spinning on an axis, whose two poles were the masculine and the feminine, what is attracted and what attracts, what engenders and what conceives.

All the old theogonies alike imagined the universe spinning on two fixed poles, absolute good and evil. Ormazd and Ahriman. According to that, will each of the sexes be an ideal of absolute good and a germ of absolute evil? Which would be the good? The masculine? No, there are no absolute goods or absolute evils; there are relative goods and evils. in proportion as each one of the elements, the masculine and the feminine, fulfills its end or contradicts it. If the function of the feminine element is to attract, the duty of woman is continuous attraction, since in attraction discontinuity has no place or it ceases to be attraction. Not so in man, since, if he continually let himself be attracted, he would disappear; absorbed in the attractive being, he would be consumed. The masculine function is discontinuous and occasional. The good woman, the one who fulfills her function and her end, is nothing more than woman; first girl friend, then wife, then mother; the mother is the home. Man is boy friend, husband, and father, by virtue of having been attracted by love; but the duties of his function do not demand that he exhaust himself in those activities but rather to centrifugally resist the continuous attraction that hinders his movements and to become a man in the fullness of his aptitudes and energies. Man in the home is not man; he is husband or father; man is a man before the rest of mankind and before nature. Woman forms, with her own flesh and with her own blood, the live body of humanity, a mission in which man has a paltry, instantaneous, and disdainful part. Right in this, which is nature's decree, the man finds himself free and available all through life to plan, to struggle, to create; in sum, to think, to invent history. The two poles of the universe, in Urbano's feeling, were Simona and he. Simona became the model of feminine perfection. Would he come to approximate the standard of masculinity that he had ideally proposed? The attraction toward Simona beckoned him with evermore enslaving force. It was the law, the eternal law, from which no man was exempt. There were no exceptions in this. Having just formulated this last mental affirmation, Urbano

313

stopped cold, like the builder who sees his building, raised with effort and patience, collapse. There was an exception: Paolo. At the first opportunity, taking him by the arm, and insinuating the warm words in his ear, Urbano said to Paolo, "But is it possible that you might not have ever felt, ever, the attraction of love in such degree that it might carry you away?"

"You already know that I have a girl friend," he replied, blushing.

"I'm referring to physical love, the attraction of woman."

Paolo, in a strangled voice, his head downcast, whispered, "From you, little brother of my heart, I cannot hide anything. I have a son. His mother is a villager from close by here. No one knows who the father is. When the girl gave birth, they questioned her closely, they threatened her; she declared nothing. My mother, frightened because there was a licentious girl in the neighborhood, as she said, took her to the Derelicts; my own mother. And my son to the orphanage. When she left the convent she brought the child with her. She is an irreproachable woman. To this hour nobody yet presumes who set her astray. My son is twelve. When my mother dies, I will acknowledge him. Though it is hardly permitted me to come near him, I adore him. His mother, I respect and am fond of, but it is not love. Love is the other thing." After a long silence, saturated with melancholy and ineffability, Paolo, with a brusque transition of tone, asked, "Our project of abduction is all set; it's not missing a jot. Don Cástulo, such a great critic, has not found a loose end in it. Conchona, so vigorous and sagacious, has not been able to better it. Besides, there are serious reasons (don't be alarmed! I'll tell you them later) which force us to put it into practice without further delay. What are you thinking of? What are you waiting for?"

"For you to give me your word."

"Which? That of being your capitalist partner?"

"Of course."

"But, my boy, haven't I given it to you a thousand years ago?"

"No, Señor."

"Go on, go on; you go about with your head in the clouds and you haven't heard me."

"We're still in time. Your word?"

"My word."

They embraced.

"What are those serious reasons," asked Urbano.

"*Pian, pianito,* Urbanín. Simona, does she write to you?"

"Some lines, with a pencil. Nothing else is possible. But I write her daily, thanks to the trickiness of that devastating Pentameter, who has cozened up to the lay sister of the gatehouse."

"That's what I meant. Simona tells you nothing?"

"Of what?"

"Steady; don't gallop or get skittish. In Pilares a typhus epidemic is afoot. In the Derelicts there are several cases. Pentameter has told me about it. He didn't want to speak to you himself of that so as not to alarm you. Simona must be taken out of there; notwithstanding that our plan cannot fail. It's what's called the Euclidean postulate."

"This very night."

"This very night, no; time is needed. Tomorrow night. We must talk to Conchona to make final preparations. Write to Simona, advising her of what she must do."

"At last, Paolo! You're a brave old fellow. And forgive me if I address you familiarly and give you a pull on that handlebar moustache."

Paolo smiled, with moist eyes.

It was a night of full moon. Twelve o'clock. At the foot of the cypress, wrapped in a soft eiderdown of roses, waited Simona with a small bundle in her hand and the gatekeeper sister.

"You're shivering, little one. Is it from fear?" asked the lay sister, covering the girl's hands between her own.

"It's not from fear."

"Will they take me too? Ask them to take me, precious. Virgin of the Desert; for the memory of your flight to Egypt, make them take me, make them take me! Ask the señorito, carnation of the Lord. Hoofbeats are sounding."

On the top of the wall, a man was outlined, with a black mask. He stopped, peering into the darkness of the garden. The lay sister hissed. The man, with a brusque gesture, tore off the mask. It was Urbano. In the starry silence, there was heard from the other side of the wall a cautious voice that said, "Don't take off the mask, boy; rashness can cost you dearly." But Urbano was already jumping to the ground and running to embrace Simona.

"Don't take me," sighed Simona, clutched to Urbano's breast. "Adelaida is dying. When I went away from her bed, she opened her eyes, looked at me, guessed, and pleaded: *We are separating forever; wait, wait . . . .*" Don't take me tonight, Urbano. Wait one more day. How can I leave Adelaida like this?"

"We'll pray for her," and Urbano led Simona along gently.

Another masked man had set up a ladder inside the wall and approached the gatekeeper sister, with terrifying swaggers.

"Who are you, my love or the devil?" shrieked the lay sister, crossing herself.

"Both," a voice answered her *de profundis.*

"Then the devil take me," sobbed the lay sister, seizing hold of the masked man's trousers.

"Gently, gently, bold woman, you're going to discharge the pistols in my belt," admonished the masked man.

Urbano called to the masked man to hold the ladder, while he, from above, helped Simona to climb up.

Then when the two lovers disappeared, the masked man climbed up and withdrew the ladder.

"Take me, take me, my Casín! By the nails of Christ and by all the instruments of the Passion; take me," cried the lay sister, next to the wall, stretching forth her arms.

"Sacrilege! You don't want us to damn our souls," said Pentameter, in his normal voice.

"How can I be more damned, if I must not see you again?"

"Who said so? You'll see me just like up to now, which is only a venial sin. I'll always love you; you'll never have me satiated."

"Swear it!"

"I swear! Tomorrow, at the regular time."

The cautious voice was heard again behind the wall, now sharp.

"Finish up, rogue, scoundrel. What's taking you so long there?"

"That simpleton, who thinks I'm going to leave her," explained Pentameter, now on the ground. "As if I didn't know what glory is. I deny the saying: nun's love and priest's belch, all air. Sure, sure . . . My nun, air? Nectar and celestial substance. Not an inkling did I have of what were custards, marmalades, figs in syrup, sighs (ice cream sighs), until this little nun was my concubine. Right away, sure, I'm going to leave her!"

"Shut up, knave, villain," cut in, covering Pentameter's mouth, another masked man with a wide slouch hat and a large whitish and full cape after the style of a Moorish cloak gathered behind over the barrel of a carbine slung in funeral carry.

There were also three horses with lowered heads pulling up grass.

"This masked man is Pentameter and this other one is Paolo," whispered Urbano to Simona. "Paolo, my big brother."

"Don't say real names, boy. What temerity!" whispered Paolo. "There's not a second to lose. The pursuers will soon be at our heels. Nothing to worry about. If it's necessary, we will make use of the arms. Up you go, boy. You ride the white-footed colt." This white-footed colt was a horse as old as Methuselah.

Urbano jumped up on his sumpter. Between Paolo and Pentameter they upped Simona to the horse's croup.

"Hold on tight to Urbano's belt," advised Paolo. "Are you afraid?"

Simona did not reply. She seemed to obey mechanically. Urbano reiterated Paolo's question several times. Simona, as if her spirit were coming down from far off places, inquired, "Eh? What are you saying? Who's talking?"

"If you're afraid."

"I'm not afraid of anything."

They rode in silence, under the moon. From time to time, Paolo ordered, "Stop! Didn't you hear a noise in the rear? Pentameter, dismount, stick your ear to the ground. Do you hear a noise of galloping steeds? Forward!"

Urbano caressed Simona's hands, nervously knit together over his heart.

"Your hands are frozen and I feel your breathing fiery on my neck. You're shaking. What's the matter? The fright, the emotion perhaps . . . "

Simona said nothing. Urbano had to repeat his questions with insistence, turning his head. Then, Simona, as though waking up, responded incoherently: "Nothing. Nothing. The great event."

They rode thus a long time, until a place called The Gallows Inn, where there awaited them a closed coach with a team of four horses. Paolo had chosen the place attracted by the strangeness of the name. From there Urbano and Simona had to go at full gallop for the rest of the night, to hide out a few days at the homestead of Conchona, who had already left in the morning coach to make things comfortable for them.

"Now you can say that you're safe. Thanks be given! Goodbye, goodbye, happy couple. Remember poor Paolo. Coachman, fly, though you make the team burst."

"Woman say something. Thank Paolo. He's our providence," Urbano begged Simona.

"Leave her be. Poor little thing. She will go along unconscious. How else did you want it to be? Anything else would be vulgar and improper for this adventure. Are you wearing your pistols? Goodbye. Goodbye. Goodbye. Driver, whip the chargers mercilessly."

Now the coach was rolling gently.

"Let me sleep, for God's sake: don't wake me. Poor Adelaida. We will not separate. Wait, wait. Pray for her, Urbano," said Simona, curling up against her lover.

"Dear heart," thought Urbano, "she's exhausted, feverish from exhaustion." And he kissed her with gentleness. Simona went along the whole time dreaming aloud mysterious phrases. A violet ray filtered through the little curtains of the coach. Day began to break. Urbano slept. He awoke at eight in the morning. It was a glorious day. Inside the coach, through a crack in the side, a slice of sun made its way, like a yellow and transparent glass moon. Urbano imagined it was as if they were confined in an urn with a glass cover. Simona still slept, pallid, fair and unconscious like Snow White. He went to kiss her forehead, and his lips were burned. He touched her hands, which burned him. Simona's lips, full and swollen with blood, were now like two empty veins, flattened and livid. From her half-open mouth, a fiery breath came out. Urbano shook her, alarmed: "Simona, Simona."

Simona raised her eyelids and looked cross-eyed.

"I don't hold a grudge against you, Sulforiana. I forgive you all. Barrabás, Lohengrín: up, up from my lap."

Urbano thought that Simona was going to die right there in his arms. He held her to his breast, kissing her transportedly. He saw himself lost, hurled down at the instant of reaching the height of his happiness.

Laboriously, through pines and fragrant lanes, the coach arrived at the homestead of Conchona, who had been on the lookout waiting for them, on the height of the orchards for three hours.

"Concha, she's dying on us, she's dying on us," shouted Urbano, in delirium, carrying the inert Simona in his arms. The girl still wore the uniform of the Derelicts, of Nazarene fustian and a small saffron cord at the waist. Her abundant red-gold hair had spilled down, and her feet hung down, shod in plain shoes and stockings of coarse, rough wool.

Conchona, at the head of her elders and of the ten little ones, broke out crying, making threatening warnings with her fists in the air.

"My empress, who I saw leave here and who I see come back, prostrate and a martyr! Those seven witches, cursed by God, stole you from my bosom, sipped your blood, killed you. Bring her here, Señorito, I'll take her to bed, I can do it better."

Conchona carefully took the girl and conducted her to the bedroom with two beds where Simona had lived alone, as a newlywed, which now was made up for Urbano for them to live in together, as unmarried lovers. Behind Conchona, Urbano followed, sobbing and walking unsteadily, the old people, making the sign of the cross and muttering prayers, the little ones, bawling, like in a primitive funeral, with no other religious observance than the eternal manifestations of terror and stupor.

Simona brought no clothing with her. The small bundle contained only the jewels that the grandmother had willed her.

Conchona dispatched one of the little ones in search of Don Arcadio Ontañón.

"Go quickly, or I'll fasten my talons in your behind."

The little boy took off like a javelin. Before an hour he was already back in the doctor's carriage, along with Don Arcadio, the latter with his mustard-colored cape and chartreuse parasol. The doctor examined the patient. Urbano, seizing the old doctor by the arms with rude anxiety, insisted that he tell him whether Simona would die or could be cured; when she was going to die, when she was going to be cured. Don Arcadio smiled, with good-natured sadness, and calmed him down, replying to him that there was no immediate danger. He added that, though Simona might not recover consciousness, not to be alarmed. The delirium would probably continue for some time; the illness was of a slow course. He wrote out some prescriptions, gave some instructions, and said he would return in the afternoon. Urbano and Conchona did not leave the patient's side.

"Do you know what I tell you?" whispered Conchona. "That she's not dying. My heart tells me so, and it's never fooled me."

"My heart too tells me that she won't die. I'm confident."

"I'm not dying, no. What interest do you have in my dying? You aren't going to get married that way," breathed Simona.

"She's delirious," determined Conchona. "Little angel of heaven; she still has fear deep in her soul of the seven witches. Ay, Señor! What a fright I had! I was afraid it might give me a miscarriage; so far along . . . ," she sighed, demonstratively dropping her eyes toward the cyclopean rotundity of her belly. "And thank goodness my lordyship, as he's now giving the academy exanimations, was not here, as nervous and choked up as he is."

In the afternoon, the doctor said that all was the same and that he had to cut Simona's hair, which would alleviate the delirium. Urbano did not consent to it. The doctor replied that, in all events, with the fever she would finally succumb and, if it were cut, she would then grow better. Urbano did not want to witness the tonsure, which was delegated to Conchona. The operation concluded, Urbano entered the bedroom; the floor was covered with long coppery cuttings, of a rare sheen, which Urbano recovered and kissed, burying his face in that sumptuous softness.

"Now she doesn't look like a woman; not even a little girl. She looks like a little boy," suggested Conchona.

Simona did resemble, yes, the sleeping and marble Adonis of ancient statuary.

At nighttime, Urbano went to bed with his clothing on in the bed beside Simona's. Conchona slept in the kitchen on a pallet on the earth. A low partition of crooked planks separated the bedroom from the kitchen. Within the bedroom an oil lamp in a glass on a three legged stool gave off a drowsy light. Urbano did not give in to sleep; his soul and senses suspended by the rhythm, arbitrary and strident, of Simona's breathing. In the early morning, he was in a daze. An unexpected animal's cry awoke him, between bellow, grunt, and cry. "Was it the cows? Was it the pigs? Was it the calves?

My ignorance of country things leaves me unsure." The cry went up an octave, as if it were approaching. Urbano opened his eyes. Through the cracks of the partition a reddish light came in. In the kitchen laborious breathing was heard, mixed with a kind of humming. It was Conchona's voice. Urbano arose and went to the kitchen. In the fireplace the embers shone beneath a steamy pot, set on the trivet. There was a lamp with four wicks lit. Urbano saw first Conchona's empty pallet and a sanguinary spectacle, like the vestige of a crime. Not far from the fireplace, faded into the darkness was Conchona, in a nightshirt, seated on the ground, with a piglet in her arms, which she was washing in a large tub. This piglet was the one who grunted, and Conchona spoke to it in the singsong of a lullaby.

"What's that?" asked Urbano, amazed.

"A baby. You heard me? I thought I hadn't make a racket. My sunshine; cherub! Look here."

"That's a pig, Conchona."

"Never! A pig, the child of my womb? A July sun. The spitting image of my lordyship. He's not missing anything but the eyeglasses."

"What? You mean to tell me that you've given birth all alone there, without help, without a doctor?"

"I think it was brought on because of this morning's fright."

"We must let the doctor know."

"God in heaven won't stand for any man's looking at me or touching me other than my lordyship. Call my mother in the granary, who's almost a midwife. She assisted at the ten births of my sister."

After calling the old woman, Urbano went back to bed and slept until morning, when the doctor arrived. The doctor, jokingly, praised Conchona's braveness. Insofar as the infant, he differed from Urbano's judgment; to him it did not look like a suckling pig but a newborn calf. He forbade Conchona to get up. She resisted, assuring that women of her strength do not have discomfort enough to remain a whole day in bed. Of Simona, the old doctor said that she was still the same, without worsening, and it was the best that could happen.

The following two days the illness stayed at the same point. Some moments, Simona half recovered consciousness. She recognized Urbano and Conchona (who the third day after the birth was already up and about); she spoke to them by name, but had lost the memory of the immediate past and did not notice being sick nor was surprised by the place in which she found herself. All in all, Urbano judged this a notable improvement.

The fourth day was Sunday. Late on in the morning Don Cástulo arrived in search of Conchona, calculating that the lovers by now no longer remained at the homestead. Great was his amazement and grief at finding them still there and seeing Simona in so much danger. He was a long while in fixing his attention on his wife. Rolling his myopic eyes, turquoise color, he said to her, "I don't know what it is about you, Conchita; but, you seem so different to me."

"Look well," replied Conchona, her arms akimbo.

"I'm looking, I'm looking, and I don't get it. It's as if you were missing something."

"You're the one who's missing something—a screw. Bring over your hand; touch here," and she drew Don Cástulo's hand to her belly.

"Heavens! Was it a false alarm? Has it all evaporated like a dream? Dropsy? Gas, perhaps?"

Conchona retired smiling and returned shortly with the little calf, crudely swathed in rough cloths and an old kerchief, since the layette, prepared with so much care and love, was at the Grove of Athena. Don Cástulo's heart quickened with the joyous frenzy of a tambourine on a festive morning. He felt a kind of cosmic emotion, as if he were present at the first day of the creation of the world. He wanted to take his son in his arms, but Conchona snatched him back promptly, because he held him in an unstable and ridiculous manner, like a clumsy waiter who carries an overladen tray. He bent to kiss him effusively, scratching him with his eyeglasses and making him yowl. Right away he spoke of the baptism and of the name that should be given him. He demanded a Greek name, which are the most beautiful; in this he was intransigent. Empedocles, for example.

"Never! Never! My baby, the child of my womb, with that monicker, so all can snicker at him. He might as well be a humpback," muttered Conchona, horrifiedly.

Don Cástulo enunciated other names: Pythagorus, Plato, Zeno, Pelopidas, Epaminondas.

To Conchona they all seemed execrable names. They put the matter off.

Then, Don Cástulo was troubled by an innocent remorse. He had imagined a parallelism between his life and that of Urbano, the beloved disciple. And there was a ghastly contrast. Whenever he reached a form of supreme happiness, Urbano was overcome by a terrible catastrophe. He almost felt guilty of Urbano's misfortunes. The next day he returned to Pilares with his spirit clouded, a conglomeration of happinesses and sorrows.

Simona's illness stabilized. Urbano, with the monotony of the anguish, was becoming insensible. He didn't leave the bedroom but to go to the dark kitchen and to sit with a drowsiness like mist before the fireplace. There floated in the air the smell of furze smoke and the penetrating and sleep-inducing perfume of sweet hay and green lavender, which Conchona burned as fumigant and disinfectant. It distracted him to hear the rattling that moved the covers of the boiling pots and to see the little clouds that were given off from them, tangled, floating, iridescent, like feather plumes over old helmets. Not far from the fireplace, on a pile of corn leaves on the black earth, reddened by the fire's reflection and in unchangeable digestive beatitude, slept the calf Conchona had borne. He never cried. Urbano contemplated him with apathetic curiosity. But most of the time Urbano spent in the bedroom, near Simona; near and so far, since his beloved's soul was absent. Then Urbano was reminded of his mother. When Simona got better, would she remain mentally unsound? He consulted over this cruel doubt with the old doctor, who responded that that was not very probable. He always received a breath of strength from him, which Don Arcadio communicated to him tacitly, with his doctorly evasions, his ingenuous humor, and his grave and kind look, like that of the patriarchs, full of experience and of benevolence.

The bedroom had a small window. Urbano directed his eyes toward it at length, as toward hope. Outside there hung some vine leaves with the transparency of seawater. Further off was seen a rural vignette—a fragment of meadow, some brambles, a fig tree, a background of gentle hills, a triangular sky. At every hour of the day, the picture changed in harmonies and in spiritual expression. But beneath the change, imperceptible and fluid, there endured an immutable emotion; that of life, of robust and beautiful life. He heard, aflame with enthusiasm, the birds, those troubadors, singing lays of love to life. All was springtime. And Simona was, in her springtime, asleep and as if dead, in no way other than mythical Adonis seemed dead or asleep during the winter to revive, with his perennial youth, at each new springtime. Simona was going to revive. Her death was apparent and transitory. She could not die. It was against the natural order, which is a perfect order. Through the little window, Urbano perceived with certainty the perfection of the natural order. It could not be placed in doubt. But a blackbird, perched in the fig tree, dressed in black and with a golden beak, seemed to place in doubt and to criticize, whistling ironically, the perfection of the universe. That blackbird troubled Urbano. His melody, individual and distinct, standing out from the vast harmony and anonymity of creation, became intolerable to him. He seized one of the pistols Paolo had given him and fired. The blackbird fell from the fig tree. In the glass of the little window a geometric orifice was left, through which an aromatic and warm breath of nature entered the room. "I've killed the doubt," murmured Urbano.

"Who's knocking at the door, so hard? What iron hand? I'm not opening up, I'm not opening up; I don't want to leave. Urbano, defend me. Don't open up, don't open up," stammered Simona in a fright, on hearing the shot.

Urbano calmed her down, with kisses and tender words.

"Ay, thanks!" sighed Simona, sinking once more into a deep drowsiness.

Thenceforth Urbano, at the foot of Simona's bed, remained in a cold and immovable calm, like a stone figure cut in a sepulcher, awaiting the resurrection of the flesh.

One afternoon, after his visit, Don Arcadio remained to keep Urbano company. At the supper hour, he said that he would sup on whatever there might be with Conchona's family. After supper he prolonged his stay. Every moment, he went to take Simona's pulse. He spoke in a low voice with Conchona, who, hearing him, sighed. Urbano, at the foot of the bed, looked from one to the other inalterable. The night dragged on slowly, like a black and muddy river. The doctor did not leave. A cock crowed. The doctor, from the head of Simona's bed, said to Urbano, "Brace yourself with courage. Now's the time."

"It's all right; it doesn't matter," replied Urbano, composed, "death will not separate us; it will unite us."

"What do you mean?"

Urbano pointed to Paolo's pistols, which were on a stump of wood. Don Arcadio approached him, on his face a priestly and severe expression.

"What are you saying, foolish and haughty boy? Do you believe yourself to be, perhaps, one of the poles of the universe and that the other pole is this poor girl?"

"Yes, Señor," replied Urbano dogmatically, his brow contracted.

"Lift your heart to God; don't impiously profane the divinity of the mystery, in which we must not penetrate until we are called.

Dress your soul in mourning, cry tears of blood; but, make use of your reason. You are beginning to live; you've still got everything ahead of you."

"I've got nothing ahead of me."

"If not selfishly and for yourself, you've still got everything ahead of you, for the others. Who has exempted you from your obligations to humanity?"

"For me humanity does not exist outside of Simona. You are an old monkey, Conchona is a pumpkin, her husband is an ass, her son a nursing pig," said Urbano unmovingly.

"Well if humanity for you is Simona, for your obligations to Simona you have to live. Who, if not you, is the one obligated to pay homage to her memory, to cry for her, to praise her to God?"

"Me, too, señor doctor, for I adore her," interrupted Conchona, who wrung her hands and swallowed her tears.

"Make use of your reason," repeated Don Arcadio with gentleness.

"Well, what else am I doing? My heart tells me that with time my sorrow will lessen, I will go about consoling myself, perhaps I may forget her, maybe I may come to fall in love with another. And as I do not want that to happen, as I do not want this feeling of now to be extinguished, my reason, then, dictates to me with absolute coolness what I have to do. I am much more reasonable than you."

"Concha," ordered the doctor, "take out and hide those stupid toys, which senseless men have invented to divert themselves with death and with life, heads or tails, as if life and death were copper coins which can be lost and recovered with a light movement."

Conchona went out with the pistols; a short while later she returned. Urbano had now approached to grasp one of Simona's hands; the doctor held the other, for the pulse. Conchona knelt to pray. It was as if time had stood still, wavering and timorous, on the threshold of eternity. That night never ended. When, at last, the dawn smiled in the little window, a smile dawned as well in the be-

327

nign and tired eyes of the old doctor. At eight in the morning Don Arcadio retired, saying, "A favorable reaction has set in. For the rest of the day, there is nothing to worry about. It will be a tranquil day."

It was not a tranquil day, because the calf had a clamorous colic. Conchona attributed it to her milk having gone sour because of the excitement of the previous night.

In his afternoon visit, Don Arcadio reiterated the diagnosis of the morning in still more optimistic terms. Inside of Urbano it was as if a tensed spring snapped and he recovered the elasticity and mildness of his spirit.

"It seems to me," he said, "as if the door of a cage open, my spirits soar out. I've recovered my self. I'm myself again. Forgive me, Don Arcadio, and forgive me thrice over, Concha; last night I said an impertinence to you." And he burst out crying.

How could they not forgive him? What did he know of what he was saying in those moments? He had borne himself heroically, like a hero of feeling, added the old doctor.

Simona got better day by day. In a week, she was out of danger; but she still had not acquired full awareness or memory. She began relating to the outside world. She asked since when had she been ill. When they told her almost a month, she didn't want to believe it. Her recollection was clouded from the moment in which they had lifted her up on horseback with Urbano. The whole illness was, for her, a span of misplaced time, a vertebra lost in the articulation of her memory. She had not suffered or felt anything.

It was then that Urbano learned, with retrospective horror, that Simona had had typhus.

Since Simona began to feel better, Urbano, out of a kind of inexplicable respect, did not wish to sleep in the bed alongside. Conchona slept there; Urbano on the pallet in the kitchen. Urbano saw Simona as a person returned from the dead, a messenger from the land of the shades, a different person, since she had come back in a different body; her head—covered with tiny curls, hammered in copper, and her pale face of alabaster—seemed to belong to a beautiful adolescent boy; thinner, in her slender torso feminine curves were not suggested.

Now convalescent, in colloquy with Urbano, they fantasized their coming trip as lovers. They would go to Santander in two days, stopping overnight in Unquera.

"You'll remember," said Urbano one day, "that your grandmother, before dying, asked us, in her memory, to commit some picturesque folly. I've thought that we ought to carry out her last wish. Until now, our follies have not been voluntary and free. My idea is that you go dressed as a man. No one will suspect that we are two lovers. They'll imagine us as two brothers. Do you remember how on our wedding trip the innkeeper took us for brother and sister? And that was when you went dressed as a woman. I'll write to Paolo what we are going to do. He'll enjoy it, because in the classical comedies it happened frequently that lovers traveled disguised as men; and he'll say that this is the most beautiful epilogue of the adventure. Ah! Don't let me forget to take Paolo's pistols, those stupid toys senseless men have invented, according to Don Arcadio."

How Urbano and Simona flew over time now, with the wings that imagination puts on the temples. With what celestial agility did the moment arrive when the two, with embraces and happy tears, said goodbye to Conchona, to Don Cástulo, to the beatific calf, to Don Arcadio.

Now they are in the stagecoach. Now the stagecoach starts off. Now hours and hours of traveling have gone by. Night is falling. The sky is purple. The coachman's whip resounds. The carriage wearily climbs a hill, full of turns, between high rocks and thick oak forest, where a black highwayman holds sway.

"Stop!"

The stagecoach has stopped. A man, with a red cloth tied beneath his eyes, sticks his head in the door and, pointing with a blunderbuss, courteously requests, "Would your lordships deign to get down."

The travelers come down. Two bandits order them to get in a row. A third bandit, a distance off, points the blunderbuss at the coachman. One of the bandits jumps up on the cowcatcher and ties the coachman and the helper with ropes. Then, while this bandit keeps watch with the blunderbuss, the other two go about searching the travelers. The last in the row is Urbano, the next to last Simona, dressed as a boy. Now the bandits approach to search Simona. Now they are going to lay hands on her. The blood rushes to Urbano's head. Now the three bandits are almost together. Beside himself, Urbano hurls himself on the two bandits nearest, not without first knocking down, with a blow, the blunderbuss that the other one had cocked. Instinctively, he puts into practice the gentlemanly arts of fencing that Paolo had taught him and the tricks of plebeian pugilism which he had learned from Pentameter. Now he has the two down at his feet. The other reaches to recover the blunderbuss, hardly recovered from the surprise. Urbano remembers that he has with him Paolo's pistols, one of them, that of the blackbird, not loaded. Never mind. The bandits don't know it.

"Stop!" shouts Urbano, showing the pistols. Let the blunderbuss alone on the ground; if you move I'll discharge a shot into your heart. Get up. Now then, volunteers to untie the coachman and the helper and with the same ropes to tie these men to an oak."

All is a work of ten minutes. The booty is returned to its owners. The coach resumes the weary ascent. The travelers are beside themselves with admiration and gratitude.

"What's your name, young man, so I may never forget it?"

"Juan Pérez."

"And that handsome little boy, is he your brother?"

"Yes, Señores."

"What's his name?"

"Pedro Fernández."

"How come Fernández if you are Pérez?"

"Because he's the son of another father."

In the inn at Unquera, alone now (all alone!) in a bedroom, Simona, seated on Urbano's knees and one arm around his neck, asks, "Why didn't you tell them your name? I was so proud of you."

"Because we've begun a new life. I'm not the Urbano of before nor are you that Simona. We have to find new names. We must forget the past, if we can, because at times, without wanting to . . . I'm laughing because . . . If you knew that when they pretended to marry us and put us in a stagecoach, as husband and wife, I went along wishing that bandits might come down and take us prisoners for real, you to one place and me to another! Now I remember."

"And do you remember," whispered Simona in Urbano's ear, "what day it was and what day it is today? The eighth of July. One year ago today."

"What a coincidence!"

"Coincidence, no. I've set today for our trip, and not a week ago or within a week. You didn't catch on to the reason for my whim, which had to be precisely today."

"What's this that's bulging out in the inside pocket of your jacket? What little secret?"

Simona took out a package of silk paper. She opened it. It contained an orange blossom in yellowish dust. She said, "My grandmother gave it to me, before dying, with these words: The rose he gave me with the first kiss; dust. And this blossom, symbol of constant and pure love: as the first day. Keep it all your life; leave it to your daughter. It will always be the same, and the generations of roses will pass."

"Don't feel sad, Simona. Keep in mind," continued Urbano, with a radiant smile, "that this orange blossom is waxen, fabricated by men, a manufactured product. And the rose was a live one, a rose of fire; that's why it's now ashes. And we are not figures of wax; we are two flames in the same hearth. Before going out, we'll have transmitted to others the burning torch."

Now, for the first time, they peacefully rest their heads on the same pillow without speaking, for their mouths are joined. Nevertheless, one and the other have need to say something.

"I cannot help thinking of a year ago today, my Simona. I wouldn't feel so happy today if then I hadn't felt so miserable. Your choice of date has been a heavenly inspiration and not a whim, as you've said. Not a whim."

"Yes, a whim, because . . . do you know? . . . now I have whims. Do you understand? . . . A child, yes, a child of my flesh; not as before, a child of my dreams.